Prophecy

Also by S. J. Parris

Heresy

Prophecy

{ A Thriller }

S. J. Parris

DOUBLEDAY

New York   London   Toronto   Sydney   Auckland

DD

DOUBLEDAY

This book is a work of fiction. Names, characters, businesses, organizations, places, events, and incidents either are the product of the author's imagination or are used fictitiously. Any resemblance to actual persons, living or dead, events, or locales is entirely coincidental.

www.doubleday.com

DOUBLEDAY and the DD colophon are registered trademarks of Random House, Inc.

Originally published in Great Britain by HarperCollins, an imprint of HarperCollins Publishers, Limited, London.

Book design by Maria Carella
Jacket design by Patti Ratchford
Jacket photograph © Mark Owen

Library of Congress Cataloging-in-Publication Data
Parris, S. J., 1974–
Prophecy : a thriller / by S. J. Parris.—1st ed.
p. cm.
1. Bruno, Giordano, 1548–1600—Fiction.   2. Elizabeth I, Queen of England, 1533–1603—Fiction.   3. Dee, John, 1527–1608—Fiction.   4. Astrology—Fiction.
5. Christian heretics—Fiction.   6. Great Britain—History—Elizabeth, 1558–1603—Fiction.   7. London (England)—History—16th century—Fiction.   I. Title.
PR6113.E77P76 2011
823'.92—dc22   2010037694

ISBN 978-0-385-53130-6

PRINTED IN THE UNITED STATES OF AMERICA

1   3   5   7   9   10   8   6   4   2

First United States Edition

Prophecy

Prologue

MORTLAKE, HOUSE OF JOHN DEE,
SOUTHWEST LONDON.
3RD SEPTEMBER, YEAR OF OUR LORD 1583

Without warning, all the candles in the room's corners flicker and feint, as if a sudden gust has entered, but the air remains still. At the same moment, the hairs on my arms prickle and stand erect and I shudder; a cold breath descends on us, though outside the day is close. I chance a sideways glance at Doctor Dee; he stands unmoving as marble, his hands clasped as if in prayer, the knuckles of both thumbs pressed anxiously to his lips—or what can be seen of them through his ash-grey beard, which he wears in a point down to his chest in imitation of Merlin, whose heir Dee secretly considers himself. The cunning man, Ned Kelley, kneels on the floor in front of the table of practice with his back to us, eyes fixed on the pale, translucent crystal about the size of a goose egg mounted in fixings of brass and standing upon a square of red silk. The wooden shutters of the study windows have been closed; this business must be conducted in shadow and candlelight. Kelley draws breath like a player about to deliver his prologue, and stretches his arms out wide at shoulder height, in a posture of crucifixion.

"Yes . . ." he breathes, finally, his voice little more than a whisper. "He is here. He beckons to me."

"Who?" Dee leans forward eagerly, his eyes bright. "Who is he?"

Kelley waits a moment before answering, his brow creasing as he concentrates his gaze on the stone.

"A man of more than mortal height, with skin as dark as polished mahogany. He is dressed head to foot in a white garment, which is torn, and his eyes are of red fire. In his right hand he holds aloft a sword."

Dee snaps his head around then and clutches my arm, staring at me; the shock on his face must be mirrored in my own. He has recognised the description, as have I: the being Kelley sees in the stone matches the first figure of the sign of Aries, as described by the ancient philosopher Hermes Trismegistus. There are thirty-six of these figures, the Egyptian gods of time who rule the divisions of the zodiac and are called by some "star demons." There are few scholars in Christendom who could thus identify the figure Kelley sees, and two of them are here in this study in Mortlake. If, indeed, this *is* what Kelley sees. I say nothing.

"What says he?" Dee urges.

"He holds out a book," Kelley answers.

"What manner of book?"

"An ancient book, with worn covers and pages all of beaten gold." Kelley leans closer to the stone. "Wait! He is writing upon it with his forefinger, and the letters are traced in blood."

I want to ask what he has done with the sword while he writes in this book—has he tucked it under his arm, perhaps?—but Dee would not thank me for holding this business lightly. Beside me, he draws in his breath, impatient to hear what the spirit is writing.

"XV," Kelley reports, after a moment. He turns to look up at us, then over his right shoulder, his expression perplexed, perhaps expecting Dee to interpret the numerals.

"Fifteen, Bruno," Dee whispers, looking again to me for confirmation. I nod, once. The lost fifteenth book of Hermes Trismegistus, the book I had come to England to find, the book I now knew Dee had once held in his hands years earlier, only to be robbed of it violently and lose it again. Could it be? It occurs to me that Kelley must know of his master's obsession with the fifteenth book.

The scryer raises a hand for silence. His eyes do not move from the crystal.

"He turns the page. Now he traces . . . it seems . . . yes, he makes a sign—quickly, fetch me paper and ink!"

Dee hurries to bring him the items; Kelley reaches out and flaps his hand impatiently, as if afraid the image will fade before he has time to transcribe it. He takes the quill and, still gazing intently into the stone, sketches the astrological symbol of the planet Jupiter and holds it up for our inspection.

I tense; Dee feels it where his hand still holds my arm, and half turns to look at me with questioning eyebrows. I keep my face empty of expression. The sign of Jupiter is my code, my signature; it replaces my name as the sign that my letters of intelligence are authentic. Only two people in the world know this: myself and Sir Francis Walsingham, Her Majesty's principal secretary of state and chief intelligencer. It is a common enough sign in astrology, and coincidence, surely, that Kelley has drawn it; still I regard the back of Kelley's head with increased suspicion.

"On the facing page," Kelley continues, "he traces another mark—this time, the sign of Saturn." This he also draws on his paper, a cross with a curving tail, the quill scratching slowly as if time has thickened while he watches this unfold in the depths of the stone. Dee's breathing quickens as he takes the paper and taps it with two fingers.

"Jupiter and Saturn. The Great Conjunction. You understand, I think, Bruno?" Without waiting for a reply, he turns impatiently to Kelley. "Ned—what does he now, the spirit?"

"He opens his mouth and motions for me to listen."

Kelley falls silent and does not move. Moments pass, Dee leaning forward eagerly, poised as if held taut on a rope, balanced between wanting to pounce on his scryer and not wishing to crowd him. When Kelley speaks again, his voice is altered; darker, somehow, and he proclaims as if in a trance: "'All things have grown almost to their fullness. Time itself shall be altered, and strange shall be the wonders perceived. Water shall perish in fire, and a new order shall spring from these.'"

Here he pauses, gives a great shuddering sigh. Dee's grip around my arm tightens. I know what he is thinking. Kelley continues in the same portentous voice: "'Hell itself grows weary of Earth. At this time shall rise up one who will be called the Son of Perdition, the Master of Error, the Prince of Darkness, and he will delude many by his magic arts, so that fire will seem to come down from Heaven and the sky shall be turned the colour of blood. Empires, kingdoms, principalities, and states shall be overturned, fathers will turn against sons and brothers against brothers, there shall be turbulence among the peoples of the Earth, and the streets of the cities will run with blood. By this you shall know the last days of the old order.'"

He stops, sinks back gasping onto his heels, his chest heaving as if he has run a mile in the heat. Beside me, I can feel Dee trembling, his hand still holding my wrist; I feel him hungry for more of the spirit's words, silently urging the scryer not to stop there, unwilling to speak aloud for fear of breaking the spell. For myself, I reserve judgement.

"'Yet God has provided medicine for man's suffering,'" Kelley cries in the same voice, sitting up suddenly and making us both jump. "'There shall also rise a prince who will rule by the light of reason and under-standing, who shall strike down the darkness of the old times, and in him the alteration of the world shall begin, and so shall he establish one faith, one ancient religion of unity that will put an end to strife.'"

Dee claps his hands gleefully, turning to me with shining eyes and the excitement of a child. It is hard to believe that this is his fifty-sixth autumn.

"The prophecy, Bruno! What can this be, if not the prophecy of the Great Conjunction, of the ending of the old world? You read this as plain as I do, my friend—through the good offices of Master Kelley here, the gods of time have chosen to speak to us of the coming of the Fiery Trigon, when the old order shall be overturned and the world made anew in the image of ancient truth!"

"He has certainly spoken of weighty matters," I say evenly.

Kelley turns then, his brow damp with sweat, and regards me with those close-set eyes.

"Doctor Dee—what is this Fiery Trigon?" he asks, in his somewhat nasal voice.

"You could not know the significance, Ned, of what your gifts have revealed to us this day," Dee replies, his manner now fatherly, "but you have translated a prophecy most wondrous. Most wondrous." He shakes his head slowly in admiration, then stirs himself and begins to pace about the study as he explains, resuming his authority, the teacher once more. While the séance occurs, he becomes dependent upon Kelley, but it is not his habit to be subservient; he is, after all, the queen's personal astrologer.

"Once every twenty years," he says, holding up a forefinger like a schoolmaster, "the two most powerful planets in our cosmology, Jupiter and Saturn, align with each other, each time moving through the twelve signs of the zodiac. Every two hundred years, give or take, this conjunction moves into a new trigon—that is to say, the group of three signs that correspond to each of the four elements. And once every nine hundred and sixty years, the alignment completes its cycle through the four trigons, returning again to its beginning in fire. For the past two hundred years, the planets have aligned within the signs of the Watery Trigon. But now, my dear Ned, this very year, the year of Our Lord fifteen hundred and eighty-three, Jupiter and Saturn will conjoin once more in the sign of Aries, the first sign of the Fiery Trigon, the most potent conjunction of all and one that has not been seen for almost a thousand years."

He pauses for effect; Kelley's mouth hangs open like a codfish.

"Then it is a momentous time in the heavens?"

"More than momentous," I say, taking up the story. "The coming of the Fiery Trigon signifies the dawn of a new epoch. This is only the seventh such conjunction since the creation of the world and each has been marked by events that have shaken history. The flood of Noah, the birth of Christ, the coming of Charlemagne—all coincide with the return to the Fiery Trigon."

"And this transition into the sign of Aries at the end of our troubled century has been prophesied by many as signifying the end of history," Dee agrees, thoughtful. He has arrived in front of his tall perspective glass in its ornate gilt frame that stands in the corner by the west-facing window. Its peculiar property is that it reflects a true image and not the usual reversed image of an ordinary glass; the effect is unsettling. Now he turns to face us and raises his right hand; in the glass, his reflection does the same.

"The astronomer Richard Harvey wrote of this present conjunction, 'Either a marvellous fearful and horrible alteration of empires, kingdoms, and states, or else the destruction of the whole world shall ensue,' " I add.

"So he did, Bruno, so he did. We may expect signs and wonders, my friends, in the days to come. Our world will change beyond recognition. We shall bear witness to a new era." Dee is trembling, his eyes moist.

"Then—the spirit in the stone—he came to remind us of this prophecy?" Kelley asks, his face full of wonder.

"And to point to its special significance for England," Dee adds, his voice heavy with meaning. "For what can it signify but the overthrowing of the old religion once and for all in favour of the new, with Her Majesty as the light of reason and understanding?"

"I had no idea," Kelley says, dreamy.

I watch him closely. There are two possibilities here. One is that he truly has a gift; I do not yet discount this, for though it has never been granted to me, in other countries I have heard of men who speak with those they call angels and demons through just such showing stones, or else a speculum made for the purpose, like the one of obsidian that Dee keeps above his hearth. But in my years of wandering through Europe I have also seen plenty of these itinerant scryers, these cunning men, these mediums for hire, who have a smattering of esoteric learning and for the price of a bed and a pot of beer will tell the credulous man anything they think he wants to hear. Perhaps this is snobbery on my part; I cannot help but feel that if the Egyptian gods of time chose to speak to men, it would be to men of learning, philosophers like myself or John Dee, the true heirs to Hermes—not to such a man as Ned Kelley, who wears his ragged cloth cap pulled down to his brow even indoors, to disguise the fact that he has one ear clipped for coining.

But I must be careful what I say to Dee touching Ned Kelley; the scryer has had his feet firmly under Dee's table since long before I arrived in England, and this is the first time Dee has allowed me to take part in one of these "actions," as he calls them. Kelley resents my recent friendship with his master; I see how he regards me from under the peak of his cap. John Dee is the most learned man in England, but he seems to me unaccountably trusting of Kelley, despite knowing almost nothing of the medium's history. I have grown fond of Dee and would not like to see him hoodwinked; at the same time, I do not want to fall from his favour and lose the use of his library, the finest collection of books to be found in the kingdom. So I keep my counsel.

With a sudden draught, the study door is thrown open and we all start like guilty creatures; Kelley, with surprising quickness, throws his hat over the showing stone. None of us is under any illusion; what we are engaged in here would be considered witchcraft, and is a capital offence against the edicts of church and state. It would only take one gossiping servant to catch wind of Dee's activities and we could all be facing the pyre; the Protestant authorities of this island, more tolerant in some matters than the church of my native Italy, still strike with force against anything that smells of magic.

Dusty evening sunlight slants through from the passageway outside, and in the doorway stands a little boy, not more than three years old, who looks from one to the other of us with blank curiosity.

Dee's face crinkles with tenderness but also with relief.

"Arthur! What are you about? You know you are not supposed to disturb me when I am at work. Where is your mother?"

Arthur Dee steps across the threshold and at once gives a great shiver.

"Why is it so cold in your room, Papa?"

Dee casts me a look of something like triumph, as if to say, *You see? We were not deceived.* He flings wide the shutters of the west window and outside the sun is setting, staining the sky vermillion, the colour of blood.

Chapter 1

The wedding feast of Sir Philip Sidney and Frances Walsingham threatens to spill over into the next day; dusk has fallen, lamps have been lit, and above the din from the musicians in the gallery and the laughter of the guests, the young woman with whom I have been dancing tells me excitedly that she was once at a marriage party that lasted four days altogether. She leans in close when she says this and presses her hand to my shoulder; her breath is laced with sweet wine. The musicians strike up another galliard; my dancing partner exclaims with delight and clutches eagerly at my hand, laughing. I am about to protest that the hall is warm, that I would like a cup of wine and a moment's respite in the fresh air before I return to the fray, but I have barely opened my mouth when the wind is knocked out of me by a fist between the shoulder blades, accompanied by a hearty cry.

"Giordano Bruno! Now what is this I see? The great philosopher throwing off his scholar's gown and lifting a leg with the flower of Her Majesty's court? Did you learn to dance like that at the monastery? Your hidden talents never cease to astonish me, *amico mio.*"

Recovering my balance, I turn, smiling widely. Here is the bridegroom in all his finery, six feet tall and flushed with wine and triumph: breeches of copper-coloured silk so voluminous it is a wonder he can pass through a doorway; doublet of ivory sewn all over with seed pearls; a lace ruff at his neck so severely starched that his handsome, beardless face seems constantly straining to see above it, like a small boy peering over a wall. His hair still sticks up in the front like a schoolboy hastened out of bed. In all the tumult I have not exchanged a word with him since the morning's ceremony, he and his young bride have been so comprehensively surrounded by high-ranking well-wishers and relatives, all the highest ornaments of Her Majesty's court.

"Well," he says, grinning broadly, "aren't you going to congratulate me, then, or are you just here for the food from my table?"

"Your father-in-law's table, I had thought," I answer, laughing. "Or which part of the feast did you buy yourself?"

"You can leave your debating-hall pedantry at home today, Bruno. But I hope you have had enough meat and drink?"

"There is enough meat and drink here to feed the five thousand." I indicate the two long tables at each end of the great hall, spread with the detritus of the wedding banquet. "You will be eating leftovers for weeks."

"Oh, you may be sure Sir Francis will see to that," Sidney says. "Today, generosity; tomorrow—thrift. But come, Bruno. You have no idea how it pleases me that you are here." He holds his arms wide and I embrace him with sincere affection; I am the perfect height to have his ruff smack me directly in the nose.

"Watch the clothes," he says, only half joking. "Bruno, allow me to introduce you to my uncle Robert Dudley, Earl of Leicester."

He steps back and gestures to the man who stands a few feet away, at his shoulder; a man of about Sidney's own height, perhaps in his mid-fifties but still athletic, his hair steel grey at the temples but his face fine-boned and handsome behind his close-clipped beard. This man regards me with watchful brown eyes.

"My lord."

I bow deeply, acknowledging the honour; the Earl of Leicester is one of the highest nobles in England and the man who enjoys greater influence over Queen Elizabeth than any alive. I raise my head and meet his shrewd appraisal. It is rumoured that in their youth he was the queen's only lover, and that even now their long-enduring friendship is more intimate than most marriages. He smiles, and there is warmth in his gaze.

"Doctor Bruno, the pleasure is mine. When I learned of your courage in Oxford I was eager to make your acquaintance and thank you in person." Here he lowers his voice; Leicester is the chancellor of the University of Oxford, charged with enforcing the measures to suppress the Catholic resistance among the students. That the movement had gathered so much momentum on his watch had been a matter of some embarrassment to him; my adventures with Sidney there in the spring had helped to disarm it, at least temporarily. I am about to reply when we are interrupted by a man dressed in a russet doublet, with a peasecod belly so vast it makes him look as if he is with child; the earl nods politely to me and I turn back to Sidney.

"My uncle likes the idea of you. He's keen to hear more of your outrageous theories about the universe." I must look anxious, because he elbows me cheerfully in the ribs. "Leicester's friendship is worth a great deal."

"I am glad to have met him," I say, rubbing my side. "And may I now pay my respects to your bride?"

Sidney looks around, as if for someone to deal with this request.

"I daresay she is around somewhere. Giggling with her ladies." He does not sound as if he is in a hurry to find her. "But you are needed elsewhere."

He turns and bows to my companion, who has discreetly withdrawn a couple of paces to watch us from under lowered lids, her hands modestly clasped together. "I am borrowing the great Doctor Bruno for a moment. I will return him to you at some stage. There will be more dancing after the masques." The girl blushes, smiles shyly at me, and obe-diently melts away into the brightly coloured, rustling mass of guests. Sidney looks after her with an expression of amusement. "Lady Arabella Horton has her sights set on you, it seems. Don't be fooled by all the flut-tering lashes and simpering. Half the court has been there. And she will soon lose interest when she learns you are the son of a soldier, with no capital but your wit and a pittance from the King of France."

"I was not planning to tell her that immediately."

"Did you tell her you were a monk for thirteen years?"

"We had not got around to that, either."

"She might like that—might want to help you make up for lost time. But for now, Bruno, my new father-in-law suggests you might like to take a turn in the garden."

"I have not yet had the chance to congratulate him."

But it is clear that this is business. Sidney rests a hand on my shoulder.

"No one has. Do you know, he disappeared for two hours altogether this afternoon to draft some papers? In the middle of his own daughter's wedding party?" He smiles indulgently, as if he must tolerate these foibles, though we both know that Sidney is in no position to complain; financially, he needed this marriage more than young Mistress Walsing-ham, who I suspect entertains greater romantic hopes of it than her new husband.

"I suppose the great machinery of state must keep turning."

"Indeed. And now it is your turn to grease the wheels. Go to him. I shall find you later."

On all sides we are pressed by those who wish to congratulate the bridegroom; they jostle, aggressively smiling and attempting to shake his hand. In the mêlée I slip away toward the door.

Outside, the night air is hard-edged with the first frost of autumn and the grounds are quiet, a welcome relief from the celebrations inside. In the knot garden close to the house, lanterns have been lit and couples walk the neatly cultivated paths, murmuring, their heads close together.

Even in the shadows, I can see that Sir Francis Walsingham is not to be found here. Stretching my arms, I strain my head back to gaze up at the sky, the constellations picked out in bright silver against the ink-blue of the heavens, their arrangement different here from the sky above Naples where I first learned the star patterns as a boy.

I reach the end of the path and still there is no sign of him, so I set off across the open expanse of lawn, away from the lit paths, toward an area of woodland that borders the cultivated part of the garden at the back of Walsingham's country house. As I walk, a lean shape gathers substance out of the shadows and falls into step beside me. He seems made of the night; I have never seen Walsingham wear any suit other than black, not even today, at his daughter's wedding, and he still wears his close-fitting black velvet skullcap, which makes his face yet more severe. He is past fifty now and I have heard he has been ill this last month—one of the protracted bouts of illness that confines him to his bed for days at a time, though if you enquire after his health he swats the question away with a flick of his hand, as if he hasn't the time to consider such trifles. This man, Queen Elizabeth Tudor's principal secretary of state, though he may not seem an imposing figure at first glance, holds the security of England in his hands. Walsingham has created a network of spies and informers that stretches across Europe to the land of the Turks in the east and the colonies of the New World in the west, and the intelligence they bring him is the queen's first line of defence against the myriad Catholic plots to take her life. More remarkably still, he seems to hold all this intelligence in his own mind, and can pluck any information he requires at will.

I had arrived in England six months earlier, at the beginning of spring, sent by my patron King Henri III of France to stay for a while with his ambassador in London in order to spare me the attentions of the Catholic extremists who were gathering support in Paris, led by the Duke of Guise. I had barely been in England a fortnight when Walsingham asked to meet me, my long-standing enmity with Rome and my privileged position as a houseguest at the French embassy making me ideally suited to his purposes. Over the past months, Walsingham is a man I have grown to respect deeply and fear a little.

But his cheeks are hollowed out since I last saw him. He folds his hands now behind his back; the noise of the celebrations grows fainter as we move away from the house.

"*Congratulazioni*, Your Honour."

"*Grazie*, Bruno. I trust you are making the most of the celebrations?"

When he converses alone with me, he speaks Italian, partly I think to put me at ease, and partly because he wants to be sure I do not miss any vital point—his diplomat's Italian being superior to the English I learned largely from merchants and soldiers on my travels.

"Out of curiosity—where did you learn our English dances?" he adds, turning to me.

"I largely make them up as I go along. I find if one steps out confidently enough, people will assume you know what you are doing."

He laughs, that deep rolling bear laugh that comes so rarely from his chest.

"That is your motto in everything, is it not, Bruno? How else does a man rise from fugitive monk to personal tutor to the King of France? Speaking of France"—he keeps his voice light—"how does your host, the ambassador?"

"Castelnau is in good spirits now that his wife and daughter are newly returned from Paris."

"Hm. I have not met Madame de Castelnau. They say she is very beautiful. No wonder the old dog always looks so hearty."

"Beautiful, yes. I have not spoken to her at any length. I am told she is a most pious daughter of the Catholic church."

"I hear the same. Then we must watch her influence over her husband." His eyes narrow. We have reached the trees, and he gestures for me to follow him into their shadows. "I had thought Michel de Castelnau shared the French king's preference for diplomatic dealings with England—so he claims when he has audience with me, anyway. But lately that fanatic the Duke of Guise and his Catholic Leaguers are gaining strength in the French court, and in your letter last week you told me that Guise is sending money to Mary of Scotland through the French embassy . . ." He pauses to master his anger, quietly striking his fist into the palm of his hand. "And what need has Mary Stuart of Guise money, hm? She is more than generously provided for in Sheffield Castle, considering she is our prisoner."

"To secure the loyalty of her friends?" I suggest. "To pay her couriers?"

"Precisely, Bruno! All this summer I have laboured to bring the two queens to a point where they are prepared to hold talks face-to-face, perhaps negotiate a treaty. Queen Elizabeth would like nothing better than to give her cousin Mary her liberty, so long as she will renounce all claim to the English throne. For her part, I am led to believe that Mary tires of imprisonment and is ready to swear to anything. That is why this traffic of letters and gifts from her supporters in France through the embassy troubles me so deeply. Is she double-dealing with me?"

He glares at me as if he expects an answer, but before I can open my mouth, he continues, as if to himself: "And who *are* these couriers? I have the diplomatic packet intercepted and searched every week—she must have another means of delivery for her private letters." He shakes his head briskly. "While she lives, Mary Stuart is a banner to rally England's Catholics, and all those in Europe who hope to see a papist monarch back on our throne. But Her Majesty will not move preemptively against her cousin, though the Privy Council urges her to see the danger. This is why your presence in the French embassy is more crucial to me than ever, Bruno. I need to see every communication between Mary and France that passes through Castelnau's hands. If she is plotting against the queen's sovereignty again, I *must* have hard evidence that incriminates her this time. Can you see to it?"

"I have befriended the ambassador's clerk, Your Honour. For the right price, he says he can give us access to every letter Castelnau writes and receives, if you will guarantee that the documents will bear no evidence of tampering. He is greatly afraid of being discovered—he craves assurances of Your Honour's protection."

"Good man. Give him all the assurances he needs." He clasps my shoulder for a moment. "If he will obtain for us an example of the ambassador's seal, I will set my man Thomas Phelippes to create a forgery. There is no man in England more skilled in the arts of interception. In the circumstances, Bruno, I do not think it prudent that you should be seen so much with Sidney," he adds. "Now that he is so publicly tied to me. Castelnau must not doubt your loyalty to France for a moment."

Even through the dark, my face must betray my disappointment; Sidney is the only person I truly consider a friend in England. We had first met years ago in Padua, when I was fleeing through Italy, and renewed our friendship in the spring, when we had travelled to Oxford together on Walsingham's business. The adventures we shared there had only served to bring us closer. Without his company, I will feel my state of exile all the more keenly.

"But I have found you another contact. A Scotsman named William Fowler—you will meet him in due course. He is a lawyer who has worked for me in France, so you will have plenty to talk about."

"You would trust a lawyer, Your Honour?"

"You look amused, Bruno. Lawyers, philosophers, priests, soldiers, merchants—there is no one I will not make use of. Fowler is well connected in Scotland, among both our friends and those loyal to the Scottish queen, who believe he is a friend to their cause. He has also insinuated himself with Castelnau, who believes Fowler to be a secret Catholic unhappy with Her Majesty's government. He has the knack of making himself all things to all men if necessity demands. Fowler is well placed to convey your reports from inside the embassy without you compromising your position." He pauses and lifts his head; strains of music and laughter drift faintly toward the house and he seems to remember the occasion. "For now, this is all. Come—we should be merry today. You must rejoin the dance."

We turn to face the lit windows across the lawn, his hand lightly on my back. Out here, so far from the City, clean night scents of earth, grass, and frost carry to us on the breeze. Even the Thames, running its sluggish course beyond the line of the trees behind us, smells fresh here, so far to the west of London. We are only a mile from Dee's house; I am surprised that he has not been invited. He is, after all, Sidney's old tutor and a friend of sorts to Walsingham. As if reading my thoughts, the principal secretary says, casually, "You are spending a good deal of time in Mortlake lately, I hear?" It is not really a question.

"I am writing a book," I explain, as we begin to move slowly together in the direction of the music. "Doctor Dee's library has been invaluable."

"What manner of book?"

"Of philosophy. And cosmology."

"A defence of your beloved Copernicus, then."

"Something like that." I did not want to say too much about the book I was working on until it was completed. The ideas I was attempting to put forward were not just controversial but revolutionary, far beyond the theories that Copernicus had proposed. I wanted at least to have written it before I was obliged to defend it.

"Hm." A heavy silence. "Be wary of John Dee, Bruno."

"I thought he was Your Honour's friend?"

"Up to a point. In matters of cartography, or ciphers, or the reformation of the calendar, there is no one in the kingdom whose knowledge I prize higher. But lately his talk runs much on prophecies and omens."

"He believes we are living in the end times."

"We are living in times of unprecedented turbulence, that much is certain," he replies brusquely. "But Her Majesty has enough to fear without Dee whispering these apocalyptic forecasts in her ear because he wants to make himself indispensable to her. As do we all, I suppose, in our way," he concedes, with a sigh. "But then his influence filters down even to the Privy Council chamber and suddenly she will not allow any decision without first consulting a star chart. It makes the business of government very difficult. Besides," he lowers his voice, "it is my firm belief that Almighty God has written some secrets into the Book of Nature that are not supposed to be unlocked. From what I hear, Dee's newest experiments come dangerously close to crossing that line."

There is no point in asking how he knows of Dee's experiments; Walsingham's eyes and ears encompass all of Europe and even the colonies of the New World. It should be no surprise that he knows what goes on a mile from his own house. Yet Dee has been so scrupulous about secrecy where his scrying is concerned.

"There are some at court who feel he has too much influence over Her Majesty, and must be removed from favour," Walsingham continues.

"Your Honour included?"

His teeth shine briefly in the dark as he smiles.

"I have a great respect for John Dee, and I would not do anything to hurt his reputation. The same is not true of some others on Her Majesty's Privy Council. Lord Henry Howard is publishing a book, I am told, to be presented to the queen—a fierce attack on prophecy and astrology and all those who claim to tell the future, calling them necromancers, accusing them of speaking with demons. He does not mention Dee by name, but the intent is clear enough . . . If Dee can be tainted for witchcraft, so much the worse for those of us known as his friends—me, Sidney, the Earl of Leicester. The Howards are dangerously powerful, and the queen knows this well enough. You may like to mention this to Dee the next time you are using his library."

I incline my head to show that the warning is understood. As I bow and prepare to take my leave, I glance up to see a figure haring across the grass to us, a short riding cloak flapping behind him. He drops breathlessly to his knees at Walsingham's feet, and even in the thin silvered light I can make out the royal ensign on his livery, beneath the spattering of mud that shows he has ridden hard to get here. He mutters something about Richmond, a matter of urgency; there is alarm in his bulging eyes.

I step away discreetly so that he may deliver his news privately, but Walsingham calls me back.

"Bruno! Wait for me a moment, will you?"

I stand a little way off, stamping my feet against the chill and rubbing my hands while the man rises to his feet and imparts his news in frantic bursts, Walsingham canted over to receive it, his hands still folded immobile behind his back. Whatever news this messenger has brought from the royal household must be serious indeed to interrupt a man's family wedding feast.

At length, Walsingham murmurs a response; the messenger bows and departs in the direction of the house with the same haste. Walsingham raises his hand to beckon me over.

"I am needed at Richmond Palace on a most grave matter, Bruno, and I want you with me. It will be preferable to disturbing the celebrations. We must leave quietly, without attracting attention—that fellow is gone to instruct the servants to make a boat ready. I will tell you as much as I know while we travel." His voice is tight but controlled; if something distressing has befallen Her Majesty, Walsingham is the man she relies upon to bring order, discipline, calm.

"Will you not be missed?" I gesture in the direction of the wedding feast.

He laughs, briefly. "So long as I leave my steward in charge with the keys to the wine cellar, I doubt anyone will notice. Come, now."

He leads me around the back of the house and through the garden to the little wharf where lights are bobbing gently, reflected in the black water. I must wait for him to tell the messenger's tale in his own time.

Chapter 2

A violent death, the fellow said." Walsingham has to raise his voice over the rhythm of the oars as the servant doggedly ploughs the small craft westward against the tide. The wind blows the spray sideways into our faces. In daylight we could ride the distance from Barn Elms to Richmond Palace in half the time, covering the ground as the crow flies across the deer park, but in darkness the river is the surest way, though it loops its course lazily around the headland.

"But of some special significance, for them to disturb Your Honour?" The wind snatches my words away even as they leave my mouth.

"One of Her Majesty's maids of honour, apparently, killed within a stone's throw of the queen's own privy apartments, under the noses of the yeomen of the guard and the serjeants-at-arms—you may imagine the entire household is in an uproar. But it is the manner of this death that makes my lord Burghley summon me with such urgency. We will learn more anon."

He sits back and points up as the white stone façade of the palace looms ahead, a pale shadow under the moon, its chapel and great hall rising to an imposing height either side of the gatehouse with its warmly lit windows. From the range that flanks the river, a forest of slender turrets rises against the clouds, all topped with gilded minarets, onion-shaped, like the palace of an Eastern sultan. A servant is waiting for us at the landing stage behind the palace where a row of wooden barques are tethered, the water slapping idly at their sides; he welcomes the principal secretary with a bow, but his face is strained. Here, where the royal apartments face the river, he shows us to a little postern gate set into the wall. By the door stand two men, each holding a pikestaff, who move aside to let the servant pass. He bangs hard on this door and calls out; a small grille is slid open and a series of brusque, whispered exchanges follow before the door is opened wide and a short, round-faced man with feathery white hair under a black skullcap strides through, his arms outstretched, his face creased in a harried frown. He embraces Walsingham briefly, then catches sight of me and the anxiety in his drooping eyes intensifies.

"This is . . . ?"

Walsingham lays a hand on his arm to placate him.

"Giordano Bruno. A most loyal servant of Her Majesty," he adds, with a meaningful nod.

The older man considers me for a moment, then a light of recognition steals over his face.

"Ah. Your Italian, Francis? The renegade monk?"

I incline my head in acknowledgement; it is not a compliment, though it is a title I wear with some pride.

"So the Roman Inquisition likes to call me."

"Doctor Bruno is a *philosopher*, William," Walsingham gently corrects.

The older man reaches out a hand to me.

"William Cecil, Lord Burghley. Francis has spoken highly of your talents, Doctor Bruno. You served Her Majesty well in Oxford this spring, I understand."

I feel my chest swell and my face flush at this; Walsingham is miserly with his praise to your face, which makes you strive for it all the more, yet he has talked about me favourably to Lord Burghley, the queen's lord high treasurer, one of her most influential advisers. You fool, I chide myself, smiling; you are thirty-five years of age, not a schoolboy praised for his penmanship, though this is exactly how I feel. I continue to beam to myself even as Burghley's face turns sombre again.

"This way, gentlemen. Let us not waste time."

Inside the palace, the air seems stiff with fear. Faces, half hidden, peer anxiously out of doorways as our footsteps echo along wood-panelled corridors lit by candles whose flames waver in the disturbance we make, sending our shadows looming and shrinking along the walls as Walsingham and I follow Burghley's purposeful strides.

"I almost forgot, Francis," he says, over his shoulder. "How was the wedding?"

"Well enough, I thank you. I have left the party in full spate. Heaven only knows what will be left of my house when Sidney's youngbloods have finished their roistering."

"I am sorry, truly, to draw you away," Burghley replies, lowering his voice. "If the circumstances were not so very . . . well, you shall see. Her Majesty asked for you in person, Francis." He hesitates. "Well—to be honest, she called first for Leicester. But I thought the earl, after a day at his nephew's wedding feast . . ."

Walsingham nods.

"I thought you were the man to take charge, Francis. The queen is rightly afraid. This thing has happened within her own walls and its implications . . ." The words die on his lips.

"Understood. Show me this deed, William, then take me to the queen."

He brings us up two flights of stairs where the panels are painted in scarlet, green, and gold tracery, then along a more richly furnished and considerably warmer corridor, hung with tapestries and damask cloths; I guess we are nearing the site of the queen's private apartments. On the way we pass three more armed men in royal livery. Burghley pauses outside a low wooden door where a stout man stands guard, a sword at his belt. The lord treasurer nods to him, and he steps back; Burghley rests his hand on the latch and his shoulders twitch.

"Your discretion, gentlemen."

The door swings open and I follow Walsingham through into a small chamber, well lit by good wax candles, where a body lies in repose on a bed whose curtains have been drawn back. At first I think it is a young man; the breeches and shirt are a man's certainly, but as we step closer I see the long fair hair spread over the pillow, threads of gold glinting in the candlelight. Her motionless face is swollen and purple, with the popping eyes and bulging tongue that tell of strangulation. The white linen shirt she wears has been ripped down the front, though the two halves have been arranged to preserve her modesty, even in death. She looks young, no more than sixteen or seventeen; her slender neck is ringed with dark bruises and ugly welts and her breeches are torn, the silk stockings muddied and snagged. I glance from one to the other of my companions and understand with a jolt that I am flanked by the two highest officials of the queen's Privy Council. This is no ordinary death.

Walsingham pauses for a moment, perhaps out of respect, then walks around the bed, examining the body dispassionately, as if he were her physician.

"Who is she?"

"Cecily Ashe," Burghley says. He has closed the door behind us and stands by it, twisting his hands together; perhaps he feels we are committing an impropriety, three men gathered to stare at the barely cold body of a young woman. "One of Her Majesty's maids of honour, under the care of Lady Seaton. Her Majesty's lady of the bedchamber," he adds, for my benefit.

"Ah." Walsingham nods, and clasps his hand across his chin, obscuring his mouth. I have noticed that he does this when he does not wish to betray any emotion. "Ashe . . . Then she would be the eldest daughter of Sir Christopher Ashe of Nottingham, would she not? Poor child—she has not been at court even a year. The same age as my Frances."

We stand silent for a moment, all our thoughts following Walsingham's to his seventeen-year-old daughter, the new bride who, perhaps even now, is being led to the marital bed by Sir Philip Sidney, a man eleven years her senior and with notoriously vigorous appetites.

"Almost the same age as my Elizabeth was when she died," Burghley adds softly. Walsingham glances at him; there is a moment of unspoken sympathy as their eyes meet and I sense that these two men share an understanding deeper than politics.

"The clothes?"

"Ah, yes." Burghley shakes his head. "The usual trouble, I suspect. Trying to steal out undetected to a tryst with someone she should not." He makes it sound as if this is a common problem.

"Has she been violated?"

Walsingham's tone is brisk again; Burghley gives a little cough.

"She has not yet been officially examined by the physician, but the body was found with the breeches and underclothes torn, the shirt ripped apart likewise. There are bruises and bloody marks on her thighs. She was laid out in the form of a crucifix, with her arms outstretched. There is something else you should see." Taking a deep breath, he crosses to the body and, taking one corner of the torn material gingerly between his forefinger and thumb as if it might scald him, he folds down the left side of the shirt to expose the girl's small, pale breast.

Walsingham and I both gasp simultaneously; there is a mark cut into the soft white flesh, over her still heart. The lines have been traced into the skin carefully and the blood blotted away, so that the mark stands out in jagged crimson lines, a shape that looks like a curved figure 2 with a vertical line bisecting its tail. This mark is unmistakably the astrological symbol for the planet Jupiter. He shoots me a questioning look, swift as blinking, but Burghley's sharp eye notes it.

"That is not all," says the lord treasurer, as he covers the girl again.

"In each of her outstretched hands she held these objects." From the wooden dresser beside the bed he holds up a rosary of dark wood adorned with a gold Spanish cross, and with the other hand he presents Walsingham with a small wax effigy, about the size of a child's doll.

"Dear God," Walsingham breathes, holding up the figurine for me to see. It is crudely made, but unquestionably an imitation of Queen Elizabeth; red wool for hair, a cloak fashioned from a scrap of purple silk, a paper crown on its head, a sewing needle protruding from its breast, where it has been stabbed through the heart. We both look at Burghley, who nods, once. No ordinary murder indeed.

"Who found her?" I ask, breaking the silence.

"The queen's chaplain," Burghley replies, turning away from the corpse.

"What was the chaplain doing in her chamber?"

"Oh—she was not found here," he says, with a tight little laugh at the implication. "No—the body was outside. There is a ruined chapel behind the privy orchard—the last remains of the priory that used to stand on this site. It is separated from the palace compound by high walls and its garden grown somewhat derelict. Lately it has been said"—Burghley frowns—"that it was becoming a popular place for meetings between the queen's ladies and the court gentlemen, because it is out of the way and not properly patrolled. This sort of thing is strictly forbidden by Her Majesty, you understand. Being a man of stern propriety, the chaplain thought he would check the area as dusk fell. And he found her laid out there as I have described."

"He saw no one fleeing as he approached?" I ask.

"No one, he says, though there is an open entrance to the abandoned garden from the river. The killer could have slipped away and hidden on the bank, perhaps even had a boat tied up farther downstream. The only other way in is through the gatehouse from the privy orchard, but at that time of the evening there are always people coming and going on the palace side, including the yeomen of the guard on their watch. No one recalls seeing anything out of the ordinary. But then dusk was falling and since she was dressed as a boy . . ." Burghley sighs, runs his palm over his skullcap.

"You have set extra men-at-arms around the gates?" Walsingham asks.

"Naturally. The wharf at the back where you landed was already patrolled, as was the gatehouse at the front. But the captain of the palace guard has ordered more men to be set around the perimeter walls, and has sent a company to search the privy orchard and the deer park. Under cover of darkness, though, I fear they will have little success. The perpetrator could be long gone."

"Or he could still be inside the compound," I offer.

Both men turn to look at me; Walsingham raises his eyebrows for me to continue.

"Only, it seems this was hardly a spontaneous killing. All these devices and props were carefully prepared. And the victim was chosen deliberately too, it seems—maid of honour to the queen? This killer means to indicate a direct threat to Her Majesty, surely, and he is showing how near he can get to her person. And if the girl was dressed for a tryst, then whoever killed her either knew when and where to find her, or he was the very person she was waiting for."

Walsingham tilts his head to one side and considers me.

"You talk sense, Bruno. But let us keep such speculation between ourselves. Her Majesty will hardly be reassured to think that someone familiar to her own household may be behind this, and I must attempt to put her mind at rest."

"There is speculation enough in the palace as it is," Burghley says, his lips pursed. "The chaplain raised such a noise when he found her that by the time the news reached me, half the servants had already been to gape at the spectacle and embellished it in their own fashion before passing it on. We cannot hope to keep the details quiet now. Already the lower servants murmur of devilry, that this is the work of the Antichrist, come to fulfil the prophecy of the end times."

"The prophecy?" I look from one to the other of them, amazed.

Walsingham catches the alarm in my voice, and laughs softly.

"Did you think it was only learned men like yourself and Doctor Dee who knew of these prophecies? No, no—in England, Bruno, this year of Our Lord 1583 has been the talk of the common people long before it dawned. Even the poorest household has an almanac predicting the Great Conjunction of Jupiter and Saturn, the first of its kind in a thousand years, the dire consequences that will follow, the floods and famines and tempests and droughts, the marvels in the heavens—oh, there have been pamphlets and interludes circulating in the taverns and the market squares for as long as I can recall, promising that the prophecy of the end times will find its fulfilment in these days."

"The wars of religion in these last years have only fuelled the fire," Burghley adds, his jaw set tight.

"'When you shall hear of wars, and rumours of wars, be not troubled: for such things must needs be, but the end is not yet,'" I muse, quoting the Gospel of Saint Mark.

"These present wars began in universities and in kings' bedchambers, not in the movements of the heavens," Walsingham chips in sharply. "Nonetheless, the result has been to whip the populace into a frenzy of fear, and when unlettered people grow fearful, they fall back on old superstitions. I don't know what it is about the English, but they have a peculiar weakness for prophecies and predictions."

"We have had five people arrested this year in London alone for disseminating printed prophecies of the queen's death," Burghley adds sagely.

"The people take this nonsense about the Great Conjunction seriously—and not just the humbler sort of folk," Walsingham says, his eyes flitting to the dead girl's breast. "It will be all the easier for the secret priests to crawl out of their dogholes and turn the people back to Rome if they believe the Second Coming is at hand."

"She held a rosary," Burghley says, almost in a whisper. "An effigy of the queen killed, and in the other hand a rosary. The message is clear, is it not? The triumph of Rome and Her Majesty's death?"

"Someone wishes us to think along those lines, certainly." Walsingham sets his jaw and a nerve twitches in his cheek. "And the sign of Jupiter, too. Her Majesty is skittish enough touching these movements of the planets, thanks to John Dee. Now she will insist her fears are grounded." He sighs. "I should go to her without delay. Bruno, you can begin by talking to anyone close to Cecily who might cast some light on her movements. Say you are Lord Burghley's man. William, you will point Doctor Bruno to the right people? And have the serjeants-at-arms search every private apartment in the building, as well as the kitchens, the chapel, and every common space. If this killer is still hereabouts, he will have a bloody shirt and knife he may have tried to hide somewhere."

Burghley nods, running his hand over his head again, and looks suddenly weary. He must be a good ten years older than Walsingham, perhaps in his mid-sixties already, though he has the appearance of better health. He glances at me sidelong, his eyebrows knit in concern.

"You will find the ladies-in-waiting somewhat hysterical, Doctor Bruno," he remarks drily. "Understandable, of course, though I was hard pushed to get any sense out of them. Still—perhaps a younger man with fine dark eyes and a pleasing smile might have better luck." He smiles grimly and pats me on the shoulder as he holds the chamber door open for me.

"That is the nearest you will get to a compliment from Burghley, Bruno," Walsingham says, following behind me.

"I assumed he was talking about you, Your Honour."

Burghley throws a look of amusement over his shoulder.

"At least he knows how to flatter, this one," he observes. "Let us hope he can turn it to good use with these women."

LADY MARGARET SEATON, Queen Elizabeth's lady of the bedchamber, does not seem hysterical when I am shown into the private chamber where she waits; if anything, she seems impressively composed, you might almost say guarded. Lord Burghley introduces me as a trusted assistant, before backing politely through the double doors and closing them behind him. Lady Seaton wears black as if she is already in mourning and sits back among her cushions, regarding me with shrewd eyes. She is older, some way through her forties, closer to the queen's own age, and though her fine skin begins to show the marks of time it is clear that she must have been considered a beauty in her youth. Two younger women sit on floor cushions on either side of her chair, clutching at her hands, both dressed in gowns of white silk and weeping copiously. At length she raises a hand and the girls make an effort to dampen their sobs.

"What are you?" she asks, in a clear voice. There is something accusatory in her tone; I sense that her apparent dislike is not personal, but that she is acutely conscious of her station and would prefer to have been sent someone with more authority.

"I am an Italian, my lady. Lord Burghley has asked me to see if you can recall anything that—"

"I mean by profession. You are not a courtier, I don't think. Are you a diplomat?"

"Of sorts, my lady."

She rearranges her broad skirts, rustling the silks ostentatiously while avoiding my eye.

"How odd, that Burghley should send a foreigner. But continue."

"The young lady, Cecily Ashe—do you have any idea whom she might have been meeting in the ruined chapel this evening?"

"The papists have done this, you know," Lady Seaton snaps, leaning forward. At the same time, I note that the redheaded girl kneeling by the left side of her chair bites her lip and drops her eyes to the floor.

"Why do you say so, my lady?"

"Because of the sacrilegious nature of it." She looks at me as though this should be obvious. "I suppose you are one, or have been?"

"Once. But His Beatitude Pope Gregory had me excommunicated and wishes to burn me. This is why I now live under Her Majesty's kindlier skies."

"I see." Her expression changes to one of curiosity. "What did you do to upset him?"

"I have read books forbidden by the Holy Office. I abandoned the Dominican order without permission. I have written that the Earth turns around the Sun, that the stars are not fixed, and that the universe is infinite." I shrug. "Among other things."

She considers this with a slight wrinkle of her nose, as if a bad smell had drifted into her orbit.

"Good heavens. Then I'm not surprised. To answer your question, I have no idea why Cecily should have been in that chapel. I last saw her at about four o'clock this afternoon, when she was engaged under my supervision with the other maids of honour in preparing the queen's jewels for the evening. There was to be a musical recital in the great hall after supper. Master Byrd was to play." Here she pauses, and there is a minute tremor in her voice. The red-haired girl stifles a sob. "Cecily retired to dress with the other girls before Evensong, and that was the last time I set eyes on her."

"But evidently she slipped away to meet someone, disguised as a boy. Do you know who that might have been?"

Lady Seaton's eyes narrow.

"Preposterous," she says eventually, though her voice remains steady. "The very suggestion. These girls are under my direct authority, Master . . ."

"Bruno."

"Yes, so the idea that I should be so lax with their honour and reputations is deeply distasteful to me, especially in the circumstances. Her Majesty does not tolerate immorality at her court. Whatever your customs in Italy, the queen of England's maids of honour do not engage in trysts in broad daylight for all to see."

I am tempted to ask whether they always wait until dark, but sense that she would not respond well to mockery. The red-haired girl darts a furtive glance upward and catches my eye for a moment before quickly looking away, evidently distressed.

"I can only assume that she was crossing the courtyard and was dragged into the chapel garden by her assailant," Lady Seaton asserts, nodding a full stop, as if this is the last word on the matter. Then her face softens into something like regret. "Cecily was a particular favourite of Her Majesty's, you know. She liked Cecily to read to her from Seneca in the evenings. Cecily had the best Latin of any of the girls."

"*Seneca?*"

"Oh, yes, Master Bruno—no need to look so astonished. Our sovereign is highly educated and she expects the same standards of her attendants. She will not have girls who can't read to her and understand what they read."

I glance down at the red-haired girl, who blinks up at me again, biting her lip. She is the one I need to speak to, if I can only find a way to get her alone. I wonder if she reads Seneca. She looks barely old enough to have learned her letters.

"Why was she dressed in men's clothes?"

"I cannot account for that, Master Bruno. The girls are high-spirited, they do sometimes get up to games and pranks. Dressing up, and so on . . . ." The words die on her lips. It is clear that she will swear black is white if she must, rather than willingly offer anything that might reflect badly on her own vigilance over the dead girl.

"Thank you for your help, my lady." I bow and make as if to leave, then turn back, as if struck by an afterthought. "There is no reason to suppose that Cecily had any loyalty to the Roman faith?"

Lady Seaton is so outraged by this that she rises to her feet, though the vast bulk of her farthingales means she almost becomes stuck in the chair, so the gesture loses some of its impact. She shakes off the girls' hands on her arms.

"How dare you, sir! Her family's loyalty to the queen is impeccable, and if you think I would not have been able to sniff out a papist right under my own nose—"

"Forgive me. I was only thinking aloud. She was found with a rosary in her hand."

"Planted on her by the papist conspirators who carried out this heinous deed!" She points a finger into my face. "I think you should leave, sir. You come here charged with finding poor Cecily's killer and instead accuse her of whoring and popery!"

I murmur an apology for any offence caused and retire, backing through the doors in a low bow. As I leave, I catch the red-haired girl's eye and try to convey by a look that I would welcome any confidence she may choose to share. It is not clear if she has understood.

The many fine tapestries hanging on the walls keep the corridor free of draughts, but I hear an insistent wind worrying at the window frames as I settle myself almost out of sight in a bay opposite the stairs, where I can watch the door to the chamber I have just left. Walsingham will be some time with the queen, I suppose, and there is nothing for me to do but wait and hope that the young maid of honour with the red hair will show herself at some point, without the company of Lady Seaton.

Minutes pass, and more minutes. Distant creaks and footfalls tell of activity elsewhere in this warren of passages, but my corridor remains empty. Cupping my hands around my face to the windowpane I can make out, under the moonlight, the expanse of the palace compound ahead of me, the great hall on the west side, and the chapel on the east, connected to the complex of privy apartments by a narrow covered bridge that spans the moat dividing us from the great court. The palace is well protected, bordered on one side by the deer park and another by the river, and all its gates and entrances heavily guarded against intruders. But the truth is that any would-be assassin has ample opportunity to run at Queen Elizabeth during her open procession from the Chapel Royal to her chambers of state every Sunday, or her summer progressions around the country, or any of her many other public appearances. Walsingham frets endlessly over her faith in the love of her subjects—naïve, in his opinion—and her desire to show herself unafraid among them; but she insists that she will not be cowed by whispered threats. She likes to meet her people face-to-face, to give them her hand to kiss. Perhaps this is because Principal Secretary Walsingham does not tell her everything he hears regarding plots hatched in the seminaries in France, now filled with angry young Englishmen in exile, who believe that the Papal Bull of 1570 declaring Elizabeth a heretic also gave them, in not so many words, a mandate to kill her on behalf of the Catholic church.

But tonight's murder is not the reckless act of a hot-blooded youth willing to martyr himself for his faith; there is a chilling touch of theatre about it, a degree of planning designed to inspire real fear. Fear of what, though? The Catholics? The planets? There is a message, too; Burghley reads it straightforwardly, but I am not so sure. The sign of Jupiter troubles me, perhaps only because it comes so near to me and Doctor Dee and our secret work. I stretch my legs out in front of me and sigh. After my experience in Oxford, I had hoped for some respite from the undercurrents of violence that attend the court of Elizabeth. I am a philosopher, after all; what I really wish for is time to work on my book in peace, for as long as King Henri III of France sees fit to go on paying for me to live here with his ambassador. When I agreed to work for Walsingham shortly after my arrival in England, I had thought it would be merely a question of keeping my eyes open at the embassy, watching who among the English nobles came to dinner there, who stayed for Mass, who grew close to the ambassador, and who was corresponding with whom among the Catholics in exile. Now, for the second time, I find myself caught up in a matter of violent death and I am not sure what is expected of me.

My thoughts are disturbed by the soft click of a door opening at the end of the passageway; I shrink back into the window seat and lean my head around cautiously, but in the dim light I can only make out the figure of a woman, too slender to be Lady Seaton. She carries a candle in a holder and walks briskly toward me; as she passes under a sconce of candles on the wall, I catch a flash of red-gold under her white linen cap and whistle softly through my teeth. She gives a little cry and immediately stifles it with her hand; I press my finger to my lips, uncross my legs from the seat, and we both freeze, still as marble, waiting to see if any guard comes running. A moment passes before we are satisfied that no one has heard.

"I waited for you. Can we speak privately?" I ask her, my voice barely escaping my lips.

She hesitates for a moment, then glances over her shoulder before nodding. Holding her finger to her lips, she gestures for me to follow her, and leads me down the staircase, along another passage and into an empty gallery, unlit except for the moonlight that spills through the diamond panes, casting pale shapes on the wooden boards, faintly coloured where the windows bear heraldic emblems of stained glass. Almost as soon as the doors swing shut behind us, she appears to regret her decision; her eyes open wide in fear and she looks frantically about her.

"If they should find me here—"

I make soft reassuring noises, such as you might make to a skittish horse, while guiding her away from the door toward one of the large windows.

"You were friends with Cecily?"

She nods, with emphasis, then smothers a sob behind her handkerchief.

"What is your name?"

"Abigail Morley."

"You know more than Lady Seaton, I think, Abigail," I prompt gently.

She nods again, disconsolate; she will not meet my eye and I guess that she fears disloyalty to her dead friend.

"Did Cecily have a lover? Did she tell you she was going to meet someone? If you know anything, it may help to catch him."

Finally the girl raises her head.

"Lady Seaton says it was black magic."

"People talk of magic to cover their ignorance. But you know better, I think."

Her eyes widen in amazement at this and she almost smiles; the audacity of someone questioning her mistress's authority. She is standing close to me and I notice that she is pretty in that milky, English way, though there is something bland about her features that does not move me. I prefer a woman with more fire in her eyes.

"We are not allowed to associate with the gentlemen of the court," she whispers. "It is strictly forbidden. Even the merest rumour could have us sent straight back to our families in disgrace with no chance of return, you understand?"

"That seems hard."

The girl shrugs, as if to say things have always been arranged like this.

"Being maid of honour to Her Majesty is the surest step to making a grand marriage at court. This is why our fathers send us here, and lay out their money for the privilege. Cecily told me her father paid more than a thousand pounds to get her a place."

"Poor man. A double loss for him, then. But how are you supposed to make these grand marriages if you are not allowed near the courtiers?"

"Oh, the marriages are made for us," she says, with a little pout. "Between our fathers and the queen. And naturally no man wants to know us if there are rumours flying about the court concerning our virtue. Besides," she adds, slipping into a sly grin, "Her Majesty is renowned as the Virgin Queen, so she thinks we should all follow her example. She should really know that all the tricks of secrecy make it the more exciting."

"Like dressing as a boy?"

"Cecily was not the first girl to have tried that. You're just noticed less—it makes it simpler to slip away. Men have it so much easier," she adds, with a pointed look, as if this imbalance were my fault.

"Well, I'm afraid your poor friend is beyond any disgrace now. So she did have a sweetheart?"

"She had met someone," the girl confides. "Quite recently—for the last month she was all smiles and secrecy, and quite distracted. If Lady Seaton chastised her for not having her mind on her duties, she would blush and giggle and send me meaningful looks." A resentment has crept into Abigail's tone.

"But did she tell you who he was?"

"No," she says, after a slight hesitation, and in the silence that follows her eyes dart away. "But in the maids' chamber at bedtime, she would hint that he was someone very important—someone she evidently thought would impress us, anyway. He must have been rich, because he bought her beautiful presents. A gold ring, a locket, and the most exquisite tortoiseshell mirror. She was convinced he meant to marry her, but then she always was fanciful."

"So he was here at court?" In my haste I inadvertently clutch at her sleeve, startling her; quickly I withdraw my hand and she takes a step back.

"I assume so. He must have been a frequent visitor, anyway, because lately she would often go missing at odd times, and she would come back all flushed and hugging her secret, though she made sure we all knew. She begged me to tell Lady Seaton she was feeling unwell, but the old woman is no fool, as you saw—she was growing suspicious. Cecily would have been found out sooner or later—or ended up with a full belly."

"But someone found her first," I muse. "So she never mentioned his name? You're certain? Or anything that would identify him?"

She shakes her head, firmer this time.

"No name, I swear. Nothing except that he was unusually handsome, apparently."

"Well, that would narrow it down in the English court."

She giggles then, finally looking me in the eye; at the same moment, the sound of footsteps echoes along the passageway outside and the laughter dies on her lips.

"Have you told anyone else of this?" I hiss. She shakes her head. "Good. Say nothing about the secret suitor—neither you nor any of the other girls who knew about it. And tell no one that you spoke to me. If you remember anything else, you can always get a message to me in secret at the French embassy. I have lodgings there."

Her eyes grow wider in the gloom. "Am I in danger?"

"Until they know who killed your friend and why, there is no knowing who might be in danger. It is as well to be on your guard."

The treads—two people, by the sound of it—grow closer; just as they stop outside the doors to the gallery I motion to her to keep back in the shadows, out of sight. Then I open the door just as the guards are about to reach for the handle, affecting to jump out of my skin at the sight of them.

"*Scusi*—I was looking for the office of my lord Burghley? I think I have become lost in all the corridors." I offer a little self-deprecating laugh; they glance at each other, but they lead me away without looking farther into the room.

"Lord Burghley, my arse. You'll answer to the captain of the palace guard first, you Spanish dog," says one, as he drags me roughly toward the stairs. "How did you get in here?"

"Lord Burghley let me in," I repeat, with a sigh; in six months in England I have learned to expect this. They regard all foreigners—especially those of us with dark eyes and beards—as Spanish papists come to murder them in their beds. I will find my way to Burghley eventually; what matters is that no one should know the maid Abigail has spoken to me. Cecily's mystery inamorato may not know that she kept his identity a secret; there is every chance he may want to silence her friends too. Assuming—and I have learned to assume nothing without proof—that he is connected to this bizarre display of murder.

Chapter 3

SALISBURY COURT, LONDON.
26TH SEPTEMBER, YEAR OF OUR LORD 1583

"Cut off both her tits, the way I heard it." Archibald Douglas leans back in his chair and picks his teeth with a chicken bone, apparently satisfied that he has delivered the definitive version. Then he remembers another detail and sits forward in a hurry, his finger wagging at no one in particular. "Cut off both her tits and stuck a Spanish crucifix up her. Fucking brute." He slumps again and drains his glass.

"Monsieur Douglas, *s'il vous plaît.*" Courcelles, the ambassador's private secretary, raises his almost invisible eyebrows in a perfect mannerism of shock that, like all his gestures, appears learned and rehearsed. He passes a hand over his carefully coiffed hair and tuts, pursing his lips, as if his objection is principally to the Scotsman's vulgar turn of phrase. "*I* was told by a friend at court she was strangled with a rosary. On the steps of the Chapel Royal, if you can believe it." He presses a hand to his breastbone with a great intake of breath. He should be in a playing company, I think; his every move is a performance.

Across the table, William Fowler catches my eye for the space of a blink before he glances away again.

"These reports do have a tendency to grow in the telling," he says evenly, looking at the ambassador. He too speaks with the Scottish accent, though to my foreign ears his conversation seems more comprehensible than the broad tones of Douglas. Fowler is a neat, self-contained man in his mid-twenties, clean-shaven with brown hair that hangs almost into his eyes; his voice is restrained, as if he is always imparting a confidence, so that you have to lean in to listen. "I have been a frequent visitor to the court on official business these past days, and I'm afraid the truth is less sensational." But he doesn't elaborate. I have noticed that Fowler, my new contact whom I have met for the first time this evening and have not yet spoken to alone, has a talent for implying that he knows far more than he is prepared to say in company. Perhaps this is why the French ambassador is drawn to him.

Why Castelnau tolerates Douglas, on the other hand, is anyone's guess. The older Scotsman is some kind of minor noble, about forty years of age, with prematurely greying reddish hair and a face hardened by drink and weather, who has attached himself to the embassy with the promise of supporting the Scottish queen's claim to the English throne. Improbable as it seems, he is a senator in the Scottish College of Justice and said to be well connected among the Scottish lords, both Catholic and Protestant; he comes personally recommended by Queen Mary of Scotland. For the ambassador, these connections must be worth the price of feeding him. I have my doubts. Given that I too have been obliged to survive these past seven years by seeking the patronage of influential men, perhaps I should be more charitable to Archibald Douglas, but I like to think that I at least offer something to the households of my patrons in return for their hospitality, even if it is only some lively dinner-table conversation and the prestige of my books. Douglas brings nothing, as far as I can see, and I am not persuaded by his professed interest in Mary and her French supporters; he strikes me as one of those who will always agree with whoever happens to be pouring the wine. It irks me that

Claude de Courcelles, the ambassador's too-pretty secretary, tars me with the same brush as Douglas; Courcelles is responsible for making the embassy's books balance, and he looks with undisguised resentment on those he views as leeches. I am often forced to remind him that I am a personal friend of his sovereign, whereas Douglas—well, Douglas claims to be a friend of many influential people, including the Queen of Scots herself, but I cannot help wondering: If he is so popular among the Scottish and English nobles, why does he not beg his dinner at one of their tables once in a while? Why, for that matter, is he never in Scotland at his own table?

The murder at court has been the chief topic of conversation at dinner this evening, eclipsing even the usual preoccupation with the Scottish queen and the ambitions of her Guise cousins. That night at Richmond Palace, I told Burghley and Walsingham of my conversation with Abigail; since then, the maids of honour have been given extra guards and the men at court are being questioned again but, naturally, when it comes to forbidden affairs, people are conditioned to lie. Walsingham grows increasingly anxious; the queen's household at Richmond numbers upward of six hundred souls. Though the hierarchies are strictly defined—each senior servant responsible for the duties of those below him or her—how can so many people be made to give true accounts of their movements on one evening? Queen Elizabeth, for her part, chooses to believe that a crazed intruder broke into the palace compound; her solution is to move the court earlier than usual to her central London palace at Whitehall, which is not so exposed to the open country and easier to defend. She will not admit the possibility that the killer might still be living among them. Walsingham had said he would send for me if he needed further assistance. Meanwhile, he said, I should return home and turn my attentions to the conversations behind closed doors at the French embassy.

In the wood-panelled dining room at Salisbury Court, the candles are burning low and the clock has already struck midnight, but the dishes with the remains of Castelnau's grand dinner still litter the table, their sauces long cold and congealed. The servants will clear the board in the morning; after the meal is when the ambassador addresses himself to private business with his guests. Now that England's most influential and restless Catholic lords gather so often around Castelnau's table, it makes sense not to risk these discussions being overheard by servants; after all, says the ambassador, you can never be too careful. This means that we must all try to ignore Archibald Douglas toying with the carcass of a chicken, or wiping a finger through cold gravy and licking it while he delivers his half-formed opinions.

Michel de Castelnau, Seigneur de Mauvissière, pushes his plate away from him and rests his elbows on the table, surveying his company of men. He is remarkably hale for a man of sixty winters; you have to look hard for the flecks of silver in his dark hair, and his dour face with its long bulbous nose is brightened by keen eyes that miss nothing. Castelnau is a cultured man, not without his vanities, who likes his supper table busy with men of wit and progressive ideas, those who are not afraid of controversy and enjoy a good argument in the pursuit of knowledge, whether in the sciences, theology, politics, or poetry. I still do not see where a man like Douglas fits into this scheme, except that he has Mary Stuart's personal blessing. In the low amber light, our shadows loom large behind us, wavering on the walls.

"A virgin defiled in the very court of the Virgin Queen." The ambassador's gaze travels steadily over each of us in turn. "My friends, this was done to slander the Catholics. Why else? Crucifix, rosary—it matters little. The details may differ in the reports but the intent is the same: to stir up fear and hatred—as if more were needed. *The Catholics have done this*, the English are saying in the street. *The Catholics will stop at nothing, they mean to kill our Virgin Queen and make us all slaves to the pope again.* This is what they are saying." He puts on a peevish, whining approximation of an English voice to simulate the common gossips. Courcelles laughs sycophantically. Douglas belches.

"What *I* hear," says a new voice that cuts through the silence like a diamond on glass, "is that her body was marked all over in blood with symbols of black magic." He looks directly at me as he says this, the one who has spoken in that clipped, aristocratic tone, the one who sits half in shadow at the far end of the table. Everything about him is sharp; pointed face, pointed beard, brows like Gothic arches, eyes hard as arrow-heads. He has been unusually silent this evening, but I can feel the resentment emanating from him like the heat of a fire every time he turns those narrowed, unblinking eyes on me.

Castelnau casts a nervous glance my way; despite his secretary's misgivings, the ambassador has never been other than a genial, even kindly, host to me since I arrived in April as his houseguest, at his king's request, but I know this part of my reputation troubles him. In Paris I taught the art of memory—a unique system I had developed from the Greeks and Romans—to King Henri himself, who called me his personal philosopher; naturally this elevated position drew envy from the learned doctors of the Sorbonne, who whispered into every ear that my memory techniques were a kind of sorcery, born of communion with devils. It was these rumours, together with the rising influence of the hard-line Catholic faction at the French court, that led to my temporary exile in London. Castelnau is an honest Catholic; not an extremist like the Guise crowd, but devout enough to be worried when people joke to him about keeping a sorcerer in his house. He is another who warns me that my friendship with Doctor Dee will not do my reputation any favours. I suspect he says this because his close friend Henry Howard hates Dee, though the cause of this passionate hatred remains a mystery to me.

Lord Henry Howard continues to stare at me from under his arched brows as if his position demands that I account for myself. "Did you not hear any such reports, Bruno?" he adds, in his smoothest voice. "It is your area of expertise, is it not?"

I smile pleasantly as I return his stare, unyielding. It would shock him to learn that I alone among the company saw the dead girl with my own eyes, but naturally no one at Salisbury Court knows I was there that night, any more than they know the truth about my work for Walsingham. Castelnau thinks that my acquaintance with Philip Sidney works to his own advantage; occasionally I feed him snippets of disinformation from the English court that support this illusion. Poor, trusting Castelnau; it gives me no pleasure to deceive him, but I must shift for myself in this world and I believe my future is safer with the powers of England, not France. I have no such qualms about informing on the likes of Henry Howard; a dangerous man, as Walsingham warned me. Since the execution for treason of his eldest brother, the late Duke of Norfolk, this Henry Howard, at the age of forty-three, is now the senior member of the most powerful Catholic family in England. He is not to be underestimated; unlike many of the English nobles, he has an excellent mind and has even taught Rhetoric at the University of Cambridge. Sidney says the queen appointed him to her Privy Council because she knows the wisdom of keeping one's enemies close, and because she likes to keep her more puritanical ministers on their toes.

"My lord is mistaken—I am only a humble writer," I reply, holding out my hands in a gesture of humility. "Like your lordship," I add, because I know the comparison will annoy him. It works; he glowers as if I have questioned the legitimacy of his birth.

"Oh, yes—how does your book, Howard?" Castelnau asks, perhaps grateful for the distraction.

Howard leans forward, an accusing finger raised to the ceiling.

"This murder—*this* was precisely the point of my book. When the queen herself leans so openly on divination and on conjurors like John Dee, her subjects are encouraged to follow suit. Since she has led them all away from their proper obedience to the pope, is it any wonder they clutch at supposed prophecies and any old grandam's tales of stars and planets? And where there is confusion, there the Devil rubs his hands with glee and sows his mischief. But people do not take heed."

"You are saying, if I understand you, my lord, that this murder occurred because people have not read your book thoroughly?" I ask, all innocence. Castelnau flashes me a warning look.

"I am saying, *Bruno*"—Howard enunciates my name as if it set his teeth on edge—"that all these things are connected. A sovereign who turns her face from God's anointed church, who claims all spiritual authority for herself but will not walk out of doors without consulting the constellations? Prophecies of the end of days, the coming of the Antichrist, rumours of wars—the proper order is overturned, and now madmen are emboldened to slaughter the innocent in the name of the Devil. I'll wager it will not be the last."

Douglas snaps his head up at this, as if the conversation at last promises more of interest than his chicken carcass.

"But if the reports are to be believed," I say carefully, "it seems rather that this killer did his work in the name of the Catholic church."

"Those who have slipped out from under the authority of Holy Mother Church will always be the first to blaspheme her," Howard counters, as quick as if we were fencing, a thin smile curving his lips. "As I suppose you would know, Master Bruno."

"*Doctor* Bruno, actually," I murmur. I would not usually insist, but I happen to know from Walsingham that, while he may have a family title, Henry Howard holds only the degree of master. Among university men, these things matter. From his expression I can see that I have scored a hit.

"*Alors . . .*" Castelnau smiles uncertainly, holding out the wine bottle as a distraction, peering across our glasses to see who needs more drink. Douglas, the least needful of the company, thrusts his glass forward eagerly; as the ambassador passes the bottle down the table, we all jump like startled creatures at the soft click of the door, our nerves set on edge by the secretive nature of these meetings.

The company breathes with relief as the newcomers enter. Despite the late hour, it seems they have been expected, at least by our host. At first you might take them to be a couple, they step into the room so close and conspiratorial, until the young woman draws down her hood and moves immediately toward Castelnau with her arms outstretched; he stands and greets his young wife with a spaniel look in his eyes. When she moves into the light you see that she is not quite so young as you might at first think; her figure could be a girl's but her face betrays that she is the wrong side of thirty. Even so, that makes her nearly three decades younger than her husband; perhaps this accounts for the spark in his eyes. She places a delicate hand on her husband's shoulder, then raises her eyes briefly to look around the table. Marie de Castelnau is petite and slender, like a doll, the sort of woman men rush to protect, though she carries herself with the poise of a dancer, in a way that suggests she is well aware of her own allure. Her chestnut hair is bound up and caught in a tortoiseshell comb at the back of her neck, though loose strands tumble around her heart-shaped face; she brushes one away as she unlaces her cloak and takes in the assembled guests.

I catch her eye; she holds my gaze for a moment with something like curiosity, then demurely returns her attention to Castelnau, who pats her hand fondly. Walsingham was right: she is very beautiful. I try to smother that thought immediately.

"You have found our dear Throckmorton, then," the ambassador says, beaming at the young man who came in after his wife and now hovers by the door, still wearing a travelling cloak. "Close that behind you and come, take some wine." He gestures broadly to an empty chair. Courcelles is despatched in search of another bottle; the secretary is not too proud to take on a servant's duties when secrecy is at stake. For my part, I am surprised that I have been allowed to stay for what is evidently a clandestine meeting; Henry Howard may dislike me, but it seems Castelnau's faith in my loyalty to France, if not necessarily to Rome, is untarnished. My heartbeat quickens in anticipation.

"He came in by the garden?" Castelnau asks his wife anxiously.

"I came by Water Lane, my lord," the young man called Throckmorton says, as he takes the seat that was offered. He means that he entered the house the back way, from the river, where he would not be seen. Salisbury Court is a long, sprawling building at least a hundred years old, which has its main door at the front on Fleet Street, by the church of St. Bride's, but its garden slopes down as far as the broad brown waters of the Thames; anyone wishing to visit the embassy in private can land a boat at Buckhurst Stairs after dark, pass up Water Lane, and be admitted through a gate in the garden wall, without fear of being seen. This

Throckmorton seems young; his beardless face is narrow and elfin, framed by fair hair long enough to curl over his collar; he has a pleasant, open smile but his pale eyes dart around nervously, as if he half expected one of us to assault him while he was looking the other way. Seated, he unfastens his cloak; his eyes linger on me as an unfamiliar face, questioning, though not hostile.

"Doctor Bruno, you have not met Francis Throckmorton, I think?" Castelnau says, noticing the direction of the young man's gaze. "A most valuable friend to the embassy among the English." He nods significantly.

Howard regards the new arrivals without smiling, then cracks his knuckles together.

"Well then, Throckmorton," he says, without preamble. "What news from the queen?"

He means the other queen, of course: Elizabeth's cousin Mary Stuart, whom they believe is also the rightful queen of England, the only legitimate Tudor heir. *They* being the extremists of the Catholic League in France, led by the Duke of Guise (Mary's cousin on her mother's side), and those English Catholic nobles who see the tide in their own country turning against them, and gather around Castelnau's table to grumble and agitate for something to be done. Except that, at the moment, Mary Stuart is not queen of anything; her son James VI rules Scotland under Elizabeth's watchful eye, and Mary is imprisoned in Sheffield Castle, sewing, precisely so that she can't inspire a rebellion. This measure has apparently done nothing to lessen the number of plots fomenting in her name on both sides of the English Channel.

Throckmorton lays his hands flat on the table, palms down, and allows his gaze to travel around the company once more, then he draws himself up as if he were about to embark on some great oratory, and smiles shyly.

"Her Majesty Queen Mary asks me to convey that her spirits are greatly lifted by the love and support she receives from her friends in London and Paris, and very particularly by the fifteen hundred gold crowns my lord ambassador so generously sent to aid the comfort of her royal person."

Castelnau inclines his head modestly. Howard sits up, amazed.

"You *spoke* with her?"

"No." Throckmorton looks apologetic. "With one of her ladies. Walsingham has ruled that she may not have visitors for the present."

"But she may have letters?"

"Her official letters are all opened and read by her gaolers. But her women bring my correspondence in and out secretly, hidden in their undergarments." He blushes violently at the thought, and hurries on. "She is confident that her keepers have not yet found a means to read these. And she is permitted to have books." He gives Howard a significant look. "In fact, she most particularly asks that you send her a copy of your new book against prophecies, my lord Howard. She finds herself most eager to read it."

"She shall have it by your next delivery," Howard says, leaning back, his satisfaction evident in his smile.

"She is also particularly anxious," Throckmorton continues, looking hopefully from Douglas to Fowler, "to have news from her son. To know the King of Scotland's mind."

Castelnau gives a short, bitter laugh. "Wouldn't we all like to know that? Where will young James nail his colours, when he is finally made to choose?" He produces an exaggerated shrug.

"He does not write to his mother directly, then?" Howard frowns.

"Infrequently," Throckmorton says. "And when he does, he writes in the language of diplomacy, so that she can't be sure of his intentions. She fears that his loyalties are not wholly where they ought to lie."

"King James is seventeen," Fowler says, in that quiet, authoritative voice, so that everyone has to lean toward him. He dresses plainly, with no ruff, just a shirt collar protruding above his brown woollen doublet. In a small way, this pleases me; I have an instinctive mistrust of dandies. "He has only just emerged from the shadow of his regents—what seventeen-year-old, having tasted independence, would willingly hand over the reins again to his mother? He will need a more material advantage than filial sentiment if he is to be persuaded to support her cause. Besides," he adds, "he was not one year old when he last saw her. She may believe they have a natural bond, but James knows he stands to gain more from a queen on a throne than from one in prison."

"Well, Monsieur Throckmorton, you may assure Queen Mary that at this very moment, her son entertains at his court an ambassador of the Duke of Guise," Madame de Castelnau interrupts, looking out from under her fringe of lashes, "who will offer him the friendship of France if he will acknowledge his proper duty as Mary's son."

There are murmurs of surprise at this from around the table. Fury flashes briefly over Castelnau's face—this is clearly the first he has heard of it and, as far as he is concerned, France's friendship is not in Guise's hands to give—but I watch him master his anger, ever the professional diplomat. He does not want to reprimand his wife in public. She does not look at him, but there is a quiet triumph about the set of her mouth as she lowers her eyes again to the table.

"In any case," the ambassador says brightly, as if he has been having an entirely different conversation, "there is every reason to believe we will soon have a treaty that will give Queen Mary her liberty peacefully, restore her to her son, and allow France to preserve our friendship with both England and Scotland."

"Treaties be damned!"

Henry Howard throws back his chair and pounds a fist on the table so suddenly that again we all jolt in our seats. The candles have burned down so far that his shadow leaps and quivers up the panels behind him and creeps over the ceiling, looming like an ogre in a children's tale.

"In the name of Christ, man, the time for talking is over! Do you not understand this, Michel?" Howard bellows, leaning forward with both hands on the table to face down the ambassador, while Courcelles makes little ineffectual flapping gestures at him to lower his voice. "Are you so comfortable now at the English court that you do not feel which way the wind is blowing in Paris?"

"The King of France still hopes to forge a political alliance with Queen Elizabeth, and it is my job to make every effort to secure this while I represent his interests," Castelnau says, keeping his patience. But Howard will not be placated.

"The French people want no such alliance with a Protestant heretic, and your King Henri knows it—he feels the might of the Catholic League rising up at his back. No more treaties or marriages or seeking to appease and befriend the pretender Elizabeth—there is only one path left to us now!" He thumps the table again for good measure so that the plates rattle.

"As I recall," Castelnau says stiffly, maintaining his composure, "you were my greatest ally not so long ago when it came to the marriage negotiations between your queen and my king's brother."

"For the sake of appearance. But that was doomed before it began." Howard waves an arm in grand dismissal. "The Duke of Anjou never really wanted to marry Elizabeth—she's at least twenty years older than him, for pity's sake. I mean—would *you?*" He looks at the men around him, inviting scorn; Douglas responds with a lascivious cackle. "And the minute she sniffed her subjects' unrest at the idea," Howard continues, "she sent him packing. She will make no marriage now—and even if she does, it will never be with a Catholic prince. She has seen where that leads."

"Nor will she have an heir now, at the age of fifty," Marie de Castelnau points out, scorn in her voice. "France's best hope is to put Mary Stuart on the throne of England and from there let her work on her son as a mother and as a Catholic sovereign, to bring him back to his natural obedience. *Et voilà!*" She holds her hands out to us with a delighted smile, as if she has performed a conjuring trick, though her hands are empty. "The whole island united again under Rome."

"*Et voilà?*" I look at her, incredulous. "Problem solved? You talk as if they were chess pieces—move this one here, take this one off the board, let this one see he is threatened. *Fin de partie.* Is it so simple, madame, do you think?"

Marie presses her lips together until they turn white, but she returns my stare, defiant. Howard glares.

"You presume to speak—" he splutters, but Castelnau holds up a hand. He looks tired.

"Go on, Bruno," he says gently. "You have hardly spoken. I would like to hear what you have to say. You knew King Henri's mind as well as any of his councillors."

I can feel Fowler's eyes on me. Without turning in his direction, I know he is willing me to be circumspect, not to compromise my privileged position at this table by appearing hostile. Yet Castelnau expects me to be outspoken; he would be suspicious if I did not take the role of devil's advocate, I think.

"I say only that these queens are not dolls to be moved around at will." As I say it, I have a sudden image of the Elizabeth doll clutched in the dead hand of Cecily Ashe, the needle sticking from its breast. I shudder; the memory makes me falter. "This glorious reunification under Rome could not be achieved without great bloodshed in England. I hear no one mention that."

"Such things are taken for granted, you damned fool," Howard growls.

"Do you make bread without crushing the grain?" Marie says, half smiling, still pinning me with her stare. She has neat, white teeth; it seems she is not afraid to use them.

"The queen of the Scots will not shy away from spilling blood when it suits her, I assure you," Douglas declares confidently to the room, rousing himself from his own thoughts to pour another large glass of wine, which he drinks off almost in one go. "Now, I could tell you a story about the queen of the Scots." He laughs into his empty glass.

"Really? Is it the one about the pie?" Courcelles says, with a stagy roll of the eyes.

"Aye." Douglas's eyes light up. "After her husband died, there was a great feast—"

Courcelles holds up a hand.

"Perhaps on another occasion. I *think* Madame de Castelnau might not appreciate it."

"Oh. Aye. Sorry." Douglas glances at Marie and touches his fringe with a self-mocking grimace.

A brief, uncomfortable silence follows; everyone turns to look at him and I sense that I have missed something. A glance passes between Marie and Henry Howard but I cannot read its meaning. Her cheeks are flushed with excitement among the moving shadows that sculpt out the lines of her face, her eyes bright and determined, her lips softly parted, glistening. She sees me watching her and lowers her eyes modestly, but she glances up again to see if I am still looking.

"The seminaries in France are still working tirelessly to send missionary priests here undercover, my lords, and the Catholic network for their continued support remains strong," Fowler says, and the company turns to regard him. "We may pray that their endeavours succeed in bringing souls back to the Holy Roman Church—"

"Yes, Fowler, I admire your piety, and I'm sure we are all praying for the same thing," Howard cuts across him, impatient. "But they are gutting every Jesuit missionary they catch on the scaffold at Tyburn like pigs on a butcher's block, as a warning to potential converts. It is time to accept that this country will not be made Catholic again by politicking nor by preaching. Only by force."

"Then—forgive me if I seem slow—but you are talking about an invasion?" I turn, wide-eyed, from Howard to Castelnau. It is not really a question; the ambassador's face answers with a look of helpless sorrow.

"Michel—is this wise, that he sit here with us?" Howard snaps his fingers toward me, impatient now. "We all know this man is wanted by the Holy Office on charges of heresy. Tell me—where do you think his loyalties naturally fall, in this enterprise? Hm? With Rome, or with his fellow excommunicate Elizabeth?"

"Doctor Bruno is a personal friend of my king," Castelnau says quietly, "and I will vouch for his loyalty to France myself. His ideas might occasionally seem a little"—he searches for the diplomatic term—"*unorthodox*, but he remains a Catholic. He attends Mass regularly with my family here in the embassy chapel, and always observes the terms of his excommunication. Which is something we may resolve in time, eh, Bruno?"

I assume what I hope is an expression of piety and nod gravely.

Howard scowls but says nothing more, and I feel a sudden rush of affection for the ambassador, and a corresponding pang of regret for my own deception. Whatever unfolds in this case, I determine that Walsingham will know the ambassador argued for peace. Castelnau, like King Henri of France, is a moderate, the sort of Catholic who believes that faith should be able to accommodate a variety of viewpoints. He is a man of integrity, in his way; he would not choose war, but perhaps he will not be given a choice. His wife, on the other hand, looks as if she can't wait.

"Listen," she says now, clasping her hands and allowing her bright eyes to sweep around the company before adding, "my lords, friends," with a calculated lowering of her lashes. "We have come together around this table from different backgrounds, but we all share one common goal, do we not? We all believe that Mary Stuart is the rightful heir to the English throne, and that she would restore the Catholic faith that unites us, is it not so?"

There is a swell of murmured assent from the company, some more enthusiastic than others; I catch Fowler's eye again and look quickly away.

"Besides, Mary Stuart on the English throne would better serve the interests of our respective nations," Marie continues briskly, stretching out her elegant fingers and affecting to examine the colourful array of rings she wears. "This joins us in our purpose as much as our religion. We must take care to remember what makes us natural allies, even when we may disagree, or we shall lose all hope of success." Here she looks up and aims the full beam of her smile at me, before turning it on the rest. I watch the ambassador's wife with fresh curiosity. Whatever her reputation for piety, there can be no doubting her political acumen; beneath the smiles and the modest blushes lies a steely force of will that contrasts with her husband's habit of trying to balance all interests harmoniously. I steal a glance at Castelnau; he pinches the bridge of his nose between his finger and thumb and looks weary. It seems the balance of power in the embassy has subtly shifted since Marie's return.

"Shall I fetch fresh candles, my lord?" Courcelles murmurs; without our realising it, the feeble flames have almost died and we are sitting in near darkness.

"No." Castelnau pushes his chair back and rises heavily. "We will retire. My wife is not long returned from Paris and she needs to rest. Tomorrow evening my chaplain will say Mass here before supper. Good night, gentlemen. I think, Claude, that Monsieur Douglas may need a guest room." He nods down the table to where Douglas appears to have fallen asleep facedown on his hands. Courcelles makes a little moue of disgust.

Our host holds the dining-room door open for us, bidding us a good night as we file past him into the corridor. I am forced to halt abruptly as Henry Howard, in front of me, embraces Castelnau in the French style, though with a very English lack of warmth.

"Speaking of natural allies—you know we must talk to Spain if this is to proceed," he hisses in the ambassador's ear as he leans in. "Sooner rather than later."

Castelnau sighs.

"So you say."

"Throckmorton carries letters from Mary to Spain's embassy as well. Oh—you didn't know?"

Castelnau looks wounded at the news, as if he had just learned that his wife was unfaithful. He is still clasping Howard by the arm.

"She involves Mendoza? But the man is so . . . ."

"Forthright?"

"I was going to say uncouth. For an ambassador."

"Mendoza is a man of action," Howard says emphatically, then bows curtly and leaves, the implicit criticism still hanging in the air.

Outside in the passageway, once we are out of earshot, Howard rounds on me, pointing a finger heavy with gold into my face.

"You may have duped the French king and his ambassador, Bruno, but you should know that I do not like the look of you at all."

"I can only apologise, my lord. These are the looks God gave me."

He narrows his eyes and leans back to give me a long hard appraisal, like a man who suspects he is being sold an unreliable horse.

"I hear what is said of you in Paris."

"And what is that, my lord?"

"Don't toy with me, Bruno. That you practise forbidden magic."

"Ah, that."

"And it is said you converse with devils."

"Oh, all the time. They often ask after your lordship. They say they are keeping a place warm for you."

Howard steps even closer. He is taller than I, but I do not step back. His breath is hot in my face.

"Joke all you like, Bruno. You are nothing but a glorified jester, just as you were at the French court, and a licenced fool may say anything. But when King Henri no longer has the power to protect you, who will be laughing then?"

"Can a sovereign lose his power just like that, my lord?"

He laughs then, low and knowing.

"Watch and wait, Bruno. Watch and wait. Meanwhile, I shall have my eye on you."

There are footsteps on the boards behind us; Howard breaks off, gives me a last blast of his disapproving glare, then hastens away, calling for a servant to bring his cloak. I turn to see William Fowler with Courcelles beside him.

"Good night, Doctor Bruno," Fowler says, his smooth face inscrutable in the candlelight. "It was a pleasure to meet you."

Likewise, I assure him, my own expression as neutral as his. He reaches out to shake my hand and there is a paper folded into his palm; I tuck it into my own with a finger and bid him a safe journey as I turn toward the staircase, wishing that I could walk with him now so that we might talk openly and together make some sense of what we had heard that night.

Chapter **4**

It feels as if I have barely closed my eyes when there comes a soft, insistent knocking at the door of my chamber. Dawn is just creeping around the edge of the shutters; only bad news brings callers this early. I bundle myself into a pair of underhose and a shirt to unlatch the door for my impatient visitor, steeling myself, but it is only Léon Dumas, the ambassador's clerk, who hurtles into the room so quickly in his haste not to be seen that he almost knocks me backward and cracks his head against the sloping ceiling. Here on the second floor of the house, under the eaves, the rooms are designed for people of my height, not his.

Dumas rubs his forehead and sits heavily on my bed. He is an earnest young man of twenty-seven, tall and skinny with thinning hair and slightly bulging eyes that give him a permanent expression of alarm— though I cannot help feeling that this has intensified since I persuaded him to share with me the ambassador's correspondence. Now he looks up at me with those big eyes and a pained frown, as if the knock on the head was my doing as well. He is fully dressed.

"Léon. You are up with the lark—is something the matter?"

He shakes his head.

"I only wanted to warn you—my lord ambassador has already gone down to his private office to make a start on the day's correspondence. He was up half the night reading the letters from Mary Stuart that Monsieur Throckmorton brought from Sheffield, and now he sets about writing his replies. He wants them delivered to Throckmorton's house at Paul's Wharf before nightfall today—apparently Throckmorton rides for Sheffield again tomorrow at first light."

"Good. So Throckmorton expects you sometime this afternoon?"

"I believe so. Castelnau will spend the morning writing his letters and ciphering them and I must be there to assist him. Then he will leave me to write out the fair copies while he and the rest of the household are dining, and when he has eaten he will approve and seal them and I will be despatched."

"So . . ." I run over the timing in my mind. "We will need to work quickly. Have you seen the letters from Queen Mary?"

He shakes his head, a nervous, twitching motion.

"No. But the packet is in his writing desk."

"Read them while he is out. If you do not have time to make a copy, at least get the sense so that you can relay it. But it may be that she has sent him a new cipher—they change it often for fear of interception. That we must copy, if it is there."

Dumas swallows hard and nods, sitting on his hands.

"If I don't have time to make two copies of his reply before he wants it sealed?"

I pace the room for a moment, considering.

"Then we will have to pay a visit to our friend Thomas Phelippes on the way to Master Throckmorton. Don't look so alarmed, Léon—Phelippes is so gifted in the art of interception, I suspect he may be a wizard. No one will see anything amiss."

Dumas looks miserable and jiggles on his hands more vigorously.

"But if we should be caught, Bruno?"

"Then we will be thrown out into the street," I reply solemnly. "We will be forced to join a troupe of travelling players. We can offer ourselves to play the ass for Christ's entry to Jerusalem on Palm Sunday."

"Bruno—"

"Ah—I know what you are going to say. Very well—you can be the front legs."

"Must you turn everything to a joke?"

Despite himself, he smiles, while I remember Howard's sharp insult from last night. *A glorified jester.* Was that really how they spoke of me in Paris? Queen Elizabeth keeps an Italian fool at court, who goes by the name of Monarcho; am I to be compared with him? It stung because I recognised the truth of it: with no money, land, or title to my name, I must make myself indispensable to men of wealth if I hope to thrive, and I have learned the hard way that most men of wealth would rather be entertained than enlightened. But might I not hope to do both? That, at least, was the intention of the book I was now writing, which would set forth my new ideas about the universe in a style that could be read outside the universities, by ordinary men and women, in their own language.

I sit beside Dumas on the bed and put my arm around his shoulder to chivvy him into better spirits.

"*Courage, mon brave.* Think of the coins chinking in your purse, if nothing else. You could hop across the river to Southwark and find yourself a willing girl in one of the bawdy houses. That would put a smile on your face. Besides"—I turn with a sigh toward the window, where a pale light slides through the gap in the shutters and slants across the bare boards—"I don't yet know what we are involved in here, Léon, but if we do our work carefully, a great many people may end up owing us their lives. Including," I add, in a whisper, as the young clerk's eyes threaten to pop out of his head, "the English queen herself."

I STEP OUT at around eleven into a golden autumn morning, as if the halfhearted English sun were belatedly trying to atone for its absence all through the cold, damp summer. In the embassy garden at Salisbury Court, the trees are a riot of colour, almost luminous against the blue with the dusty sunlight behind them: crimson, ochre, burnt amber, delicate greens still lingering from the summer, all gaudy as the coloured silks Sidney and his friends wear to parade around court. I am dressed, today as every other day, in black; a lone sombre shadow in this landscape of colour. For thirteen years I wore the black habit of the Dominican order; later, when I scraped a living teaching in the universities of Europe, I put on the black gown of doctors and academics. Now that I am free of the constraints of a uniform, I still wear black; it saves me the trouble of thinking about it too much. Fashion has never held much interest for me; sometimes I wonder how the young dandies can move about freely in their costumes, puffed up as they are with ballooning breeches and sleeves, slashed so that the rich linings show through in contrasting colours, or choked by their vast ruffs of starched lace. My only indulgence with the retainer Walsingham pays me is to buy clothes of good-quality cloth, shirts of fine linen under a black leather jerkin, cut to fit close to my body, no material wasted. Sidney teases me that I am wearing the same clothes every time he sees me. In fact, they are many different copies of the same clothes; I am fastidious about clean laundry, and change my linen far more often than most of the Englishmen I know. Perhaps this comes from those months I spent running from the Inquisition when I first fled the monastery at Naples, when I slept in roadside inns in the company of rats and lice, sometimes walking miles in a day to put enough distance between myself and Rome, with only the clothes on my back. To recall that part of my life even fleetingly makes me start to itch all over and want to change my shirt.

Through the scattered patterns of bright leaves I walk the length of the garden as the morning grows warmer, a book unopened in my hand. Beyond its boundary wall I hear the cries of boatmen on the river, the soft lapping of the waves against the muddy shoreline. Fowler's note asked me to meet him at three o'clock today at the Mermaid Tavern on Cheapside; there is nothing for me to do until Dumas has finished copying out the ambassador's secret letters and is ready to take them to young Master Throckmorton. If luck and timing are on our side, we can take the letters to Walsingham's man Thomas Phelippes in Leadenhall Street on the way, have them opened, copied, and resealed, then Dumas can deliver the originals to Paul's Wharf while I take the copies to Fowler at the tavern.

I have spent the morning in my room, trying to make some progress on my book. Since my return from Oxford in the spring, this has been my chief occupation; the work that I believe will turn all the established knowledge of the European academies on its head. In the same way that Copernicus's theory that the Sun and not the Earth lies at the centre of the known universe sent ripples through Christendom, forcing every cosmologist and astronomer to reconsider what they believed to be fact, so my treatise is nothing less than a new and enlightened understanding of religion, one that I hope will open the eyes of those men and women who have a mind to comprehend it to the possibility of unity. My philosophy is nothing less than a revolutionary understanding of the relationship between man and that which we call God, one that transcends the present divisions between Catholic and Protestant that have caused so much needless suffering. I have some hope that Queen Elizabeth of England has a mind equal to understanding my ideas, if I could only secure a chance to present them to her. To this end I have been passing my days as often as I can in Dee's library, immersing myself in the surviving writings of Hermes Trismegistus and the Neoplatonists, as well as other secret volumes full of hard-won wisdom and ancient knowledge, books of which Dee holds the only copy.

But since the night of Sidney's wedding and the murder of Cecily Ashe, I have been drawn back from the world of ideas to the present violence I hope one day to end. My mind will not settle, so I have brought a book out to the garden, where all I do is scuff the scattered leaves and dwell on the image of Cecily Ashe stretched out on a bed in Richmond Palace in her gentleman's clothes, her bruised and distorted face, the mark cut into her breast. The death is no longer my business, I suppose, and yet the image of her corpse nags at me; last night I dreamed about the murder, dreamed I was chasing a shadowy figure with a crucifix through an abandoned graveyard until finally he turned through the mist and I glimpsed beneath his hood the face of Doctor Dee.

This murder reminds me too closely of the deaths I witnessed in Oxford in the spring; this was not violence done in the heat of the moment but a cold-blooded killing meant as a symbol, a warning. But of what? And if it had been the young suitor Abigail had mentioned, what calculated planning he must have put into his work! To woo a young woman for the best part of a month with sweet words and expensive presents, with the intention all along of leaving her cold body as a blank page on which he would write his own message in her blood. I picture the girl Cecily, the way Abigail had described her delight in her secret liaison, the innocence of that first love at seventeen, never imagining that she was inviting her own destruction. Perhaps inevitably my thoughts follow this path to another young woman whose life had been destroyed by falling in love: Sophia, the girl I had known in Oxford who had briefly touched my own heart, though I did not know then that she had already given hers to a man who betrayed her and almost killed her. As if to prolong the discomfort, my memory gropes further back, to Morgana, the woman I had loved two years earlier when I lived in Toulouse. She was in love with me, but as I had neither the money nor the position to marry her, I had slipped away quietly one night to Paris without saying goodbye. I had thought I was doing the right thing, leaving her free to make the marriage that would please her father and give her a life of ease, but she too had died before her time. Was her life also cut short because she made the mistake of falling in love?

I will never know, but I remember the look that passed between Walsingham and Burghley across the body of Cecily Ashe and feel a profound wash of relief that I have no daughter to fear for. Despite the unseasonable warmth, I shiver. The fragility of these girls, how vulnerable they make themselves when they put their trust in men. If I were a praying man, I would pray that the maid Abigail remains safe. As it is, all I can do is hope that the killer believes his message has been understood. If not, he may feel the need to write it again.

All this musing has brought me to the end of the garden. Turning back along the path toward the house, I am almost bowled over by a small beribboned dog chasing a ball made of rags and chased in its turn by a girl of about five years who comes flying through the piles of leaves, her hair and her blue gown whipping behind her. The ball rolls to my feet and I snatch it up just before the dog reaches it. I hold it aloft and the dog's yapping grows frantic as it leaps and twists off the ground, its eyes fixed on my hand. The little girl slows to a halt in front of me, her expression wary; I lob the rag ball to her over the dog's head and the child is so surprised that she catches it, more by accident than by design. The dog flings itself at her and she scoops it up into her arms, giving it the ball, which it worries with a comical growl, as if it had subdued a great enemy.

"*Pierrot, tu es méchant!*" the child scolds.

"Pierrot?" I ask, crouching so that I can look her in the eye. "He's a boy?" She nods, bashful. "So, the ribbons?"

"He likes them." She shrugs, as if this should be obvious. A woman's voice comes from beyond the wall.

"*Catherine! Catherine, viens ici! Où es-tu?*"

Marie de Castelnau appears in the archway that divides this part of the garden from the more manicured paths nearer the house. The rich light touches her hair as she brushes a stray curl away from her face, giving her a faint halo; she is frowning but as her gaze alights on me and her daughter, her expression softens and she slows her pace toward us.

"*Ah. Monsieur l'hérétique. Bonjour.*"

"Madame." I bow.

She bends to the child and lays a hand on her shoulder.

"Catherine, take Pierrot inside. Look—your shoes are all dirty now and it's nearly time for your lesson. You can play in the garden afterward, if you have worked hard."

Catherine sticks out her bottom lip.

"I want to have my lesson out here." She points at my book. "*Monsieur l'hérétique* is allowed his books outdoors."

Marie glances at me and smiles, half apologetic, before turning back to her daughter.

"Well, *Monsieur l'hérétique* is allowed to do all sorts of things that are not proper and you had better not follow his example. He is very wicked." She winks.

The child looks up at me, her mouth open, waiting for confirmation or denial; I make my eyes wide and nod.

"I'm afraid it's true."

She giggles.

"Go on, off you go," Marie says, sharper this time, patting the girl's back. Catherine scampers away, the little dog bleating at her heels.

"I'm sorry—my daughter thinks that is your name now." Castelnau's wife laughs and falls easily into step beside me, folding her arms across her chest, as we begin to walk slowly back toward the house. "It's what King Henri calls you. It is meant affectionately. On his part, I mean," she adds hastily, glancing quickly sideways and then back to her feet.

"You spoke to King Henri about me?"

She laughs again, a gentle, fluting sound.

"No. But your name came up often when I was with Queen Louise. I have known her since we were girls. The king misses you, apparently. He says there are no original thinkers left in Paris now that *Monsieur l'hérétique* has abandoned him for London."

"Well, it is kind of him to say so." We walk in silence for a few paces, the sun warm on our faces.

"I must say, I was intrigued to meet you," she continues, after a moment, and there is a silkiness in her voice that sounds a warning note. "Queen Louise said you were a great favourite among the ladies in Paris."

"Was I?" This is news to me; there were idle flirtations at the Parisian court, but nothing worth the notice of the queen consort, as I recall. After my experience in Toulouse, I had vowed to devote my energy to writing and to harden my heart against the possibility of love.

"Oh, yes, indeed," Marie says, lightly touching my arm and allowing her hand to rest for a moment, "because you were a great enigma, apparently. There were many stories told about you, but no one ever got close enough to sort the truth from the rumours. And of course you frustrated all the ladies by never choosing any of them, which only fuelled the gossip."

"I had not the means to marry."

"Perhaps you had not the inclination?" she says, with a sly smile. I pause and look at her. Does she mean what I think?

"There have been women," I say, defensive. "I mean to say, I have loved women, in the past. But I have always had the misfortune to fall for the ones I cannot have."

She smiles, as if to herself. "Isn't it always more interesting that way? But I did not mean to imply what you thought." A brief hesitation. "You know it is said of Lord Henry Howard, though?"

"What—that he doesn't look at women?" I recall Howard's fist thumping on the table the night before, the blaze of his eyes. Perhaps that would account for his air of suppressed rage.

"He has never married. Although," Marie adds, leaning in with a confidential air, "it may only be that he has been put off marriage by example. You have heard why his brother was executed?"

"Treason, I thought?"

"Yes. But the exact nature of his treason—you did not know? The Duke of Norfolk intended to marry Mary Stuart and so become King of England when she returned to the throne, after they were rid of Elizabeth."

She nods enthusiastically, waiting for a response, her blue eyes lit up with the thrill of her story, as if she has told me something she should not. She is standing inappropriately close, her hand still on my arm, and we have now walked far enough to be visible from the house. Instinctively I glance up and see a figure standing silhouetted there, watching us, but though I shield my eyes and squint, I cannot make out who he is. Immediately I take a step back from Marie, as if her mere proximity makes me guilty of something. I am already betraying Castelnau on one front; the last thing I want is for him to suspect me of dealing dishonestly with him on another.

"Henry Howard does not wholly trust you," she says, her tone suddenly serious. "Because of your breach with Rome. But my husband defends you and says you are a true Catholic and a friend to France, whatever strange philosophies you may toy with. And Howard responds that if you were a true Catholic you would have been reconciled to the church by now."

"What are you asking me?"

"I don't know. I suppose I find you something of an enigma too. They can't both be right. I must confess that I have never met a true Catholic who was happy to be excluded from the church. Why do you not repent and find a bishop to give you the sacrament of reconciliation?"

"I was excommunicated for leaving the Dominican order. If the excommunication were lifted, I would be obliged to return, and I fear I am not made to be a monk."

She gives me a knowing look, half smiling, at this; she assumes I mean for the obvious reason. She assumes wrongly: I mean because I cannot accept being told what to think. A monk copies the wisdom that already exists; he is not supposed to discover a new philosophy of his own.

"Well, *Monsieur l'hérétique*—I shall not give up on you. I will pray for your soul. Perhaps with patience and prayers, we may bring you back to the fold."

She laughs then, and skips ahead of me, holding her skirts away from her shoes to kick at fallen leaves. I do not know what to make of this woman. Perhaps she just enjoys gossip and is starved of company at the embassy, but she strikes me as too shrewd for that and there is something in her manner that makes me guarded. I can't be sure if she is flirting with me to amuse herself, or if she suspects me to be more or less than I appear and is trying to catch me out; either way, I determine that I must not be flattered or beguiled by her attentions into giving anything away. One thing at least is certain: there is a great deal more to Madame de Castelnau than a pious Catholic wife. But her news about Howard's brother is worth knowing.

"So is the position still vacant?" I call out, as she pauses to pick a sprig of purple heather from a bush at the side of the path. "Mary Stuart's husband, I mean?"

She turns, shredding the plant between her fingers and scattering the pieces.

"Why, are you interested?" Her clear laugh rings across the garden. "I must warn you, Bruno—that lady's husbands are unusually prone to misfortune. The first died of an abscess, the second she had blown up, and the third died insane in a Danish prison. And the Duke of Norfolk lost his head for merely aspiring to be the fourth."

At that moment the figure watching from the house detaches himself from the wall and is revealed to be Claude de Courcelles, his blond hair reflecting shards of light as he bounces down the steps toward us.

"Madame, your daughter is looking for you to begin her lessons." He effects a fussy little bow, impeded by his ruff, and sends me a scathing glance. Marie tosses her head and tuts.

"Where is her governess? She should be dealing with her. Can I not have a moment's peace?" With a rustle of satin, she hitches up her skirts to climb the steps to the house. "By the way, Courcelles," she says airily, over her shoulder, "Bruno is thinking of marrying the Scottish queen. What do you say to that?"

"My congratulations." The secretary offers me a thin smile, hard as ice. "Although you may find she prefers a gentleman of *independent means*."

"I hear she is not that choosy," Marie calls from the doorway. "Apparently she is monstrously fat these days."

Courcelles and I watch her lithe figure disappear into the recesses of Salisbury Court and exchange a glance. With exaggerated courtesy, he gestures for me to lead the way.

"YOU'VE HEARD THE news from court, I suppose?" Fowler says in his lilting accent, as I slide into the settle opposite him at the Mermaid. The tavern spans the fork between Friday Street and Bread Street on Cheapside, east of the great church of St. Paul's, and is popular with merchants and professionals; most of the men crowded around the wooden tables are dressed in well-cut cloth with feathers in their caps and meet here to argue over deals and contracts, shipments, lawsuits, loans. Behind the hubbub of lively conversation and the occasional oath you catch the chink of coins. The air is warm and yeasty; after casting my eyes around for some moments I have found the Scotsman tucked into a table at the back of the taproom, sitting in a spill of sunlight scored with diamond shadows from the windowpanes. The high-backed wooden settles effectively barricade us in our corner from any prying eyes or sharp ears. When I shake my head, he leans in closer, pushing his fringe out of his eyes. "I was at Whitehall this morning. They have arrested Sir Edward Bellamy for the murder of the queen's maid."

"Really? Was he the girl's lover, then?"

"He says not, but it turns out to be his clothes she was wearing when they found her. The young fool forgot that his monogram was embroidered on the shirt."

"But he denies the murder?"

"Naturally. He says they were old clothes the girl asked him to sell her, but apart from that they had barely spoken before. It's true that it's an old trick these maids use for slipping out in disguise, but it seems he is not believed about the rest. They have dragged him kicking and screaming to the Tower and the girl's father has ridden down from Nottingham breathing hellfire and demanding satisfaction. Poor fellow will have made a loss on his investment."

Fowler makes a grim face and sits back while a serving girl arrives to fill our pots of beer from an earthenware jug. She attempts to exchange pleasantries but soon concludes that my companion and I are too sober and dull to be out for any merriment. When she has gone, he raises his beer toward me.

"Your good health, Doctor Bruno. I am glad we finally have the chance to talk. I have heard glowing reports of you from our mutual friend." He arches his eyebrow to indicate the secrecy that binds us.

"Likewise, Master Fowler." I clink the pot briefly with his. He gives a curt nod, indicating the table with his eyes, and slides one hand underneath it onto his lap. It takes me a moment to understand him; feeling a little foolish, I draw from inside my doublet the copies of Castelnau's letters lately made at the house of Thomas Phelippes and slip them across my lap into Fowler's waiting palm. With practised fingers, he tucks them deftly away inside his clothes and wraps both hands around his tankard of beer. I glance briefly over my shoulder around the tavern, but the exchange appears to have gone unnoticed.

"Thank you. I shall take these back to Whitehall this afternoon," he murmurs, barely audible.

"May I ask you something?"

"Please." He opens his hands in a welcoming gesture.

"What exactly do you *do* at court?"

For the first time, he laughs, and his face relaxes. His fringe falls across his brow again as he dips his head and he pushes it back, revealing keen blue eyes.

"I make myself useful. You know how it works at the English court—the same as anywhere else, I suppose. Noblemen send their sons to recommend themselves to the queen in the hope of advancement.

The difficulty is that there is only one queen and dozens of hopeful courtiers all chasing her favour." He pauses to take a draught. "So you end up with a lot of young gentlemen who have nothing to do all day but hang about the galleries and halls in the hope that the queen might pass by at some point and take notice of them. In the meantime, there is ample opportunity for them to gamble away their fathers' money, or trap themselves in a hasty marriage because they've got some girl with child, or bluster their way into dangerous duels. And when they find themselves in trouble, they are often too afraid or ashamed to ask their fathers for help."

"Which is where you come in."

"Which is where I come in. They are very inexperienced in the world, some of these young lads, and often lonely—they want advice and someone to listen. And I have good connections in the City—I know lawyers who can make unwanted marriage contracts go away, find solutions to bad debts, that kind of thing. People who can arrange loans discreetly. This way, I learn everybody's business around the court, their affairs, their complaints, their alliances, sometimes even the state of their souls. All those snippets of information that interest our mutual friend."

"I can see how that would be useful. And they trust you, these courtiers?"

"They are grateful to me. I am known to keep a confidence. But I suspect at least half of them don't even remember my Christian name, which is all to the good."

I regard him with interest. His face is beardless, his hair mid-brown, and his skin pale. Only his eyes are particularly memorable; they burn with an intense light, sharp and alert. With his soft manners, he melts easily into the background, the ideal observer. I begin to understand his value to Walsingham.

"But with all the confidences that come your way, you heard nothing to make you suspect this Sir Edward before he was arrested?" I ask, keeping my voice low.

"He was one who lived quietly. He always seemed a gentle sort."

Fowler looks perplexed for a moment, then drains his pot and raises a hand for more beer.

"Do they suspect a religious motive for the killing?"

"I know no more than I have told you. Apparently he has a cousin who was once fined for refusing to attend church, but then most families have one of those. Edward Bellamy was not among those suspected of dangerous papist leanings, if that's what you mean. But I daresay they will get a confession from him in the Tower, one way or another. They will want this business wrapped up quickly so the queen may sleep easy in her bed."

His fingers curl slowly into a fist and stretch out again as he says this; I wince. It is better not to think about what they do in the Tower. In the summer I saw a prisoner after the interrogators had finished with him; death would have come as a blessing. This thought triggers another memory.

"Is he a handsome man, this Sir Edward?" I ask, as the serving girl reappears with her jug. Fowler looks surprised, and amused.

"I can't say I've considered him in those terms. It's not how I usually assess young men."

"Nor I," I add hastily. "I only wondered—you know: if he had seduced the girl or forced her."

Fowler is still looking at me with a curious expression.

"Now that you mention it—I don't suppose he would be accounted handsome to women. He has a slight disfigurement—what we call in English a harelip—and he is rather sickly looking. Not that a spell in the Tower will do much for his looks, either." He picks up his beer and we consider this in silence for a moment. Then he leans in closer. "But we must concentrate on our own business. Any further news from the embassy, besides these?" He pats his breast, where he has tucked the letters inside his doublet.

"Nothing much since last night."

Léon Dumas and I had walked to Thomas Phelippes's house after dinner with the packet for Throckmorton to take to Sheffield Castle,

Dumas fretting and griping the whole way and continuing to do so all the while Phelippes was expertly removing the seals from Castelnau's letters to Mary so that we could make our own copies for Fowler to pass on to Walsingham. To my eyes the resealed letters bore no trace of having been intercepted, but Dumas was almost feverish with anxiety when he set off again to Paul's Wharf to make his delivery; I had to buy him a drink and wait for him to calm down before I was willing to send him on his way.

"Turn up on his doorstep in this state and you may as well hang a sign around your neck saying 'I've given all these to the Privy Council first,'" I told him. Dumas had wrung his hands. "What if she can tell they've been opened?" he bleated. "Queen Mary, I mean? Castelnau will kill me!"

"By the time they get to Mary, they will have been through so many people's hands, how could anyone point to you?" I sighed. "Besides, Castelnau could not kill a soul," I added. "Although I wouldn't put it past some of his friends."

Now the originals have been taken to Throckmorton in time for his departure tomorrow and Dumas is on his way back to the embassy. Thus far, the system is working smoothly. I wrap my hands around my mug and lower my voice.

"The ambassador sends Mary a long letter—four pages, all in code. But his clerk has managed to take a copy of the new cipher, so that should be straightforward. It's in the package you have. And Lord Henry Howard sends her a copy of his book against prophecy in which he signs himself '*votre frère.*'"

Fowler nods. "How touching. He would have been her brother by marriage, if his own brother's plot had succeeded. Was there anything concealed inside the book?"

"No. Phelippes checked when he opened the package."

Fowler grows thoughtful. "Then the book itself must contain some message, or some significance. One of us will have to read it. You are the scholar, I believe."

I roll my eyes in mock protest. "I'll find myself a copy. At least I will be better armed to argue with him over dinner next time."

Fowler smiles, but lifts a finger in warning. "Be very careful around Howard, Bruno. He believes his family has suffered more than any from the Protestant reforms and he is quite willing to be ruthless in return. The Howards forfeited the lands and titles of the Duchy of Norfolk when his brother was executed, and he has been biding his time for revenge."

"And now he wants a war."

Fowler grimaces.

"It begins to look that way. None of them really cares about Mary Stuart; they all use her as an excuse to pursue their own interests. But they are quite willing to plunge England into war to achieve them. Has Mendoza visited Salisbury Court yet?"

"The Spanish ambassador? I am not sure I would recognise him."

"Oh, you'll know Don Bernardino de Mendoza if you see him. Looks like a bear, voice like a war drum. As soon as he comes to speak privately with Castelnau, let me know and I can tell our mutual friend. If Howard and the Duke of Guise can secure Spanish money, all this talk of invasion might grow into more than words."

"Isn't the talk of treason enough, if the queen knew?"

He gives a brisk shake of his head. "The queen will not make accusations against Howard or Mary Stuart—nor the ambassadors of France or Spain, for that matter—without absolute proof that they mean her or the country harm. They are all too powerful. And I mean proof that can be held in front of their faces in a court of law. Our friend wants this business to progress far enough that someone spells out their intentions on paper and signs their name to it."

"It's a dangerous game to play." I find myself unreasonably irritated by the easy assurance with which he asserts Walsingham's wants, as if he is privy to the principal secretary's innermost thoughts on a daily basis. I recognise also that this is only jealousy on my part; an irrational wish that I were as intimate with Walsingham, or as trusted.

"Certainly." Fowler presses his lips together until they almost disappear. "Though it's no game. I understand from my sources in Paris that Guise is already mustering troops, to be deployed whenever they have the word that England is ready."

His sources in Paris. He talks as if he is an old hand at this intelligence business, though he can't be more than twenty-six or twenty-seven.

"Have you served him long? Our friend, I mean."

He shrugs.

"A few years."

"And how did you come to be involved in all this?" I ask, waving a hand vaguely to indicate the web that Walsingham weaves around himself, and which we do not name.

His mouth curves into a half smile.

"Adventure, at first, I suppose. My father is a respectable Edinburgh burgess who intended me for the law. But when I arrived in Paris a few years ago to pursue my studies, I was surprised by the number of disaffected young Englishmen I found there—converts out of Oxford and Cambridge, tempers running high, all ready to whip up a Catholic rebellion against the English queen." He pauses to take a drink. "Of course, it's easy to talk about revolution among your fellows from the safety of a Paris tavern, and it was mostly bluster, but I soon came to see that one or two among them were sincere, and knew something of significance. All I had to do was sit quiet and nod in the right places, and they assumed I was of their mind." He glances around cautiously. "But I was also sharp enough to realise that what I learned among them might be of considerable value to others, so I waited until I gathered a hoard of useful tidbits and then I presented myself at the English ambassador's house. It was he who put me in touch with our mutual friend. Afterward I returned to Scotland and set myself to work cultivating friendships among the few prominent Scottish Catholic lords, those who favour Mary Stuart. I travel back to Edinburgh now and again to keep up with the politics there. It's essential to our friend to know their intentions, and it seems I have successfully passed myself off among the Catholics there and here as one who supports their cause."

"Very enterprising of you."

He inclines his head as if to say, *Perhaps.*

"It was the first time in my life I felt I'd chosen a path for myself, instead of following what my father laid out for me. That was exciting to me." He shrugs, implying that I am welcome to think what I like of this.

"And what of your religion?"

"Religion?" He looks surprised. "It was never my principal motive, strange as that may sound. Yes, I was raised in the Protestant church, but I have often felt I have more in common with moderate Catholics than with the more extreme devotees of my own faith. Excessive religion of any kind is dangerous, in my view. Elizabeth Tudor understands this, I think."

I nod, with feeling.

"And you?" he prompts. "I know you call yourself a Catholic at Salisbury Court."

"It's a question of freedom," I say, after a while, looking into my mug. "There is no freedom of thought under the rule of the Inquisition, no freedom to say *What if?* and then to imagine or speculate, and in such a climate, how can knowledge progress? The book I am writing now, for instance—in my own country I would be burned just for setting those ideas on paper. So when Wal—, when our friend approached me, I agreed because I thought the intellectual freedoms of Elizabeth's England worth defending."

"But you have still not told me your religion," he says, with a knowing look.

"I have been charged with heresy by Catholics in Rome and Calvinists in Geneva," I counter, smiling, "and when it comes to factions, I side with neither. My philosophy transcends both. But for that, you will have to read my book."

"I await it eagerly," he says, lifting his mug with a mischievous glint in his eye.

We sit in companionable silence for a few moments, finishing our beer.

"But don't you ever feel . . ." I shake my head, lay my hands on the table. "I don't know. Guilty?"

He regards me with those clear, serious eyes.

"For betraying trust? For having more than one face? Of course," he says, and smiles sadly. "To feel no guilt would mean you had no conscience, and our friend would never trust a man with no conscience, for there would also be no loyalty. I placate my conscience with the thought that if I must betray someone on a personal level, I do it for the good of the country."

I nod, thoughtfully; this is the argument Walsingham has always presented to me. What he doesn't tell you is that personal relationships are often the more compelling, and that to betray someone whose trust you have won pulls against human nature.

"You feel this keenly though, I think," Fowler whispers, studying me carefully. "You are fond of the ambassador."

I acknowledge this weakness with a tilt of my head.

"He is the one good man in Salisbury Court."

"He is trying to please too many people," Fowler says, as if this is the definitive judgement on the matter. "That is what will undo him. But guard yourself against sentiment, Bruno. If he ends up assisting with plans for a Catholic invasion, he is a traitor, regardless of his good intentions."

"I know this." I catch the sting in my voice; again, I find I resent his tone of seniority, and am ashamed of myself for it. Does he imagine I need to be told how to perform my role in the embassy? Perhaps I am being oversensitive; it is a valuable warning for anyone in our business, as I learned to my cost in Oxford.

"Of course." Fowler sits back, holding his hands up as if to mitigate any offence. "And for now, it is all about the letters. This enterprise depends on you and your friend the clerk."

We pay for the beer and press our way through the crowded tavern, emerging into the slanting afternoon light. The weather has improved the mood of the Londoners; as we walk down Friday Street, people smile and greet one another, remarking on the unseasonable warmth, instead of shoving you aside with their usual grim-faced determination. Fowler and I walk in silence at first, subdued by our conversation; only now, as I watch the passersby cheerfully going about their business, am I able to understand the weight of the work we are engaged in. We are talking about nothing less than a possible invasion, by France or Spain or both, whose ultimate aim is to unseat Elizabeth and bring England back under the control of Rome. And what will become of her Protestant subjects then, these ruddy-faced market traders and broad-hipped goodwives merrily sidestepping the horseshit on the cobbles as they wave to one another and call out for the hundredth time that you'd think it was July, wouldn't you?

Sidney and Walsingham were both in Paris during the St. Bartholomew's Day massacre of 1572, when ordinary Huguenot families were systematically slaughtered in the thousands by Catholic forces and the city's gutters ran with Protestant blood. This, I know, is what Walsingham fears above all: the same happening in the streets of London if the Catholics take power again. In Paris, there are plenty of people who murmur that the Duke of Guise was responsible for the bloodshed on St. Bartholomew's Day.

"This is where I leave you," Fowler says, as we reach the corner of Watling Street. "If you need to get a message to our friend, you can reach me at my lodgings close by the cock pit on St. Andrew's Hill." He pauses, laying a hand on my arm. "Watch who comes to Mass at Salisbury Court this evening. See if Howard brings any Englishmen we don't already know about. And keep an eye on Archibald Douglas. He is not quite the drunken boor he pretends to be."

"Then he is a master of deception," I say. "I wonder that Castelnau and Howard put up with his manners."

"They tolerate him because Mary Stuart tells them to. And Douglas trades on the fact that she is deeply in his debt. You know it was he who engineered the murder of her second husband, Lord Darnley?"

"The one who was blown up?"

"The very one." Seeing my eyes grow wider, he smiles. "That is why

Douglas may not go back to Scotland—there is a warrant out for his arrest. He is a notorious intriguer, and suspected of other political conspiracies to murder besides. And he is devilishly clever in the way he works his hooks into people—witness the fact that King James likes him, though he is suspected of murdering James's own father. Women apparently find him beguiling."

"There is no accounting for women's likes," I say, picturing Douglas's three-day growth of silvered stubble and his belches. Fowler rolls his eyes and nods wholeheartedly, as people step around us. "What's the story about the pie?"

"Ah, you had better have that from the horse's mouth." He grins. "Only Douglas can give that tale the savour it deserves. I'm sure your chance will come. Well—we shall meet again soon, Bruno. Meanwhile, bring me word if any Spanish envoy sets foot in Salisbury Court. Good luck." He nods briefly, turns on his heel, and is swallowed into the colourful jostling crowds.

THE SUN HAS sunk lower over the rooftops as evening eases in, washing London in forgiving amber light that flashes from windowpanes as I make my way home through the city. On a day such as this, I begin to think I could perhaps learn to feel at home here. Above me, a riot of painted signs creak gently in the breeze, emblazoned with bright pictures proclaiming apothecaries, chandlers, barber-surgeons, merchants of cloth and wine, and taverns named for animals of every kind and hue—black swans, blue boars, red foxes, white harts, hounds, hares, cocks, and even unicorns. At each side of the thoroughfare a steady stream of people press by: street vendors crying their wares, men with cages of squawking chickens swinging from poles across their shoulders, women with baskets of oranges balanced on their heads and peddlers with wooden trays fastened around their necks full of all kinds of oddities—combs, quills, buttons, brushes and knives, sometimes all jumbled together. In the vast churchyard of St. Paul's, which is more like a marketplace, beggar children thread barefoot through the crowds, importuning the better-dressed ladies and gentlemen, while on one corner a ragged man stands playing a battered old lute and singing a forlorn song, hoping to be thrown a few coins. The smell of cooking meat fights with the stink of rotting refuse, and the richer sort hold pomanders and posies of flowers close to their noses to keep the vapours at bay.

As I cross the courtyard, past where the former shrines and chapels are now fallen into disrepair or turned into stalls for booksellers and traders, a pamphlet seller steps in front of me, thrusting his wares in my face. I almost dismiss him, but the image on the front of his pamphlet catches my eye and I take one to look more closely. Here, again, are the symbols of Jupiter and Saturn conjoined, beneath a bold title: *End of Days?* The fellow selling it holds out a hand for his penny, his fingers waggling impatiently. He has his hood up, despite the sun; a wise precaution, since I can see at a glance that neither the printer nor the author has dared put his name to this piece of work, meaning that it is printed illegally. Intrigued, I scrabble for a coin and walk away, bumping into people as I read the thing. The anonymous author writes with a doom-mongering tone: he has attempted to cast the queen's horoscope from her nativity and tie his dramatic predictions to the coming of the Fiery Trigon, the terrifying alignment of the great planets whose symbols decorate the front. Queen Elizabeth's days are numbered, he writes; God will smite England with war and famine and her disobedient subjects will cry out for a saviour. Inside, there is a woodcut of a devil prodding a man with a pitchfork. I tuck the pamphlet into my jerkin to save for Walsingham, though I imagine if he has not already seen it, he soon will.

I HAVE BARELY closed the front door behind me at Salisbury Court when Courcelles materialises out of the shadows beside the staircase, as if he has been waiting for my arrival.

"There is a boy here says he has a letter for you," he announces, resting one delicate white hand on the carved wooden eagle that decorates the end of the banister. "He has been here the best part of the afternoon and, try as we might, we could not persuade him to leave it for you, not even for a shilling. Nor will he tell us who sent him. He says his instructions are to put it into your hands alone and it was a most urgent and confidential matter." His fine eyebrows arch gracefully as he says this; evidently he expects me to offer some explanation.

"Then I had better see him," I reply evenly, though my pulse quickens. I think first of Walsingham, then Sidney, then Dee; any one of them might want to contact me as a matter of urgency, but Walsingham would surely not arouse suspicion by sending an obviously secretive message directly to the embassy, and Sidney is still on his honeymoon, as far as I know. That leaves Dee, and my gut clenches; has Ned Kelley done something to him?

Courcelles presses his lips together and points me in the direction of the stables at the side of the house. There I find a skinny boy of about twelve years old sitting miserably on a straw bale, picking at his fingernails while the stable hands jeer at him in French. He shows signs of having been in a scuffle.

"I am Bruno. You have something for me?"

He leaps to his feet as if stung, and pulls a crumpled letter out from inside his jacket. He wears no livery but he is not poorly dressed. He beckons me closer and passes me the letter as if it contained secret intelligence.

"From Abigail Morley." His voice is barely a whisper. "She said I must only put it in your hands, sir, though they tried to take it from me." He glances resentfully at the stable boys, who twist awkwardly and look away.

"You did well." I find a coin for his trouble and see him out of the side gate, before pausing in a pool of shadow, away from curious eyes, to tear open the letter. It is written in an elegant, curling hand; Abigail asks me to meet her tomorrow at eleven in the morning at the Holbein Gate, Whitehall. She says she is afraid.

Chapter 5

PALACE OF WHITEHALL, LONDON.
28TH SEPTEMBER, YEAR OF OUR LORD 1583

Another morning of empty blue skies and warm light; I take a wherry upriver to Whitehall, landing at Westminster Stairs, the nearest public jetty to the palace. The River Thames is wide and calm, jewelled with reflections of the sun and white ripples where the breeze ruffles the water's surface, and I lean back in the boat as the oarsman heaves his way through the flotilla of small craft transporting goods and passengers up and down London or eastward, out toward the docks.

From the stairs I walk back up King Street past the boundary walls of the palace to the Holbein Gate, a vast, imposing structure that spans the main thoroughfare out of London to the west, joining the sprawling privy apartments and state chambers of Whitehall with the tiltyard and the park of St. James on the other side. Three storeys of red brickwork and white stone, with an octagonal tower at each corner in the English style, and grand rooms above the main archway, the gatehouse is patrolled by palace guards and always densely crowded, as all travellers on the road must be funnelled through it to pass in either direction. Abigail has cho-sen wisely; often the best place to pass unobserved is in a crowd.

From somewhere nearby a church bell chimes the hour of eleven and I wait, hesitant, by the passageway through the eastern tower of the gatehouse, which is reserved for those on foot. Through the central arch-way, carts pulled by horses or mules churn up clouds of dust from the dry road as traders bring their goods into the palace or on toward the city. People bustle past with bundles or packs and I press myself back against the wall, out of the way; suddenly an old woman with no teeth thrusts a filthy hand into my face, demanding money or food, and I jump back, startled. I know from experience that if I reach for a penny, a hundred more beggars will stream in an instant from the shadows with their hands out, but there is such desperation in her face that I cannot refuse; she folds her fingers with their swollen joints painfully around the coin I slip into her palm, clutches at my jacket, and pulls me toward her.

"When hempe is spun, England's done," she croaks into my face, so that I have to reel back from her stinking breath. "Take heed, sir. The signs are all about us." She points one trembling, crooked finger to the sky, then releases me and scuttles back into the crowd.

I stare after her, puzzling over her words, when another figure wrapped in a thin cloak approaches and guiltily I regret my generosity; here they come already, and I don't have enough coins to part with them all. But this woman sidles up to me, reaching inside her clothes, and from the depths of her hood whispers my name in an educated voice.

"Abigail!"

"Shh. We must not be seen. Walk with me into the passage for a moment."

We step into the shadow of the tower archway; immediately the deep chill of damp stone settles on my skin. The passage through the tower is not wide and we are jostled and shoved, with the occasional curse, as we huddle at one side. Abigail keeps her hood pulled up around her face.

"They have the wrong man," she whispers, without preamble. "I didn't know who else to tell."

"How do you know?"

"Because Sir Edward Bellamy tried to court me once, and we laughed about it—I mean, Cecily and I. It was cruel of us, but he is such a poor figure of a man. No woman would want him, for all his lands, unless she were past caring." She rubs self-consciously at her throat as she says this. "But Sir Edward is a gentleman and does not deserve to have this pinned on him. He was not her secret sweetheart, I would swear to it."

"But her lover was not necessarily her killer. It need only have been someone who knew she had a tryst that evening. The lover could have been one of Sir Edward's friends, perhaps?"

The bottom half of her face is visible below the hood; she chews her lip doubtfully.

"I just do not believe he could kill anyone, or be party to it. He is so mild-mannered."

"Quiet men have murdered before."

She shakes her head decisively.

"It doesn't feel right. He sold Cecily his old clothes so she could disguise herself as a boy—that much I believe. But I think the palace guard were just glad to make an easy arrest so the queen will think they are doing their job. Anyway, I did not ask you here for that. There is something else."

She beckons me closer and from inside her cloak draws out a little velvet bag tied at the top with ribbon.

"Lady Seaton went through Cecily's things to give her father when he came." She speaks so low that her face is almost touching mine to make herself heard. Her breath is warm on my cheek. "But I suspected she was looking for something that might give away Cecily's affair. She found nothing. She didn't know about the cushion."

"What cushion?"

"It was one of Cecily's most beloved things—a little cushion that she embroidered as a child. A Bible text, flowers, you know the sort of thing. She kept it on her bed—I thought it was just a sentimental keepsake, for when she was homesick, but one day she showed me how she would unpick the seam and hide her secret gifts inside the cushion cover."

She holds out the bag; I weigh it in my hand. It is light and chinks softly as I move it.

"These are the presents from her admirer, everything she had sewn inside the cushion. I don't know what use they may be—I can see no clue in them, but perhaps you might find something. Especially since every-one seems determined to find Sir Edward guilty—it would be a terrible thing if he were to take the punishment for it." She tugs at my sleeve, and there is something childlike in the gesture. "There is a design on the ring, an emblem. It is not the Bellamy arms, though it is no one's I recognise. But you could give it to Lord Burghley—he might know."

"He might. Have you told anyone else about these things?"

She bites her lip and looks away, but then she shakes her head firmly. Again I have the sense that she is holding something back.

"I almost did when they arrested Sir Edward, but I could not approach Lord Burghley myself. Besides, I remembered what you said. If the killer is someone inside the court, he might know that Cecily was my friend, might he not? So he might think she had told me her secrets and want to stop my mouth too?" She raises her face to me and in the dim light I see how pale she is, how her lips are trembling, though she tries to fight it.

"You are brave to have brought me Cecily's things—thank you. I have no doubt that they will be invaluable." I place my hands on her small shoulders to reassure her. "As for the danger, I think it more likely that this killer, if it is not Sir Edward, will be glad to let another man take the blame and remain in the shadows. Why would he risk drawing attention to him-self with another attack when he has the chance to get away with murder?"

"I suppose that would depend upon why he killed Cecily in the first place," she says sensibly. "I mean, a man might kill a woman because she is with child and he doesn't want to marry her—you hear such stories. There was a great deal of that kind of talk at first around court. But that spectacle he made of her body"—she shudders—"makes me think it must be something else. What if he killed her because she knew something she should not? He would want to silence her friends then, sir, would he not, in case she had shared confidences?"

Looking down at her earnest face, I begin to think that I have underestimated Abigail Morley. These have been my own thoughts; I have even wondered about Lady Seaton, whether her defensive manner on the night of the murder was all to do with the fear of salacious gossip, or whether it masked another motive. I squeeze the girl's shoulders gently.

"Why do you say that? Did Cecily give you reason to think she was guarding dangerous secrets?"

"It was only that"—she hesitates, glances around—"since she met this man, she had begun to talk a lot of prophecies."

"What kind of prophecies?"

"Oh, you know the kind of thing, they're two a penny—that the queen's days are numbered, that England will be destroyed. You hear such stuff on every street."

"I heard one just now, I think, from an old crone. 'When hempe is spun, England's done.'"

Abigail nods enthusiastically.

"That is a favourite among the servants. You know what it means, of course?" She drops her voice. "It's the Tudor line. Hempe stands for Henry, Edward, Mary and Philip, and Elizabeth. The old grandams quote it to predict England's downfall when the last Tudor dies. Cecily knew them all."

"But she only showed an interest in such things recently?"

"This past month or so. I wondered what ideas this man had been putting in her head. I would tell her, 'Cecily, some of these things you're saying could be treason!' She just laughed at that, as if she didn't care, and told me everyone was talking of it."

"Did she mention religion? Or who she thought should take the throne instead?"

"No, nothing like that. It was more of a personal resentment," Abigail adds, then claps a hand to her mouth. "I don't know if I should tell you this."

"Abigail." I look her directly in the eyes. "It would be as well to tell me anything that might help. Why did she resent the queen?"

"When Cecily first came up to court, last year," she whispers, drawing in closer to me as a group of boys in the garb of apprentices elbow their way past, "she had a sweetheart from home, some gentleman's son she'd known since she was a child. He got himself to London in the hope of seeing her, but when Lady Seaton heard of it she told the queen and they had him turned away. Cecily was forbidden even to write to him. He wasn't highborn, you see. She forgot him quickly enough, but she didn't forget her resentment of the queen for it. And she was afraid the queen might interfere with this new man as well." Her eyes flit from side to side. "For being too highborn for her."

I cannot help but laugh at this.

"I had no idea love was so minutely calibrated. Must you all measure your husbands' status so carefully?"

She giggles, sounding for a moment lighthearted.

"I may not choose my husband for love, but I shall make damned sure I choose my lover carefully. What? Would you look so shocked?" she adds, in response to my expression, which makes her giggle all the more. "No need to be such a prude, even if you were once a monk."

"Are you going to stand there blocking the way all day, then?" grumbles a heavyset man in a coarse smock as he lumbers past, knocking Abigail hard enough that she stumbles into my arms as I try to stop her falling. Startled, she regains her balance and brushes herself down as we look at each other, then quickly glance away.

"I should probably—" she says, gesturing back toward the palace wall.

"Yes. But take care, Abigail. Make sure you do not go about the palace alone. Someone at court knows who killed Cecily and why, and you are right—he may be watching you. Be wary about whom you trust."

"It is hard to know whom to trust at court after this." She laughs, a nervous, high-pitched sound, her fingers twisting at the strings of her cloak. "I mean, how do I even know that I can trust you?"

"You can trust me, Abigail. I have no pledge to give except my word." Gripping her shoulders a little tighter, I make her look into my eyes. She searches them with her pale green gaze, and eventually she nods.

"Yes—it is odd, for all the women say never trust foreign men, especially those from Spain or Italy. But I feel I can trust you. Will you let me know if you learn anything more? It would help me to feel safer."

I am about to promise, when two young dandies in puffed satin push roughly by us, this time jostling Abigail into the wall.

"Hey! Watch yourselves!" I call after them; the shorter of the two, who wears a scarlet cap with a peacock feather, turns at my accent.

"Do you speak to me, you Spanish whoreson?" He pauses, spits on the ground, and seems about to come back for me, but his friend restrains him, and with a last filthy look, they resume their walk.

"Fools," I mutter, though I am grateful that they were not spoiling for a fight in the street. "Thank you for trusting me. And, Abigail—you must let me know if you remember anything more that Cecily told you. It could be essential."

I speak gently, but she understands my implication: I think she is keeping something back, some clue to the identity of Cecily's lover, out of either fear or misguided loyalty. She smiles hesitantly and I realise I am still holding her by the shoulders; our eyes meet again, for slightly too long. For a moment I entertain the absurd thought that, once this business is resolved, I might ask to see her again. There is something about her expectant eyes that makes me wonder if she has thought the same. I could hardly be considered the grand match her father has in mind, but has she not already made it clear that she would have different criteria for a lover? I push to one side the uncomfortable suggestion that her father is probably not much older than I am. Embarrassed by my unspoken thoughts, I release her and she draws her hood up closer.

"The perfume is disgusting, by the way," she says, as she turns to leave, nodding to where I have stuffed the velvet bag inside my jerkin. "Only a man could possibly think a woman would want to wear that." She laughs then, and with a little wave, steps out of the archway into the bright light of the morning.

I watch her as she disappears into the throng, then turn and make my way back in the opposite direction. It is only when I emerge into the light at the other end that I sense someone behind me; quick as blinking, I spin around, but there are dozens of people in my wake, none of them paying the slightest attention to me other than to tut at the fact that I have stopped dead in the path, interrupting the flow of human traffic again. I turn urgently left and right, craning my neck above the crowd, knocking into people as I go, but all I can see is a steady stream of faces coming toward me from the gatehouse passageway. None of them makes eye contact. It is possible that I imagined the sensation. Yet I know, instinctively, that there was someone at my back, just now, watching me, and he must have seen me talking to Abigail Morley.

I HAIL A boat back to Salisbury Court, thinking that it would be harder for anyone to follow me inconspicuously by river, but although I spend the journey peering out at the other wherries and their passengers until even the boatman grows nervous and asks what is the matter, I see nothing to give me any cause for concern. By the time I arrive back at the embassy, I have almost persuaded myself that I was mistaken.

Halfway across the first-floor gallery, with my fingers burning to examine the contents of the velvet bag, which I have not dared to open in any public place in case I was being followed, I hear a woman call my name. So fixed am I on reaching the privacy of my room in order to examine its contents that I nearly curse aloud at being detained. Marie stands in the doorway behind me, regarding me with her head on one side, her daughter's little dog clasped in her arms. Reluctantly, I turn and bow.

"Madame."

"Who was your mysterious letter from yesterday, Bruno? We are all dying to know." She advances on me, smiling coquettishly, and stops a little too close. She wears a dress of blue silk, and on her bodice is pinned a large jewelled brooch, studded with rubies and diamonds that glint and sparkle in the sun. The dog stretches out its small head and licks my hand in an enquiring manner. "I have speculated that you have some besotted English girl sending you verses, but Claude is quite convinced that it is something more intriguing. Who would be sending Bruno letters, he wonders, that could not divulge his name? Or *her* name." She widens her eyes in an affectation of intrigue.

I smile politely, but this is worrying: it will not do me any good to have the household speculating on my communications, especially in the midst of such conspiracies as I heard the other night. I begin to think it was a mistake to suggest that Abigail contact me here. Thinking as quickly as I can, I compose my expression into one of regret.

"I only wish you were right, madame, but I'm afraid there is no besotted English girl. The letter came from a young man at court who has read one of my books and wishes to become my private student."

"One of your *books*?" She looks disappointed.

"As unlikely as that may seem."

"Student of what?"

"Of the art of memory. Just as I taught to King Henri in Paris."

"Oh." She considers this. "Then why the secrecy?"

"Because ignorant people mutter that the techniques of memory owe something to occult sciences. I expect he is being cautious. Though I assure you there is no truth in that," I add, hastily.

She continues to study me with her head tilted, as if I make more sense viewed at an angle.

"Well, then, Bruno," she says, at length, "I insist that I become your private student too. I would like to learn your system. You can sort out the payment with my husband—although he may feel that the board and lodging you already receive are wages enough."

"Madame, I am not sure that would be—"

"Don't be tiresome, Bruno. It would be perfect—it is not as if you are employed elsewhere, and I must fill my time somehow while Catherine is with her governess. Besides, my memory is quite shamefully poor. I came after you to tell you something, and now I have quite forgotten what it was. You see? I need you." She smiles up at me with a twitch of her eyebrow, all innocent and knowing. Looking for a distraction, I reach out to stroke the dog and she does the same, with the result that her hand lightly caresses the top of mine; I pull my own hand back as if burned, and she blushes and drops her gaze. Christ, I think: the idea of trying to teach her anything, alone in a room, is more daunting than any task Walsingham could ask of me. I am reassured by the thought that Castelnau would never sanction it.

"Anyway, where are you heading in such a hurry?"

"Oh—just to my room. I had one or two ideas while I was out walking and I must write them down before they evaporate."

Her laugh is musical. "You are not a very good advertisement for your own memory techniques, Bruno."

"You have been warned."

"Oh, I am not deterred. I only feel sorry for your young student—I hope he is not wasting his money. What was his name?"

I hesitate only for the space of a breath, but she is sharp enough to notice.

"Ned. Ned Kelley. Well, madame, I must—" I gesture toward the door at the other end of the gallery. It is a handsome room, running the length of the house at the front, with tall windows along the walls on both sides. Sunlight plays along the darkened panelling, dust dancing in perpetual motion in glittering shafts. The same light falls sidelong on Marie's face and I have an urge to reach out and touch her cheek, not from desire but merely to see how soft it feels, lit up and golden. I take a step back as if to leave and she reaches out and grasps my sleeve.

"There—now I have remembered what it was! The ambassador wishes to speak to you in his private office—he has been asking for you all morning but no one knew your whereabouts." She says this as a kind of accusation.

"Then I will go to him shortly," I say, feeling the shape of the bag still pressing against my chest under my jerkin. "First I must change my shirt."

She looks at my collar doubtfully.

"While you are there, tell him I wish to take lessons in your arcane magical arts."

"Madame, there is no magic involved, whatever they say in Paris—" I begin, earnestly, but then I catch sight of her impish smile.

"Oh dear, Bruno—you are too easy to tease. I think I will enjoy our lessons."

I reply with a curt bow, leaving her standing in a ray of light with her jewels glittering, still laughing to herself.

THE VELVET BAG, when it is opened, reveals the items Abigail mentioned to me before: a gold signet ring with an engraved emblem; a tortoiseshell hand mirror, beautifully smooth; a small glass vial of perfume in the shape of a diamond, of the kind that women wear around their necks, with a gold clasp and a chain attached at the top. Love tokens, clearly expensive, but what can these trinkets tell me of the story of Cecily Ashe and her lover? One by one, I hold them up to the light and examine them. The ring's design is of a bird with outstretched wings and a curved beak, an eagle perhaps, and around the edge letters are carved in mirror image, so that they would read true when pressed into warm sealing wax. I frown for a moment, trying to decipher the motto, until I realise it is written in French: *Sa Vertu m'atire*. "Her virtue draws me"—or perhaps "its virtue." But the word *attire* is misspelled—a curious mistake. You would think if you were having a gold ring engraved, you would make sure the goldsmith carved it correctly; nor would any craftsman worth his fee want the expense of making such an error. So, I think, rotating the ring again while my eye follows the letters around, what appears at first glance to be a mistake must be by design, and therefore perhaps the motto has a hidden or coded meaning. If this is the case, it is not giving itself up to me easily; I am no nearer than Abigail to knowing whose emblem this is, though it seems the giver of the ring had a French connection. That hardly helps, of course—half the nobility have some French ancestry and everyone of the gentry class and above learns at least a few words.

The little mirror is the least interesting object. I turn it over in my hands but it yields nothing; the tortoiseshell is so highly polished that you can see your face almost as well in its swirling patterns of tawny brown as you can in the silvered glass. Frustrated, I put it to one side and open the perfume bottle. Raising it to my nose, I understand immediately Abigail's complaint. Beneath the scent of rose water is a hint of something bitter, a sour vegetable smell that makes you wince. But Abigail is wrong about a man's ignorance of perfume; the giver of these gifts was clearly a man of taste and considerable generosity, so why would he present his love with a perfume that was so obviously unappealing? Tipping the bottle, I wet the end of my finger with a tiny drop of the colourless liquid and raise it to my tongue, but as I am about to taste it, there comes a sudden rap at the door.

"Bruno? Are you in there?"

Dumas. I scrabble to stuff the gifts back into the velvet bag and in my haste I knock the little mirror to the floor, where it lands with an ominous crack.

"One moment!" Cursing silently, I retrieve it and turn it over to see with great relief that the glass has not broken, but the fall seems to have damaged the frame; it feels looser, as if the glass might slip out. But there is no time to look closer; I push the bag under the pillow of my bed and unbolt the door for Dumas. He stands, twisting his hands, with the face of a startled hare.

"My lord ambassador sends for you. I don't know what it is about. Do you think he has discovered our . . ." He falters, looking for the right word.

"Business? Well, let's not immediately jump to the worst conclusion, eh." I give him a good clap on the shoulder for encouragement as I pass him in the doorway, though the fact that Castelnau has been looking for me all morning worries me, too. Dumas watches while I lock the door of my bedchamber. Secrets must be guarded closely in this house.

CASTELNAU LOOKS UP from his desk as I enter his private office, and his expression seems serious, though not angry.

"Bruno! What an elusive man you are. Take a seat, will you?" He indicates a chair by the empty fireplace, inlaid with tapestry cushions. Dumas hovers behind me, shifting from one foot to the other, as if unsure whether he is expected to stay. "Léon, you have work to do, don't you?"

Dumas scurries back to his small desk in the corner. Castelnau waves a hand in his general direction.

"Don't worry about him, Bruno. I have no secrets from Léon—do I, Léon?" He smiles genially. Dumas makes a noise that is somewhere between a squeak and a cough. I send him a hard stare behind the ambassador's back. I have never seen a man wear his conscience so plainly on his face; if only Courcelles could give him a few lessons in oily insincerity, our operation would be much the safer.

"Will you take a glass of wine?" Castelnau says, reaching for a Venetian decanter on his desk. I decline, claiming the hour is too early. The ambassador looks disappointed; nevertheless, he pours himself a generous glass and pulls up the chair opposite mine. "You have been on my mind a great deal these past couple of days, Bruno," he begins, then pauses to drink a long draught. "I know you will have been troubled by what you heard at dinner the other night."

"Unless I have misunderstood, my lord, it sounds very much as if Lord Henry Howard is trying to start a war."

Castelnau sighs. He looks tired; for the first time since I have known him, he is beginning to show his age. I wonder if this is the effect of the Scottish queen's intrigues or the return of his wife.

"You have not misunderstood. My wife, as you have seen, is a great supporter of the Duke of Guise, but I want you to know that I do not favour any such enterprise nor does King Henri—though he has his own difficulties at the moment. I need you on my side, Bruno, to advocate tolerance, diplomacy, negotiation, when they start up their talk of invasion. Stand with me—we need to remain in their confidence. I am doing my best to urge everyone to be patient."

"Perhaps they feel they have been patient long enough."

"Hm." He tips back his glass and drains it, then shakes his head. "If only Elizabeth had not been so stubborn about marrying the Duke of Anjou—then our two countries would have had a solid alliance. But I see now that she was making fools of us all. She has never had any desire for marriage. In that, at least, she shows wisdom."

He adds this last so vehemently that I suspect he is no longer thinking about the queen. From what I have seen of Marie de Castelnau, I find it hard to imagine that his own marriage gives him any peace of mind.

"Henry Howard is powerful in this country just as the Duke of Guise is in France," Castelnau continues. "Powerful enough to make their respective sovereigns afraid. But not as powerful as they would like to be. So now they look for a secret alliance with Spain to fund their plans."

"A grand Catholic reconquest."

"I know you are no zealot for the Catholic church, Bruno," Castelnau says, leaning forward and fixing me with his large, sad eyes, his glass clasped between his hands. "But the tide is turning. The Protestant faith is weakening—in France, in the Netherlands, and in this island too. It flourished for a season, but it couldn't compete. I would wager that by the end of this troubled century it will be remembered only as an experiment, a warning to our sons and daughters. All the omens point to the coming of a new era. We must be ready."

"Then you think this war inevitable, my lord?" I rub my brow with my thumb, confused. "In that case, why argue against it?"

"No. I think the reassertion of Catholic supremacy inevitable," he says, his face stern. "King Henri has given too much freedom to the Protestants in Paris, and I do not think he can resist the rise of the Duke of Guise. But perhaps both sovereigns can be persuaded to submit to the Catholic powers without war. That is my hope. So you see my difficulty, Bruno. I must not appear too firmly set against this invasion, in case Guise gains power in Paris. But neither must I commit myself or France to it—as a diplomat I must urge all parties to peaceful means." He shakes his head at this conundrum and looks away to the window. I understand what Fowler meant when he said Castelnau was trying to please too many people.

I am framing a reply when the door is suddenly flung open with such force that the timbers shudder on their hinges. On the threshold stands a man who almost fills the doorway, arms folded across his broad chest, black beard bristling. His scowl could blister the paint on the portraits that line the walls. Dumas visibly shrinks farther into his corner. Castelnau assumes the smooth face of diplomacy and rises to his feet, addressing the visitor in Spanish.

"Don Bernardino. This is an unexpected pleasure."

"Save your flattery for the English, Castelnau. We both know that it is neither. But I bring you news that will light a fire under your backside." The Spanish ambassador turns and skewers me with his black glare. "Who is this?"

"Giordano Bruno of Nola, at Your Honour's service," I offer, also in Spanish, as I stand and bow.

Mendoza's eyes narrow; he nods slowly.

"So this is King Henri's Italian heretic. I have heard them talk of you. I suppose you think you are safe here." He turns back to Castelnau, his eyes blazing scorn, and points a stubby forefinger at his face. "This is your problem, Michel—you keep men like this in your house, feed them at your table, and then you wonder why no one will take you or your sovereign seriously. My King Philip"—here he stabs the finger forcefully into his own chest—"is pouring out Spanish money and men to fight heresy, while your King Henri opens his purse to patronise it!" He directs a furious look at me; I return it as blandly as I can while letting him see that I am not cowed. "Send him out," Mendoza says, with a flick of his hand, as if he were in charge. "And him." He points at Dumas, trembling behind his little desk in the corner. "What I have to say is not for the ears of servants."

Castelnau nods me toward the door with an apologetic expression. Dumas follows, arranging his papers into a pile as he stands while Mendoza looks on, huffing impatiently.

Outside, in the corridor, Dumas turns his anxious eyes on me. "What do you suppose his news is?" he whispers.

"If I had to guess, I'd say Philip of Spain has agreed to invest in Mary Stuart's enterprise. If I am right . . ." I let the sentence fall away. "The stakes are much higher than we imagined. We must not fail now, Léon."

Entering the first-floor gallery on the way back to my room, I encounter Marie and Courcelles standing together in a bay window, their heads bent close, talking quietly. They fall silent as soon as they see me; Courcelles stumbles back with a guilty look. It is a gesture I recognise; perhaps this is how all men behave around Marie. There is something in her way of talking and touching that makes you feel you have been inappropriately intimate. She, on the other hand, seems blithely unaware of this, or she affects to be.

"Well, Bruno?" she calls lightly, as I quicken my steps, hoping to pass them without being detained. "Did you ask him?"

"Ask him what, madame?"

"Honestly, Bruno—I begin to think I should be teaching *you* about memory. About our lessons."

"Ah. I'm afraid I did not have the time. We were interrupted."

"Oh? By whom?"

"By the Spanish ambassador."

"Mendoza is here?" She exchanges a glance with Courcelles. "Excuse me, gentlemen." With a swish of her skirts, she strides the length of the gallery and disappears. Courcelles looks at me and gives one of those infuriating Gallic shrugs.

THE VELVET BAG is still safely tucked under my pillow. In the light that slants through my dormer windows, I lay out the three objects again on the bed. The mirror glass has been loosened by its fall, and as I fiddle with the tortoiseshell backing to see if I might fix it, I realise with a jolt that it is designed to be taken apart. Carefully, I work the glass from side to side until it eases out from the casing. Behind it, there is a square of paper. With trembling fingers, I unfold it and smooth it out, and my heart catches in my throat. Someone has written the all too familiar symbols of Jupiter and Saturn, and below them, a date: 17th November. Nothing more. I turn over the paper, raise it to my face, and sniff it, in case some other unseen message has been written there in orange juice, but there is no scent. My heart hammers against my ribs; I don't know what I have uncovered here, but surely this has some bearing on the murder of Cecily Ashe. The date holds no significance for me, but taken together with the planetary symbols, it must hold a meaning for whoever sent this secret note to Cecily, hidden inside the glass of her mirror. Presumably it also meant something to her when she received it, although she could hardly have guessed it was a date she would not live to see.

If the mirror held a secret message, might the other gifts also have some significance beyond themselves, that only the giver and receiver would recognise? The ring, with its misspelled motto—that, surely, must be a deliberate mistake? *Sa Vertu m'atire*—but whose virtue? Cecily's? Or someone else's? The ring will only fit my little finger; my fingers are slender, but this ring was not made for a man's hand. As I slip it on and turn my hand to look again at its inscription, I notice a red blotch where I dipped my forefinger into the perfume. The skin is raised up in a kind of welt, which itches and burns when I rub it. Hardly what you want in a perfume, I think, and I am relieved that I didn't taste it; it must be cheaply made, though that seems strange, given how costly the bottle and the other gifts look. Then, in an instant, understanding dawns, and I have to get up, clutching the bottle in my fist, and pace the room, sweat prickling under my collar. I need to talk to someone about these ideas; ordinarily I would find Sidney, and for the first time, I truly begin to feel his absence. I don't even know if he and his new wife are in London, but even if they were, I cannot expect to continue as close to him as I was in Oxford if I am to go on being trusted here, within the walls of the French embassy.

Who, then, can I talk to? I can't go directly to Walsingham with this, even though it was he who involved me in the death of Cecily Ashe; at least, I don't want to go to him until I am certain my theory is right. There is William Fowler, of course; Walsingham has sent him to me as a substitute for Sidney and I suppose I must confide in him, though Fowler's inscrutable neutrality hardly inspires affection like Sidney's colourful braggadocio. Sitting down heavily again on my bed, I realise that I miss my friend; his marriage has made me feel all the more acutely how alone I really am in England. But there is another reason why I don't want to talk to Fowler, apart from the fact that his remit is only to convey my intelligence concerning the plots brewing in Salisbury Court, and it is a matter of personal pride: Abigail Morley has trusted me with Cecily Ashe's secrets and I want to be the one who unravels them. I want to prove my abilities by finding this killer, without involving someone like Fowler, who I can't help regarding on some level as a rival for Walsingham's approbation, even though we are supposed to be working together.

I walk to the window and lean on the sill, gazing out at the afternoon sky, now fading to a burnished auburn. My room overlooks the back of the house; from here I can see down the gardens as far as the great brown stretch of the Thames, broad as a highway, its sluggish waters reflecting the sinking sun. If I am honest with myself, I am afraid. Whatever the outcome of these plots with Mary Stuart, my own future hangs in the balance; I can see this much clearly. If this invasion, which at the moment sounds like the late-night revenge fantasy of disenfranchised men and a furious captive queen, should somehow become reality, I would not stand a chance in a newly Catholicised England. But if—as I sincerely hope—these plots are thwarted, it seems impossible that Castelnau could continue here as ambassador with any credibility once his involvement is known. And if he should be expelled, I must make sure that I am valuable to Walsingham and the English court for my own sake, not just for my access to the embassy and its intrigues. If I could discover who killed Cecily Ashe, I reason, Queen Elizabeth could not doubt my usefulness.

Then it occurs to me: there is a friend I can talk to, someone who has precisely the skills needed to test my theory about the perfume and the ring, and who also understands discretion. I have neglected him in the flurry of these past days, but he is the one person who knows more about the Great Conjunction than anyone in London. Tomorrow, then, I will return to Mortlake, to the house of Doctor Dee.

Chapter 6

MORTLAKE, SOUTHWEST LONDON.
29TH SEPTEMBER, YEAR OF OUR LORD 1583

octor Dee's library is, to me, one of the uncelebrated wonders of
this rainy island. His entire house is a sprawling hotchpotch of
extensions, additions, new wings and secret rooms, so that it is impossible from the outside to tell the shape of the original cottage that once
belonged to his mother, buried somewhere deep within the labyrinth. All
these addenda were designed by his own hand according to his own esoteric precepts, to serve some particular purpose of his work, and the
library is the culmination of his achievement. His collection of books
and manuscripts, and indeed the room itself, is grander than the college
libraries I saw in Oxford; at vast expense he has had built the new vertical
shelving popular in the European universities rather than the old-style
lecterns, so that the books may be displayed to better advantage from
floor to ceiling, around the walls. This does not necessarily help the visiting scholar, since there appears to be no obvious method to cataloguing
the works, unless it is some arcane system that exists purely in Dee's own

head, for he can put his hand immediately on any work you care to name, and remembers exactly where to replace it.

There are shelves crammed with ancient maps and charts rolled on wooden spindles and stacked horizontally; cases with ancient manuscripts of vellum and gilt illumination, saved from the destruction of England's monastic libraries; there are books that Dee crossed a continent to find, books which cost him a year's income, books bound in calfskin of rich brown with brass bindings, books which in another country would see him burned at the stake. Here you can find the *De occulta philosophia* of Cornelius Agrippa of Nettesheim, the *Liber experimentorum* of the mystic Ramon Llull, Burgo's *Treatise on Magic*, the writings of Nicolaus Copernicus, and Abbot Trithemius's studies of cryptography; you can, if the subject interests you, find books on mathematics, metallurgy, divination, botany, navigation, music, astronomy, tides, rhetoric, or indeed any branch of knowledge that at some time has been committed to pen and ink. In one corner of the room, he keeps a pair of painted globes mounted on brass stands, one showing the Earth and the other the heavens, a gift from the great cartographer Gerardus Mercator; in another, a quadrant five feet tall, and other devices of his own construction for measuring the movements of the planets.

Beyond this cavernous library, with its vaulted wooden ceiling, where you often encounter travel-weary scholars and writers who have crossed seas or ridden for days to consult some book of which Dee owns the only known copy, lie the inner rooms, where only his most trusted friends and associates are admitted: his alchemical laboratory and his private study, his sanctum.

"Some sort of poison, you think?" Dee murmurs, canted over the workbench in his laboratory. He holds up the glass perfume bottle to an oil lamp that hangs from a hook above him, so that its facets reflect fragments of light as he turns it curiously from side to side. Outside, the weather is still bright with the last warmth of summer, but in this room the shutters are always closed. Standing in Dee's laboratory gives you the sense of being trapped in the belly of a great beast, with the dark and the heat from the several fires continually burning, and the fact that the room seems to pulse with autonomous life: six stills of various sizes, with vast interconnected vessels and flasks of clay, glass, or copper, puff and bubble constantly, as if engaged in an ongoing conversation with one another. Clouds of steam float across the ceiling and disperse in clammy rivulets down the peeling walls. Today there is a filthy smell in the room, a decaying, barnyard stink.

"Oh, that," Dee says, grinning mischievously like a small boy caught out, when he sees me wrinkling my nose. "I am experimenting with distilling horse dung."

"For what purpose?"

"I won't know that till I see what we get from it. Now."

He unstops the perfume bottle and sniffs the liquid with the practised nose of a vintner assessing a new wine. I am amazed he can smell anything over the boiling horse dung.

"Hm. They've mixed it with rose water. But you're right—there's something else in there. Acrid. Show me the finger again."

He draws my hand into the light. Though the redness has faded where I touched the perfume, a small blister has risen. Dee nods thoughtfully. "Any number of common plants or berries might have that effect, if the sap was concentrated. Could cause considerable discomfort if it was rubbed over delicate skin, as perfume is. It's a spiteful trick, if nothing else."

"And if someone drank it? Could it be poisonous?"

He frowns. "Depends on what the base substance is. But why would he imagine the girl would take it into her head to drink the perfume?"

"Perhaps it was not intended for the girl."

"But why would *anyone* drink perfume?"

"They wouldn't. Unless they were unaware that it had been added to their food or cup. Which would be an easy thing if you came into contact with them every day."

Dee's eyes gape and he stares at me, appalled, as he understands my meaning. "The queen?" His voice comes as barely a whisper. "You're suggesting that girl intended to poison the queen?"

"I don't know. It's only a theory." I pace about between the stills, trying to breathe through my mouth as I talk, to avoid the manure fumes. "It seems, as you say, oddly spiteful and pointless to give a woman poisoned perfume that will make welts rise on her skin. But what if Cecily knew that the perfume was never meant to be worn, if her suitor gave her the bottle for another purpose? Think, Dee—there are any number of desperate men ready to assassinate the queen for the liberation of the Catholic church."

Dee nods, sanguine. "They arrested a fellow only last month on the road from York with two loaded pistols, boasting to all and sundry that he was going to kill Elizabeth to restore England. He was obviously mad, poor devil. They hung and quartered him anyway, to make an example."

"But not everyone is so hotheaded. A sharper man might reason that a better way to get to the queen is by turning someone she trusts to his cause. A maid of honour like Cecily Ashe would have had ample opportunity to slip something into the queen's wine, if she was provided with it."

I can tell he is not convinced.

"Well, Bruno—before we run away with these theories, let us have a better idea of what is in this bottle." He hands me the perfume and crosses to a wooden crate tucked into a corner of the room, behind a vast belching conical pot half the height of a man, suspended on a brass frame above a fire. When he lifts the lid of the crate there is a sudden scratching and scuffling, accompanied by furious squeaks. Dee reaches in and pulls out his hand clasped around a struggling brown mouse. "Now then." He looks up and catches sight of my expression. "They multiply like the plague in the outhouses—I have the kitchen boy catch me a supply for the laboratory. You'd be surprised how varied their uses can be. *What*, Bruno?"

"It seems a little cruel." I shrug.

"The pursuit of knowledge is often brutal," he says blithely. "But that is science. And you would hardly want me to test it on a servant, now, would you? Hold the mouse." He passes the lithe, wriggling body into my hands. I feel the tiny heart pattering against my fingers, the warmth of its frantic life. The tail whips back and forth as Dee moves unhurriedly from bench to bench, gathering pieces of apparatus—a glass tube, a funnel, a small box with a hinged lid. He instructs me to hold the creature on its back. It likes this even less and nips me sharply; I curse and almost drop it as a bead of blood swells on my finger.

"Keep it still," Dee says impatiently, as if I were the one playing up. With some difficulty, he inserts the tube into the mouse's mouth, which the poor animal resists with all its meagre force, squealing pitifully, until I am afraid I will crush the life out of it in my attempts to subdue it. Dee attaches the funnel to the neck and pours in some liquid from the perfume bottle. A considerable amount of it spills out; it is questionable whether the mouse has swallowed any, but Dee opens the lid of the little box and tells me to put the creature inside.

"And now we wait," he says happily, as if he had just put a batch of cakes in the oven. "In the meantime, Bruno, I too am troubled by something that I must share with you. Come."

He leads me through the door at the back of the laboratory into his private study, where I had last joined him and Kelley for their séance. I am relieved to see that Kelley is not there.

"She has summoned me to Whitehall this very evening," he says, motioning me to a chair with one hand and worrying at the point of his beard with the other. "I do not think this is good news. Walsingham rode over to see me yesterday. He showed me this." He crosses to his desk and holds up a copy of the same pamphlet I had bought for a penny in St. Paul's courtyard, with the signs of Jupiter and Saturn printed boldly on its front page. "Francis wanted to warn me," he continues, quietly. "What with the girl's murder at Richmond, it seems the world is gone quite mad with talk of prophecies and apocalypse, Fiery Trigons and Great Conjunctions. *This* sort of thing"—he slaps the paper with the back of his hand—"abounds, fuelling the common people's fear and unrest. The Privy Council feels it is getting out of hand and must be stopped." He sighs, with a rattled dignity, and lays the paper back facedown on the desk.

"But none of that is your doing."

"Quite right. I am only the messenger." He spreads his hands wide in a gesture of humility. "But apparently Lord Burghley talks of introducing new legislation that would make it illegal to cast the queen's horoscope. He thinks that will put an end to these feverish predictions of her death. I don't see that it will help—already a man stands to lose a hand for writing that kind of filth, and still they print them, and fools read them."

He sits heavily and leans forward over his knees, clasping his hands together, prayerlike, and staring intently into the near distance as if he saw someone there who was trying to speak to him. I adopt the same position in silent sympathy; I can see his predicament. Poor Dee: if it is against the law to cast the queen's horoscope, she can hardly go on employing a private astrologer, and royal patronage is almost his only source of income. He has a wife and two young children to support, not to mention that idler Ned Kelley, who has attached himself to Dee's household; on top of that, alchemy and book collecting are not cheap pursuits. He needs a reliable flow of money to fund his experiments and maintain his library, and he also needs the queen's protection from those who whisper against him.

"Henry Howard is behind this," Dee mutters darkly, as if he has followed my own thoughts, his gaze still fixed on the same spot. "He will not rest until he sees me banished from court and out of the light of her favour altogether."

"Henry Howard?" I look at him, puzzled. "He has something to do with these pamphlets?"

"No—it is he who leads the charge against them!" Dee cries, leaping from his chair and striding again to the desk, where he picks up a small, leather-bound book which he waves at me as if in evidence. "He rails against all forms of knowledge that he has not the capacity to understand, he talks of summoning demons, he argues that it is the queen's toleration of astrologers like me that has led to the present frenzy of prophets and fortune-tellers sowing fear and disbelief up and down the land. No one at court wants to be seen disagreeing with his book. But the idea that Henry Howard should set himself up as the champion of cool reason! Listen to this, Bruno." He flicks through a few pages, clears his throat and reads. " 'Certain busybodies in the commonwealth, who with limned papers, painted books, figures of wild beasts and birds, carry men from present duties into future hopes.' He means me, of course. Or this: 'the froth of folly, the scum of pride, the shipwreck of honour and the poison of nobility.' All of it aimed at me, you see, and there is much more I could read you."

I reach out for the book quickly before he can carry out this threat. The title is stamped in gold on the front: *A Defensative Against the Poison of Supposed Prophecies*. "Why does Henry Howard hate you so much?"

Dee sits down again and folds his hands.

"He was my pupil once," he says, with a trace of sadness. "He came to me secretly, hungry for the kind of knowledge that you and I know can be dangerous in the wrong hands. This would have been ten years ago, just after his brother was executed—he was about your age then. A fearsomely clever young man, he was, and on his travels he had encountered philosophers and magi who had shown him the writings of Hermes Trismegistus. He desired to become an adept."

"And you agreed?"

"He was a talented scholar, and he paid generously, perhaps because he wanted it well hidden that he was coming to me. But . . ." Dee spreads his hands in a gesture of regret. "The great mysteries of the ancient philosophies must be approached with humility. I soon saw that Henry Howard's ambition far outstripped his wisdom."

"Literal, in what way?"

"He became obsessed by the lost book of Hermes. Ah, I see you smiling, Bruno. Aren't we all, you are thinking? But I ask you—that lost fifteenth book, what do you understand it to contain?"

"No one knows for certain," I say. "That is its irresistible lure. We know only that the great philosopher and astrologer Marsilio Ficino refused to translate it for Cosimo de' Medici because he was afraid of the consequences for Christendom."

"Precisely. Because the lost book is believed to set forth the mystery of man's divinity. It is the culmination of the Hermetic magic."

"They say it holds the secret of becoming equal to God," I whisper, picturing Howard's pointed face, his beady eyes.

"But where you and I understand that to mean through enlighten-ment or gnosis, Howard's interpretation was much more literal," Dee says, leaning farther in with a meaningful nod. "That was what troubled me."

"Literal, in what way?"

"It was not divine knowledge Howard aspired to." He lowers his voice. "It was divine immortality."

We fall silent for a moment, watching each other. Twice I open my mouth to say this is impossible, but each time something about Dee's earnest grey stare deters me. His faith in magic, if by that we mean a world that lies beyond the bounds of our present knowledge or philoso-phy, is simpler and more trusting than my own. If the universe is infinite, as I believe, then it must surely contain an infinite number of possibilities that we have not yet imagined or attempted to harness, but the more I consider this, the more I discover in myself an instinctive scepticism toward the easy claims of alchemists and mountebanks and those who perform tricks of mind reading from the backs of carts to a willing crowd. Could a man truly achieve immortality? And could one book really contain the key to open that door? Rumours and mythologies grow around lost books; they acquire extraordinary powers in their absence. But the lure of immortality—I can see how that would draw a man like Henry Howard.

"So what happened?"

Dee sucks in his cheeks.

"It was not just the Hermes book. It became increasingly clear that Howard's interest in magic was not about knowledge but about power."

"Does the one not lead to the other?" I say, with a sly smile.

"For those who have the wisdom to use both judiciously. But not in the simplistic way he imagined. His eldest brother had just been executed, don't forget—the Howards had lost the best part of their lands and titles. He wanted a means of controlling and manipulating his way back to eminence. I glimpsed in him a ruthlessness that made me deeply uneasy. In the end, I told him that I could not go on teaching him."

"I imagine he took that badly."

"Oh yes. The Howards do not like to be thwarted. First, he offered more money. When I continued to refuse, he threatened me."

"With violence?"

Dee tugs at his beard and raises his head toward the window, a weight of great sorrow in his eyes.

"Nothing so crude. He simply said he would destroy me. He said he would work against me like a subtle poison, so that not even those I counted my friends would acknowledge me. He dared me to put him to the test."

"But that was ten years ago," I say, meaning to be reassuring.

"Yes, and here I still am. Oh, there has been much muttering against me over the years by the ignorant and the envious—that I conjure demons, speak with the dead, perform any number of forbidden and grisly rituals at dead of night with mummified corpses or stillborn children or I know not what. Thus far, Her Majesty has never paid attention to such foolishness." He lays a hand on my arm. "But I have never imagined that Henry Howard forgot his hatred or his threat. People like you and me, Bruno—we walk as if on fragile ice. We work at the very edge of knowledge, and that frightens many people. We can never know when the ground might fall away beneath our feet."

He looks so melancholy that I press my hand over his and clasp it for a moment.

"So, Howard's response was to turn violently against all forms of occult knowledge?" I say, indicating the book. Dee frowns.

"Publicly, yes. But I have always wondered if he hasn't secretly pursued his desire, using his piety against it as a cover. Henry Howard is nothing if not tenacious. Some fourteen years ago, it was thought that a copy of the lost manuscript of Hermes had been found. This part of the story you know, Bruno, from that rogue Jenkes."

I nod, with feeling; Rowland Jenkes, the dealer in esoteric and forbidden books who had tried to kill me in Oxford.

"Well, then," he continues, "you remember that Jenkes thought he had found the book buried in an Oxford college library. He wrote to me, knowing of my collection, and I travelled to Oxford to meet him. From what he let me see of the manuscript, I was sufficiently convinced to pay him a high price for it."

"You read it, then?" I sit forward eagerly.

"Only a small part of it," he says. "I can't say for certain, but I believed it was by Hermes Trismegistus. My plan was to bring it back to London and immediately make a translation. Only I never had the chance. As you know, my servant and I were brutally set upon and robbed on the road the moment we left Oxford, and the book was taken."

"Jenkes told me about that," I say, nodding. "But he swore the theft was not his doing."

"At first I assumed it must have been, so that he could sell the book again," Dee says, absently rubbing at the back of his head as if the tale has opened the old wound. "I returned to Oxford to recover—I was quite badly injured in the attack—and confronted him, though of course he denied everything. But as time passed, it occurred to me that there were others besides Jenkes who wanted that book, and who would have had the means to pay spies in my household and villains to steal it from me on the road."

"Henry Howard?" I look down at the book in my hands.

"I have no proof. It is only a suspicion. But for years afterward I asked everyone I knew, every collector and dealer in antiquities and manuscripts in England and all those I knew in Europe, and no one had heard any further word of the Hermes book. You can bet that if Jenkes had hired thieves to get it back, he would have attempted to trade it on for more profit.

Which makes me believe it was stolen from me by someone who had no interest in selling it, but who wanted to keep it, to study its content."

"I suppose the only way to be certain is to try and kill Henry Howard," I say, keeping my expression serious. "If he proves to be immortal, we may reasonably assume he took the book and found it to be authentic."

Dee chuckles softly. "Don't tempt me, Bruno. In any case, this brings us no nearer to solving my dilemma."

"I thought that *was* your dilemma?"

"I'm afraid it is more specific. Yesterday"—he hesitates, glances at the door—"Ned Kelley had a horrifying vision. He fears that the spirits have granted him sight of what will come to pass, and I must decide whether to warn the queen."

I want to tell him not to be a fool; my cynicism about Kelley tightens in my chest like a hard bud, but Dee's eyes are wide and his lips trembling slightly. More gently, I lean in toward him.

"Go on."

He takes a deep breath.

"In the showing stone, much as it was the time you observed, a spirit appeared to Ned as a red-haired woman in a white gown, with the symbols of the planets and all the signs of the zodiac embroidered on it. In her right hand she held a book and in her left a golden key."

Kelley's figures are always holding a book, I think to myself. Perhaps his imagination is running dry. "This is no figure I recognise," I say shortly, though the moment he mentioned a red-haired woman my mind snapped instantly to Abigail Morley.

"But there is more. She did not speak, but in the vision she unlaced her bodice and opened it for him—"

"I bet she did."

"Don't mock, Bruno," he says, hurt. "Wait until you hear. On her breast she had a symbol engraved in blood . . ."

"Was it the sign of Jupiter, by any chance?" I say, unable to keep the sarcasm from my voice. But Dee looks stricken.

"Sweet Jesus. No—but you are close. It was the sign of Saturn. How on earth could you know?"

I rise, infuriated, cross to the window, and turn sharply back to him.

"He has plucked this detail straight from the murder at court! Come, John—the man is a charlatan. He is playing you like a harp—can you not see it?"

"But Ned goes nowhere near the court or those circles. How would he learn of a detail like that?"

"It is the talk of London!" I cry, exasperated. "He only has to step out of doors to hear people gossiping about it in the streets. He has picked up a handbill from somewhere, read the lurid descriptions, and thought it would make a neat picture for his next invention! Do not lose sleep over it, for heaven's sake."

"Now, Bruno." He looks weary. "I know you do not like Ned, but really—he is a very gifted scryer and you insult me to suggest otherwise. He speaks with the spirits in their own heavenly language. I have heard him."

"He is a criminal! Have you not seen his ears? That's what they do to those who forge coins, is it not? And if he can counterfeit money, why not visions, and languages?"

"Ned has led a hard life and has made his mistakes, but all that is in the past. He is an honest fellow now, Bruno. It is not for us to judge."

I run my hands through my hair, grasping at handfuls; there will be no reasoning with him. "Christ's body, John! You are entitled to make some judgement of a man if he is living off you. You are too softhearted."

Dee smiles fondly. "This from the man who could not bear to hurt a mouse."

We stare at each other, the mouse suddenly remembered. Dee rouses himself with surprising speed from his chair and hurries back through to the laboratory, his robe whipping behind him; I follow at a clip. Here among the stills, with their soft, intestinal murmurings, the atmosphere is more humid now, and more fetid. The room smells like a farm in a midsummer thunderstorm.

Dee lifts the lid and holds the small wooden box up to the lamp. The mouse lies motionless, its tiny feet splayed outward. A pool of thin, watery shit spreads around its tail, a similar one of a reddish liquid around its head. Its eyes bulge unnaturally, like the glass eyes of a stuffed creature.

"Interesting," Dee muses, nodding as if pleased with this result, his head almost touching mine as we lean in. "The substance has worked quickly—see, where it has voided its stomach from both ends. I must confess I was not persuaded by your theory, Bruno, but it seems you were right."

"What substance would have this effect?" I ask, peering closer, half hoping to see the mouse convulse or twitch.

"Hard to say. Something like yew, or black bryony possibly, both easy to come by at this time of year, easy to extract."

"And would it work in the same way on a person?"

"Not so quickly, especially if it was diluted with rose water. But in essentials, I should think so, in a large enough dose. It's clearly had a violent purgative effect. I'll cut this creature up and have a close look at the innards, although I won't have time before I go this evening. But Bruno"—he turns to me, his eyes wide again with dawning fear—"if your guess is correct, someone must warn the queen immediately."

"No!" It comes out more sharply than I intended. "I mean to say—all we know for certain is that a bottle of poison was given to one of the queen's maids in the guise of perfume. That girl is now dead, but we know nothing of who gave it to her or why. Until we have some definite ideas, it is best the queen should not be alarmed and the court thrown into uproar. She is already heavily guarded. Besides," I add, "the person who gave me the perfume might be compromised."

"You don't understand, Bruno." He clasps my shoulders and gives them a little shake. "Ned's vision, the red-haired woman, her downfall. It all fits. I fear Her Majesty is in terrible danger."

I do not want to ask, but know I must. "What was the end of the vision?"

"After she revealed her breast with the sign of Saturn carved into her flesh, she held the book and key aloft and opened her mouth as if to give a great speech, but before she could utter a word, she was pierced through the heart by a sword and then swept away by a raging torrent." His grip tightens and his eyes wildly search mine; clearly he expects a better response.

"Well, he certainly has a sense of drama. Where *is* Kelley, by the way?" I glance around the laboratory, as if the scryer might be hiding behind one of the larger stills.

"Oh, I have not seen him since yesterday evening. He was so shaken by the vision that he needed to go away for a while to recover." He sees my eyes narrow. "He has done it before, Bruno. If the session with the spirits has taxed him too hard, he will disappear for a few days so that he can come back refreshed."

"Really. It must be exhausting for him." I frown. "And he never tells you where he goes?"

"I never ask."

I place my hands on his shoulders in return; we stand for a moment locked in this half embrace while I look into those melancholy grey eyes, so full of wisdom and yet, in some ways, so blind.

"Do not, under any circumstances, try to tell the queen about this vision this evening," I say gently, as if admonishing a child. "If any harm really were to befall her, they would say you foresaw it by the power of the Devil, and in the much more likely event that nothing happens, you will be taken for a false prophet, no better than these pamphleteers. I do not pretend to understand Kelley's motives, but we do better to concentrate on what we know of real dangers to the queen"—I nod toward the perfume bottle on the workbench—"than on whatever dreams he may or may not see in the stone."

Dee is about to protest, but suddenly it seems a great weariness comes on him, and he hangs his head instead.

"Perhaps you are right, Bruno. Better not to give my enemies more arrows to aim at me."

I glance sideways at the stiff little body of the brown mouse in the box, remembering its pulse in the palm of my hand. How quickly a life is snuffed out, I think. If only we could catch the soul as it took flight, follow its journey, and return to chart the territory, like the adventurers to the New World, like Mercator with his globes. But the mouse has not been sacrificed in vain. It has proved, if nothing else, that the queen's enemies almost managed to reach into her bedchamber. But how to begin to find them?

As I am taking my leave at his front door, I suddenly remember a question that Dee, if anyone, might be able to answer.

"The seventeenth day of November—has it some astrological significance? I have tried to think, but I don't have charts with enough detail here to calculate whether it will be the occasion for anything of note in the heavens."

Dee chuckles. "I don't know about the heavens, but any Englishman will tell you that here on the ground it is Accession Day. The anniversary of Her Majesty's accession to the throne, you know—since 1570 she has declared it a public holiday, with pageants and processions to celebrate her glorious reign. Street parties and so on. It should be a sight worth seeing this year, being the twenty-fifth since her coronation. Why do you ask?"

I hesitate, wondering if I should tell him about the paper hidden inside Cecily Ashe's mirror, but I fear he would come instantly to the same conclusion as I, except that he would tie it to Kelley's ridiculous invention and feel compelled to warn the queen, in that slightly hysterical way he sometimes has. My mind turns over quickly, even as Dee looks at me expectantly. Did whoever gave Cecily a vial of poison disguised as perfume also send her the date on which he intended her to use it? Was Elizabeth's twenty-fifth Accession Day supposed to be the day of her death? The uproar this suggestion would cause at court would create such noise and smoke as to obscure any trace of the real plot; besides, something had obviously gone badly wrong if that was the intention. Cecily Ashe was dead, and the poison safe in Dee's laboratory. Did this mean the would-be assassin would find another means to strike at the queen on Accession Day? There is no doubt in my mind now that Cecily was killed by the man who gave her those gifts, who had involved her in a plot to poison the queen and then left her corpse holding an effigy of Elizabeth stabbed, a reminder of the task she had somehow failed to carry out.

"Bruno? You look troubled." Dee's frown grows fatherly with concern. "Is something the matter?"

"No, no—I heard the date mentioned by one of the embassy servants and wondered why it was important." I search his face and am seized by a sudden affection for him; impetuously, I grip him by the shoulders and kiss him on both cheeks. He looks surprised, but pleased. "Remember—no mention to the queen of any visions," I add over my shoulder, as I turn to go.

I HAD PAID the boatman who brought me to Mortlake to wait, since wherries are harder to come by this far upriver. We have progressed perhaps twenty minutes on our journey back toward London, when I notice another small boat keeping pace with ours at a distance of about fifty yards. It has only one passenger, a man, as far as I can tell, wearing a travelling cloak and a hat pulled down around his face, but they are too far away for me to see him clearly.

"Has that boat been behind us all the way from Mortlake?" I ask the boatman, who squints at it from under his cap.

"That one? Yes, sir—it was moored up just along the bank from where you come down."

"All the time I was on shore?"

He shrugs.

"Couldn't rightly say, sir. A good part of the time, at least."

"With that same passenger? Or did he get on at Mortlake?"

"Didn't notice."

"But it left at the same time as us?"

"Must 'a done, if it's behind us now."

"Slow your pace," I instructed. "Let them catch us up."

The boatman obeys me and eases off his oars; the boat behind us appears to do the same, so that the distance remains. I tell my boatman to stop rowing altogether; he complains that the current is too strong and we will be brought into the bank. The other boat moves closer to the opposite side, away from us. The farther we travel downriver, the busier the water becomes, but our two boats continue to follow the same course; I crane over the side but still cannot get a good view of the passenger who I am now certain is following me. At Putney, the other ferryman suddenly weaves his craft across the river and pulls it in at the landing stairs; my boatman pulls doggedly onward, and I can only see the man in silhouette as he disembarks. There is nothing to distinguish him; he appears to be of average height and build, and he keeps his hat pulled down as he climbs the stairs and disappears. Clearly someone was interested in my visit to Dee. I recall the sensation I had of being followed yesterday at Whitehall; could it be the same person? But who would have an interest in my movements, to spend that much time tailing me to Mortlake? A cold shiver prickles at my neck. Unless it is someone who saw me talking to Abigail yesterday and is following me precisely because he fears that she has passed on to me something that she knew. And if that is the case, it means the man I have just seen stepping lightly up the stairs at Putney could only be the killer of Cecily Ashe. If it is so, I think grimly, Abigail may be in immediate danger—as may I, for that matter, though I am probably better equipped to look after myself. Perhaps I should warn her—but how am I to get a message to her at court without arousing further suspicion? I have no means of contacting the kitchen boy who brought her message last time—and no means of knowing whether he might have alerted anyone else to her meeting with me in the first place, intentionally or otherwise.

When the boat has finally delivered me back to Buckhurst Stairs, and I have paid the boatman his considerable fee for the long journey, I return to find Salisbury Court silent, its halls and galleries unaccountably empty. This suits me; I manage to reach my room without being detained by Castelnau's summons or his wife's aggressive flirting. But even before I insert the key into the lock, I am struck by a feeling of unease, as vivid as if I had glimpsed a presence in the corridor; I whip around to right and left, but the landing remains as unnaturally still as the rest of the house. Chiding myself for growing skittish, I attempt to turn the key and it will not move. I turn the latch; the door is already open. Every muscle in my body tenses; the hairs stand up on my skin and my hand goes instinctively to the knife I carry at my belt. I left this door locked, I would swear to it on everything I hold dear; I am diligent to the point of obsession in this matter. I have never, in six months, gone out and left my chamber unlocked—there are books and writings in my chest that would not be regarded sympathetically by anyone in this devoutly Catholic household. How naïve I have been not to have considered that someone in the house must have a duplicate set of keys for all the rooms. Silently cursing my own stupidity, I slowly ease the door back and then kick it violently, springing over the threshold with my knife drawn.

But the room is empty, untouched, just as I left it, the bedsheets folded back neatly, some papers arranged in two separate piles on the writing desk where I had been working, the quills, inkpot, and penknife scattered beside them. For a moment, I doubt myself; perhaps in my haste to get to Dee this morning, I really did forget to lock the door. Still the sense of unease persists; I turn slowly, taking in the room, the details of its sparse furnishings, racking my brain to see if anything looks out of place, half expecting some movement out of the shadows. It is only when I cross to the desk that I notice immediately that the papers are out of sequence. Clearly, whoever has been in my room failed to consider that I am famous in France for my prodigious memory as well as my heresy. Quickly I sift through the notes; there is nothing here that is too contentious, some mathematical calculations on the motions of the Moon and the Earth, and a series of diagrams measuring how the heavenly bodies reflect light, but nothing that could have me arrested. Nevertheless, the topmost papers are not the ones I was working on recently. This thought leads me to check the carved wooden chest where I keep my more inflammatory books. The padlock that holds its iron clasps is intact, but there are tiny scuff marks in the dust around it that suggest it has been moved a fraction. Someone has given it some attention very recently.

At the far end of the room there is another chest, somewhat larger, where I keep my clothes. It emits a faint gust of amber when I lift the lid, from the pomander I keep in there to discourage moths. Here too, I see subtle evidence of interference. My clothes have been taken out and replaced, hastily folded. I lift up a fine wool doublet and smooth it down, refolding it carefully. Nothing appears to be missing, but the chest has clearly been searched. This is even stranger; I can see that there might be some among the embassy's household—Courcelles, for one—who feel they have a right to sneak in and investigate what I read and write under their roof, but I cannot imagine any reason why anyone here would have the slightest interest in looking through my clothes. Only someone who was looking for something very particular would bother to search there.

At least, I think with some relief, as I tuck the doublet back into the chest, I had taken the velvet bag containing Cecily Ashe's love tokens with me. This thought makes me freeze for a moment; but that is impossible, clearly. No one in the household could know anything about my presence at Richmond Palace on the night of the murder, nor about my contact with Abigail Morley. Standing, I brush myself down and shake my head briskly, to dislodge such foolish thoughts as if they were flies. The encounter with the man in the boat has made me see shadows where there are none, and even there I have no firm proof that I was followed. Still, I think, as I step out onto the landing and make doubly sure that I lock the door behind me—I have not imagined the intruder in my room, and someone in the embassy knows who it was.

The silence persists throughout the house; it is as if the apocalypse has occurred while I was out, the other inhabitants of Salisbury Court gathered up and only I left behind. I do not encounter another soul or hear so much as a footfall on my way to Castelnau's private office at the back of the house, and when I knock on his door, the only sound is the echo of my knuckles on the wood.

When I push open the door, however, I see a figure outlined against the window; he starts and turns, expectant, and I recognise him as the young man Throckmorton, the courier. When he sees me, his elfin face tightens, wary.

"Good day, Master Throckmorton. My lord ambassador is out?" I keep my voice light. I see his eyes flicker for the merest instant to Castelnau's desk. He bows slightly, and clasps his hands behind his back.

"The household is hearing Mass at present. I am waiting for him to return."

"Ah. You do not join them?"

"I have only just now arrived," he says, and again his gaze strays almost unconsciously to the ambassador's desk. "I was not expected today, so I did not like to interrupt." He smiles, but it appears strained.

"I had thought you on the road to Sheffield," I say; our haste in delivering the letters two days ago was, I believed, because Throckmorton rode for Sheffield the following morning. What has happened to delay him—some concern over the correspondence, perhaps?

"I had to postpone my journey. Unforeseen circumstances. I ride on the second." He is cautious with me in his turn. Even here in the embassy, it is wise not to speak too openly. I decide to take a chance.

"Because of Mendoza's news?"

"You know of that?" He looks immediately suspicious.

"I was here when he visited Castelnau yesterday." I affect a lack of concern, picking up a quill from the ambassador's desk, turning it between my fingers, and replacing it, all the while not looking at him. "Interesting developments."

I glance at Throckmorton; he seems relieved, and visibly relaxes.

"Yes, indeed," he says. "With Spanish troops and money, we have a real chance of success. I had not expected King Philip to agree so quickly."

So my speculation was correct. Throckmorton has the same gleam in his eyes that I observed in Marie de Castelnau when she talked of the glorious enterprise of restoring England to Catholic rule. His smooth face with its clear, wide-set eyes is lit with a boy's excitement at the prospect of some adventure, his enthusiasm clearly undampened by any personal experience of war or massacre. Where does a young man like this, with his cultured accent, his well-cut doublet of dark green wool, and his expensive leather boots, acquire a taste for enforcing his religion with Spanish warships?

"Your family has suffered a great deal, then, I suppose?" I lift the lid of an enamelled inkwell and affect to give it all my attention.

"My family?" He sounds bemused. "Why would you say that?"

I turn to look at him.

"Only that I imagined all Englishmen who conspire against their queen must have reason to resent the Protestants. Like my lord Howard."

Throckmorton tilts his head to one side.

"You don't think a man would want to fight for his beliefs alone? For what he holds to be true?"

I shrug.

"It is possible. But revenge or gain are stronger motives, from what I have observed."

He regards me with suspicion for a moment.

"Perhaps you have never believed anything with enough passion to fight for it."

I smile, ignoring the implied slight. It is true, I would like to tell him, that I have never considered the lives of innocent people a price worth paying for any belief of mine, but I must maintain my fiction.

"I do, of course, or I would not be here. But then I was raised a Catholic. I was only curious as to what makes a young Englishman turn against his own country."

He looks a little abashed at this; I sense I have touched a sensitive area.

"My family were all loyal Protestants, Doctor Bruno," he says, with a hint of defiance. "My uncle, Sir Nicholas, was a diplomat for Elizabeth, in France and Scotland, where he became a friend of Mary Stuart. Though he never shared her faith, he supported her right to succeed Elizabeth and publicly opposed her imprisonment."

I nod, as if impressed.

"I studied in France after Oxford," he continues, "and there I met many Englishmen in exile who favoured the cause of Queen Mary. Through them I was introduced to Madame de Castelnau." You might have missed it, if you were not paying close attention, the almost imperceptible softening of his voice. Perhaps he is driven not by revenge but by subtler motives. I want to smile, but I keep my face earnest and attentive. He would not be the first man—or woman—to change his religion for the sake of desire. Presumably Marie used her considerable powers to draw him into the embassy cabal.

"So you converted to the Catholic faith in France?" These seminaries of Rheims and Paris are the thorn in Walsingham's side, cauldrons of Catholic missionary zeal brewing up plots and conspiracies heated by the youthful rage of English students craving a taste of rebellion. First Fowler, now Throckmorton; both sons of good families, both resisting the prosperous but uninspiring course mapped for them. One becomes a spy, the other a traitor, all in the name of adventure, the desire to prove themselves. I was about this Throckmorton's age when I defied the Inquisition and fled my monastery in Naples; I cannot pretend that the prospect of risk doesn't quicken the blood.

"God by His grace showed me the way to the true church." Throckmorton says this as if it is a phrase he has carefully learned from another language. "I came back to England to be of what service I could to Queen Mary's cause. Madame de Castelnau recommended me to her husband." Again, the slight change in tone when he mentions her, the lowering of the eyes, the faint spread of a blush.

"Do your family suspect?"

"My father and uncle are both dead. I wish my uncle in particular could have lived to see these times." His voice grows wistful. "He was suspected of involvement in the Duke of Norfolk's plans to marry Queen Mary, in '69, you know."

"Henry Howard's brother? Really?" I forget for an instant to disguise my interest, but he is less guarded now that he has warmed to his theme.

"He was their go-between for a while, I understand. The whole family fell under suspicion for it, but they never found any evidence to charge him. I was fifteen at the time, but I remember it well." His face tightens again at the memory.

"A family tradition, then." I smile, to put him at ease, but he barely notices, glancing anxiously past me to the door.

"If Mendoza does not replace me."

"Replace you?"

Throckmorton scowls.

"He fears my face will become too familiar around Sheffield Castle. He says he's worried I'll be searched and the correspondence discovered, so he talks of using one of his own couriers. But they don't know the terrain like I do, and they don't know how to get the messages to Mary's women." He bridles at the suggestion; I see he fears being deprived of his role.

"Perhaps he also wishes to keep his correspondence separate from the French?" I offer. "Maybe he doesn't trust this embassy, and thinks you are too much Castelnau's man?"

Again his eyes slide inadvertently to the desk, but he reins them quickly back and begins to pick at a loose thread on his sleeve.

"This is why I need to speak to the ambassador. There is bad blood between him and Mendoza, as I'm sure you know, but that must not be allowed to infect these plans. I am Mary's man, if I am anyone's."

Mary's or Marie's, I wonder.

"Well, then, I shall leave you in peace to wait for him," I say, moving toward the door.

"What about you, Doctor Bruno?"

"Me?" The question stops me as I reach for the latch, and the roots of my hair prickle; I turn to find his pale eyes fixed on me, questioning.

"Yes. Whose man are you?"

"King Henri of France," I say, as lightly as I can. "He is my patron while I live in England, and I will give myself to whatever cause his ambassador believes to be in France's best interest."

He studies me for a moment through narrowed eyes.

"Then for you it is a matter of politics, not religion? Restoring Mary to her throne, I mean?"

I smile.

"If there are men whose religion is free of politics, Throckmorton, they are not to be found in the embassies of Europe. They are probably in a desert cave somewhere, praying and wearing animal skins."

He laughs at this, and gives a little bow as I take my leave, hoping that I have assuaged any doubts he might have harboured about me, at least for the moment. I retrace my steps through empty corridors toward the back of the house, to the small annexe that Castelnau's predecessor converted into the embassy's private chapel. Queen Elizabeth permits the celebration of Mass within the embassies of those countries who still cleave to Rome, but participation is strictly limited to embassy staff and servants, and foreign nationals baptised in the Catholic faith. In practise, the embassy chapels are crowded with those English Catholics, friends of the ambassadors, for whom taking the sacrament in their own houses would be punishable by imprisonment or death.

I take up a position in a window seat opposite the door of the chapel and wait so that I can observe them leave. Among my duties for Walsingham I am expected to note who attends Mass here and pass on the names of any unexpected visitors. A slow monotone is just audible from inside, the words indistinct, punctuated at intervals by the muffled responses of the communicants. A fly buzzes idly against the glass, lemon-coloured light pours through in oblique lines, illuminating the rushes on the floor.

Minutes pass, I lose track of how many, the intonations continue, then silence falls and finally the door opens and they pour out, whispering among themselves with a slightly frantic relief like children released from school: the butler, the housekeeper, the cook, the rest of the household servants. Then those who were sitting nearer the altar: Courcelles, Archibald Douglas (which surprises me; I had not known he attended

Mass), Lord Henry Howard, naturally, and behind him, a tall young man with a long, equine face and high forehead, then Castelnau and his wife, followed by a diffident Spanish priest, who scuttles by with his head lowered and his hands clasped before him. Though Mass is legal for those who live here, they all carry themselves as if they have been caught out in some immorality, glancing sidelong at me and scurrying past with downcast eyes; all except Marie, who flashes me a coquettish smile.

"Ah, Bruno—I'm afraid you've missed Mass today," the ambassador says, pausing with an apologetic smile, as if it were his fault; Courcelles offers a derisive snort.

"My apologies—I have only just come in," I say, with a brief bow. "Throckmorton is waiting in your office, my lord."

"Throckmorton?" Castelnau stops abruptly and exchanges a look with Howard. "What on earth?"

I only shrug and shake my head.

"He has some urgent matter to discuss, I suppose."

"Then I had better hear it." Castelnau quickens his pace.

Howard pauses to glower at me, his gaze scanning me from head to foot with his now-familiar contempt. I meet his eye, because I want him to know that I am not intimidated by either his person or his position, and as I do so a sudden anger burns in me at the idea of this man coolly hiring thugs to attack Doctor Dee and his servant on the road from Oxford, the idea of him poring over the stolen book by the light of a candle, intent on the pursuit of immortality. But this, too, is only speculation; I compose my expression. Howard looks away and my attention shifts to the young man with him. He appears in his mid-twenties, expensively dressed in a velvet doublet with a wide starched ruff like any other courtier of his age, but there is something unexpectedly familiar about his face, with its thin moustache that looks as if it has been painted on with a fine brush.

"Haven't we met?" I ask him, when he turns and meets my stare with his dark eyes. He seems surprised to be so bluntly addressed; behind him, Howard draws a sharp breath at my breach of etiquette. The young man's hesitation is so slight as to almost go unnoticed, except that he bites his lip and his eyes flit away from mine for the space of a blink.

"I don't think we have had the pleasure of being introduced," he replies. His voice is politely bland.

"My nephew Philip Howard, Earl of Arundel," Howard says brusquely; then, gesturing to me, "this is the ambassador's houseguest, Giordano Bruno, the Neapolitan." He says "houseguest" as if he were presenting me as Castelnau's whore. The young man nods and offers an expressionless smile, and it is then that I place him: he was one of the two young courtiers that shoved past me and Abigail yesterday at the Holbein Gate. Not the one who called me a Spanish whoreson, but the tall friend who stopped him from coming back and adding injury to his insult. I am certain that the young earl recognises me too; maybe he denies it out of embarrassment at his friend's behaviour. Englishmen love to abuse foreigners in the street, as I have learned more times than I can count since I arrived, but here, as the guest of a foreign embassy, perhaps he prefers not to be associated with such bravado. I only bow, and say nothing.

"Oh, Bruno—I almost forgot," Castelnau says, turning back as he reaches the end of the corridor. "Tomorrow there is to be a grand concert at the Palace of Whitehall, with new music by Master Byrd sung by the choir of the Chapel Royal. Her Majesty Queen Elizabeth has graciously invited all the ambassadors of the countries of Catholic Europe, perhaps in order to demonstrate that while she retains such a prominent Catholic as her court master of music, she cannot be regarded as an enemy of the faith."

He smiles; Howard grunts his disdain.

"In any case," Castelnau continues, flapping a hand to show he is in a hurry, "Marie and I would be glad if you would accompany us. I have been remiss in not presenting you at court sooner."

I open my mouth to thank him, but he is already sweeping on his way to Throckmorton. I lean against the wall. To be officially introduced to the court of Elizabeth, perhaps even to the queen herself—what might this mean for me? In the end, I reflect, I am no different from any of the young courtiers Fowler described, hanging about vainly hoping for that source of all patronage and benefit to shine the beams of her favour in my direction. But there is also the possibility that I could make contact with Abigail, warn her of what Dee found in the vial of perfume, press her again for anything more she might remember. The key to this mystery lies at the heart of Elizabeth's court, in its most intimate chambers, and now I have the chance to take at least one step closer to that inner sanctum.

Chapter 7

L amps are lit on either side of the stairs, though it is not yet dusk, the sun hanging low over the city to the west, scattering amber light over the water. Marie steps lightly down to the boat, a short cloak of white fur wrapped around her shoulders over her evening gown of peacock-green silk, her hand resting lightly on her husband's arm as she skips from the last step into the craft; her clear laugh rings out as she almost loses her balance and clutches at the hand of one of the oarsmen to steady herself. She seems giddy tonight, bubbling with high spirits, flushed with the prospect of an evening at court. Hardly surprising, I think; she is a beautiful woman, with the blush of youth still on her skin, who loves more than anything to be admired, and there is little enough opportunity for that around Salisbury Court. No wonder she feels the need to exercise her charms on me and Courcelles. The ambassador's secretary steps down to stand beside me now, watching Castelnau and his wife as they settle themselves into the embassy barge for the trip upriver to Whitehall. He is dressed in some fussy suit of dark red; an evening breeze with just a catch of autumn chill lifts his fine blond hair away from his face, and I notice again how exceptionally handsome he is, though I find something too feminine about his full mouth, his almost beardless chin, his laconic pout. He glances sideways at me and back to the river.

"Nice to see you made an effort to dress for the occasion, Bruno," he murmurs. I am wearing a neatly cut doublet and breeches of fine black wool, just as I wear every other evening.

"In my experience, it is politic not to compete with the ladies on occasions like this," I reply pleasantly, folding my hands behind my back and surveying the traffic on the water. "They don't appreciate it."

Gulls cry and wheel, arcing gracefully over the river to the far bank as the waves lap gently at the foot of the landing stairs. Courcelles looks down at his own clothes, suddenly doubtful.

"Bruno, Courcelles—get in the boat, for goodness' sake!" Castelnau calls, clapping his hands. "It will not do to arrive late!"

I settle myself opposite Marie, who smiles and leans forward; as she does so, my eye is caught again by the jewelled brooch pinned to her bodice. Its shape seems oddly familiar, and as I focus on its outline instead of the shifting glitter of the diamonds, I notice that it is a bird with a curved beak, rising up from its nest with wings outspread. It takes a moment before I realise where I have seen this bird before, and I almost cry out; it is identical in design to the emblem carved into the gold signet ring given to Cecily Ashe by her mysterious lover. Instinctively my hand moves to my breast, where I carry the ring in a pocket inside my doublet, in case my room should be searched again.

"See something to interest you, Bruno?" Marie says sweetly. I glance up to meet her arch expression and become aware that I have been shamelessly staring at the brooch, which she has attached to the side of her bodice, where the smooth white hemispheres of her breasts swell unmissably over the low neck of her corset. She gives me a look of mock reproach, as if I were a naughty schoolboy; I feel the hot rush of blood to my cheeks. A quick glance at the ambassador reassures me that he has caught none of this; he is busy outlining the arrangements for our return journey in minute detail to Courcelles, whose darting glance tells me that he, at least, has half an ear on our conversation.

"Your brooch," I say hastily, pointing, which only makes me feel clumsier.

"Ah. Beautiful, isn't it?" she says, in the same silky voice. "It is very special to me. It was a gift from the Duke of Guise when I left Paris." She touches it lightly and allows her fingers to drift, almost absently, across her décolletage. I allow my eyes to follow her hand and rest with it on that pale expanse of skin, the fine line of her collarbone and the crescent of shadow that dips between her breasts. At length I wrench my eyes upward and find hers fixed intently on me.

"Really? Forgive me"—I hear a slight tremor in my voice, and curse it—"only I thought I recognised the design."

"The phoenix?" She tilts the brooch slightly, bending her head down toward it. "You may well have seen it in France—it is the emblem of Marie de Guise, the duke's aunt. The brooch passed to him when she died."

"The duke's aunt? So—the mother of Mary Stuart?"

"Of course. The phoenix was her particular symbol. Because she herself had risen from the ashes so often, you see. Hard fortune could not crush her. Mary Stuart has adopted it too, I hear, to symbolise her own forthcoming return from prisoner to queen. Soon to be effected, if God wills it."

She smiles, deliberately provocative, showing her neat white teeth; I murmur my assent, but my mind is racing. There is no doubt that the bird is identical to the symbol on the ring. A phoenix—what I had taken for the branches of the bird's nest, I now saw were flames tapering around it as it lifted its broad wings in triumph. As the boat's oars settle into a steady rhythm, and the wind across the river grows chilly the farther we move into midstream, I turn away from Marie and fix my eyes unseeing on the south bank, while in my mind I conjure a picture of the letters around the phoenix emblem on the signet ring. *Sa Vertu m'atire.* I have no difficulty with this—my memory system is built on techniques of visualisation—and as I picture the letters, it is all I can do to keep myself from crying out and striking myself for my own stupidity, for suddenly what was obscure seems as blindingly clear as the gold disk of the sun, suspended before us in the violet sky. Not a code but an anagram. The letters swirl and rearrange themselves in my mind's eye so smoothly I believe a child could have solved it: *Sa Vertu m'atire* becomes, almost perfectly, Marie Stuart.

I bite down on my knuckles and hunch forward over my knees, lest I give away my agitation with my body, for with this realisation comes another, more chilling: the ring given to Cecily Ashe was more than a lover's trinket. It must have been a pledge, acknowledgement of an explicit connection with Mary, Queen of Scots, or with her supporters. So was the poison in the perfume bottle also given in Mary's name? Then the implication can only be that Cecily was in some way involved with the plots against Elizabeth on behalf of Mary Stuart, and as far as I know, those plots all revolve around the French embassy and those who gather in its chapel and dining room. I turn my face out of the wind and back to Marie, as if seeing her properly for the first time.

"Something wrong, Bruno?" she asks, moving to lay a hand softly on my arm. "You look distressed. Was it something I said?"

"No—no, thank you." I withdraw my arm gently, seeing that Castelnau has looked up and noticed her gesture. "I am not made for water travel, that is all. I only have to step into a boat for my stomach to turn somersaults."

"That must be inconvenient for you, given all your long journeys by river," Courcelles observes drily. I snap my head around.

"What do you mean?"

"Nothing." He shakes his head briskly, as if he should not have spoken. "Only that you are so often out of the house these days. And you seem to go everywhere by boat, that is all—I wonder your purse can bear the cost."

"I have letters of introduction to book collectors in London so that I may continue with my own work," I say, with a shrug. "The river is the quickest way around, after all, and I prefer to travel at my own expense, without the need to borrow your master's horses. For that, I try to overcome my poor sea legs. Does this trouble you?"

He gives another tight shake of the head and clams up then, so I do not press him. But the little barb he could not resist has given him away. How does he know, and why should he care, where I travel and how? Was he the man in the boat? Could he have been set to follow me to Mortlake by those in the embassy who doubt my loyalty? But that is clearly impossible—he was at Mass with the family yesterday when I arrived back from Dee's house after being followed by the stranger who landed at Putney. Even so, Courcelles is clearly taking an interest in where I travel. I slide a glance at him and experience a little shiver of distaste. I must not be so complacent as to think that any of my movements go unobserved here.

Castelnau distracts us with a commentary on the fine houses whose gardens run down to the river behind high walls as we pass, with details of their occupants: those roofs belong to Somerset House, where the queen had lived as a princess before her accession, now a lodging for foreign diplomats; here you may see the great gatehouse tower of the Savoy Hospital, which the queen's grandfather founded for the care of the poor, and beyond it, the landing stairs leading to the magnificent grounds of York Place, once the residence of the great Cardinal Wolsey, but commandeered by the queen's father as a gift to his—here Castelnau checks himself, remembering his professional obligation, and omits the word *mistress*—to his second wife, he continues, the queen's mother, Anne Boleyn.

Courcelles appears visibly bored by the guided tour, but to Marie and me, who have not been in London so long as to have learned the stories written in its stones, the ambassador's archive of details is fascinating. The mossy brick walls and thickets of chimneys seem to gather colour and life as he speaks of the histories played out in the halls and galleries within. Marie seems especially taken by the fate of Anne Boleyn.

"To think," she says, to no one in particular, gesturing at the walls of

York Place as the efforts of the oarsmen carry us around the curve in the river and the house recedes from view, "so many years the king loved her, and fought to make her queen, and she waited for him, looking out of those very windows. And everyone was opposed to the marriage, but they could not deny the force of their love. He undid his kingdom for that woman. It's so romantic. Don't you think?"

She turns and addresses this question to me, all innocent wide eyes and softly parted lips. I notice how this appears to annoy Courcelles. This is part of her game, I suppose, to play us off one against the other, to inspire us to rivalry. Presumably she does the same with Throckmorton, when he is present, and other men too, no doubt. She does not seem to realise that I have not agreed to take part.

"And as soon as he had her, he started engineering ways to have her head cut off," I say, smiling. "Desire attained very quickly sours."

"That is rather a cynical view of love, Bruno," she chides.

"It is based on observation. Like all my hypotheses."

"Look, here is the palace," Courcelles chips in, and we turn to watch the low, red-brick walls of some outbuildings at the water's edge give way to higher fortifications of pale stone and, just ahead, a structure jutting out into the water with lanterns hung all around it.

Castelnau raises a hand for silence and allows his gaze to travel slowly over us, so that we all have the opportunity to note his grave expression.

"We will have no conversation tonight with Henry Howard and his party beyond a civil greeting," he warns, lowering his voice. "The English court, and especially Her Majesty, must have no reason to suspect that we have any special dealings with him. Are we clear about this?" Though he says "we," he appears to be addressing this directly to his wife. We nod dutifully.

"Pull in at the Privy Bridge," Castelnau commands the oarsmen, and Marie begins smoothing her skirts and arranging her cloak anxiously.

The Privy Bridge is not so much a bridge as a kind of pier or jetty, elevated on wooden stilts and built up with a covered walkway that looks like a small house, so that the royal party can avoid the elements on their way to the barge. Tonight the walls of this building are hung with scarlet-and-gold banners embroidered with the queen's arms, the lion and dragon rampant rippling as the breeze catches them. At the end of the bridge, a flight of steps lead down to a landing stage, and here two men in the queen's livery are waiting to help visitors disembark. Castelnau hands Marie out of the boat and follows; Courcelles and I fall into step behind them, and I pause for a minute on the stairs, looking up at the palace wall ahead. This is to be my first introduction to the English court, perhaps even to Elizabeth herself, and I am gripped by a strange apprehension.

We are led along a passage and across a broad paved courtyard, surrounded on four sides by grand ranges in red brick, with crenellated balustrades at the roofs and tall mullioned windows edged in pearl-white stone. At the entrance to every doorway and in the cloistered shadows you cannot fail to notice the number of tall young men, armed and wearing tabards bearing the royal standard.

"Elizabeth grows fearful," Courcelles observes quietly, nodding toward one of the granite-faced men. "There are not usually so many of the palace guard on display."

"Perhaps she has reason," I say. He responds with a grim laugh.

From the high open doorway of the great hall spills a babble of music and talk, together with the drifting perfume of some scented oil burning to sweeten the air. On the threshold, Castelnau turns and points a finger into my face, so suddenly that I almost trip over him.

"And no trouble, Bruno." He smiles, but the warning is meant.

I understand him. I am here by his invitation and this is no small thing; I have a reputation in Europe for courting controversy, but this evening I am representing the French embassy and, by extension, King Henri himself. I would be expected to conduct myself meekly at the best of times, but in the present circumstances, it is vital that Queen Elizabeth continues to think well of Henri of France and his ambassador. As Castelnau sees it, their relationship may be all that stands between England and war. Courcelles smirks, but I merely nod obediently. Castelnau, satisfied, turns, adjusts his doublet, and prepares to make his entrance. As he does so, Marie turns back to me and winks.

But the splendour of the spectacle before us drives all other thoughts from my mind. The hall arches overhead, the upper portion of its walls all light from the high pointed windows of stained glass, drawing the eye upward to the dark wood spans of the great hammer-beam roof, with its elaborately carved tracery and gilded spandrels. From each of the wall braces hangs a coloured banner embroidered with some royal insignia in golds, crimsons, azures. The lower parts of its long walls, where I can glimpse them through the crush of people, are decorated with exquisitely detailed Flemish tapestries depicting scenes from the Old Testament, bordered with gold damask. Courtiers in silks and velvets of all hues gather in groups or mingle around the room, glancing at one another and parading their finery; the men wear puffed knee breeches with white silk stockings to show off their calves, doublets with sleeves slashed to reveal the jewel-coloured lining, and wide starched lace ruffs that give them the air of birds fanning out their feathers in a mating display, with cuffs to match. Over one shoulder they drape short capes of velvet fastened with gold or jade brooches, and as they lean in to converse, the long peacock feathers on their caps nod and sway, and sometimes become tangled up with one another. Some of them carry silver pomanders at their belts, and the air is thick with spiced perfume; they all, without exception, carry ornamental swords, swinging by their thighs in elaborately embellished scabbards. I am surprised that a queen who lives under permanent threat of assassination should tolerate her courtiers coming armed into her presence, but perhaps even she dare not part a gentleman from his weapon. Sidney once told me that she had forbidden duelling among the gentlemen of the court, with a penalty of losing one's right hand. The awkwardness of their costumes obliges these courtiers to walk with their legs slightly parted, in an exaggerated swagger; there is something comical about their strutting and their anxious glances to one side and the other to make sure they are being noticed. I can only imagine what they would be like if there were more women present.

A group of musicians play subtle string compositions in a vaulted alcove set before one great window that stretches from floor to ceiling. The effect is magnificent as the setting sun slants low through the patterned panes, illuminating the musicians' heads and shoulders before painting its coloured geometry over the rush-strewn floor.

Marie's head swivels from left to right and back, bright-eyed as a child at a carnival, and I smile to myself. This is certainly the place to be if you are a young woman seeking male admirers. There is a noticeable surfeit of young men in the hall. It is said that the queen does not like to have to compete for the attention of her courtiers—still less as she ages—so they are encouraged to leave their wives at home; certainly the few women present are older, nearer the queen's own age, strapped tightly into bodices above broad farthingale skirts, their faces stiff with paint. Already Marie is drawing glances as we progress slowly through the crowd; though she holds tight to her husband's arm, I notice that she smiles to herself and does not lower her eyes as she ought when she finds herself the object of some gentleman's hungry stare.

I crane my neck and scour the crowds for familiar faces, but there is no sign of Abigail. At the far end of the hall, nearest to the musicians, seating has been arranged on a platform in front of the panelled wall, with a gilded throne in the centre; I presume that the queen and her attendants will make a grand entrance before the concert proper begins, with her ladies in her wake. The likelihood that I will have the chance to speak to Abigail alone is small indeed—court etiquette demands that I stay close to Castelnau and wait for his introduction—but perhaps I may be able to get a message to her requesting another meeting. I still suspect that she is holding something back, and my recent discovery about the ring makes it all the more urgent that I persuade Abigail to confide any more secrets. But beyond this, since her unexpected remark about finding a prospective lover, I have been intrigued by the possibility of seeing her again; at times I catch myself wondering if she might have said this for my benefit, though at others I tell myself I am being ridiculous.

Nonetheless, I cannot suppress a frisson as I cast my eyes around the glittering crowd for a possible glimpse of red-gold hair.

Just then, the knot of people ahead of us parts and I spot, across the room, a dangerous confederacy: Henry Howard and his nephew Philip, Earl of Arundel, deep in conversation with Don Bernardino de Mendoza and Archibald Douglas, whom I almost don't recognise. He appears to have had a shave and a haircut for the occasion and looks younger and markedly cleaner than the last time I saw him. Castelnau dips his head in greeting; Howard responds with a curt nod, and turns back to say something to Mendoza, who whispers back, still staring at our party. Over Marie's head, Castelnau glances at me, and there is fear in his eyes.

But he continues to weave his way toward the dais, keen to secure us a vantage point near where the queen will be sitting, the better to catch her eye; as I follow him through the crush, to my delight I spot Sidney standing with his uncle, the Earl of Leicester, the two of them head and shoulders above everyone else. Sidney's hair sticks up more wildly than usual, as if he has just stepped out of a strong wind; I try to catch his eye as his gaze travels the hall. When he eventually notices me he smiles warmly, but he makes no move in my direction, and I remember with a pang that here in public, especially under Castelnau's nose and with Courcelles watching me like a cat, I must keep a wary distance from those closest to Elizabeth. The Earl of Leicester is imposingly aristocratic in an elaborately embroidered doublet of plum velvet; he keeps his arms folded tightly across his chest as he too scans the crowd, his face with its high cheekbones and thin lips set in an earnest expression, his eyes alert. Presently he leans in to Sidney and says something that makes them both laugh; I turn away, biting down the regret that I can't join my friend. It strikes me that, of all my acquaintance in England, there is barely anyone I can talk to openly. In this great jostle of overdressed men, I feel suddenly isolated, and weary of acting a part.

But these thoughts are dispelled as the musicians cease their tune and into the silence that follows there rises one clear note of eight trumpets together. As if at some unspoken command, the crowd falls back to either side to create a path from the main entrance to the raised seats at the far end of the room, and I see that a carpet has been laid up the centre of the hall. Castelnau eases us through so that we stand at the front, nudging Marie forward. A hush descends on the hall, before the trumpets ring out their signal again and the double doors are flung open; the courtiers drop as one to their knees, and, glancing up, I see the white skirts of a girl scattering rose petals over the carpet to either side as she processes slowly up the aisle formed by the kneeling guests.

Raising my head as far as I dare, I look up past this girl and set eyes, for the first time, on the Queen of England. Since even before I arrived in her realm, I have carried the image of Elizabeth Tudor in my mind as a symbol of possibility: the Protestant monarch who has dared to defy three successive popes over the twenty-five years of her reign. It is foolishly presumptuous, I know, but I always believed that, if I could only find a way to make her listen or read my words, she would feel some instinctive affinity with me. Like me, she has been excommunicated for heresy and declared an enemy of the church for her ideas; the Holy Office seeks her death as it does mine; despite the best efforts of her more rational advisers, such as Walsingham and Burghley, she encourages men like John Dee and takes a keen interest in his esoteric pursuits. If any sovereign is suited to be the patron of a heretic philosopher with unorthodox and provocative views, it is surely this open-minded, unashamedly intellectual woman who, behind the generous smiles she bestows now on her fawning courtiers, must have a will of steel to have ruled so long alone in a world of men.

Elizabeth Tudor walks at a stately pace, upright in her bearing and surprisingly graceful in her movements, given her years and the obvious weight of her ornate gown, with its skirts of thick scarlet-and-gold brocade, the scarlet bodice all embroidered with tiny garnets and pearls. At her neck she wears a small ruff of starched lace, with a stiff collar, a delicate structure of wire and finer lace, standing up behind her head; three long ropes of pearls are fixed at either side of her collar and hang in tiers across her front. Her dark red hair is an extraordinary confection, piled high and pinned in loops on top of her head, so that she must hold her neck almost without moving to maintain her balance. I suspect it is a wig. Her entire posture is an exercise in regal control. Behind the white veneer of ceruse that coats her face, her expression is inscrutable, her eyes, lips, and brows painted in like a mask. She is not beautiful, but in her face is a refinement that goes beyond beauty, a look of purpose and self-possession that makes beauty seem trivial. In her hands she carries a fan of tall red feathers with a mother-of-pearl handle and she moves, as do her ladies, in a fine cloud of perfumed powder. For one ridiculous moment I find myself hoping she will glance to her left and see me, but she continues without haste toward the seats, smiling at the kneeling crowd, but always maintaining that inward-looking poise. As they pass in her wake, I notice the maids of honour, all dressed in long gowns of white silk, following her steps impeccably while their eyes stray feverishly around the room, alighting here and there on young men before flitting coyly away. Behind the maids march the older attendants, the seven ladies of the bedchamber, among them Lady Seaton, who happens to glance down as I look up; our eyes meet and she frowns with what I take for curiosity, before returning her gaze to the front, arranging her face back into its habitual, slightly sour expression.

It is only when the queen has mounted the dais and taken her throne with her maids gathered around her that I notice Abigail Morley is not among the women and immediately my chest clenches.

Walsingham, Burghley, and a number of other grave-looking, silver-bearded men in black—the statesmen of the Privy Council, I presume—take up their positions at the sides of the dais, hands clasped behind their backs as if they were on duty. If Walsingham notices me, he gives no indication. Elizabeth gestures for her subjects to rise, which they do with varying degrees of stiffness, and when the rustling has died away, she stretches out a hand.

"My lords, ladies, and gentlemen," she begins, in a clear voice, pitched low for a woman but carefully measured, familiar with public speeches. "I have invited you here to enjoy some new compositions by

Master Byrd, sung by the choristers of our Chapel Royal. The beauty of music, both sacred and secular, transcends all bounds of race and religion, and is for all." With this, she gives a nod, and the main doors of the hall open once more.

"She says this to appease the Puritans," Courcelles whispers at my back. "There are plenty in her council who think polyphonic music among the worst sins of Rome."

I nod, but my attention is on the man now walking up the central aisle toward the dais; short, with brown hair swept back from his forehead and a neatly trimmed beard, only his darting eyes betray a restless energy as he leads the choir—thirty men and twelve boys—toward the alcove in front of the grand window where the musicians had played. This William Byrd is watched around the clock by Walsingham's agents; he makes no secret of his Catholic faith, and his position as gentleman of the Chapel Royal only protects him so far. But the fact that Elizabeth not only disregards his religious disobedience but continues to exalt him so publicly is read by some as a sign of ambiguity in her own faith, or merely as an indication that she knows her own mind and will not be bullied by extremists of any faction.

An expectant silence falls over the court as Byrd waits for his choristers to settle themselves in lines. When he is satisfied, he raises both hands and pauses at full stretch, his arms taut as a bowstring; the audience holds its breath and for the space of a heartbeat we all seem suspended in time, caught between one moment and the next. Then Byrd lowers his hands in a sweeping gesture and a note breaks forth from the smallest boy, pure and clear as birdsong, its sweetness echoing to the beams of the roof. Barely has he begun his note when the other voices join him, layering their harmonies piece by piece over one another, the bass notes holding firm and melancholy beneath the soaring, liquid music of the boys' voices. The song is a prayer for the queen, though the words slide through the melodies like water pouring over a fountain of glass. The effect is so beautiful, so otherworldly, that the hairs on my neck prickle and stand up. I glance sideways at Marie and her expression takes me by surprise; her head is tilted back, her eyes closed, her lips softly parted, as if she is allowing the music to ravish her. Seeing her so seemingly transported, I revise my opinion of her; I had thought her too superficial to be moved by beauty, unless it was her own reflection in a glass. Perhaps I have judged her too harshly. Then I have to look away; there is something so provocative about the curve of her exposed throat, the moistness of her open mouth, her pale eyelids, that I experience a sudden surge of desire that rebels against my will and my better judgement. I cannot allow myself to indulge those thoughts about my host's wife.

Searching for distraction, I allow my gaze to wander again around the hall, observing the faces, the variety of responses, from immersion to undisguised boredom; suddenly, in the corner of my eye, I am aware of a commotion near the dais. Standing on tiptoe, I am near enough to see that one of the yeomen of the palace guard, evidently in a state of some urgency, has approached Lord Burghley and is whispering frantically in his ear. Edging back, I insinuate myself between Courcelles and Castelnau so that I have a clearer view of Burghley through the heads of the audience. His face is drained of colour; I see him cast around and gesture for Walsingham, a small, tight movement of the hand. Walsingham excuses himself, squeezing past his companions on either side to join Burghley, who draws him close in whispered conference. Eventually Walsingham looks up, his eyes rake the crowd for a moment, and as soon as I catch the frozen expression on his face, I feel a sudden lurch in the stomach, a certainty of horror.

By now several people are turning to look at the source of the disturbance while the singers' fluting voices still rise to the rafters. Elizabeth herself has noticed and leans forward, hands resting on the arms of her throne, to see who dares interrupt the concert, with a look of irritation that quickly turns to concern as she sees her two senior statesmen huddled with the soldier. Walsingham holds up a hand to her, a gesture that says, Don't worry, we have this under control. But his face is tight with anxiety and now he raises himself on tiptoe, searching the crowd again, as if he hoped to find someone in particular. Then he leans in to the soldier, whispers some hasty instructions, and the three of them—Burghley, Walsingham, and the guard—leave the hall by a side door.

I try to concentrate on the music but the blood is hammering at my temples: the palace guard, his look of fearful urgency; Burghley and Walsingham and their strained expressions. Something terrible has happened, I am certain of it, and try as I might to rein in my worst imaginings, my mind returns again and again to the absence of Abigail among the queen's maids and the suspicion that someone had been watching our exchange at the Holbein Gate. But I can hardly leave the concert and follow Walsingham; publicly I am no one here, only an insignificant guest of the French ambassador. It is not my place to ask questions. The choir continues its ethereal song; there is a movement, another disturbance, at the other end of the hall, opposite the dais, but when I crane my neck to look, I see that it is only servants bringing in candles, which they fit into wall sconces between the tapestries as the last of the daylight is dying. Then I notice that, behind the servants, armed men have unobtrusively slipped into place either side of the main doors, and still the singing continues. My palms are sweating; I wipe them on my breeches and fix my attention on the choir, but my mouth is dry. Another motet begins and fades to its bittersweet, plaintive close.

"Giordano Bruno?"

His breath is hot on my cheek, his voice barely audible. In the corner of my vision, a bearded face appears so close to mine that I can't focus.

"Don't turn or speak, sir. In a few minutes, find a moment to slip through the door behind you, as discreetly as you can. Principal secretary's orders."

He moves away as invisibly as he arrived, without my even having seen his face fully. I wait until I am sure that Castelnau, Marie, and Courcelles have their eyes fixed on the choir and take a short step backward, then another, until I am hidden by other guests. A side door is built into the panelling; as I approach, the guard there holds it open a fraction and I back through the narrow gap. On the other side, a tall young man, bearded and wearing a black suit, waits for me. He has the appearance of a clerk.

"This way." He gestures to the corridor ahead.

"Can you tell me what this is about?"

He shakes his head, his mouth set in a grim line, and motions for me to continue down the passageway that leads away from the great hall toward a warren of state apartments. When we need to turn a corner, he places a palm lightly on the small of my back to show me the way. At the end of another corridor he stops outside a door and knocks, before ushering me into a small, sparsely furnished office with tall windows. The Earl of Leicester leans against the wall by the window, looking out at the darkening sky as if deep in thought while shadows carve deep hollows around his eyes and the sharp bones of his face; Walsingham paces, one hand clasped across his mouth and chin; Burghley stands by the writing desk, watching the door, his skullcap awry and his white hair sticking up in tufts where he has run his hands through it. Beside him, to my immense surprise, stands the skinny boy who brought me the message from Abigail three days ago. He wipes his hands repeatedly on a streaked apron that suggests he works in the kitchens, and by the look of his face he has been crying. As the guard shuts the door softly behind me, the boy points at me and cries, accusing: "That's him, sir! That's the man!"

Chapter 8

Lord Burghley's face constricts in an expression of distress. I suspect it is mirrored on my own face, though I don't yet know why. No one moves.

"You're quite sure? This is the man who gave you the message for Lady Abigail?"

Walsingham speaks sharply and the boy looks confused; his eyes flick wildly from me to Walsingham to Burghley and back, as if between us we are trying to trick him.

"No! Not the message—that is to say—the message came from him, but it wa'n't him who gave it to me."

"You are not making any sense, boy."

"He told me the message came from Master Bruno—the man who stopped me in the yard," the boy says, a note of panic rising in his voice. "I couldn't rightly see him in the dark, but he had an English voice. *This* is

Master Bruno," he adds, pointing again. "It wa'n't his voice. He's not English."

"We know that." For a moment Walsingham betrays his impatience, then he masters himself and his tone softens. "We need to understand what happened tonight. Jem, is it?"

The boy nods unhappily.

"Good. Then, Jem—tell us again. A man you don't know stopped you earlier in the yard by the kitchens and asked you to give a message to Abigail Morley from Master Bruno. Is that right?"

"Yes, sir."

"And you didn't see this man clearly?"

"No, sir. The candles hadn't been lit yet and it was shadowy. And he had a big hat, pulled down over his face, and his collar all up like this, sir." He tugs at the neck of his dirty tunic to demonstrate. There is a pause. "He might've had a beard," the boy offers, hopefully.

Walsingham rolls his eyes.

"He *might* have had a beard. Well, at least we can rule out the women and children."

"Not *all* the women," Leicester says under his breath, from the window. I catch his eye and he smiles, briefly; despite the tension in the room, I return it. It is almost a relief. Burghley sends him a reproachful stare.

"And what was the message, exactly?" Walsingham continues.

"To tell her—to say that Master Bruno wanted to meet her in secret at the kitchen dock before the concert. He said it was urgent. Then he gived me a shilling." The boy glances around again nervously, as if afraid he might be asked to give up the coin.

Walsingham frowns.

"And you delivered this message straightaway? To Her Majesty's private apartments? How did you manage that?"

"I took up some sweetmeats, sir. Then the guards can't stop you— you just say the queen's asked for 'em, they don't know otherwise. The girls—Her Majesty's maids, I mean—they often get messages in and out by us kitchen boys." He bites his lip then, looking guilty. "I got as far as I could and got one of them to fetch Abigail."

"And how did she seem when you gave her the message?"

"Frightened, sir," the boy says, without hesitation. "She said she'd come directly, and not to tell anyone else about it."

"And this was before the concert began? How long before?"

"I couldn't say, sir." The boy looks at his frayed shoes. "I don't know how to read the time. Not long, though—there weren't many people left in the kitchens, I know that. They gived us the night off because she had her supper early, on account of the music. Her Majesty, I mean. And there was already people arriving."

Walsingham gives me a frank look.

"I never sent any such message tonight," I say, trying not to sound defensive. "Will someone tell me what has happened?"

"They've killed her," the boy blurts, glaring at me with accusing eyes. "And if it wa'n't you, then it was the other feller, and if it wa'n't him, then it was the Devil himself!"

I find, when I hear the words spoken aloud, that I had expected this, or something like it; the sense of foreboding that had taken root when I first noticed Abigail's absence in the queen's train had been steadily growing in my imagination, but the bluntness of the boy's outcry still shocks me. So the killer has found his way to Abigail, I think, as my mind fumbles blindly to make sense of the boy's story, and though the message was not my doing, the circumstance is indisputably my fault.

Leicester stirs unhurriedly from his place by the window, stretching out his long limbs as if this were his cue. He nods to Walsingham and then gestures toward the door with the slightest movement of his head. Walsingham holds up a forefinger, signalling for him to wait.

"You've been very helpful, Jem," Walsingham says gently to the boy. "I have one more question. Do you think this man waited for you especially to take his message?"

"Well—yes, sir." The boy blinks rapidly, as if he fears another trick.

"Because of me taking the message before, see? I suppose he must have known, somehow."

"What message before?" Walsingham's voice is sharp as a blade again.

"From Lady Abigail to him." He points at me. "In Fleet Street, sir. I had to wait half a day in the stables with them French boys threatening to knock me down." He bares his teeth, as if the memory of it still stings.

"Thank you. I'd like you to go with the serjeant now, Jem. We may have some more questions for you. If you can remember any more details about the man with the hat—anything about his voice, his face, his figure, anything at all that might help us—I would be very grateful."

"It's my fault, i'n't it?" The boy looks suddenly to Burghley, who has a grandfatherly air that makes him less severe than the others. "If I hadn't taken that message, she wouldn't 'a died, would she? I'm to blame—for a shilling!" He bunches his fist against his mouth and looks as if he might cry. "She was always kind, the lady Abigail. Not like some."

Burghley lays a hand on his shoulder.

"It's no one's fault except the wicked man who killed her. And with your help we shall find him, so he can't hurt anyone else."

The boy gives me a last look over his shoulder as the guard leads him away.

When the door is firmly closed, the three members of the Privy Council turn their eyes sternly upon me.

"Message, Bruno?" Walsingham folds his arms across his chest.

As succinctly as I can, I outline my dealings with Abigail Morley, from the kitchen boy's visit to our meeting at the Holbein Gate, when she gave me the bag of Cecily Ashe's treasures and I first suspected we were being watched, to the discovery Dee and I had made about the perfume and my most recent guess at the significance of the gold ring—which I take from inside my doublet and hand to Walsingham. He turns it over between his fingers, nodding gently, as I continue my story. When I come to the end, they regard me for a moment in silence; I can almost read the separate workings of their minds in their faces.

"They'll have to release Edward Bellamy from the Tower." Burghley speaks first, squeezing his plump fingers together anxiously.

Walsingham turns on his heel and paces the width of the room, his hands flexing and uncurling. I have never seen him so rattled and working so hard to contain it. Eventually he stops and turns on me with an expression so fierce it startles me.

"You did not think to pass any of this on to me, Bruno? You appoint yourself this girl's sole confidant, regardless of the fact that you already suspect the killer has an eye on her? Why did you not come to me immediately?"

"Your Honour, I—" I spread my hands out in apology, feeling once again like a schoolboy. "I did not want to cause unnecessary panic until I was sure about the perfume bottle. The engraving on the ring I only worked out this evening."

"It is my responsibility to judge whether panic is necessary or not. Those objects should have been brought straight to me," Walsingham says again, his voice tight.

"I thought that until I was certain, the fewer people knew of this, the better."

"Including me, evidently."

"Peace, Francis." Burghley extends a hand toward him. "The girl said nothing even to Lady Seaton and she would have been too intimidated to approach the Privy Council. She confided more readily in Bruno, and he was sensible to test his theory before coming to us." He turns to the rest of us. "This serves at least to prove that the killer is familiar with the court and its ways." He shakes his head, and his face seems paler. "No matter how many extra guards we place around Her Majesty, he knows how to slip right under their noses. Kitchen boys, indeed."

"What happened to her? Abigail?" I hear my own voice falter and there comes a sudden memory of the warmth of Abigail's breath on my cheek as she whispered the secrets I persuaded her to part with. She had thought I was the one person she could trust; someone knew that, and used the knowledge to kill her.

Walsingham glances at Burghley, then crosses to me and places the flat of his hand between my shoulder blades. "Come, Bruno. I want you to see this. We will need every last grain of intuition we possess between us. My lord of Leicester—you had better return to the hall and reassure Her Majesty. She saw the guard enter and she will be anxious enough already, but I think it best the recital is allowed to play out without interruption."

Leicester gives a terse nod, his handsome face creased in a frown. He turns to me.

"Your theory, Doctor Bruno, if I have understood correctly," he says, his eyes searching my face, "is that the first murdered girl, Cecily Ashe, was being set up by her lover as part of a plot to poison the queen, and that this plot is somehow connected to the Guise plans of invasion being cooked up at Salisbury Court?"

"That is how I read it, my lord."

"So she was killed because those who were directing her feared she would betray them?"

"I believe so."

"And Abigail Morley possibly knew enough to identify the lover, or so he thought, therefore he killed her as well?"

Again I nod.

"Then we have all the suspects right here, within these walls," he says, looking around at the two statesmen. "Everyone we know is party to this plot of a French and Spanish attack is at court this evening for the concert. The guests were gathered at least three-quarters of an hour before the queen made her entrance—any of them could have had time to slip out unnoticed in the crowd. At this very moment, there could be a man in that hall who quite literally has blood on his hands."

Walsingham looks uneasy; Burghley tuts.

"What would you have me do, Robert—publicly arrest Henry Howard and the Earl of Arundel, not to mention the French and Spanish ambassadors, before the whole court on suspicion of murder, with barely a shred of evidence?" Burghley shakes his head. "In any case, it is hardly to be supposed that any of them are committing murder with their own hands, even if there is a connection. They'll have been safely mingling in the hall in full view of three hundred people while some accomplice despatched that poor girl, you can be sure of it."

"It would be expedient if we could get the guests from the hall to their boats and horses without alerting them to any of this," Walsingham says, brisk now. "I will instruct the guards to move people swiftly along once the recital is finished."

"She will want to see Dee," Leicester says, looking at Walsingham with an expression I cannot read.

Walsingham closes his eyes for a moment, as if testing the weight of this further complication.

"So she will."

"She has been greatly agitated since his visit yesterday, as we all know. And now, with this—" Leicester breaks off, gesturing vaguely toward the door. "Well, it seems more than coincidence. Though she will no doubt take it as prophecy."

"Good God. Dee's vision. I had not thought of it until this moment." Burghley presses his hands together as if in prayer, his forefingers touching his lips. "I suggest John Dee be questioned immediately. And not necessarily by one of his friends," he adds with a warning glance at Leicester. In response to my quizzical look, he turns to Walsingham. "We should take Bruno now. Time runs at our heels."

Walsingham nods.

"Quite so. Even Master Byrd's motets cannot go on all night."

Along a series of corridors, past tapestries and torches flaming in wall brackets, he leads me at a trot, with Burghley following, carrying a light. At every corner the guards appear even more numerous than when I arrived, and there is a tension on their faces that adds to the atmosphere of dread that seems to have infected the palace. We pass into a part of the complex that is clearly the domain of servants and tradesmen, the people behind the scenes whose tireless work allows the glorious pageant of state to run smoothly. Here, too, guards are stationed; as they hear our footsteps their hands move immediately to their pikestaffs, but they step back, respectfully lowering their eyes when they see who it is striding so purposefully and stony-faced toward them.

I follow Walsingham across a dimly lit yard, where barrels are stacked in one corner and timber in another; two men are moving a pile of sacks into one of the outbuildings by the light of a small lantern. Still Walsingham has not said a word; I desperately want to ask him about Dee, but the principal secretary's expression is so forbidding I hold my tongue. On the right-hand side of the yard runs a long, two-storey building of red brick with a series of tall chimneys. Here Walsingham slows his pace and pauses by a semicircular grille built into the wall at ground level, rising to the height of a man's waist. Through the iron bars that close it off from the yard, I hear the gentle lapping of water below.

"The palace kitchens," Walsingham says, gesturing to the building, his voice low. Bending slightly, I see that this grille is the end of an arched tunnel that runs through the middle of the kitchen building, its other end opening onto the river itself. The daylight has almost seeped from the sky entirely, and the tunnel yields only blackness. This, I suppose, is the kitchen dock. At a respectful distance, a huddle of servants whispers urgently between themselves, keenly watching our arrival. From among them I hear the stifled sound of a woman's sob. Another guard, leaning against the wall by a small door to the left of this grille, pulls himself quickly to attention as he sees Walsingham approach, then at a nod opens the door for us. Walsingham gestures for Burghley to come forward with the torch. The door opens onto a stone-flagged passageway in the kitchen building, where a faint smell of cooked meat and herbs lingers as if ingrained in the brick walls. Almost immediately there is another door on the right, which Walsingham opens slowly and then turns to me.

"This is not pleasant, Bruno, particularly as you knew the girl. But I want to know what you make of this murder. I am sorry to ask this of you," he adds, in a gentler voice. I nod silently and he reaches out for the torch from Burghley.

We step into what looks like a storeroom, perhaps twelve feet across and twenty feet long, empty except for a stack of wooden crates against the wall and an unmoving figure laid out upon the stone floor, ghostly in a white dress. Walsingham moves forward and crouches beside the body, holding up the torch so that its wavering flames illuminate the pitiful end of Abigail Morley.

The bodice of her dress has been roughly torn down the middle and ripped apart to expose her torso. From her left breast a dagger protrudes, plunged into her flesh almost down to its handle. Straight into her heart, I think; I have a disturbing sensation that I have been here before, that I have already seen this image as if I had lived through it once in the recent past. As I draw closer and kneel on the floor, I realise that the body and the flagstones around it are soaking wet, matted strands of her red hair spread around her head. Walsingham brings the torch nearer and motions silently for me to look again at her breast. On the right side, opposite the dagger, a mark has been crudely carved into her pale skin: an upright cross with a tail curving to the right, like a lowercase *h*: the astrological symbol for Saturn. I breathe out carefully, trying to slow the hammering in my chest. In an awful moment of clarity, I understand why the Earl of Leicester spoke of Doctor Dee and something more than coincidence. I have not seen this image before, but I have heard it described, before the event. Abigail has been killed almost exactly according to Dee's description of Ned Kelley's latest vision in the stone.

Finally I force myself to look at Abigail's face, bleached and tinted orange in the torchlight. I am amazed at how serene she looks for someone who has so recently met a violent death. This in itself strikes me as odd; during my years on the road I saw the corpses of men stabbed with blades and there was no such placid expression, rather a twisting of the features, their death throes written into their final expression.

I gesture for Walsingham to hold the torch up to her face; he does so, both of us kneeling now in the water that has slopped around the body, pooling in the worn dips of the old stones. Abigail's unseeing eyes are fixed on nothing, but the whites are bloodshot, the left one entirely red.

There is bruising around the mouth and nose, but no marks on the neck as there were with Cecily Ashe.

"She was in the water?" I ask, my voice coming out as barely a whisper.

"Tied by the hands to one of the mooring rings at the dock here. One of the kitchen girls found her when she noticed the door to this room had been left open. She says she saw the loading-bay doors open and then something white floating in the water, like a ghost." He grimaces.

"She was meant to be found, then. But from her face she didn't drown," I say, almost to myself. "I think she was smothered, then stabbed very precisely after she stopped moving. He must have been waiting and taken her by surprise when she appeared—" I break off. When she appeared expecting to meet me.

Walsingham rises stiffly to his feet.

"He came in here, I think." He holds up the torch and I see that on the opposite wall from the door where we entered is a wide set of double doors with a heavy bolt across them. Walsingham beckons to me, then hands me the torch and draws back the bolt, opening the right half of the doors, which swings inward. I see that they open directly into the arched tunnel running under the building, with two wide stone steps leading to the water. The tunnel is the width of a small barge and its arched roof perhaps ten feet high, clearly built to allow boats carrying supplies to be brought directly from the river to the palace kitchens where they can be unloaded into this room. As the end of the tunnel is blocked by the metal grille, it would be impossible to gain access to the palace except through these double doors.

"This door was open when she was found," Walsingham says. "So I surmise he came in by boat, the same way he escaped, and she must have opened the door for him herself." He rests a hand on the doorframe and peers out over the black water softly slapping against the steps in the little channel. "She was floating here, right by the dock." He points to the water just beneath the step. "You're right—this was meant as another display. If he had not tied the body up she might have sunk or drifted out of the tunnel into the river—he intended for her to be found quickly. Perhaps even while the concert was in progress."

"Again the mark of the prophecy—Saturn this time. He wants to leave no doubt that these deaths are connected. And this dagger—" I pause again, looking up at Walsingham as another memory surfaces. "The doll! Cecily Ashe was found holding a doll with red wool for hair that we assumed was intended as an image of Queen Elizabeth. It was pierced in the heart with a needle."

"I remember it well." He rubs the back of his hand across his chin. "Made like a witch's poppet. Her Majesty was deeply disturbed by it. And now he has taken to using human dolls. But the intent remains the same, do you not think—to mimic the death of the queen?"

"As heralded by the Great Conjunction of Jupiter and Saturn," I muse.

"I recall Her Majesty pointing out this girl to me once when her ladies were gathered in the presence chamber," Burghley offers from the doorway. "She asked me if I did not think the girl the very likeness of herself in her youth. The comparison amused her. And indeed, when you looked closely, it seemed there was a distinct resemblance, though it was just the red hair, I suppose. Poor child."

"And yet . . ." I shake my head as I shift my position by the body; my knees are growing numb from the wet stone. As I continue to stare at Abigail's marble face, I realise that my attention has grown analytical, my reasoning mind has taken over from the emotion I felt at her death a moment earlier. "Something is not right here."

"You certainly have a gift for understatement, Doctor Bruno," Burghley says drily.

"I mean to say—my theory must be wrong. Now that I look closely, the facts do not support it."

Walsingham gives an unexpected bark of mirthless laughter. "It is a rare man who can admit that, Bruno. Most of my acquaintance strain always to bend the facts to their theories. Explain yourself."

"It doesn't make sense. I had believed that Cecily Ashe was killed because she had been part of a conspiracy to murder the queen and she had perhaps changed her mind, or somehow become a threat to that plot and the other people involved. And now Abigail, who was suspected of knowing her friend's secrets, and who may well have been seen talking to me, is also dead. But then, why, in both cases, leave the bodies where they will be found, within the court, and displayed so as to point explicitly to the queen's death at the hands of Catholic assassins? If the very purpose of killing these girls was to silence them, to protect the conspirators . . ."

"Perhaps the purpose was to punish them publicly," Walsingham says sagely. "If the killer knew or suspected it was too late to keep them silent, he may have chosen to make an example of them instead, for their betrayal."

"And jeopardise his own plot in doing so?"

"Perhaps there is more than one plot," Burghley suggests.

"God's blood, William, there are a hundred plots, perhaps a thousand!" Walsingham exclaims, pressing the palm of his hand to his forehead and beginning to pace again in the confined space between the open loading bay and Abigail's body. "Most of them at the level of that sorry fellow picked up on the road from York, waving his pistols and ranting. But when we have a bottle of poison almost in the queen's own bedchamber, brought there by a girl who owns a ring bearing the impresa of Mary Stuart, and Howards lurking about the French embassy talking of an invasion force, I think we may safely assume we are dealing with one extremely serious conspiracy to regicide and war."

"Then I ask again—why call attention to a plot to kill the queen if these deaths are to safeguard one?"

"I don't know, Bruno—to sow fear and confusion? To lead us in one direction while they attack from another? In any case, I thought you had made it your business to solve this without anyone's help." The quiet anger in his voice is unmistakable. He makes a gesture of exasperation with both hands, waving the flaming torch alarmingly; its guttering light briefly illuminates a glint of something at Abigail's neck. I reach forward to touch it and instinctively my outstretched fingers shrink from the chill of her skin; again I recall how close she stood to me under the Holbein Gate, the warmth and solidity of her flesh that time I clutched at her arm when we first spoke in the queen's privy apartments at Richmond. All that eager life, pinched out as easily as a candle. I set my face firm and reach out a second time, willing myself not to recoil; from her cold flesh my fingers hook out a sturdy gold chain fastened at her throat. Its pendant has slipped round behind her head and become tangled in her hair; impatiently I fumble to free it, a few strands of red-gold hair coming away in my hand with the chain. Attached to it is a lozenge-shaped locket, also carved in gold.

"Look at this." I hold it out to Walsingham, as if to make amends.

He turns it over in his fingers, looking at me expectantly.

"I never saw her wear this before," I add.

"She may have saved her best jewels for court occasions. You open it." Walsingham holds the light steady; even Burghley draws closer to see. The catch is delicate and my fingers clumsy; Burghley starts to hop from foot to foot, puffing through pursed lips.

"We should not stay too much longer—the concert will be almost over."

Walsingham ignores him and bends closer, so that the heat from the torch almost scorches my face. I work my fingernails into the clasp and at last it springs open. The right half of the locket reveals an enamelled painting, seemingly undamaged by its recent immersion. It shows a red phoenix, its head turned to the left and its wings outstretched, in a nest of flames. Inside the left half, two initials are finely engraved, a capital M entwined with a snaking S. I pass it to Walsingham; even with the play of shadows on his face, I see him blanch.

"What is it, Francis?" There is a new note of anxiety in Burghley's voice.

Walsingham clenches the locket in his fist.

"Mary Stuart. Always Mary Stuart. So this girl was also part of the plot. By Christ, have they recruited the whole of the queen's household?"

"The locket was not Abigail's," I say, hearing my knees click as I finally stand, shaking out the stiffness in my legs.

"How do you know?"

I tell them about Abigail's oddly furtive manner at the Holbein Gate. "She mentioned a locket when she first told me about Cecily's secret suitor and his gifts, but there was no locket in the bag of love tokens she passed to me. My guess is that she decided at the last moment to keep it for herself. That's why she seemed guilty."

Walsingham considers this for a moment.

"Perhaps she was foolish enough to wear it about court before today," he says. "If our killer—or at least, the one who hires the killer—is indeed a courtier, he may have seen it around her neck and recognised it as the locket he gave to Cecily."

"In any case, my lord Burghley is right," I say, glancing at the lord treasurer. "There is more than one man behind these murders. Whoever stopped the boy Jem in the yard could not have got back out to the river and rowed up the kitchen channel in time to meet Abigail. I'd bet he delivered the false message from me, then walked calmly back to the hall while someone else waited out on the river with a boat. And I'd wager anything that at the moment she was killed, the man in the shadows was applauding the choir in full view of the queen and the whole court."

Walsingham sighs as he pulls the door of the loading bay shut and secures it with the bolt. The smell of the river recedes a little.

"I need proof, Bruno. Suspicions are no good when they touch people as powerful as those we have in mind here. A ring, a locket—Her Majesty will not move against her cousin for such trinkets, and in any case, Mary Stuart will only say they were stolen by those who wish her harm. It seems certain that whoever is directing these murders is a familiar face at court. And he is clever. He may still be plotting to attack the queen by another means. Who *was* Cecily Ashe's lover?" He grips my shoulder and gives it a little shake, his face close to mine.

Burghley coughs discreetly.

"I think we really must return. The concert will be almost over, and the French ambassador's party will be wondering at Doctor Bruno's absence. Francis—you return with Bruno to the hall. I will endeavour to see that those servants and guards who know of this terrible business are kept at a distance until the guests have all departed. Let the rumourmongers wait until tomorrow, at least, before their tongues run riot." He sucks in his cheeks, and motions for us to leave first.

Walsingham and I pass through the kitchen yard, now almost entirely blanketed in darkness, and back to the passageway by which we had come.

"He is following you, Bruno, this killer," he says in a low voice, over his shoulder. "He knew that kitchen boy had been to Salisbury Court."

"Unless he was at Salisbury Court already."

"That nest of vipers. That is where the proof is to be found, I have no doubt of it. Keep your eyes sharp as a falcon's, Bruno—only you can lay your hands on the evidence that will condemn one or all of them for treachery. But be careful. He must know you are hunting him. And if you come across anything else—however trivial it may seem—bring it straight to me, by any means you can. Understood?"

"Yes, Your Honour." I lower my head, chastened.

He stops walking, turning to face me so abruptly that I bump into him. "There is something else I must ask you, Bruno." He glances around and lowers his voice yet further. "Have you ever heard John Dee speak of visions? Glimpses of the future granted him by angels, that sort of thing?"

I hesitate, possible answers caught in my throat. Against my advice, Dee must have recounted Kelley's vision of the red-haired woman in the white dress to the queen when she summoned him the previous evening. The old fool, I think; too proud, too eager to impress. I would bet, too, that he did not mention Ned Kelley but took credit for the vision himself; he would have wanted the queen to believe he alone had the gift of speaking with angels, though he would have presented the image as some kind of metaphor, no doubt, a sign that the heavenly guardians had care of her royal person. And now, only one day later, the vision is fulfilled horribly, almost to the letter. Did Dee not say Kelley described the red-haired woman being swept away by a great torrent, and Abigail's body found floating in the water? This must have been what Leicester meant when he spoke of more than coincidence. In a flash of understanding, I see that he is right: Ned Kelley knew. There can be no other explanation: he described the murder of Abigail Morley before it happened, and it was no angel or demon who imparted the knowledge. No wonder the cunning man has run away.

"Bruno?" Walsingham bends closer to look into my face, a warning in his eyes.

"He has mentioned something of the kind," I mutter, not wanting to seem that I am withholding more secrets from him. "He has a showing stone which he believes to yield images, if the circumstances are apt."

"Speak plainly—you mean he is conducting séances to contact spirits. It's all right, Bruno—you are not betraying him. You and I are of the same mind—we both want to protect Dee. But he has invited a deal of trouble for himself." He sighs and checks again to make sure we are not overheard. "Yesterday evening, Doctor Dee shared with the queen a vision he had lately seen, of a red-haired woman with the mark of Saturn on her naked breast, pierced through the heart and carried away by a great river. He told her it was a vision of the desires of her enemies, vouchsafed by her guardian angels so that she might be on her guard. Or some such nonsense. This morning Her Majesty saw fit to relate that vision to the Privy Council. She did so out of mischief, I believe, to irk Henry Howard. She has always made it her business to mock publicly all threats of danger to her person, whether based on real intelligence or fantasies like this one of Dee's, to show the world that she is unafraid. She could not have known—well, you see the difficulty, Bruno."

I nod. I see it very well. John Dee unknowingly predicted the murder of Abigail Morley and the queen's most senior advisers know it; the obvious conclusion will be that this foreknowledge in some way implicates him. Why could he not have listened to my advice?

"He told me as well," I whisper, leaning closer. "But he did not tell you the whole truth. The vision was not his, though he would have wanted the queen to believe that he has that gift. He keeps a scryer in his house."

I tell him, as briefly as I can, about Ned Kelley, his clipped ears, his portentous visions of spirits in the crystal, the way he has insinuated himself into Dee's household, his disappearance after prophesying something very like the death of Abigail Morley. When I have finished my account, Walsingham presses his lips together and shakes his head.

"Poor Dee," he says eventually, with a note of compassion. "So passionately seeking after the unknown, he misses what is right under his nose. He had ever the fault of trusting those who should not be trusted."

"If it were not for the detail of the water, I would have said Kelley got his prophecy from some penny gossip sheet," I say. "But he told Dee he saw the woman swept away by a torrent of water, and then Abigail's body was found in the channel by the dock. A needless delay on the killer's part, to tie her to the mooring ring, unless there was something symbolic about it."

"We must find this fellow Kelley, by whatever means. He *will* tell us where he gets his foreknowledge, willingly or otherwise. It is not from any spirit in a stone, that much is certain."

"Your Honour does not believe that the world contains more than our eyes alone reveal?" I ask, with a half smile. His face remains grave.

"Not in the sense that Dee or the queen believe it, nor even you, Bruno. I have seen enough of life to believe that God gave us reason to use it, and that evil is conceived solely in the hearts of men. But this Kelley must be questioned. I will send forces to smoke him out."

I shake my head.

"He will go to ground if you pursue him with force. It must be done subtly—he will only give up his secrets by coaxing or trickery. Let me try with him. He dislikes me, but he might at least be persuaded that I am on his side."

Walsingham nods, and lays a hand on my shoulder.

"Very well, Bruno. But find him quickly. Burghley will have sent for Dee tonight. The Privy Council will have to question him, and it will not look good for him once the details of this murder are known."

We proceed along the painted corridors until the strains of the music can be heard once more, the fluting voices seeming more ethereal than ever by contrast with the scene we have just witnessed. As we turn a corner, a young man in the livery of the palace guard comes hurtling toward us with urgent steps, shouldering his way past me and mumbling an apology without looking back; as I recover my balance, the stumble causes a memory to jolt back.

"Philip Howard!" I whisper, stopping short.

"What?" Walsingham turns, his eyes narrowed.

"Philip Howard was at the Holbein Gate the day I met Abigail." I lower my voice until it is barely audible. "He and his friend pushed past us, but he might well have been watching before that. He fits the description of Cecily Ashe's lover too—he's handsome and titled, just the sort of man a young girl couldn't resist showing off to her friends about. And he has a connection to Mary Stuart through his uncle and the embassy."

Walsingham presses his lips together.

"The Earl of Arundel is another one we cannot possibly accuse without iron proof. I will have him watched. Now, Bruno, you must return to your party. The ambassador will be curious about your absence. I leave you to find something plausible to tell him." He pats me on the shoulder once, then directs me to a side door back to the hall, where two guards with pikestaffs now keep silent watch.

I SLIP IN as quietly as I can through the back of the crowd, most of whom have their attention politely fixed in the direction of the choir, and find myself on the opposite side of the hall from which I left. A few heads turn at the sound of the door, but their curious glances last only a moment. On the dais, I notice that the chair to the right of the queen's, where one of her ladies had been seated, is now occupied by Leicester, who leans in toward her, his expression solicitous. Elizabeth's own face, beneath its mask of ceruse and rouge, is impossible to read, but her eyes do not flicker from the singers; in her unwavering attention, she seems to set an example to her subjects. Through the heads of the audience, I catch a glimpse of the vigorously waving arms of Master Byrd. Only now, as I fold my arms across my chest and stare hard at the floor, breathing deeply, do I realise how I am shaking.

"Doctor Bruno. You look as if you have seen a ghost."

The clipped voice at my shoulder, instantly recognisable; I turn to see Lord Henry Howard standing at a distance from his party and regarding me with interest. I drag my hand across my face as if this will pull my expression into some semblance of normality, and attempt a cordial acknowledgement. Howard has had his beard trimmed for the occasion; it makes his looks spikier than ever. His black hair is neatly combed back, and in his hands he holds a velvet hat trimmed with garnets and an iridescent peacock feather.

"Or perhaps I should say a spirit?" he adds, with the same feigned politeness, turning the hat slowly between his fingers.

I am still in shock, and though I can barely feel my legs, it occurs to me that the knees of my underhose are wet from kneeling beside the body. It is unlikely that Howard will look closely enough to notice, but it does not help me to feel any more at ease in his presence. In fact, I am so conscious of my soaking knees that it takes me a moment to register what he has said.

"I'm sorry?"

"You are spending a great deal of time in Mortlake, I understand, in the library of our friend Doctor Dee?" he goes on. "So the ambassador mentioned."

"I sometimes use his library for research," I say slowly, hardly able to bend my mind to caution at this time. Howard arches one of his elegantly pointed eyebrows and gives me a long look, as if to tell me not to be disingenuous.

"So he's conjuring spirits now, is he?"

"I don't know where your lordship has that idea," I say, but I hear the waver in my own voice; all I want is for him to stop this needling and leave me in peace so that I might gather my thoughts before I rejoin Castelnau.

"He has been sharing his prophetic visions with Her Majesty," Howard says, his eyes roving over the heads of the crowd to where the queen sits on her dais with Leicester. "For her part, she chooses to ridicule them by sharing them with the Privy Council. You may imagine how we all laughed." He turns abruptly to look at me. "But of course, if Dee is attempting to speak with spirits, he could be arrested for witchcraft. I doubt she could save him then."

"My lord, I know nothing of this."

"You are close to Dee, are you not?"

"I respect him as a scholar. But I must say, John Dee strikes me as too sensible a man to attempt anything of that kind."

"What, summoning devils, you mean? In a showing stone? Or animating statues?"

At these words, I cannot quite keep my face from reacting; immediately, his eyes light up, knowing he has scored a hit. I take a deep breath. Either Henry Howard has decided to extend his hatred of Dee to all Dee's known associates, or he has been given reason to believe that Dee and I might be intimate enough for the old magus to have divulged the secret of Howard's own quest for the Hermes book. And if that is the case, what has happened to give him such an idea? Has Castelnau really mentioned my trips to Mortlake, or is it possible that Howard has been following me? Though he too was hearing Mass at Salisbury Court when I returned from Mortlake yesterday, he could easily have set some servant to watch my movements. I meet his mocking gaze briefly, but I am too badly disconcerted by the evening's events to stare him down with my usual bravado. Animating statues is an overt reference to the Hermetic magic, and he expects me to rise to it. I decide my best course is to feign ignorance and say nothing.

"You had better take care, Bruno," he says eventually, when it becomes clear that I am not going to respond. "The reputation you enjoyed in Paris as a black magician already begins to spread in whispers through the English court." He gestures at the people around us.

"I wonder how that could have come about," I say, with flat sarcasm.

"Oh, rumour travels with winged sandals, like Mercury, does it not?" He smiles like a cat. "Stand too close to John Dee and you may find he drags you down with him. There is enough fear and mistrust of stargazers and magicians at court for that. The people clamour to be told the future, then they turn like a pack of dogs on the one who shows them. Even monarchs."

"Is that a warning, my lord?"

"Let us call it a piece of advice."

"If I should encounter any stargazers or magicians, I will pass it on."

He is about to reply, but at this moment the voices of the choir fade to their valedictory note and the assembled crowd erupts into enthusiastic applause. The queen gestures for William Byrd to step up to the dais, where, on bended knee, he is permitted to kiss her extended hand before standing to face the court and take a bow. Amid the continued applause, he leads his choir in procession back through the throng as the high double doors are flung open for their departure.

When the choir has departed, Queen Elizabeth rises to her feet and the court drops as one to its knee, until she holds up a hand and motions for us to stand again. The musicians resume their places and take up a gentle background tune as the queen, assuming a gracious smile, as far as her tight face paint will allow, arranges her train and beckons her maids to take it up, before stepping down with dignity from the dais; it is apparently her custom after such occasions to take some time to mingle with her subjects, allow them to bow and flatter and even, if they dare, petition her. At this cue, eager courtiers press forward, jostling one another for the chance to exchange a few words with their sovereign. Fortunes have been won and lost on the strength of such brief conversations, if the queen is in a mood to be pleased by a well-turned compliment or an appealing face; it is an opportunity not to be missed, and these English-men know it. I watch with growing admiration the way she moves among them; if Leicester has told her that another murder has been committed within the walls of her palace this evening, she gives no sign of it, and her resolve seems designed to ensure that the courtiers and guests gathered in the hall should have no inkling of it either. I notice that Leicester keeps close behind her, one hand resting lightly on the hilt of his sword.

Mendoza appears at Howard's side, lays a hand on his shoulder, and casts a dismissive glance at me.

"Ah, *el hereje*," he remarks, with a nod, as if it pleases him to have invented a nickname for me. He speaks in Spanish, in a low voice muffled further by his copious beard. "Look there, where your ambassador struggles so anxiously for an audience with the English queen."

I follow the movement of his head to see Castelnau, pushing as politely as he can toward Elizabeth, his expression almost pathetically hopeful as he attempts to catch her eye.

"He would tread on his own child's head just for one of her smiles," Mendoza sneers. "He still thinks he will broker a treaty between France and England, does he not?" He fixes his small, black eyes on me.

"I am not the person to ask, señor."

"Don't give me that, Bruno! You were a confidant of the king of France and it pleases the ambassador to involve you in affairs of state, though God only knows why. Tell me—has Castelnau told the French king that Guise is amassing troops against England?"

"That I do not know." I have grown so used to deception that even when I am able to answer a question honestly, I sound implausible. "But I think it unlikely."

"Why do you say that?"

I hesitate.

"For the sake of his wife. And because for the moment he would not want to give King Henri more reason to fear the Duke of Guise."

"And because he still thinks he can engineer a satisfactory outcome between all parties, no? He imagines he is controlling this enterprise—balancing one set of interests against another?"

"Perhaps." I recall what Fowler had said about Castelnau trying to please too many people.

"It is touching, his faith in diplomacy." Mendoza shakes his head. "I shall almost be sorry to see him disillusioned. But you are an astute man, Bruno. Astute enough not to yoke yourself to a monarch whose days are numbered."

"Do you mean Elizabeth or Henri?"

"Either. Both. A new day is dawning. Men like you and Castelnau will need to decide where you stand. If you have any influence over him, you would counsel him well not to let his king hear what is discussed in the embassy. *Entendido?*"

He draws himself up to his full imposing height and puffs out his chest, his beard bristling. He does not intimidate me, but I am in no state at present to argue with him. I merely nod my agreement and take the opportunity to slip away backward into the milling crowd.

"Bruno."

I turn in the direction of the murmur, and there, leaning against the wall between the hanging tapestries, is William Fowler, dressed in a neat suit of grey wool, with a matching cap clutched between his hands.

"What did Howard want?"

"To remind me again how much he hates me," I say, glancing over my shoulder at Howard as he and Mendoza confer, their dark heads together, while the courtiers around them press toward the queen. My head is spinning; I am not sure what to make of my brief exchange with Henry Howard. He must fear that Dee has told me something I could use against him and was warning me that he has the power to bring me and Dee down together, but I cannot escape the implication that he has been watching me closely. The thought makes the hairs on the back of my neck prickle; was it Howard, then, or someone working for him, who saw me with Abigail at the Holbein Gate? Instinctively I glance over my shoulder again; for the first time since this business began, I feel a chill of real fear.

"But has something happened?" Fowler whispers, edging closer around the back of a couple of spectators. "I saw you come in looking white as a corpse. I wondered if perhaps—"

I give a tight shake of the head, to indicate that I cannot speak of it there.

"The queen's advisers were coming and going half the concert too," Fowler persists. "I noticed Walsingham leave." There is a note of anxiety in his voice, which I recognise because I have felt it myself; it is the fear of missing some important moment, of being left out. This time it is I who know more than he, I who am in Walsingham's confidence, and despite the circumstances, this pleases me.

"Bruno, are you all right?" he persists. "You look terrible. Does it have something to do with Howard?"

"Meet me tomorrow," I hiss, through my teeth. "Two o'clock. Not the Mermaid—some other place."

He thinks for a moment, then sidles even closer.

"The Mitre, Creed Lane. The back room." He slips past me as he says this and melts into the crowd in that way of his, like a grey cat into the shadows.

I work my way between shoulders toward Castelnau's party. The ambassador is still fighting for a position near the queen; Marie and Courcelles are huddled together, whispering. Courcelles is the first to notice me, with a wrinkle of his delicate nose.

"Where have *you* been?" he demands. I gesture with my head toward the royal party, as if nothing is amiss.

"QUEEN ELIZABETH HERSELF?" Marie says, apparently impressed, pulling her cloak tighter around her shoulders with a little shiver. The wind is up over the river, carrying the first scent of frost. The boat's lanterns sway in time with the soft ripple of the sculls in and out of the water. I think of Abigail's killer rowing away downriver, leaving her lifeless body floating in the kitchen channel, her red hair spread out around her, waving like waterweed.

"Did you hear that, Michel?" Marie nudges her husband and nods back to me, her eyes gleaming in the lamplight. "The Queen of England wants to learn Bruno's memory system, and it was I who asked first. How very fashionable you have become, Bruno!"

Courcelles eyes me coldly. "But the queen did not know you would be attending the concert. It seems strange that her people should have been awaiting you with such alacrity."

"She has heard of me through Sir Philip Sidney," I say, trying to keep my voice steady. "He knows something of my work and has apparently mentioned it to Her Majesty."

He continues to regard me with that same sceptical expression. I am conscious that to insist too much on my story will only compound his suspicions. I care little what Courcelles thinks for himself, but I cannot have him dripping doubt into Castelnau's ear, now that my place at Salisbury Court has become so essential to Walsingham.

"Did you have the sense that something was going on tonight, though?" Courcelles persists, addressing his question to the whole group. "All those guards. And the queen's advisers running in and out. The Earl of Leicester whispering in her ear. It was odd—as if something was amiss but they were trying to pretend all was as normal."

Castelnau looks perturbed. "I noticed nothing amiss."

"Nor I," I say hastily.

"You were not there," Courcelles points out.

"It is a shame they made you miss the whole concert, though," Castelnau says thoughtfully, in a manner that suggests he is not wholly persuaded by my story. "I have not heard its like. They must have had a great many questions to ask you, eh?"

"The queen is enthusiastic about my art of memory, it seems, but her advisers had heard some unfortunate rumours regarding my methods."

"That it's black magic by any other name?" Courcelles says, one eyebrow arched. "All of Europe has heard those rumours."

"Something of the sort." I shoot him a withering smile, but it is lost in the dark. "In any case, they wanted to put their minds at ease that I was not a danger to the royal person or to the reputation of her court."

"It is a marvellous opportunity," Castelnau says thoughtfully. "They do seem to like you, these English. I suppose it is your reputation as a rebel against the pope." His eyes drift to the middle distance and I wonder if he is still questioning my excuse, or calculating how my favour at court might work to bolster his own standing with the queen.

"Perhaps, my lord." I begin to fear that I may eventually trip myself up with my cat's cradle of lies.

"Well, the queen will have to wait her turn," says Marie, leaning forward with a disarming smile. "I requested that you tutor me before she did, and I stake a prior claim." She lays a hand on my arm. "We shall begin tomorrow morning, while Catherine is with her tutor. No—I shall hear no excuses, Bruno." She turns to her husband, her eyes eager, her hand in its green silk glove still resting lightly just above my wrist. "Won't that be something for this tedious English court to talk about, Michel— that the wife of King Henri's envoy shares a teacher with the Queen of England!"

"I thought you disapproved of the Queen of England," Castelnau says mildly.

"*I* thought *you* disapproved of Bruno," Courcelles adds, with a pointed look.

I return his glance with equanimity, but his words offer a useful warning. I do not know Marie de Castelnau. I do not know her intentions with regard to me, nor the root of her interest in my work; I know only that she is fiercely committed to the Catholic cause of Mary Stuart and the Duke of Guise. For so many reasons, I must not let her catch me off guard even for a moment. I hope briefly that the ambassador might forbid it, on grounds of propriety.

Castelnau appears to be thinking, then allows the beam of his patriarchal smile to sweep slowly across me and his wife. "If it would interest you to learn, my dear, I'm sure Bruno would see it as a service. Heaven knows we could all do with a better memory."

This appears to be the last word on the matter. Marie gives my wrist a little squeeze before settling back among the cushions, lamplight playing over the satisfied curve of her mouth as the oars continue to splash their steady rhythm through the black river. From under the fine curtain of his hair, Courcelles continues to study me with his fox eyes, just waiting for one false move. I watch the water part over the blades in silver rivulets and picture again the marble-cold face of Abigail Morley, who died tonight partly because of me.

Chapter 9

As if waiting for its cue, October blows in on gusts of a bitter east wind. The cornflower-blue skies over the city now churn with bruised, angry-looking clouds and the dead leaves scratch the paths and windowpanes. A fire has been lit in the small parlour where Marie wishes to conduct our first lesson; I have had no choice but to agree, though I am itching to get to Mortlake in pursuit of Ned Kelley. Last night I slept badly, the image of Abigail's soaked and mutilated body laid out in my dreams and my waking thoughts, my conscience tormented by the thought that I should have done more to protect her. If I had gone to Walsingham sooner, instead of being so determined to prove myself alone, would she have been safer? Such questions are fruitless, yet they prodded at my mind all night, sharp and insistent, like devils in woodcuts of hell prodding with their pitchforks at the souls of sinners.

Marie stands by the window, her hair bound up, no doubt aware that her figure appears to advantage silhouetted against the grey light. As I close the door behind me, she leaps forward, eyes gleaming, and clutches at my sleeve.

"Another girl was killed at the palace last night, Bruno, did you hear?" There is relish in her voice.

"That—that is terrible. Where did you hear of this?" It takes every ounce of my skill to bend my face to the appropriate expression.

She shrugs. "One of the servants. Went out to the market this morning and all of London is abuzz with it, apparently. Another of the queen's maids, they said, killed just like the first, with astrologer's marks cut into her."

Gently, I remove her hand from my arm and take my place on a settle by the hearth, stretching my hands out toward the dancing flames. I cannot picture Marie rising early to gossip with the servants, but it is not impossible. If she is telling the truth, it means the news has travelled surprisingly quickly, defying all Walsingham's and Burghley's efforts to contain it. *If.*

"I thought they had apprehended the killer?"

"I know!" Her eyes widen, excited. "It seems they have the wrong man, or else there is another murderer. To think it must have happened while we were all listening to the music—isn't that horrible?" She produces a theatrical shiver. "It's funny, you know, because I noticed a fuss—some of the queen's advisers coming and going, I thought it odd that they should disturb the concert. Then the Earl of Leicester came in looking very agitated and sat with the queen—I suppose they must have discovered the body then? It must have been exactly the time you were out being quizzed about your memory system, I suppose? Did you hear nothing?"

I think I catch a deliberate edge to her voice when she says this, and look up sharply, but she merely returns my gaze and folds her hands together demurely in front of her.

"I noticed the palace guard going to and fro with some haste, but I saw nothing out of the ordinary. I was taken to a private office and questioned about my work. Whatever else was happening, it must have been in another part of the palace." I shrug, as if to say I am not much interested.

"Who questioned you?" Her voice is light, but her eyes fix hard on mine, so that to look away would immediately make me seem shifty.

"Lord Burghley."

"Ah." She nods and smiles, then moves to sit beside me on the settle, arranging and smoothing her skirts carefully until she is satisfied. She runs a forefinger along my wrist. "You would not lie to me, would you, Bruno?"

My skin shivers and tightens to goose bumps at her touch. "Why would I want to lie?"

"I don't know. Perhaps you have a woman you are hiding from us?" She glances up sidelong with a mischievous smile.

"At the court?" I force myself to smile. "I'm afraid not. There is no woman. My life is far less exciting than you imagine, madame. It is mainly spent in libraries among dusty manuscripts."

She smiles, catlike, and arranges her hands in her lap. I breathe out slowly; it seems that, for now, the questioning is over.

"Well, then—let us see if we can liven it up. Come, Bruno. You are the master and I your acolyte. I am in your hands. Mould me as you will."

Her expression is all sweetness; only the dangerous glitter in her eyes betrays a mischief I prefer not to dwell on. The only way through this is for me to appear as naïve and as literal as possible, to keep all conversation on the surface and pretend to be so blockheaded as to miss any implied double meanings on her part.

Then there is the matter of my memory system, and how much I should impart. The rumours that chased me from the Parisian court were all true, of course; my *ars memoria* is so much more than a useful tool for orators or those who wish to improve their powers of recall. It is an art of deep magic, refined over years of study, worked on through all my long months as a fugitive in Italy and later in the libraries and archives of Geneva, Toulouse, and Paris. It is, though I say so myself, a profound achievement, though few will have the capacity to comprehend it fully; my system is the first of its kind to marry the classical art of memory with the system taught by Thomas Aquinas and passed down in the teachings of my former order, the Dominicans, but to add to these the most powerful ingredient of all, the ancient Egyptian wisdom of Hermes Trismegistus. Without this element of magic, my work would have held no interest for King Henri of France, a man who hungers after esoteric knowledge with an enthusiasm that almost makes up for his lack of talent. Marie de Castelnau was a confidante of King Henri's wife; how much, then, might she already know? Again, the sense that this is some kind of trick hangs over me, setting my teeth on edge.

Even so, we must start somewhere. I hold out to her a large sheet of paper on which I have drawn a diagram, and sit back with some satisfaction while she takes it and reads, turning it this way and that as she narrows her eyes to make out the tiny inscriptions.

"In God's name, Bruno," she says, at last, having turned the paper in a full revolution. "How is anyone supposed to make sense of this?"

"It is not for all to understand."

She appears to like this.

"That I can see. It is only for adepts, so King Henri says. I want to become an adept." She flicks the paper with a finger, then crosses her ankles and rests her chin on her hand. "Where do we begin?"

Where indeed? For a moment I am tempted to laugh. My system is infinitely complex; I have not fully penetrated its mysteries myself. The diagram, laid out according to the rules I explained in my book *On the Shadows of Ideas*, published in Paris shortly before I left (and one of the principal reasons for my flight), shows a series of concentric wheels, divided according to the twelve signs of the zodiac, separated further into subdivisions, which can be arranged in seemingly limitless configurations to embrace the sum of human knowledge. On these wheels are represented the properties of elements in the natural world—plants, animals, minerals; on a higher plane come the inventions of men, the spectrum of all the arts and sciences; beyond these, the images of the mansions of the moon, the planets, the constellations, and the houses of the zodiac. Finally, and most powerful of all, there are the names and images of the thirty-six decans of the zodiac, which no man before me has dared invoke; it was this element that had the learned doctors of the Sorbonne and the ecclesiastical authorities in Paris muttering against me for sorcery, because they lacked the light of true understanding. My system, correctly understood, becomes a means of connecting all that is contained in the universe, in one golden chain of ascent from the lowest substance through the imagination of man and up to the gods of time, who inhabit the infinite space beyond the spheres of the planets, who move and influence everything we know as the heavens and the Earth. And the man who can fully embrace the knowledge contained in this system therefore holds the entirety of the known universe within his own mind, and can rediscover his own divine nature, that part of himself that once communicated freely with the Divine Mind and with the gods of time, before that knowledge was lost to us. He would become more than an adept—he would become like God.

This is what Dee and I mean when we speak of entering the Mind of God, though we disagree about the nature of the decans. He, afraid to stray too far from the conventional forms of the Christian religion, calls these spirits "angels"; it is these he seeks to speak to through his misguided faith in Ned Kelley's scrying. But I know that the likes of Kelley will never find a means to reach the decans. Before the great civilisation of Egypt crumbled and so much of its wisdom was lost, priests and magi knew the secret of communicating with the gods of time and of harnessing their powers. These secrets were closely guarded in the temple archives, and when the last priests fled, they carried the scrolls that preserved their knowledge with them to far corners of the known world. One of these priests was Hermes Trismegistus—who some believe was the deity Thoth, scribe of the gods. So the names of the decans have been passed down to us through the writings of Hermes, though his precise instructions for communication and ascent are still lost to us, contained—I believe—in the missing fifteenth book of his writings, the book Dee believes could be in the possession of Henry Howard. My memory system is the closest approximation I can devise without the great key described in that book. Even so, it is sufficiently steeped in ancient knowledge to see me burned, as King Henri and I both knew.

Marie is still looking at me. Firelight softens the right side of her face, licking a warm glow along her cheek and collarbone. The room is too dim, or the day is; there is something too intimate about the shadows, the amber light. I lean across, pointing to the outermost wheel of the diagram, uncomfortably aware of her intense gaze in the stillness.

"Any memory system is based on symbolic pictures, since our minds are better suited to recalling images," I begin, not quite meeting her eye. "These images here are classified according to their common properties. So, for example, in this circle you see arranged the stones and minerals associated with the planet Mars—"

"There was much talk of your knowledge in Paris, you know," she interrupts, twisting a stray curl around her finger. "They said you were teaching King Henri to call down demons, so that he could side with the heretic Elizabeth against the pope."

"Well, the ignorant have to fill their time somehow. Now, these wheels can be turned to create different series of connections—"

"It was one of the things the Duke of Guise used to stir up unrest against the king," she interrupts again. "He said you were manipulating Henri by sorcery, converting him to your heresies so that he would protect you from the Inquisition. That was one of the reasons King Henri banished you from court. Did you know that?"

"King Henri didn't *banish* me," I say, needled. "I wanted to visit England. The idea was mine."

She laughs, mocking.

"If that's what you want to believe. Henri was afraid of the Duke of Guise. The French people do not want a weak king, Henri knows this. They want a sovereign who will defend the Catholic faith, not one who humours Protestants and dabbles in witchcraft. Oh, yes, there was much talk about you in Paris, Bruno, even after you left. Some said you killed a man in Rome." She tilts her chin and raises an eyebrow, as if daring me to confess.

"Do I look like a murderer to you, madame?" I smile, but my palms are prickling with sweat. Philip Sidney had made a joking reference to this once, but he had heard the story in Italy; I had not thought it had pursued me through Europe and across the sea.

She laughs again, this time with more warmth.

"No. But then you do not look like I imagine a sorcerer either, nor a heretic, nor a monk."

"Because I am none of those things, madame."

"Oh, do stop the *madame*. It makes me feel a hundred years old. I am Marie. Just Marie." She studies her fingernails for a moment, then raises her eyes to meet mine again, a curious half smile playing about her lips. "Who *are* you, Bruno? No one knew in Paris. No one knows at Salisbury Court. Everyone wants you at their supper table, for your wit and your daring ideas, and all the women try to catch your eye, but you keep your distance from everyone, you will not let anyone close enough to see you truly. So stories grow to fill the spaces in our knowledge."

"I am only the man you see before you," I say, spreading my arms and holding out my hands as if to prove that I have nothing concealed. "No mystery."

She looks at me for a long time, as if trying to read something encrypted in my eyes. Determined not to seem suspicious, I hold her gaze. There is only the sound of the logs crackling in the hearth and the rise and fall of our breathing. I realise afresh how very beautiful she is, how confined she seems here, and how dissatisfied with her lot: her aging husband, preoccupied with affairs of state, and her young daughter. I remembered how brittle her movements had seemed when I saw her with her child, how forced, as if she were performing the role of mother unwillingly. For a moment I consider the path set out for a young woman of noble birth: how briefly she is allowed to shine, to be publicly paraded and admired among her own kind, for precisely as long as it takes to find her a suitable husband. Her wedding day is the zenith of her short flowering; after that she is expected to fade again into the background, to cover her hair and content herself with the reflected glory of her husband and children. For a woman like Marie, such self-effacement must fit like a hair shirt.

This game she is playing with me—the flirtatious comments, the touches, the knowing way she parcels out her attentions between me and Courcelles—is all a means of creating some drama for herself, now that she is no longer centre stage. Briefly I pity her, until I remember how callously she had talked of holy war at the dinner table, and how she wears the Duke of Guise's emblem as a badge of honour—the same emblem that was found with both the dead maids. Whether she knows it or not, Marie is somehow connected to the murders. But perhaps even this enthusiasm for the Franco-Spanish invasion is for her just another way to feel she is acting on the world, instead of hearing about it through the muffled walls of her tapestried rooms.

"I don't believe you," she says eventually, shaking her head with that same amused smile. "Whatever you are, Bruno, you are more than you seem on the outside. Though the outside is perfectly acceptable." She spreads out the paper with the diagram across both our laps and makes a show of studying it, tracing her finger slowly over the circles, her arm pressed against mine. My body is rigid with the effort of not responding. "*Did* you teach King Henri magic?" she whispers, as if this proximity might persuade me to open up.

"No."

"Does Elizabeth want you to teach her magic? Is that what your secret talks were about?"

"No." So this is what she wants to discover, is it? I wonder if someone has put her up to it—Henry Howard, perhaps, to discredit the queen.

"It is common knowledge she keeps an astrologer."

"This is not astrology." I tap the diagram. "It is a means of organising the mind."

Her fingertip lingers over the central circle.

"Are these the names of demons?"

I force a laugh; it comes out as a strangled squeak.

"Again, no. These are the thirty-six decans of the zodiac, three faces for each sign. They are also symbols, memory pictures, if you like."

She murmurs some of the names softly, like a litany: *Assican, Senacher, Acentacer, Acecath, Viroaso*. The hairs on my neck prickle at the words in her mouth; the air seems to settle on us like velvet. Then she turns and slowly raises a hand to my face, her thumb running softly along my cheekbone, then along my lower lip, and there is such longing in her eyes that it startles and confuses me. The firelight is reflected as dancing points of light in the depths of her pupils; I am caught, motionless. Just as her face begins to move inevitably toward mine, and I know that I am helpless to resist the pull of it, a log collapses in the grate with a great crack and flare, spitting cinders over the stone hearth. We both jump at the noise; the spell is broken and I take the opportunity to stand abruptly, snatching the paper away in my haste.

"Marie . . . I can't. Your husband—I am a guest in his house. It would be—" The sentences hang there, unfinished.

She twists on the settle, her body squirming first one way, then the other; when she looks up, her eyes are flashing. Her pride is wounded, and so she turns her anger on me; her cheeks are flushed and her mouth pressed into a white line.

"One word to my husband," she says, her voice tight as wire. "I only have to say one word of this, that you tried to touch me, and you would be thrown out of this house. Where would you go then?" When I do not respond, she raises her head, defiant. "Back to Paris in disgrace. I could destroy you if I chose."

"I suppose you could. But what would that satisfy? I have done nothing to hurt you, Marie."

She says nothing, only looks away, her teeth clenched.

"What is it you want from me?" I say, as gently as I can.

She shakes her head, still turned resolutely toward the fire. I cannot read her; my suspicion remains that she meant to use her charms to coax some secret or other from me, believing I would be weak enough to give in, but there is always the outside chance that she felt something sincere, or believed she did. Either way, no woman takes being scorned lightly, and a woman whose pride is hurt can be dangerous. I kneel on the floor before her, placing my hand lightly over hers. She does not remove it, though she still will not look at me.

"Marie." I pause, choosing my words carefully. "I was a monk for thirteen years. I have learned a little about mastering desire. And however beautiful you are, and you *are*"—here she deigns to look at me, finally, though her eyes are still cold—"I owe the duty of loyalty and respect to your husband and to King Henri, who is his master and mine. Nor would I wish to lose your respect." If I ever had it, I add silently.

She purses her lips, as if weighing my speech, and eventually seems to approve it with a curt little nod. A thin wave of relief washes through me; I know as well as she how difficult she could make my life at Salisbury Court if she set her mind to it. For a moment I remain kneeling while I consider how to proceed, unwilling to make any sudden move that might inflame her anger again.

"Perhaps it is best we leave the lesson for today?" I suggest timidly; she nods and at that moment there comes a sharp knock at the door. I jump back, letting go of Marie's hand, but not fast enough to be missed by Courcelles, who strides in without waiting for an invitation, his sharp eyes taking in the tableau at one sweep. Marie at least has the grace to look guilty for a moment, before a malicious smile curves across her face as she looks up at him.

"Lesson going well?" he asks, in a voice like satin wrapped around a steel blade.

"Yes, thank you, Claude," Marie says lightly. "Did you want something?"

"Yes, madame—the child Catherine's governess has asked me to fetch you. She refuses to settle to her lesson."

I watch Marie's face and note that her first, uncensored reaction is irritation. I see it tighten her features, before she remembers herself and arranges her expression into an approximation of motherly concern.

"Does she expect me to do everything? What is she employed for?" she says, standing and smoothing down her dress. She hesitates briefly, as if unsure whether to acknowledge me or not, then juts her chin forward and sweeps from the room without glancing at either of us. Courcelles turns to me with a look that could crack marble.

"I thought your tutelage was supposed to improve her memory?" He rests a hand on the latch. "It seems to be having rather the reverse effect—apparently neither of you remembered that she is a married woman. I wonder what her husband would say to that."

"No doubt we will learn when you tell him," I say without looking up, folding away the diagram of my memory wheels before he can see it.

"Oh, it won't be me who tells him, Bruno. I am discreet as the grave." He leaves a pause, perfectly timed. "Not unless you give me good reason to think my lord ambassador should be informed."

"There is nothing to tell," I say bluntly, rising to my feet.

"I'm sure. But my lord ambassador is a sensitive man on that point, for obvious reasons. By the way, did you hear—there has been another murder at court, just like the first?"

"So I heard. A great tragedy."

"Last night, if you can believe it, while we were all at the concert. Well—all except *you*, I should say."

"An extraordinary coincidence."

He produces a dry laugh. "No such thing as coincidence—isn't that what you fairground stargazers say?" With a final toss of his hair, he stalks out, leaving me with the uncomfortable knowledge that I am more vulnerable than ever at Salisbury Court.

Chapter 10

M ary Stuart won't be happy."

Thomas Phelippes doesn't raise his eyes as he makes this observation; instead I watch them flicker with quick lizard movements over the lines of numbers written in the letter he has just expertly unsealed. Walsingham once told me that Phelippes only had to read a cipher once or twice to have it by heart; he said this with almost fatherly pride. If he weren't such a phenomenon as a code breaker, Walsingham had added, with an indulgent laugh, he could make a fortune in a travelling fair with his feats of memory. Naturally, I am fascinated by the reports of this man's prodigious powers of recall, but he doesn't have the kind of demeanour that invites intimate conversation. In fact, he seems singularly ill equipped to deal with other people; he rarely looks directly at you, shifting uncomfortably unless he has been asked to explain some piece of his business, when he holds forth at length in his curious monotone, firing the information at you with barely a pause for breath. Here, in the dim back room of his house on Leadenhall Street, shuttered and lantern-lit even in the day, to protect his secretive work, he seems like a woodland creature, content to hide in its burrow. If Nature has blessed him with exceptional gifts of intellect, she has sought balance by withholding from him any physical charm; the man is short and squat, with a heavy jaw, a flattish nose, and the scars of smallpox on his cheeks.

"Mary Stuart is never happy," I remark, as his keen gaze continues to search the letter that I know comes from Lord Henry Howard, and is on its way to Francis Throckmorton for delivery on his next trip to Sheffield Castle. Idly, I pick up a block of sealing wax from Phelippes's broad desk, examine it, put it back. In the corner of the room, Dumas is making a hasty copy of one of Castelnau's letters to Mary before he delivers the original, his nib scratching frantically like a mouse trapped behind a panel. Phelippes reaches over without looking up and replaces the wax in the exact spot it had been, a fraction of an inch to the left, with a little irritated click of the tongue. Then he picks up a book from his desk and leafs urgently through the pages, glancing from it to the paper in his hand. As he lifts the book up, I see that it is Henry Howard's *A Defensative Against the Poison of Supposed Prophecies*.

"Good read?" I ask.

Phelippes lifts his head sufficiently for me to catch the look of disdain on his face.

"It's the cipher," he mutters, as if it were hardly worth the effort of explaining this to someone so wilfully stupid. "The book *is* the code. It's one of the most basic devices. That's why he sends her a copy. See here, where the numbers are set out in groups of three?" He tilts the paper toward me enough for me to see what he means, the lines of figures squeezed together in Howard's cramped handwriting. "Page, line, word. You see? Meaningless to anyone who doesn't know the edition the numbers refer to or doesn't have a copy, and in theory endlessly varied, because one need never use the same reference for the same word twice.

But Howard in particular is lazy. He frequently uses the same page reference for common words rather than looking for other examples. Makes my job easier, anyway."

"So you have memorised these page references?"

"A good number of them, yes."

If he catches the tone of admiration in my voice, he gives no sign of it, nor does he speak with any trace of pride. He is merely stating facts. He crouches closer over the letter, rifling through the pages of the book at the same time.

"For instance, I will have to double-check some of these words against the book but the gist of this letter is Henry Howard saying he knows nothing about any ring. Apparently Mary sent him a valuable ring that belonged to her mother, with a family crest engraved. In a green velvet casket. Weeks ago, this is. She wanted him to use it as a seal to guarantee his letters were genuine, but he protests he never had any such casket nor ring from her. You'd think they were betrothed, all this giving and receiving of rings." Phelippes barks out a sudden laugh, the sound unnatural in his throat.

"Except that Howard never did receive it," I murmur, my mind spinning into action. The ring Mary had sent as a gift to Henry Howard had ended up being given as a love token to Cecily Ashe—it could only be the same one—but by whom? If all Mary's correspondence to Howard comes through the French embassy, then the package containing the ring could have been intercepted either before it was passed on to Howard— by Throckmorton, say, or someone at Salisbury Court—or else Howard is lying to Mary, and he was the one who gave the ring to Cecily. Or his nephew, Philip Howard, who I have already marked out as fitting the description Abigail gave of Cecily's lover. I shake my head; again, the question remains: Why give a token so clearly identifiable, one which, if found, would point straight back to the conspirators around Mary Stuart? It seemed almost like a deliberate betrayal of Mary.

The room is oddly still; I glance up and realise that Dumas has stopped his scribbling. Instead he is staring at me, his face white and strained, his eyes bulging more alarmingly than usual. I send him a quizzical frown; he only bites his lip and mouths the word "time."

He is right; he must take the packet of letters to Throckmorton and I have Fowler waiting for me at the Mitre. We work as fast as we can in this back room of Phelippes's house, but there is always the fear that someone from Salisbury Court will have seen Dumas meet me at the Lud Gate or noticed our detour through the city to Leadenhall, particularly now it seems certain that someone is watching my movements. Already the best part of the day is gone, thanks to Marie and her diversions, but I still have hopes of making my way to Mortlake in pursuit of Ned Kelley, or clues to his whereabouts. Phelippes seems to have frozen at his task; I give a small cough behind my fist but he merely blinks.

"Almost there," he says mildly, still staring fixedly at the letter, and I realise he is memorising the numbers. I would love to ask him his technique, but do not want to break his concentration. When he has jotted down what he needs, he refolds Howard's letter and arranges the instruments of his other skill, the forging of seals: several bars of wax, a candle, a selection of small silver-bladed knives, some no bigger than the nib of a quill. He takes a moment to compare the new wax, matching the colour carefully to the original seal. I watch, mesmerised, as his quick fingers deftly reattach it, part heating the underside and adding just enough fresh wax to press it home without cracking the surface or disturbing the cords set into the original wax. Any careless move at this crucial stage could damage Howard's seal so that the tampering became evident; Mary's sharp eyes would be looking for any such sign of treachery. I find I am holding my breath in sympathy, anxious not to make any move or sound that might distract Phelippes, but he seems oblivious; for a thickset man, he has surprisingly delicate fingers, long and white like a seamstress's. With his little knife he prods and tweaks the soft wax until he is satisfied with its appearance. He replaces the letter inside the oilskin wrapping of the package Dumas must deliver to Throckmorton imminently.

At the edge of my vision I can see Dumas fidgeting; he is anxious to be gone. When he has handed over the letter he has been copying and the packet for Throckmorton has been resealed satisfactorily, Phelippes ushers us out of the back door of his house, bidding us good day with an awkward twitch of his shoulders, eyes still turned to the ground.

We cross a yard and emerge into a side street that leads us out by the little churchyard of St. Katharine Cree. A cold gust throws a handful of raindrops into our faces and Dumas shivers, a violent tremor that rattles through his thin body. He seems unusually tense; as we step out into the street, our collars pulled up against the squall, a boy dashes suddenly from the mouth of an alley and Dumas leaps a foot into the air like a rabbit, clutching at my sleeve.

"Are you all right, Léon?" I ask, as the boy swerves between puddles and disappears behind houses on the opposite side of the street. Dumas looks at me with an oddly pleading expression, as if there is something he wants to say, then shakes his head tightly, mumbling that he must hurry. I, too, am already late for my meeting with Fowler; earlier this morning I had regretted the necessity of seeing him, adding another distraction to my day, but now I feel something approaching relief. Walsingham's anger at the palace has taught me that I cannot hope to find this killer alone, and the quiet, composed Scot, with his network of contacts and his knowledge of Salisbury Court, may be just the confidant I need. Walsingham has as good as instructed me to share my information, and the prospect of sharing the burden is no longer unwelcome.

I lay a hand on Dumas's shoulder and he flinches. We must part ways here, I west to Creed Lane, he south to Paul's Wharf and Throckmorton's house.

"I will see you back at Salisbury Court."

He looks around briefly, then leans in toward me.

"They will know now, won't they? That the letters have been opened?"

"What makes you say that?"

"The ring. If the casket and the ring has been stolen from inside the package, they will start looking for anyone who might have had the chance to do so." He is clutching at my sleeve again, his eyes bright with panic.

"Slow down, Léon—the ring could have disappeared at any stage in its journey. Or it may not have disappeared at all. There is no reason to think we will be under any more suspicion than we are now."

But he is not convinced; in fact, he looks more stricken than I have ever seen him. If his fear gets the better of him and he tries to pull out of the arrangement to avoid discovery, we could lose our access to Mary's correspondence with Salisbury Court and with it any advance information about the invasion plans or concrete evidence of plots against the queen. This must not be allowed to happen; the entire operation depends on Dumas's peace of mind, and it is up to me to reassure him.

"We must remain calm, Léon, and give nothing away from our behaviour. You and I will speak of this further. Come to my room when you can," I say, clapping him on the shoulder again, "but for now, God-speed." And I watch him as he sets off south toward the river, his shoulders hunched against the rain. As I turn to make my own way up the hill, I am certain I see a flicker of movement, a figure darting away into the shadows behind St. Katharine Cree. My stomach twists for a moment, as my hand reaches for the bone-handled dagger I carry always at my belt, the only possession I took from the monastery of San Domenico Maggiore in Naples the night I fled. But as I draw level with the churchyard I can see no one; two men are walking eastward toward me, deep in conversation, and I pull my shoulders back and breathe deeply. London is full of people going about their business, despite the rain, and I must guard against becoming as nervous as Dumas, leaping at shadows. I pull the peak of my cap down against the weather and walk on, though I keep one hand on the dagger, just in case.

CREED LANE RUNS to the west of St. Paul's churchyard, and the narrow street is already thronged with people as I approach the sign of the

Mitre, jostling one another with sharp insults as they try to protect themselves and their wares from the weather. Just as I reach the door of the tavern, a hand clamps down on my shoulder; again, I start, my hand instinctively tightening around the knife as I turn to find the grinning face of Archibald Douglas only a few inches from mine, his breath already thick with the fumes of drink but his eyes bright and mischievous.

"Bruno! I thought it was you. Recognised your hat through the crowds. What brings you to this part of town?"

I look at him through narrowed eyes, immediately alert. Douglas has never to my knowledge seen me wearing a hat, and in any case, mine is of black leather, the same as every second man in London. Could it possibly be *Douglas* following me?

"Books," I say, hastily recovering myself. "I wanted to look at the booksellers' stalls outside St. Paul's."

"I'm not sure they sell your kind of books on public stalls," he says, winking broadly and hooking his arm around my neck as he pushes the door open. "Come on, let me buy you a drink."

I am wary of his sudden appearance and unprecedented display of bonhomie, but since I was so obviously on my way into the tavern, it is impossible to refuse his offer without looking suspicious myself, so I shrug and allow him to usher me through the door into the steaming taproom, where the smell of wet wool vies with the warming aromas of pastry and yeasty beer.

Douglas shoulders his way through the press of damp bodies sheltering from the cloudburst, calling for beer as a put-upon girl eases past, splashing from the four tankards she carries, two in each hand, and cursing as she does so.

"Watch you don't get your pockets picked in here," he says to me, over his shoulder, then he pauses, looks over my head across the other side of the room, makes a face, and mutters, "Fuck." When he reaches a corner table, he motions to the other drinkers to shove up along the bench, let us sit down; grumbling, they obey. There is something oddly compelling about Douglas's presence; though I don't like him, neither do

I want to be on the wrong side of him, and since he is so entangled with the conspirators at Salisbury Court, it would be foolish of me not to use this opportunity to take a close look at him. Still, I can't escape the sense that it is he who has decided to take a look at me.

When we are seated and drinks set in front of us, he leans in, beckoning me closer.

"You'll never guess who I just saw over the other side of the room." Without waiting for me to answer, he breathes, in a gust of beer fumes, "William Fowler."

"Fowler? Really?" I concentrate on the tankard in front of me. Poor Fowler. I wonder if he noticed me come in with Douglas, having kept him waiting for more than half an hour. I can only hope he understands that, in our business, plans have to change at a moment's notice.

"Aye. What do you make of him?"

"Who, Fowler?" Douglas's question pulls my attention back; he is tilted forward eagerly, and his eyes are fixed sharply enough on mine. I shrug. "I barely know him. He seems like a quiet sort."

"Aye." Douglas nods, and takes a noisy draught. "That's the thing, though, isn't it? Keeps to himself, right enough." He taps the table with an ink-stained forefinger. "My lord Howard suspects someone is tampering with the correspondence. To Queen Mary, I mean."

"What makes him say that?" I am forced to lean nearer to him; between his Scots accent and my Italian one, and the general hubbub of talk in the tavern, the conversation is not easy to follow.

"He says there are things missing. Disappearing, you know. So he concludes someone has a hand in the packets that come from Sheffield Castle."

"What things?"

Douglas shakes his head. "Letters and packets that should have come to him from Mary. He didn't say any more than that. But naturally he's looking at Salisbury Court." He lets this fall casually, glancing away to the next table as he says it, but immediately my sinews stiffen.

"Howard has no reason to suspect anyone at the embassy," I say, trying to keep my voice level. Bitter experience has taught me that when you are accused of anything, regardless of whether you are innocent or guilty, it is almost impossible to deny the accusation without sounding as though you are protesting too hard. It was for this reason that I chose to run away from my monastery rather than stay and face an interrogation by the Father Inquisitor.

Douglas laughs aloud then, a big open-throated guffaw.

"Come now, Bruno, don't pretend to be simple. You're famed for defying the Holy Office. You're a defrocked monk, for Christ's sake! As far as Howard is concerned"—here he lowers his voice—"you're an enemy of the Catholic faith, not an ally. I'm not saying that's my view, I just think you should know what Howard feels. He's furious with Castelnau for allowing you into those meetings at the embassy."

"Well, I hate to disappoint him, but my first loyalty now is to whoever puts a roof over my head and bread in my hand."

"Aye, I'll drink to that," he says ruefully, raising his tankard.

"I know nothing of Mary's letters, save what I learn around the table with the rest of you." I look him in the eye as frankly as I know how. "Are you of the Catholic faith yourself?"

A smile curves one side of his mouth.

"Aye. I suppose you could say I've thrown my lot in with the Catholics. But I think of myself as a pragmatist. I know how to read the weather, my friend, and I don't need any stargazer or ancient prophecy to tell me Elizabeth's star is waning." He glances suddenly to each side, but no one appears to be paying attention to our conversation. "I know how to make my services indispensable to those on the way up, then I call in the favours when they're established. Henry Howard has no illusions about my piety, but he knows I wouldn't jeopardise my own position. Queen Mary vouches for me and that's good enough for him. No—it's Fowler I've wondered about. He has a lot of friends at court. Castelnau thinks that works in our favour, but I have my doubts."

"I heard you already made yourself indispensable to Queen Mary once," I say, partly to change the subject. Too much speculation on

Fowler's trustworthiness among the regulars at Salisbury Court could lead to unwelcome attention.

He grins broadly then, slapping his hand on the table and calling across the mêlée for more drink.

"You refer to the unfortunate and untimely death of Queen Mary's late second husband, Lord Darnley, at Kirk o' Field, I take it?" He drains his tankard and then regards its empty interior with mild disappointment for a moment. "It is said they found my shoes at the scene the next morning. Is that proof, I ask you? Could have been anyone's shoes—it's not as if I'd embroidered my bloody name on them. But you try telling that to the Privy Council of Scotland. Of course, there was my erstwhile servant who testified against me on the scaffold, but a man will say anything with a rope around his neck, won't he? Ah, thank you, my lovely." He turns the beam of his smile upon the serving girl, who sets down two new pots of beer before us. I have barely touched my first, but he appears not to have noticed.

"What was the story about the pie?" I ask.

Another great bark of laughter.

"Ah, the pie. I'll tell you. Mary Stuart, when she learned her husband was dead, invited a host of ladies to attend a ball at her court and they danced the night long, all of them *stark naked*," he whispers, pausing for effect. "And you know what they did next? Cut off all their hair."

"Their hair?" I repeat, frowning.

"On their quims, you numpty." He gestures to his crotch, in case I am in any doubt. "Then they put the hair inside a fruit pie and fed it to the gentlemen guests, for their amusement. That's the woman they want to put on the throne." He pushes his fringe out of his eyes and nods, apparently delighted with his tale.

"Is that true?"

He lays a hand flat over his heart.

"True as I'm sitting here, son."

"Gentlemen. I bid you good afternoon. I thought it was you."

I start and look up at the unexpected voice; Fowler has appeared through the shifting huddle of damp coats to stand by our table. He smiles uncertainly.

"Oh, hello. Here's a coincidence. Master Fowler—good day to you." Douglas raises his cup and smiles, politely enough, but it doesn't touch his eyes. Fowler inclines his head with no obvious warmth. There seems to be some unacknowledged mistrust or animosity between the two Scots, giving the lie to the idea that compatriots far from home will always be drawn to each other. I attempt to convey apology to Fowler with my eyes, but with professional sangfroid he just murmurs, "Bruno," with a nod, before turning his attention back to Douglas.

"What brings you here, Archie?" he asks.

"Oh, business," Douglas says airily. "Always business, Fowler, you know me. And our friend Bruno has been browsing for books in St. Paul's churchyard. Speaking of which"—he reaches inside his doublet and pulls out a sheet of paper, folded and crumpled—"did either of you see this?" He smooths it out on the table before him; another pamphlet, this time with a woodcut of the astrological sign of Saturn. Douglas pushes it across to me and I open it, with Fowler reading over my shoulder. Inside is a crude drawing of a dead woman, a sword protruding from her breast. The gist of the text is that the second murder of a royal maid must be read as a clear sign from God that Elizabeth's reign, and with it what the anonymous writer calls the "Protestant experiment," is nearing its end. The killings, with their markings that so clearly refer to the Great Conjunction and its apocalyptic prophecies, are signs of God's wrath toward the heretic queen, who in her rebellion against God looks for guidance to magicians and servants of the Devil like John Dee rather than to the wisdom of the pope. If it is not the Devil himself carrying out these murders by his own hand, then it is certainly someone moved and guided by satanic powers.

"Put that away," Fowler hisses, casting his eyes quickly around the room before squatting by the table. "It's illegal even to possess printed prophecies now—you don't know who's watching."

"These murders are doing our job for us," Douglas remarks, ignoring him and prodding the pamphlet, his voice barely raised above a whisper. "Undermine the people's confidence in her, that's all it needs. You'll find there'll be very little resistance to a change of sovereign once they have proof that the Almighty's set his face against her."

"You underestimate the stubbornness of the English," Fowler mutters, shaking his head. "And their dislike for Rome. Remember the discontent in the streets when it was thought the queen might marry a Catholic Frenchman, the pamphlets that appeared then?"

"Oh, aye?" Douglas straightens, as if squaring up for a fight, then remembers where he is and drops his voice again. "And you underestimate the number of simple folk in the kingdom, William. There's far more of them love Rome than you think. People miss the reassurances of the old faith. They miss their wooden saints and pilgrimages and the comfort of confession, penance, and absolution." He points a finger in Fowler's face. "They knew where they were with the old faith, and simple people like certainty. You set foot in any of the wee towns and villages around the country—no one's read bloody Erasmus or Tyndale. They go to church where they're told because they can't afford the fines, but in their hearts they've never stopped believing the miracle of the Mass. Even the churchmen. And if they hear news that the Devil is cutting a swathe through the court because their sovereign flirts with sorcery, they'll be glad of the chance for a new one, believe me. There's enough simple folk to fuel an uprising when the day comes, if they're encouraged in the right way."

He sounds as enthused about this prospect as if he had planned it himself, and he is right that these murders at court, if the news spreads in the right way, can only be useful to the conspirators if there is to be an invasion of Catholic forces. But once again I am brought back to the same question: If the murders are part of the Catholic plot, why dress them up so obviously to look like a Catholic plot? What is to be gained by such an elaborate double bluff?

"I wonder if this murderer knows he is helping our cause," I say tentatively, still looking down at the pamphlet. The news must have travelled with wings for a pamphlet to have been written and printed less than a day after the murder. But again, there were enough servants at Whitehall who witnessed the events of the previous night to make this possible, and plenty of people who were sufficiently opposed to Elizabeth to risk their lives by printing such material.

"Of course not." Douglas glances around. "This is just some lunatic who hates women. But I'm saying we can turn it to our advantage."

"A lunatic inside the court, it seems," Fowler adds, folding his hands together. "Everyone was gathered there last night for the concert."

Douglas shrugs.

"No better time to break in, then, when all eyes are turned elsewhere," he sniffs. "Anyway—that's not my concern. It's in our interest to ensure *this* kind of thing"—he waves the pamphlet—"finds as wide an audience as possible. Spread the fear. Undo her popularity among her subjects first." He levers himself out of his seat, pulls his cloak around his shoulders and, almost as an afterthought, empties his second tankard of beer, slamming it down on the table. "Which reminds me—I have matters to attend to. A pleasure, gentlemen. Until some other evening, no doubt." He replaces his shapeless wool cap, touches the peak of it with a mock bow, and is absorbed into the crowd.

"I take it you're paying for his, then?" says the serving girl, appearing at my elbow with her hand out impatiently for coins. Only then do I realise that Douglas, having invited me for a drink, has left without paying, an outcome I probably should have foreseen.

Fowler smiles ruefully as I count out money for the beer.

"You are not yet familiar with the ways of our friend Douglas, I see."

The girl turns the coins over in her palm and looks at me suspiciously, clearly wondering if I might have tried to deceive her with some dubious foreign currency. Satisfied, she gestures toward the tankards. I look at Fowler, who holds up a hand to decline.

"Thank you, no. This place is giving me an aching head. The sky is clearing a little, I think. We could walk."

"I'm not sure Douglas counts himself much of a friend of yours," I say, as we squeeze through to the door. Fowler is right; the sky is still streaked with threatening grey and the wind chivvies leaves along the gutters, but the rain has abated for the moment. The cobbles are slippery with horseshit and sodden straw, and I step carefully to avoid the foul brown stream running down the gutters at the edge of the street.

"No, I don't suppose he does." He pulls up his collar and we fall into step in the direction of St. Paul's churchyard; among the crowds, there is hardly a better place to pass unobserved, though I keep one hand tightly around my purse. "I know too much about Douglas, that's the problem. When a man flees to another country to reinvent himself, the last thing he wants is to find someone from home, who could spill the whole of his history at any moment. Imagine if someone who remembered you from Italy showed up at Salisbury Court." He smiles, but I recall Marie de Castelnau's sly allusion to the dead man in Rome, and wrap my arms tight around my chest to suppress a shiver.

"In any case, we had best be on our guard," I say, as we slip through the gates into the shadow of the great cathedral, whose walls rise two hundred feet above us, its broken spire poking like the stump of a finger into the sodden sky. "They suspect someone of tampering with the correspondence." As we saunter by the booksellers' stalls, their trestles pulled in out of the earlier rain, I tell him of what passed in Phelippes's workshop, the missing ring, and the conspirators' growing concern over their communications with Mary. I am struck, in the retelling, by the realisation that Henry Howard did not confide in Douglas about what he believed had been stolen; clearly there are secrets within secrets fermenting behind the closed doors of Salisbury Court. Phelippes's offhand joke about betrothal floats back into my mind with sudden significance, so that I stop dead for a moment. If Howard is conducting his own private correspondence with Mary Stuart, could it be that he aspires to finish what his brother started? It would be a momentous gamble; if these invasion plans stand even a chance of succeeding, then any man who marries

Mary could expect to become king of England when she is crowned. Could he be courting her with his private coded letters? Such an aspiration would not be beyond Henry Howard.

"Bruno?" Fowler has stopped too and is looking at me with concern. I decide to keep this line of speculation to myself.

"So Howard thinks it is me, it seems, and Douglas wants to believe it is you," I say, as we round the apse at the east end of the building and find ourselves at the back of a crowd gathered at the small outdoor pulpit that marks St. Paul's Cross. Buffeted by the wind, the people huddle stoically, craning forward to catch the words of the preacher before they are snatched away into the air. I can barely see the man in his domed pepper-pot stand over the hats of the crowd, but from the fragments of his sermon that reach us, it seems he is preaching against divination, fortune-telling, and, yes, ancient prophecies. He is shouting something about King Saul and the Witch of Endor, his words whipped away by the wind. I presume the sermon has been officially commissioned; aptly, since the churchyard is the prime market for illegal pamphleteers, peddling hand-bills like the one Douglas just showed us, slipping through the crowd among the men who sell you prohibited holy relics from inside their coats.

"What of your nervous friend Dumas, the clerk?" Fowler asks. "Has anyone pointed the finger at him?"

"Not yet. He has kept his head down."

"Good. Then at the moment, their suspicions are only born of mal-ice. We may hope to shrug that off easily enough. What matters is that no one should think to look in Dumas's direction. If anyone questions him, we are finished."

"Quite right," I say, with feeling. Dumas would fall apart at the first accusation; at all costs, he must remain below their line of sight. Then I recall the figure I thought I saw slipping behind the church on Leadenhall Street when Dumas and I left Phelippes's house, and the coincidence of Douglas's sudden appearance at the very place where I was meeting

Fowler, and again a sense of unease prickles at the back of my skull. It is impossible to know who to trust.

"What of this new murder, then?" Fowler whispers, as we tuck ourselves into the fringes of the preacher's audience. "It must have happened right under our noses. Was that why you were called out of the room?"

In a low voice I tell him all that happened the previous night at Whitehall, including my previous dealings with Abigail, the murder of Cecily Ashe, and my suspicions that the murder of both maids is bound up with the plots brewing at Salisbury Court. When I have finished, he gives a brief whistle, shaking his head, his eyes still fixed on the pulpit.

"Sweet Jesus," he murmurs. "Bruno, this plot is bigger than we imagined. You think they do mean to kill Elizabeth? I had thought the Duke of Guise wanted to take her prisoner, if this invasion succeeds, to try her publicly for heresy, make an example of her."

"Perhaps they feel it would be more likely to succeed if the country has no sovereign to rally behind," I whisper back. "It would leave England in disarray, entirely vulnerable. As a prisoner, she would inspire loyalty, the way Mary does now. Dead, she can do nothing."

"The people would cry out for a strong monarch then." Fowler squints into the wind. "My God. So you think one of our friends at Salisbury Court is the killer?"

"Behind the killings, at any rate, if not holding the knife himself. I don't see how it can be otherwise. Cecily Ashe was given the ring Mary Stuart sent Howard; it must be as a token of her part in the conspiracy. And the man who gave it to her has to be the man who killed her, probably out of fear that she would betray the plot."

"And the same man murdered the girl Abigail?"

"Abigail must have been killed because she was Cecily's friend, because the killer thought she knew something of his identity or the plot. But it's my belief that she was killed because he saw her talking to me that day." I lower my eyes, take a deep breath. "And the one person who was there and saw us was Philip Howard. He fits Abigail's description too."

Fowler frowns.

"But the Earl of Arundel was at the concert last night, I saw him. They all were, now I think of it."

"He would have only needed a few minutes before it started to find the kitchen boy and make sure she had the message to meet at the kitchen dock. Then his accomplice would have known where to find her."

"All we really know about this man," Fowler says slowly, rubbing his forefinger across his chin, "is that he is an eminent figure and young women regard him as handsome. But you might reasonably say that of any of the men who gather around the ambassador's table. Courcelles, for instance, is of noble birth and considered very attractive to women, I believe. Madame de Castelnau certainly thinks so, you only have to see the way she looks at him. And he'd have ample opportunity to spirit away a package sent to the embassy."

"By that token, so would Throckmorton, and he is a good-looking boy, I suppose."

"But Throckmorton is never here for long enough to plot a regicide or two murders, he is always on the road to Sheffield. He could have taken the ring from the package, I suppose, but I don't believe he has the ingenuity. He's one of those who will happily obey as long as someone tells him where to go, but he does not invent plots for himself." He shakes his head. "That only leaves Douglas and Henry Howard."

"Douglas?" Incredulous, I forget to keep my voice down; a woman in front turns and pins us with a stern look, her finger to her lips, though how she can hope to hear the sermon over the crowd's cheerful jeering and whooping, I have no idea. I consider Douglas for a moment, and wonder if Fowler might have a point. He may have that weathered look and greying hair, but he has a strong jaw and a mischievous gleam in his eye that goes with a sense of being at ease in his skin; it's possible that a green girl might describe him as handsome. And even Henry Howard, with his pointed beard and pointed eyebrows, has a certain commanding presence that might be attractive. In any event, it seems clear that such a subjective description will not be much help to us.

"Who is to say what women find handsome anyway?" Fowler whispers, as if reading my thoughts. "There may even be those who say so of you, Bruno," he adds, with a sideways smile.

"*Grazie*. You're not so bad yourself," I reply with a grin, though my mind flits unavoidably to Marie and her attempt to seduce me. Whatever her motive, I do not think it was my face.

"Listen to us—debating who is handsome and who is not, like a pair of old priests at the Southwark boy houses." Fowler gives a grim laugh. "We'll need better evidence if we are to find this man. But where to start?"

"I know where I mean to look," I say, through my teeth.

The preacher at St. Paul's Cross appears to have reached some kind of conclusion; a smattering of applause erupts, as if for a travelling show, then the crowd around us begins to break and dissipate, like ink in water, of its own accord, drifting in twos and threes away from the pulpit. Clouds are scudding up across the sky from the river, and the wind has lifted; the air smells of rain again. Fowler pulls his cap down and we turn away, back toward the south side of the cathedral and its bustle of merchants, peddlers, and cutpurses. There is a strange kind of relief that comes from talking, even if no solution is found. I feel lighter for confiding in Fowler, and curse myself again for my stubborn desire to find Cecily's killer without help. Perhaps if I had been less preoccupied with my own success, Abigail might not have paid the price. The weight of remorse sits like stones in my stomach when I picture her body laid out on the cold floor of that storeroom, and the determination to see this man brought to justice burns with a new intensity.

"Listen, Bruno," Fowler says gently, laying a hand on my arm. "You want it to be one or other of the Howards. I don't blame you—there is much to dislike about them. But we need to keep our eyes and our minds open. There is something strange about this. If poisoning the queen was always a part of this Guise invasion plan, then why has no one mentioned it at any of Castelnau's secret meetings? And if the murder of Cecily Ashe was to protect their mission, why do they all behave as if it is news to them?"

These are questions that touch on my own misgivings. I crane my head skyward; the light is fading and I must make haste if I am to find a boatman who will take me as far as Mortlake this evening.

"One or more of them is dissembling," I offer. "But the group that gathers at Salisbury Court has been brought together by Castelnau. It does not necessarily follow that all its members will like or trust one another. Perhaps those who are plotting Elizabeth's death are brewing their own plans and merely using the French invasion as a vehicle." Again, I consider the possibility that Henry Howard may be courting Mary Stuart with his eye on the throne, but I say nothing to Fowler. Perhaps it is childish, but I want the credit for suggesting this theory to Walsingham.

"True," he says thoughtfully, squinting up at the sky. "I have the impression Henry Howard would rather be directing this enterprise himself, but the authorities are rather too interested in his family's business for him to take full control without being discovered. He needs the cover of the French embassy to communicate with Mary's supporters in Paris, but you can see he doesn't like Castelnau involving the likes of you and me."

"What's your relationship with Howard?" I ask, curious.

Fowler shrugs.

"He tolerates me because Castelnau has persuaded him I have useful connections at the Scottish court and, as you know, any intelligence about King James's inclinations with regard to his mother's claim is worth a great deal to the conspiracy. I do not think Howard mistrusts me as such, but he never seems at ease when I am there. I sense that he doubts the loyalty of anyone who does not share the ferocity of his own motives."

"Then he must doubt all of us," I reflect. "No one else has such a personal vendetta against Elizabeth and her government as he."

He nods, with feeling.

"What's more, as you saw the other night, he has lost patience with Castelnau's insistence on diplomatic relations. With Spanish money committed, Howard may be tempted to despatch with the French embassy altogether and pursue his course with Mendoza." He presses his lips together. "In the Spanish ambassador he has found an ally as ruthless as he."

I picture Howard huddled with Mendoza at the Whitehall concert, their dark heads bent close together, the contempt they both turned on me when I approached. I am about to reply when a movement catches my eye; I turn, but the churchyard is a constant tide of bodies, eddying around one another, many with their hoods pulled up or hats pulled down against the wind. It is impossible to tell one from another, and yet for a moment there, I sensed that prickling sensation of being watched. Is he here? Or am I growing as skittish as Léon Dumas?

"Well, we may learn more tomorrow night at Arundel House," Fowler mutters, as we pass the magnificent doors of the south transept and turn our steps away from the churchyard. "The Earl of Arundel is giving a supper party for the usual guests."

"I fear I am not at the top of the Howards' invitation list."

"I'm sure the ambassador can find a way to include you. Speak to him. And let us keep our wits sharp. Which way are you walking?"

I pause, glancing toward the mouth of a narrow alley that leads between timber-framed buildings to a lane that will take me down to Paul's Wharf. "To the river. I will see you soon, no doubt."

"Are you heading west? Perhaps we could take a boat together?"

"Mortlake. But I think it will be quicker if I go alone. I mean no offence," I add, quickly, "only I am late already. And we should be careful." I glance over my shoulder.

"Mortlake? You are not going to see Walsingham?" He drops his voice again.

"No. An acquaintance who lives nearby."

He gives me a long look through narrowed eyes, as if he suspects this is not the whole truth. Perhaps he imagines I am attempting to pass him by, taking some juicy scrap of information to Walsingham that I have kept back from him. Such doubts has our master bred into us; instinctively we sift every man's words for double meanings, even those we are supposed to trust.

"Godspeed, then—you have a long journey." Fowler hesitates, as if he has grown suddenly shy. "I am glad we spoke of these matters, Bruno. Ours can be a lonely task at times, do you not feel? It is my hope that we can combine our wits and energies to find Walsingham the proof he needs to bring all these intriguers to justice. Well. You know where I am if ever you need a confidant, or some company." Then he claps me on the back, pulls up his collar, and walks away briskly toward Carter Lane, while I turn toward the river as fat raindrops begin to spit emphatically from the darkening sky.

Chapter *11*

Out on the river, I find a moment of calm to unravel my tangled thoughts for the first time in what seems like days. The rain clouds have hastened the dusk, and I sit in the prow of the little wherry wrapped in my cloak and a curtain of thin drizzle, lulled by the rhythm of the oars, looking out at the lights winking from windows of the riverside buildings. I have been fortunate in finding one of the few boatmen who doesn't feel the need to fill the journey with idle chatter; his lantern sways on its hook as he pulls against the tide and in the absence of voices, my thoughts return again to Marie's behaviour this morning. My refusing her, with the best of intentions, has left me at her mercy, should she decide to make trouble for me. Perhaps it would have been easier to offer her some encouragement, allow her some small measure of what she wanted. In that moment of closeness, when she had leaned in to kiss me, my body had remembered what it was to be touched. It was some months since I had kissed a woman, and that had not ended well. What I had told Marie was true—my years in the Dominican order had at least taught me to master desire, to subdue the stubborn cravings of the body. But no amount of self-discipline can blot out loneliness from the heart. The life I have chosen—or had forced upon me, I am never sure which— offers little opportunity for intimacy of any kind. A writer, especially a writer in exile, must learn to be self-contained, to be content within his own mind, and for the most part I am so. But there is always, somewhere inside, however muted, the dull ache of a longing that I sometimes fear will be a lifelong companion. If I were a different man, I might have had no qualms about Marie; a man like Douglas, I imagine, would not think twice about taking any woman who offered herself. But apart from my loyalty to Castelnau, there is a coldness in Marie that instinctively repels me, even while her obvious attractions draw me in. Inevitably, my thoughts drift back to Sophia Underhill, the last woman I had held in my arms, the one whose mind and beauty had pierced my careful defences only a few months ago. I wonder where she is now and whether she has found some happiness.

Usually when my thoughts tend along this path, I can rein them back by setting my mind to work through the ordered paces of my memory wheel. This evening the images all metamorphose into a picture of Marie's lips; as a remedy, it is not especially effective.

As a result, I arrive in Mortlake as soaked in melancholy as in drizzle. Dusk has fallen and along the riverbank the shapes of dwellings and trees grow indistinct, blurred by rain against a grey sky. I shiver, and feel suddenly very far from home. I must take hold of myself, I say sternly; my one firm purpose here is to find a killer, and self-pity is a distraction for weak minds.

At first there is no answer from Dee's house; I stand at the door for some minutes as the rain grows steadily harder, and a cold anxiety creeps up to my throat. Perhaps the whole household has been taken for questioning; perhaps Ned Kelley has returned and is keeping the door barred. I shade my brow with my hand and try to peer through one of the small casements to the side of the front door, but there is no light within. Just as I am contemplating looking for a window I can force or break to climb in, there is a creak and the door opens a crack to show the flame of a candle.

"Mistress Dee, it is I, Giordano Bruno, come to hear if there is news from court." I rush back to the porch, relieved. The face of a woman scowls at me from the darkness within. It is not Dee's wife. "I beg your pardon. Is your mistress at home?"

She turns away; I hear footsteps, voices in hushed conference, then the door is opened wider but no more graciously. Behind the sullen servant I catch sight of Jane Dee, who steps forward into the light as the door is closed behind me, the toddler Arthur hanging on to her skirts, his small oval face tilted warily up to me.

"Doctor Bruno." She smiles, but the strain shows around her eyes. The baby on her hip rubs its eyes with a small fist, knocking its linen cap awry; Jane expertly rights it with one hand, her expression tightening back to anxiety. She is about thirty years of age, not beautiful but with a kind, open face; Dee depends on her utterly and has joked that I must never think of marrying unless I can find another woman like Jane. I have the greatest respect for her; there are not many wives who would tolerate a house filled with the smell of boiling horse dung and the best of the household income going on manuscripts and astronomical instruments. Her hair is bound up untidily, with strands coming loose where the infant clutches at them, and she looks pale, older than her years. She raises her face to me and attempts another smile.

"Do you bring news about my husband?"

"No." I hold out my hands, a show of emptiness. "I came because I hoped you might have heard some."

She glances briefly at the maid, who still hovers by the door, something irritatingly furtive in her posture. Jane gestures to me with her head, shifts the baby to her other hip, and I follow her and Arthur along a passageway and into a chilly parlour, where a fire is dying in the hearth.

Jane pokes it and a feeble shower of sparks issues up the chimney; for a brief moment the logs gamely struggle back into life. She looks at me apologetically.

"Take off your wet cloak, Doctor Bruno, and stand here by our sad apology for a fire, if you will. They came for him late last night." She brushes her hair from her face and bounces the infant gently to soothe it. Arthur sits down cross-legged, close to his mother's feet, his eyes still fixed on me. "Five men in royal colours, said it was urgent. They bundled him out into a boat, hardly gave him a chance to fetch his cloak." Her mouth presses into a white line.

"Were they rough?" I lower my voice, glancing at the boy. Jane shakes her head tightly.

"No. But they were armed, if you can believe it. Why would she send armed men for my husband, Doctor Bruno, who has never done anyone a stroke of harm in his life?"

I hesitate.

"There was another murder at court. Earlier in the evening. You had not heard?"

Her eyes widen.

"I have not been out. I have had enough to do with the comings and goings here." Her face darkens. "A murder? But surely—? What has that to do with us?"

"When Doctor Dee went to see the queen the night before the murder," I begin, in the same low voice, "he described to her a vision of a red-haired woman violently killed. What he described was almost exactly what happened the following night to one of the queen's maids, who had red hair. Not surprisingly, your husband's apparent foreknowledge is a matter of interest to the Privy Council. These murders are regarded as a threat to the queen herself." I pause again, unsure how much I should divulge. Jane nods slowly, her lips still pressed tight. The baby grizzles; without looking, Jane inserts the knuckle of her little finger into its mouth, and it gnaws gratefully.

"So they believe he prophesied it by some devilry?" Her scorn is somehow reassuring.

"I think they are more interested in whether he could have learned of it by more ordinary means."

She frowns.

"But of course it wasn't his vision," she says, and the bitterness is unmistakable.

"No. The vision was told to him by the cunning man Kelley."

"Who has not been seen these past four days," she finishes. "But naturally my husband won't tell the queen that. Won't want her to think he doesn't have the gift. Poor John." She laughs sadly. "He doesn't have it and he never will. It's not something you can get from books, however much time and money you spend fretting over them. My own grandmother had it, so I should know—she could divine with the sieve and the shears, and tell dreams. But if you ask me, that Ned Kelley has no such gift either. Kelley is many things—and it wouldn't surprise me if a murderer was one of them—but he doesn't see the future nor speak with any spirits." She nods a full stop and shifts the baby to her other hip.

"We are agreed on that," I say, with feeling. "But I would like to know where Ned Kelley had his prophecy from. It cannot be coincidence. And I fear your husband's loyalty to him is more than he deserves. If John knows anything, he will not divulge it to the queen's advisers, and I fear that will be to his own cost."

Jane sucks in her cheeks and glances down at the boy, who has nudged himself a few inches nearer to my feet.

"You never spoke truer there, Doctor Bruno. It has been a sore enough subject between us these past months. God in heaven only knows how John has allowed himself to be duped by that man, I cannot account for it. Sleeping under our roof, taking the bread from our table, from the mouths of my babes—" She breaks off, realising how her voice has risen; there is a sudden colour in her cheeks. Little Arthur cranes his head up with interest.

"Who took the bread from the table?"

"Hush, my dove." Jane stops, motions to me to be silent. We all stand still for a moment, straining to hear, then she tiptoes across the room and flings open the parlour door. The scrabble of hurried footsteps can be heard retreating up the passage. Jane jerks her head toward the sound and casts me a meaningful look, as if to say, You see what I have to put up with?

"You said there had been comings and goings here," I say, as she closes the door again. "What did you mean?"

"John's library. You know how he welcomes all comers, says his collection should be for any scholar who knows how to read them with due care? All except his magic books, naturally," she adds, dropping her voice. "Well, this very morning, while John is still detained at court, a man turned up on the doorstep, well before nine, saying he had travelled a long road to consult a particular manuscript, and that he had letters from my husband granting him permission." The baby grizzles and she offers it her knuckle again. It seems less willing to be fobbed off this time, and turns its face away, its cheeks an angry red. "I didn't like to let a stranger in with John away and me here on my own with the babies, but neither did I like to turn the fellow away, for John never did, though you can imagine the sorts that fetch up at our door."

I think of Kelley, and nod. "So you let him in?"

"I didn't know what else to do." She looks up, pained.

"Did he show you these letters?"

"He showed me some papers—you have to understand I don't read well myself, Doctor Bruno, but I know my own husband's signature. So I let him into the outer library, but I told him I wouldn't know where to begin with this book he wanted. I said he'd have to look it out for himself, if he could, but as you know, John keeps no rhyme nor reason to his bookshelves."

"Did he tell you the title of this book?"

She frowns.

"I'm sure he must have, but I don't know if I recall. It was Latin." She shakes her head. "In any case, it seems he didn't find it, because I kept an eye on him. Dropped in every few minutes, you know. I'm not a fool— some of those books are worth a year's wages and I wouldn't put it past anyone to try and steal them, no matter how much of a fine gentleman they dress. John has noticed a few missing, though I put that down to our houseguest." Her lips draw tight with dislike.

"He was a gentleman, then, this visitor?" I ask, suspicion pricking. "Well dressed? What did he look like?"

"Oh, tall. He wore a hat with a great feather which he didn't take off even indoors—I thought that ill-mannered, I remember. Just shows you can have all the fine cloth you like and it won't improve your manners. He had a pointed beard, dark, cut like this in a triangle." She indicates with her free hand, taking it from the baby's mouth; it complains loudly.

"A young man, was he?"

She considers.

"Younger than John. Older than you, I'd guess. Forties, maybe."

My heart seems to contract; it sounds unmistakably like Henry Howard. No doubt there are other men who would fit such a description, but who else would take the opportunity to rifle through Dee's library, knowing he was detained? And if it had been Howard, what was he hoping to find?

"So you observed him in the library?" I make sure my voice betrays no alarm; the poor woman has enough to be anxious about. "Did you see what he read? Did he try to take anything?"

"I don't think so. But it was strange. He combed those shelves like the hounds of hell were at his heels, almost in a frenzy. And when he thought I wasn't looking I saw him trying the door to John's inner rooms, you know, where he keeps his secret books. Thank God, John had locked it up and taken the key with him. Tapping on the panelling, too, this fellow was, as if he were looking for some secret hiding place. He even stuck his hand up the chimney breast—I didn't see him do it, but when he came to leave he had soot on his sleeve." She half laughs at the man's audacity.

I happen to know, as she must, that Dee keeps certain papers in a box hidden in a recess inside the chimney breast in his own office. Whoever this man was, he clearly had a good idea of what he hoped to find, and it must have been something he suspected Dee would keep away from prying eyes.

"How long did he stay? Did he give the impression that he found what he wanted?"

"So many questions, Doctor Bruno!" Jane tries to make her voice light, but I catch the fear in it as she jiggles the baby more urgently on her hip. "He stayed until it was past dinnertime, though he didn't seem to notice. He took down one or two books and glanced inside them, I didn't see what, but that was more for show. I started to think maybe he'd come on purpose, knowing John was away, thinking he'd have free run of the place. But who could have known about that, except the queen and her people?" Her voice has risen; she looks at me as if for reassurance. "Do you know who he was? You suspect something, I can tell by your face."

"I think you should not allow any stranger in while your husband is detained," I say. "Especially not this man, if he shows up again. And I will see if someone can be sent to keep an eye on you while John is at court— it is not right that you should be left alone with the children."

"Oh, I am not alone," she says drily. "Not while I have that slattern for company."

I glance around, guessing she means the sullen maid who opened the door. I wonder that she doesn't get a different servant, since she appears to resent this one so much. Perhaps this one is all they can afford, which might explain the resentment.

"Might I look in Ned Kelley's room?" I ask. "There may be something there that will offer us a clue as to how he invents his visions, and that might be enough to clear John of any suspicion."

"Of course." She shows me to the door, hands me a candle, and points up the main staircase. "The room over the stairs. Go on in and root around all you will, with my blessing. And don't mind *her*," she adds, darkly.

Dee's house is old and crooked, the wood of the stairs and banisters dark and smoothed to a sheen by generations of hands and feet. The treads groan like living things weary with age as I climb, and from the corner of my eye I glimpse shadows at my back as the watery pool of light moves with me. Though I know there is no one in the house except Jane and her children, save for the maid, still I find I am tensed against any sudden surprises, half expecting someone to leap at me from a passage or doorway, as if Kelley might have been squirrelled away in some spidery corner all this time.

The door at the top of the stairs is not locked. It opens onto a generously proportioned room with two casement windows that must overlook the front of the house, toward the river path. Now, against the black sky, they offer only a distorted reflection of my outline with the flickering candle flame. As I turn with it slowly, the room reveals itself as a jumble of objects in the frail light: a wooden truckle bed, the sheets twisted and thrown back, as if Kelley had only moments ago leaped out of them; two chests, one locked, one spilling with clothes or linen; a table with a few stumps of candle; beside them, a pair of dice and a locket. Their shadows climb up and down the walls as the candle passes them.

I push the door to behind me and fit my candle to one of the holders from the table; setting it on the floor beside me, I kneel by the closed trunk. Its lock is old and crusted with rust, and when I insert the tip of my little bone-handled knife, it takes only a few moments of easing and jiggling before the mechanism clicks open and I can prise up the lid. My pulse jumps as my fingers brush against paper; sheaves of letters, perhaps, and, farther down, the calfskin cover of a book. I bring out a bundle of manuscript pages and examine them in the thin circle of light; what I see makes me gasp.

Here are pages of notes and drawings in a rough hand: astrological and alchemical symbols and Cabalistic codes; lists of names in a curious unknown language; geometrical designs that match the table of practice Dee uses in his séances, whose components he said were told to him by spirits via Kelley; there are star charts, and sketches of the images of the decans according to the descriptions given in the writings of Hermes; scraps of magic lore culled from books forbidden throughout Europe, and three recent illegally printed pamphlets, the kind from St. Paul's churchyard, decrying the murder of Cecily Ashe as a sign of the end of days, complete with gruesome illustrations. Most disturbing of all, at the bottom I find a series of hand-drawn images, more explicit than those in the pamphlets. They depict a young woman with flowing hair, her arms flung wide and holding in one hand a book, in the other a key, her bodice torn and her breasts thrust out, with a dagger plunged into her heart, some showing the sign of Saturn marked on her chest, others the sign of Jupiter. These pictures vary in their particulars—in one, she is standing in what appears to be a raging river, in another, she is laid out naked on something that looks like an altar, but the ravaged expression on her face remains the same. I find my insides knotted by a peculiar nausea; there is an unmissable relish in these drawings, the expression of a young man's violent fantasy. You sense that the artist has taken pleasure in illustrating not only the woman's naked body but her suffering—and Kelley, though his writing is uncultured, is not without talent when it comes to drawing; the pictures are vivid. Assuming that these are his own work, the drafts that would enable him to pronounce his visions to Dee in convincing detail.

Slowly, I fold away the drawings of the young woman and tuck them inside my doublet. These look like nothing so much as preparatory sketches for the murder of Abigail Morley, and if they can be proved to be by Kelley's hand, they may be enough to convict him, or certainly to bring him to trial. Even contemplating the possibility that Kelley could have acted out his lascivious fantasies on Abigail makes a fist of anger bunch beneath my ribs and my breath quicken; I close my eyes for a moment, forcing myself to remain calm, to act in the light of reason. But Kelley, if he was a killer, would not have the means to get near the queen's maids, unless he were the hired hand for someone better connected.

Reaching back into the chest, I lift out the two books hidden beneath the papers. The first is a bound edition of *The Book of Soyga*, copied by hand, a book of names and invocations believed to contain the original language spoken between God and Adam, a language of great power uncorrupted by man's fall. I had seen a manuscript of this book in Paris and was sceptical about its authenticity, though I knew Dee owned one and still kept faith that it contained some hidden power. When I had asked to see his copy some while ago, he had told me that it was missing. Apparently his household scryer was light-fingered as well as treacherous.

The second book takes me by surprise, for it is my own: *On the Shadows of Ideas*, the book I published in Paris last year. Turning its leaves slowly, I find Kelley has underscored the passages in which I describe the images of the decans. What Dee has taken as the scryer's divine revelations from the Egyptian gods of time is nothing more than the ability to parrot back the words he has read—words of mine, no less. When Dee is returned, I will show him this copy with its folded-back pages and notes as proof that Kelley has no more of a seer's gift than the housemaid. Perhaps this will finally persuade him that he has been deceived.

I tuck the book inside my doublet with the papers, as furious with myself as with Dee this time; I should have guessed at this the moment I first heard Kelley describing his "vision" of the decan of Aries in the showing stone. Kelley knows nothing of the writings of Hermes, any more than he speaks with spirits; his revelations are pure invention, cobbled together from scraps he has pilfered from Dee's own library.

"Those are my husband's books."

I start, almost knocking over the candle; lost in these thoughts, among the shadows, I have not heard her footsteps and her sharp voice out of the darkness sends my heart almost leaping into my throat. I turn and the Dees' housemaid is standing in the doorway, holding a small candle.

"Christ, woman, you scared the life out of me." So startled am I that it takes me a moment to register what she has said. "Your *husband*?"

"You have no right to look in those papers. Those books are nothing to do with you."

"You are wrong there, madam—this one has my name on the title page." I hold it up for her.

She only narrows her eyes and continues to glare at me, as if this might eventually wear me down.

"So Ned Kelley is your husband. Where is he, then?"

She shrugs. In the candlelight I see that she is older than I first thought, perhaps nearer forty than thirty, with the last vestiges of something that is not quite beauty but a bolder appeal.

"Away. But he will be back, and then you will be sorry."

"Will I? Tell me, when he returns, does he plan to continue cozening the man who feeds and houses him? What does he get out of this charade? Has someone put him up to it?"

"I don't know what you're talking about," she says, looking away. "I don't pry into my husband's business."

"Just as well, since his business is murdering young girls."

I have her there; she turns to me, mouth open, eyes wide just for a moment, though she pulls herself together quickly enough.

"My husband never harmed anyone, you wicked slanderer—he has his gifts from God. But who would expect anything else from a filthy foreigner. Your eyes are black as a Moor's," she adds, for good measure.

"Perhaps my great-grandmother had herself a Moor, who knows?" I say, picking up the candle and rising to my feet. These English have so little imagination. I notice her looking at the book tucked under my arm.

"Where is your husband?" I ask again. "I know some people who are very keen to talk to him about his *gifts*." I bring the candle up close to her face, but she is a tall woman, as tall as me, and sturdy; she will not be cowed. She merely looks me in the eye, insolent as a Southwark whore.

"You can't walk away with that book, you have no right—" she begins again. My patience breaks.

"Don't talk to me about rights, mistress," I say, grasping her by the upper arm and pushing her back against the doorframe, "when you and your husband feed off the generosity of a good-hearted man and his wife for your own profit. Tell me where he is." I shake her brusquely and she bares her teeth at me. I am gratified to see that she looks at least a little scared before the brazen face returns.

"Generosity, you call it? Credulity, I say. I don't know where Ned is, but I'll wager somewhere a sorcerer like you nor a fool like John Dee won't find him."

"Lucky, then, that the queen's men are better trained for searching. Especially when a man is wanted for murder."

This punctures her bluster somewhat; she tries to wrest her arm away from me but as we are both holding candles her movements are limited.

"Ned hasn't murdered anyone. That was never—"

"Never what?" I rattle her arm harder. "Never part of the deal? Maybe your husband and his paymaster have changed the deal. Well, no doubt they will get that out of him one way or another."

"Why are you hurting Johanna?" says a small voice from somewhere around my knees. I glance down and there at the top of the stairs is Arthur Dee, his earnest eyes upturned and swivelling from me to Kelley's wife. Reluctantly, I let go of her arm. She flashes me a look of triumph and makes a great fuss of smoothing down her skirts, rubbing the flesh of her arm ostentatiously as if she has been ravished. She should be so lucky, I think, with a last glance of disgust.

"Is everything all right up there, Doctor Bruno?" Jane Dee calls from the foot of the stairs.

"All is well." I bend down to the boy. "No one is hurt, Arthur. Shall we go down to your mother?"

He nods and reaches his little hand up to mine; we leave Johanna Kelley, if that is her name, replacing the items in her husband's chest with a face like storm clouds.

"I don't like her," Arthur confides as we descend, in a whisper guaranteed to carry through the house. "She struck me once and my mama called her a witch." I try to stifle a laugh.

"I imagine the slattern was not best pleased to find you going through her husband's things," Jane says, when I rejoin her in the parlour. She looks as if the thought pleases her. "If husband he is."

"She is short on civility, that much is certain."

Jane nods. "You wouldn't think she was once in service to one of the noble families. I'll bet she minded her manners a lot better then. Or maybe she didn't," she adds, significantly.

I stop, midway through pulling on my cloak.

"Really? Which family?"

"She used to be a maid in the Earl of Arundel's household, up at Arundel House on the Strand. Won't say why she left, but it's my guess she was thrown out in disgrace. There's a child, you know, a little daughter no more than Arthur's age, she leaves it with some widow out Hammersmith way. And it's not by Kelley," she says, with a nod full of meaning. "She only took up with him a year ago, from what I gather. It's my bet they're not even properly married."

"You think she got the child at Arundel House?" I stare at her, disbelieving. Another Howard connection. Could it be—I am still gaping at Jane as this new idea forms—that Kelley is working for Henry Howard or his nephew, perhaps introduced to them by his wife? My mind rushes back to my curious conversation with Howard after the concert and his oblique threat; he had specifically mentioned Dee conjuring spirits in a showing stone. Was that a lucky hit, or did he have such a detail from a firsthand report?

"I wouldn't be surprised. But she must have money from somewhere to keep it. Her clothes are good cloth too—better quality than you'd expect of her sort. Anyway, since my husband in his folly gives lodging to her so-called husband, I insisted she give us some labour in return. Don't know why I bothered. This babe'd be more use with the housework." She bounces the baby gently on her shoulder and it hiccups. "And she is stealing food from my kitchen, I'm sure of it."

I raise an eyebrow at this; perhaps, then, Ned Kelley has not run so far away after all. I do not say so to Jane; she would hardly sleep easier in Dee's absence to think of the scryer hiding in the garden.

"Do not open the door to anyone until your husband returns," I tell her at the door, patting my chest where I have hidden away Kelley's papers. "I have matter here that will vindicate John the moment it is seen by the right people, and make Ned Kelley a wanted man."

Jane snorts. "As if he wasn't that already. Don't worry about us, Doctor Bruno, we shall manage fine as we always do. It was a kindness of you to visit," she adds, with an effortful smile, pushing her hair back from her face. I catch the tiredness in her voice again. "It's dreadfully wet out there still—are you sure you must leave? You are welcome to stay if you'd rather."

I sense that she would be glad of the company, or at least the reassurance of a man's presence, but now that I have Kelley's papers, I feel I must get them to Walsingham as quickly as possible.

"I had better go. But if Kelley shows his face, or if *she*"—I nod toward the stairs—"gives any sign she knows where he is, send word to Walsingham at Barn Elms immediately. In the meantime, I will see if he can spare a man to keep an eye on the house until John returns."

"Thank you, Bruno. Here, you cannot go into the night without a lantern. Johanna!" she calls into the darkness of the stairwell. "Fetch a lantern for our guest!"

There is no response. Tutting heavily, Jane stomps away with the baby toward the back of the house. Arthur and I are left looking solemnly at each other in the hallway.

"You be sure and take good care of your mother until your father comes home," I say, bending to ruffle his soft hair. He has his mother's looks, but Dee's penetrating eyes.

The boy nods. Jane returns and hands me a lantern with a new candle.

"Return it when you can," she says. "Now go with God."

My cloak is no less damp than when I arrived, in spite of its stint by the fire, and the evening air when I step outside whips through it with a chill that pierces straight to my bones, though the rain has eased for the moment. I shiver, but make a cheerful farewell to Jane. Little Arthur remains on the doorstep waving until I am at their gate. I glance at the upper storey and am almost sure I see a figure standing at the window, silently watching, wrapped in shadow.

It is less than a mile across the spur of land that juts out, making the river loop around Barnes and Mortlake; clouds scud across the face of the moon, driven by the wind, but there is only one main road, little more than a track, that runs along by the water then cuts across. Even in the dark, it would be hard to lose my way between here and Barn Elms. Despite Walsingham's instructions to send my intelligence through Fowler, the papers I have pressing against my chest are so urgent that it would be folly to delay; I can deliver them into his hands or Sidney's and be on my way without anyone knowing I was there. The lantern held before me, its light fractured in the standing water collected in ruts on the path, I pull the cloak tighter and close the gate behind me.

I feel rather than hear him, almost the moment I step out onto the muddy lane that will lead me to the river path. He—or perhaps she—is no more than a movement out beyond the edge of sight, a stirring of the air, the soft plash of water disturbed in a puddle. I turn, slowly at first, widening the circle of the lantern's poor light as I hold my arm out, but whoever he is remains hidden. Yet I know I am not alone, and part of me curses my own recklessness as I quicken my step. What was I thinking, coming so far from the city at night, and especially since there can be no doubt that someone has been following me? But with every step I feel Kelley's papers scratch against my chest and try to ignore the rush of fear in my blood; we are one step away from discovering who killed Cecily Ashe and Abigail Morley, and I am now convinced that Ned Kelley is the evidence that ties the Howards to the murder plot. I am all but running now, fired by the thought that this might soon be resolved, but he keeps pace with me in the dark, whoever he is; I catch echoes of my own footfalls in the mud but I no longer turn. Instead I keep my eyes to my course, one hand on my knife, the lantern held in front with the other, telling myself that every step brings me nearer to Barn Elms and Walsingham. Once my pursuer sees where I am headed, surely he will drop back out of sight. Walsingham keeps armed guards at his gate; he is obliged to, given how many Catholics would like to send him early to his judgement day.

The damp breath of the night; the solid outlines of the wet trees to either side; the presence that I sense without seeing, who becomes a kind of companion in the silence. I almost begin to believe that he does not mean me harm, that he is only keeping an eye on me, tracing my path. An owl's shrill cry rips the air overhead and I gasp aloud, startled, my foot briefly stumbling in a rut; from somewhere behind or to the side I think I hear a matching intake of breath. I have run perhaps half a mile when there is a distinct human sound; not quite a word, more of a grunt, the noise of some physical effort. I wheel around, holding up the light, drawing the knife from my belt with my right hand, and as I do, I hear his movement, there comes a faint whistling in the air and some blind instinct tells me to duck; the hand with the knife flies up to my face, just before the blow catches me and knocks me to the ground.

Through the blurring shadows I can just make out the form of him as he looms over me, before the world turns to black.

Chapter 12

When the light reappears the first thing I see against the swimming shapes is his outline, still bent over me; I struggle and hear a strangled cry escape my lips, but he has me pinned down somehow and a blade of pain is slowly sawing across my forehead from the blackness where my left eye should be. My waterlogged limbs protest and give up. I seem to be sinking into the ground but I can't move to stop myself.

"He's awake." The voice seems to come from the man peering into my face; it sounds familiar but I can't open one eye and the other won't focus. I wonder in passing if he means to kill me. With some effort, I find I can stretch out my palms flat on either side of me and the ground feels smooth and cool. Then something cold and wet lands on my face and I splutter back into awareness, battling to push myself up on one elbow.

"Christ alive, Bruno, you gave us the fright of our lives there," says the man, and as the crusted blood is sponged from my good eye, he solidifies into the shape of Philip Sidney. I can't comprehend how he came to be here, so I decide not to try, though I can't deny I have not been so glad to see him since he rescued me in Oxford.

"I think you take delight in making me act as your nursemaid," he says cheerfully, as if he is reliving the same memory. "So what in God's name happened to you this time? Do you remember any of it?"

"I don't even know where I am."

"Don't try and get up." He stands, stretches his long arms over his head, but the wet cloth keeps up its gentle momentum over my face. Someone else is here, I realise, but I can't turn my head to see. "You're at Barn Elms," Sidney continues, from the other side of the room. "You were damned lucky, Bruno, if the truth be known—one of the servants found you there on the road from Mortlake on his way back from a day off. He didn't know it was you, of course, but when they brought you back to the house, Frances recognised you. Didn't you, my dear?"

"Yes, Philip," says a soft, girlish voice from above me. So Sidney's wife is my nurse. When she lifts the cloth away to rinse it, I catch a glimpse from the corner of my eye; the water she wrings out is bright crimson.

"You'd probably have died otherwise, I'd wager," Sidney says, with his usual matter-of-factness. "Did you see him? He hit you with something heavy, but it looks worse than it is, I think. Did he rob you?"

"*Merda!*" I struggle to sit up, pushing the sheet back and almost sending the bowl of water flying; white light splinters behind my eyes but I grip the bedpost until it passes. I have been undressed while I was blacked out, and I am wearing only my shirt and underhose. "The papers! Where are they?"

"What papers? Steady on, you'll start the bleeding up again."

"Who took my doublet off me?" I force myself unsteadily to my feet, but the room tips and blurs again.

"I did, you bloody fool," Sidney says. "I've been sitting with you since they brought you in. Walsingham was here a good part of the time too. We thought you might not make it." He pauses for a moment. "Still," he says, his voice brusque again, lest I think him sentimental, "should have known it takes more than a bash on the head to do for you. But you had nothing with you. No papers, no purse. Not a thing. And your doublet and shirt were undone."

I sink back onto the bed, pressing my palm gingerly to my temple.

"I was bringing them to Walsingham. He must have taken them."

"Who?"

I glance at Frances and shake my head minutely and then wince. Even this movement makes it feel as if my brains have come loose in my skull.

"My dear, go and fetch your father, if he's free, would you? Tell him Bruno's speaking again. Most obliged." He points imperiously to the door. His wife bobs meekly and leaves with her bowl of bloodied water. The door swings softly shut behind her. "She's terribly obedient, you know," Sidney observes with mild interest, as if we were discussing a horse.

The room is furnished with a large comfortable bed hung with white linen curtains, now bespattered with my blood. A tapestry of a hunt scene sways softly on one wall and candles have been lit in sconces on every side to bathe the walls in a cheerful glow, but to my bruised eyes the light appears to swim, like sun through water, and the objects around me sway and waver. I reach up to touch my swollen brow and my legs begin to tremble as I realise, as if taking a second blow, the full weight of what happened. That my pursuer left me alive may have been an over-sight on his part; perhaps he thought he had killed me, but it now seems beyond doubt that he is willing to do so.

I have barely begun recounting the events at Dee's to Sidney when the door crashes to the wall and Walsingham strides into the room, with such a degree of urgency that for a moment I think he means to sweep me into his arms. He stops just short of this, but I can focus enough to see the concern etched in his face, and feel flattered.

"Make no mistake, Bruno, I shall find the man who did this to you," he says, showing me his balled fist before enclosing it softly in his left hand.

"Or woman," I say, and my tongue feels thick in my mouth. Walsingham raises an eyebrow.

"Really? Explain." He nods to Sidney to shut the chamber door.

So I tell him about Jane Dee's mysterious visitor; about Ned Kelley's chest, the books and the drawings; I explain about Johanna Kelley's connection to the Howard family, and how my assailant must have known that I had taken something incriminating from Dee's house. Walsingham frowns and bites his lip when I tell him the papers have been taken; when I have finished, he draws a hand down the length of his face and nods.

"If this wife of Kelley's is stealing food for him, he can't be far from the place," says Sidney, folding his arms. "Either he was watching the house or she followed you herself, knowing what you'd found, is my guess."

"I wish I could have seen those pictures," Walsingham says, with a grimace. "First this business with Mary's ring, then Kelley and this Johanna woman—is Henry Howard really at the heart of all this?"

"Can't we find some pretext to arrest him?" Sidney demands. "Perhaps he will be willing to answer questions if he is afraid."

"And what pretext do you suggest?" Walsingham turns on him; it is rare to hear the principal secretary raise his voice, and I curse myself again for having lost the papers that might have helped him bring this to a close. "We have nothing to charge him with—nothing! And if the queen moves against the Howards without sound evidence, the rest of the Catholic nobles will close ranks against her, which is the last thing we want if there are envoys trying to stir them to armed rebellion. God's blood!" He pounds his left palm with his fist, pacing the room like a bear on a chain while Sidney and I watch, tense. "I cannot go on protecting John Dee from his own folly!" he bursts out eventually, as if to himself. "Conjuring spirits! He lays himself open to being abused. And if it turns out he has been harbouring a murderer in his house—" He rubs his beard, takes a deep breath, and turns back to me, attempting to impose his customary self-control. "Bruno, what do you make of this so far?"

My head still feels as if it is stuffed with wool; his voice seems to come from somewhere distant, but I gather my ragged thoughts as best I can.

"Find Ned Kelley," is the best I can manage. "Henry Howard, Philip Howard, the dead girls—somehow they are all connected, but only Kelley can link them."

Walsingham looks at me expectantly, but my vision blurs again and I have to lean back against the bedpost.

"I will send men after Kelley," he says, eyeing me carefully. "And someone to watch over Jane Dee—make sure she receives no more unwelcome visitors. John has said little, except to swear neither he nor Kelley has any connection with the murders. Now I understand why he doesn't want to talk about the nature of his relationship with Kelley— but I must question him again about these drawings. And I'll have this Johanna taken in and questioned while we are about it. Meanwhile you, Bruno, have had a lucky escape, and I blame myself for allowing you to pursue this alone. You need to rest."

"I need to get back to the embassy," I say, alarmed and standing up too fast. "I am under enough suspicion there already—I can't disappear for a night. What time is it?"

"Nine," Sidney says. "You'd better stay here, old friend—you'll frighten the life out of the ambassador looking like that."

"Bruno's right," Walsingham says, stepping closer to examine my wound in the candlelight. "His position at Salisbury Court is crucial to us now. I'll have someone take you back by river. Tell them you were set upon for being foreign."

"Wouldn't be the first time." I touch my eye again. My head feels enormous. With some effort, I stand and wait for the seasickness to pass.

"Bruno." Walsingham places his hand on my shoulder, fatherly. "You acted with your customary blend of courage and recklessness tonight. Those papers would have been like gold, and I am as distressed as you over their loss. But I would have been more distressed if we had lost you for their sake. From now on, I want you to confine your investigations to

Salisbury Court. Keep yourself armed, and if you must make longer journeys or deliver messages, go accompanied. Make use of Fowler—you are there to work together. No gadding about the countryside in the dark trying to do it all alone—*capisce?*"

I nod, painfully.

"Good." He smiles, but it only lasts an instant. "I will arrange a boat, and come with you as far as Whitehall. See if I can persuade Dee to tell me any more." He strides to the door, purposeful again, then turns back to me. "Do you think there is any truth in it, Bruno? This pursuit of commerce with spirits? It was said in Paris that you knew something of these arts."

Squinting, I try to focus until I can see his features sharply. His expression is neutral, curious. "It is forbidden by every statute of the church," I say eventually. "Theirs and yours."

"I *know* it is forbidden, Bruno—I write the laws," he says, impatient. "This is why no one will admit to it, while the country crawls with these so-called scryers and cunning men, duping the poor and ignorant. And sometimes the educated," he adds, with a wry curl of the lip. "But do you believe some men could truly have this gift, to speak with spirits—angels or demons, or whatever you want to call them? Have you ever known such a thing, or are such beliefs only remnants from our benighted past?" He searches my face, his hand still resting on the door. I can feel Sidney's eyes on me too, expectant; I know he was drawn to such knowledge when he was a student of Dee's, but since he assumed his position at court he has kept a politic distance. My poor bruised brain feels ill equipped for the subtleties such an answer requires.

"If, as I believe," I say, weighing my words, "this universe is infinite, then it follows that it must contain more than we can have so far managed to comprehend or write down. The sacred scriptures, not just of our own religion but of others besides, all speak of beings who stand between us and the divinity. Through the ages, right across the world, men have claimed to speak with them, and so to know the future. I can't judge the truth of their claims, but I am certain of this—if there are men who have such a gift, Ned Kelley is not one of them. And neither is John Dee."

"Are you?" Walsingham asks.

I hear Sidney suck in a breath through his teeth.

"Not I, Your Honour." I do not add the word "yet," though it echoes in my head.

Walsingham considers me for a moment, then nods brusquely, and sweeps through the door, gesturing for us to follow. Sidney lays a hand on my arm.

"Careful, Bruno." He lowers his voice. "Whatever the truth about this Kelley and the murders, Dee will not come out of this business well. What he has been doing is as good as witchcraft, you know that. People burn for less. The queen won't let that happen, but she will have to distance herself from him, and you could be tainted by association."

"Then Howard will have achieved his aim," I say, gripping his sleeve. "Dee will be disgraced and cast out. We must find some evidence that will tie Howard to this beyond any doubt, or Dee will be destroyed."

"You are convinced Howard is behind the murders, then?"

"I just don't know. So much points to him, and yet there is so much that doesn't make sense." I pause, remembering Fowler's warning. "But I must guard against persuading myself that it's Howard just because I want it to be him." I raise my hand again to the wound at my temple. "God, I am a fool. If I hadn't lost those papers—"

"If this fellow had had a better aim, you'd be dead," Sidney reprimands. "Forget the papers. Get closer to Howard if you can. At some point he must show his hand."

"Or kill me first," I say, looking at the smear of blood on my fingertips.

Chapter *13*

At first I can't make sense of the sound; an insistent hammering that chips through the cocoon of sleep. I wake to a new burst of pain behind my eyes, though when I reach tentatively to my temple I can feel that the swelling has begun to subside. Fragments of last night drift across the surface of my mind, assembling themselves into a vague memory of Walsingham's boat dropping me at the end of Water Lane and one of his servants accompanying me as far as the garden door of Salisbury Court. I had hoped to drag myself up the stairs unnoticed, but Courcelles was coming down at the same time; I was almost gratified by how appalled he looked at the state of me. Despite my protests, he led me straight to Castelnau's office. The ambassador accepted my story of a bar fight with English thugs without question (all we foreigners have suffered some degree of abuse from the Londoners), and could not have been kinder, though I waved aside his fuming threats to involve the law or take it up with the lord mayor; all I wanted by then was to collapse into my own bed and close my eyes.

Now I have been woken prematurely—there is barely a glimmer of light through the shutters—by this increasingly urgent knocking. For a moment it falls silent, and I think whoever is there has gone away. "Bruno! Let me in, will you?" comes a whisper, before the tapping begins again, more frantic than before. Cursing under my breath, I struggle out of the bedclothes and unlatch the door to see Léon Dumas shivering in his nightshirt, his eyes bulging like an anxious fish.

"Quick," he says, glancing over his shoulder as he slips inside, though the passageway is empty. "God's blood, what happened to your head?"

"I was set upon in a tavern. Some London boys didn't like my accent."

"Really?" He looks even more frightened. "I have been spat upon for being French, but this is vicious. Were they drunk?"

"Very. It got out of hand. I should have ignored them, but I let them get under my skin. It was my own fault."

"What were you doing in such a place, Bruno? Were you alone?" He looks so concerned that I almost want to laugh and reassure him.

"Yes. I stopped for something to eat on my way back from the library at Mortlake. You know, where I go to work on my book."

"It looks terrible." He continues to wring his hands, frowning like a helpless mother. "Have you seen a physician? I think you ought."

I shake my head and immediately regret it.

"It will mend. Was there something you wanted?"

"Oh. That. Well, it's—" He squeezes his hands together several times, then walks to the window, turns to me with an agonised expression, bites the knuckle of his thumb, and walks back. "I need your help."

"Of course. What's the matter?" I ask, striving to sound more patient than I feel.

"There is something—" He rubs the back of his neck and looks away. "I don't know how to tell you this, but I must. It weighs too hard on my conscience." He stops again and fixes those enormous eyes on me as if imploring me to extract his confession without his having to speak it aloud. My heart freezes for a moment; he is going to tell me that he has buckled under the strain of his false front and given us up, told someone at the embassy about Walsingham and the letters. Our betrayal is known—it must be. With my head in such poor shape, I can barely think ahead to the consequences for the invasion plot, and for me.

"I was sworn to secrecy but I'm afraid I will be found out soon, and then it will go worse for me. But I said to myself—Bruno will know what to do."

"What has happened, Léon?" I ask, trying to sound reassuring, though I fear I already know the answer. He appears so tense that I wonder if he might burst into tears.

"It's the ring," he blurts, finally. "The missing one, that Mary Stuart sent to Henry Howard."

For a moment, I am nonplussed.

"What about it?"

"I know where it is."

To the best of my knowledge, Mary Stuart's ring is currently in Walsingham's care. Dumas cannot possibly know this. I stare at him as he chews his knuckles again.

"It was greed on my part, Bruno, I confess it. But not for myself—all the money I sent home to my parents. They are poor." His voice rises in his own defence.

"What money? What are you talking about?"

But at that moment a floorboard creaks outside the room; I hold up my hand and Dumas stiffens, fist to his mouth.

A soft tap at the door; another dawn visitor. I have never been so popular at Salisbury Court. I motion to Dumas to keep silent in the hope that this newcomer will think I am still asleep, but this response is apparently understood as an invitation; the door eases open and through the crack slips Marie de Castelnau, her hair unbound, dressed in a loose gown that drapes suggestively over the swell of her breasts and the curve of her hips. Her feet are bare. She widens her eyes at me and presses a finger to her smiling lips, as if we are mischievous children complicit in a game; she has not yet seen Dumas. With an implausible smile, I direct her with my eyes to where he stands, looking no less amazed than if he had witnessed the Second Coming. For the moment that it takes them to register the shock of each other's presence, I am seized by the urge to laugh, but it dries in my throat at the sight of Marie's face; she seems throttled with fury and the look of hatred she trains on Dumas threatens to burn right through him and set fire to the floorboards. Dumas, for his part, wears the expression of a man who has heated irons held inches from his privy parts. Even if my head were in better shape, I am not sure I could think of any words that would undo the implications of this moment.

Fortunately, it is Marie who gathers her thoughts first.

"You," she says, folding her arms across her chest and mustering some remnants of her usual poise. "Shouldn't you be on your way to help my husband? I'm sure he has plenty for you to do."

Dumas continues to stare at her, slack-mouthed, as if she were Lucifer himself.

"Well, go on, then," she says, jerking her head toward the door. "I'm writing a letter to a friend in Italy," she adds, airily, as Dumas manages to unstick his feet from the floor. "I wanted Bruno's help with the translation. And it must be sent early today, because the messenger leaves this morning. You see?" Her clipped tone aims to tidy away any potential misunderstanding. Dumas just goes on staring, stupefied, reaching the door as if in a daze. He flings me a last panicked look and backs out tentatively, as if he is unsure whether I will be safe alone with Marie. I jerk my head at him to go; better I catch up with him later.

She watches the door click shut with a small impatient shake of her head, and places her hands on her hips.

"Why was he here at this time?"

"Dumas? He gets homesick," I say, wishing my brain felt sharper. Dumas had been on the edge of a momentous confession, and Marie's appearance had robbed me of it; now it would be impossible for me to fix my thoughts on anything until I had shaken the rest from his stammering lips. "Sometimes he just wants someone to talk to." Effortfully, I tear my gaze from the door and back to her face. Her sharp eyes assess mine for a moment, then stray to the wound on my head.

"At this hour?"

"Well—*you* are here at this hour."

Her face softens into a sideways smile.

"Perhaps I get homesick too. And lonely. Don't you, Bruno?" She seems to glide toward me, feet silent. "In any case, I should think my reasons are not the same as that clerk's. What's his name?"

"Léon Dumas." Perhaps it should not surprise me that she doesn't know the names of her husband's staff, but it seems to confirm something about her, a lack of interest in anyone not immediately useful to her. "But you have a husband," I add, trying to keep my voice level. She stands now barely inches from me and raises a hand to my brow, her face concentrated in concern. I flinch even before she touches me, and she laughs.

"Don't worry, Bruno, I am not going to hurt you. Yes, I have a husband, and I can see you have never been married, if you think it a cure for loneliness."

I clench my jaw tight as she runs a finger lightly through my hair just above the wound.

"Courcelles said you had been attacked—I was worried about you," she whispers. I wonder briefly when Courcelles found the opportunity to speak to her between my late arrival and this dawn ambush, but my thoughts are scattered by the touch of her left hand on my breastbone, as her right forefinger continues to trace a line along my temple and down my face. Again, I concentrate on keeping very still, though my nerves are burning and my throat has constricted. Her gown has slipped a little and the naked slope of her shoulder is visible. "Bruno," she begins, not quite looking me in the eye, "what happened yesterday—"

"Please—forget it happened," I hear myself say, in a new strangled voice. "There is no need to say any more about it."

"But this is just the problem, Bruno," she whispers, her breath warm on my chin. "I can't forget. I can think of nothing else. I don't know how you have done this to me." Her body snakes closer to me in a fluid, instinctive movement, fitting herself to the angle of my hip. Enough. My head clears as if doused by cold water; I step back and grasp her gently by the shoulders.

"Please, Marie, I have done nothing knowingly, and you should not be here."

"That you have not done it knowingly makes it all the sweeter," she murmurs, and through her small shoulders I can feel the pent force as she strains to press herself against me, and the heat of her body. Again, I am racked by confusion; her desire seems real enough, but I cannot shake off the suspicion that this is a performance, a trap she means to spring. Even if it is not intentionally a trap, I think, it would soon become one. I must get her out of my room before I have any cause to reproach myself.

"Marie," I say gently, and she lifts her head to look me in the eye, her expression hesitant, her lips parted and breathless. *Dio mio*. It takes every atom of self-control I possess not to simply lean in and kiss that hot mouth. "This cannot be. In your heart you know it. It would only cause pain—not just to your husband but to you and to me. Please, I implore you—try not to think of me like this, as I try not to think of you."

She shakes her head, but at least she does take a token step back.

"More pain than I feel already, Bruno? To see you every day, to live in the same house and eat at the same table and know that you do not want me as I want you? If there is a greater pain than this, I do not know of it."

Because you have never known what it is to want something and not immediately have it in your possession, I think, looking at her. For her the attraction lies solely in my continuing refusal; I am not so vain as to imagine otherwise.

"In any case," she goes on, averting her eyes, "I do not know how to live with this any longer. I begin to think that if you will not love me, then we cannot go on existing under the same roof. One of us must return to Paris."

I run a hand through my hair and take a deep breath, trying to muster a diplomatic answer. Now she speaks of love; if she truly means this, it is nothing more than an illusion she has created in her own mind. She has persuaded herself that she loves me, because I have refused her. But then, perhaps what we call love is only ever self-delusion. And if she is acting a role, is this all part of a larger ruse to get me out of the way? If she decides one of us must return to Paris, she can only mean me, and as far as I can see, there is nothing for me in Paris except the gathering strength of the Duke of Guise and his Catholic faction, waiting to welcome the Inquisition as soon as they have the chance. I wonder who might have put her up to it; whoever has the most to gain from removing me just as the invasion plot gathers momentum. Henry Howard? The Duke of Guise himself? Whoever it is, they must not succeed.

"I would never willingly cause you pain," I begin. My head is aching. "But neither do I wish to insult your husband. I don't know what my choice is, Marie—you want me to become your lover, here, under his roof? Do you think that could ever be managed without the entire household knowing that he was being cuckolded by his houseguest? Already, we have Léon Dumas speculating on why you would be coming to my chamber in the dawn, so"—I gesture to her flimsy gown, feeling myself blush—"so informally attired. There are other servants who would be less discreet. It would be an impossible situation."

Immediately I know I have said the wrong thing; her face darkens, her eyes flare, and she darts a furious glance toward the door, as if Dumas might be standing outside taking notes.

"You think he would say something to my husband? Or to the other servants? What could he say? I gave him a good reason for my visit, what cause could he have for idle gossip?" Her voice is tight with anger. I rub my brow. Does she really believe that the household staff would not find it worth commenting on, that the mistress of the house should visit the lodger under cover of darkness, barely dressed, while her aging husband snores in his bed?

"Dumas will not say a word, he is a good man and would not want to spread rumours," I say, squeezing her arm reassuringly. "But you see how it would go for us if there were a story for the servants to tell? You would not want to dishonour your husband in his own house, I'm sure, whatever else you may feel about him."

She sighs. "Michel is a good man. And he adores me, so he is often persuaded to go against his own judgement for my sake. We need him if this invasion is to succeed. You are right, Bruno, I cannot afford to lose his support now."

This is not exactly the point I have made, but I say nothing.

"But he is sixty years old, Bruno. He cannot be a husband to me in the way I need. You understand me." Her voice grows silky; again, I feel the sharp heat in my groin, the dry throat. "I want only to know that you feel the same," she adds, her voice barely audible, her eyes reeling me in.

"I—you must know that I do," I say, thinking that this is the only politic answer. If I reject her outright, she will see that I am sent back to Paris; she has as good as said so. "But you are right. I do not want to see the invasion plans fail because we could not set aside our own selfish desires for a short while. Your husband's support is essential and he must not be distracted at this stage. It would let everyone down."

She regards me with genuine surprise, which turns slowly to cautious approval.

"You know, I had wondered about your commitment to the invasion plan, Bruno. I confess that there were those among us who have doubted the truth of your loyalty to the Catholic interest—Howard and the Earl of Arundel, Claude, even me at times. I am glad to hear you prove them wrong."

I incline my head in acknowledgement.

"And as for the other matter," she says with a secret smile, lowering her voice again, "if you mean it, then we will find a way. The Duke of Guise will have no use for my husband in any case, once Mary Stuart is queen of England and Guise has asserted power in Paris."

Her certainty about this future Catholic empire, and the ease with which she talks of disposing of her husband, chill me, even while my body remains in thrall to her proximity. I regard her with a fascinated revulsion, as she leans forward and kisses me softly, though chastely, on the mouth. I neither respond nor withdraw but remain perfectly impassive, at least outwardly, hoping that I have bought myself a little more time.

"Speak to your friend the clerk," she says imperiously, at the door. "Make sure he doesn't say a word."

"I will."

She gives me a last, knowing smile, pouts a kiss and pauses in the doorway for a moment, glancing to left and right along the corridor to make sure she is not seen. Then she is gone, leaving the door banging behind her and a trace of ambergris perfume in the air of my room. I wash my hands slowly over my face and sit on the bed to compose myself. Balancing my interests here with regard to Marie and her husband will demand greater feats of diplomacy from me than anything the ambassador himself could face at court. In the meantime, I must corner Dumas alone and draw from him the rest of his garbled confession about Mary Stuart's ring.

I HAVE NO opportunity during the rest of the morning; once I have broken my fast, I take a book and lurk as unobtrusively as I may in the passage that leads to Castelnau's office, in the hope that Dumas will emerge at some point so that I can accost him. But the ambassador must have him tethered to his desk, for there is no sign of him for the best part of two hours, though Courcelles passes me twice on his way to and from a consultation with the ambassador; both times he looks me up and down pointedly and asks if I have sufficient light to read, and if I would not be more comfortable in the gallery? The third time he appears, he offers to interrupt Castelnau and send me in; hurriedly, I assure him I have no wish to bother the ambassador, and slink away to my room, Courcelles watching me retreat with his usual shrewd-eyed face of suspicion.

No matter; I will catch Dumas's eye when the household gathers at midday for dinner. My head still aches badly but the wound is mending well. In the absence of anything useful to be done until I can lure him out from under the ambassador's nose, I attempt to work a little on some notes for my book, but my mind will not fix on anything besides Dumas's story and the line of Marie de Castelnau's collarbone. So it was Dumas who took the ring. He spoke of money and greed; did he then spy the ring when Mary's correspondence with Howard came through Castelnau's office, and take his opportunity to pocket it and sell it on? Then whoever bought it from him was either the person who gave it to Cecily Ashe, or one link nearer to that person. Inwardly, I curse Marie again for her ill-timed appearance and for her unwanted attentions, even as I almost smile at the irony; never, during my lonely years as a Dominican monk, did I imagine the day would come when I would curse a beautiful woman for believing herself in love with me. But I fear her visit this morning will make Dumas's life difficult too; I don't believe he is given to gossiping among the servants, and in any case, he is too fearful at the moment to dare risk offence. His face when Marie entered was a mask of pure terror; for her part, she was clearly furious to have been caught out in her illicit venture, and will find it hard to believe that Dumas can be trusted. There are more than enough stories of servants attempting to extort money from their masters over such matters. I can only hope she will not take it into her head to preempt anything he might say by trying to discredit him with Castelnau. I push my papers away and prop my elbows on the desk, leaning my head on my hands. Marie's unwanted interest in me has now made Dumas's position as well as my own vulnerable to her whims.

These thoughts, and multiple variations on them, keep me occupied until the hour of dinner, when I am surprised and a little alarmed to find Dumas not present. The meal is simple, boiled chickens with a stew of vegetables, as Castelnau and his wife are invited in the evening to the supper at Arundel House that Fowler had mentioned, hosted by the Earl of

Arundel and Henry Howard. There has been no mention yet of my being invited, though I am almost frantic to have myself included; what better means of studying Howard and his nephew at close quarters? But I can hardly beg the ambassador to take me in front of his wife and secretary. Courcelles's idle chatter at table makes clear that he will be in attendance this evening. He is almost the only person who makes conversation over dinner; the ambassador seems withdrawn and anxious, and only speaks to affirm some piece of business or answer one of his questions. Marie sits at her husband's right hand, but keeps her eyes pointedly fixed on me from under her lashes, so determinedly that I am obliged to keep my own on my plate so it doesn't look as if we are engaged in some kind of staring contest. Whenever I glance up and her gaze locks on to mine, she gives me a secret smile—one that does not escape Courcelles, I notice, whose glowering I also affect to ignore.

When the meal is over, Castelnau motions to me as the servants bring him a bowl of water and a linen towel.

"Join me in my office when you have washed your hands, will you, Bruno? I would speak with you. Alone," he adds, with a nod at Courcelles. His chair scrapes back with a brusque movement and he strides from the room without a word to his wife.

The outer door is closed by the time I reach his study, so I knock for the sake of formality, and turn the latch as I hear his barked "Entrez!" from within. The ambassador is already seated at his desk; he gestures for me to close the door and draw up a chair opposite him, as he purposefully lays down his quill and turns over the paper he has been writing. I note that Dumas's desk is unoccupied, his chair still pushed back as if he left in a hurry.

"Bruno." Castelnau folds his hands together on the desk. There is a weariness in the gesture that is mirrored in his face; he looks drawn and pale, bruised shadows heavy under his eyes. "I have been worrying about this attack on you last night."

"It was my own folly, really. A lesson learned." I touch my finger to

my brow and smile ruefully, in the hope that he will let the matter drop; I
would prefer not to be questioned too closely on the events of the previous day.

"But can you be sure this was not a personal attack?" he says, his
frown deepening. "I mean, aimed at us? At the embassy?"

I take a deep breath.

"They were strangers, my lord. A gaggle of London apprentices after
a day's drinking. They didn't know me—they saw a foreigner and a target
for abuse to amuse one another, that's all. I was called a Spanish whoreson," I add, to bolster the tale. "I should have let it pass, but instead I
insulted them back, and they set upon me."

He gives me a long look, then shakes his head sadly.

"This city," he says, as if it were responsible for the weight of all his
burdens. "My fears are getting the better of me, Bruno, I begin to see
enemies where there are none. I worry that these preparations for war
will be discovered. It makes me anxious when people inside this embassy
are attacked in the street for no good reason. Where did you say you
were?"

"Some tavern near Mortlake. You know, my lord, that I go there to
use the library of John Dee. He welcomes visiting scholars, and he has
many books that I would not find elsewhere."

"Yes, yes." He dismisses this with a wave of his hand. "His library is
renowned. But perhaps you should not go there for a while, Bruno. I have
enough to worry about without fearing for your safety."

"I will stay away from taverns, that much is certain," I say, rubbing
the side of my face. "But my lord, the English drink too much and they
hate foreigners—this is true of every corner of London. And every street
now buzzes with talk of prophecies and planets and the end of days—all
these fears are compounded and they turn on anyone who looks different, because they are afraid."

Castelnau smiles weakly.

"And these are the people Henry Howard and my wife think will rise up gladly and join with French and Spanish troops to overthrow their queen." He shakes his head again.

"You are losing faith in the invasion plan?"

"I never had faith in it, Bruno, you know this. And the Spanish involvement makes me deeply unquiet."

"You think they mean to use it to advance their own power?"

"Philip of Spain believes himself to be the chief defender of the Catholic faith in Europe. But he also believes he has a claim on the English throne, through his late wife, Elizabeth's half sister. You may be sure he's not committing money and men just to hand Mary Stuart the crown." He grimaces. "And if the Spanish support for Guise and his followers goes beyond this invasion . . ." His voice trails off.

"You mean he might fund a Guise coup in Paris." I finish the sentence for him. It is not a question. A silence unfolds as our thoughts follow the same path: the Duke of Guise could take the French throne with Spanish support, creating a formidable alliance of hard-line Catholics to rise up, united, against the weaker countries of Protestant Europe.

"Exactly. Listen," Castelnau says, after we have taken a moment to consider the implications of this, "I need you to do something for me."

I hold out my palms to either side.

"However I may be of service, my lord ambassador."

"Go to this supper tonight at Arundel House in my place, will you?"

"In your place? Are you ill, my lord?"

An almost silent sigh escapes him, making his shoulders tremble.

"Yes. I feel a shadow of myself these past days. I do not sleep anymore, Bruno. I don't remember the last time I slept an untroubled night. It must have been before my wife returned from Paris." He lets this fall with unmistakable bitterness.

"The rapid progress of this invasion plot has placed a great deal of strain on you, my lord," I say, with a degree of genuine sympathy. "You should rest."

"How can I rest, Bruno?" he cries, raising his hands. "The Duke of

Guise is a fanatic for the Catholic cause. He would slaughter every last Protestant in Europe with his bare hands if he had the time, singing hymns to God as he did it and believing he was carving himself a place in heaven. Henry Howard is of the same mind, except that he also wants revenge against the House of Tudor. And now, Mendoza and Philip of Spain have joined the party because they sniff the chance for Spain to take the spoils at minimal cost, with France so divided. And here am I in the middle of them all, trying to represent my king's interests, to argue for clemency and moderation, while my wife throws her lot in firmly with Guise." He shakes his head.

"I am not surprised you don't sleep, my lord."

He knits his fingers together again and leans forward, pointing his two forefingers straight at me.

"There is more. Henry Howard is concerned that his correspondence with Mary is being tampered with."

"What makes him say that?" Sweat prickles under my arms but I keep my face clear.

"Mary is supposed to have sent him something that he never received." He frowns in concentration as his fingers pluck ceaselessly at the strands of his quill. "Naturally, his suspicions fall on Salisbury Court."

"But those letters pass through many hands on their journey," I say.

"Precisely. Young Throckmorton's, for a start. But it troubles me greatly that Howard now looks at us with mistrust. His influence among the English Catholics cannot be underestimated, Bruno. It is he who will galvanise them, persuade them to risk their lives and estates to help this invasion succeed. If he decides to shut me out by sending his letters via Mendoza, we lose any influence we may have over this plot and any hope of arguing for a moderate response."

He pauses to take a deep breath, pinching the bridge of his nose between his finger and thumb as he lowers his eyes to the desk. He has plucked the quill almost bald. When he speaks again, he drops his voice until it is barely more than a whisper. "But we must not exclude the possibility that this invasion plot will fail. The Spanish may not come up with the promised funds or troops. The English Catholics may prove harder to rouse than Howard hopes. Or someone among their number may betray them. These things happen," he says, as if he thinks I am about to protest.

"And if the plot should be discovered, for any of those reasons . . ." I say, thinking aloud.

"Then King Henri must not be seen to have any association with it," Castelnau finishes the sentence for me. "Or any future alliance with Elizabeth would be untenable. But neither should he oppose it outright, just in case it should succeed, or he will lose any support from the French Catholics and Guise will topple him easily." He swears an oath, softly, under his breath. "In any case, Bruno, if there is to be a Catholic reconquest of England, it must be done with as little violence as can be managed, and for that reason you and I must hold on to the trust of those who are directing it for as long as we can." He places his hands flat on the desk and straightens up, with some effort. "I do not feel well enough to face Howard and Mendoza tonight. I will send my apologies, and you will go to Arundel House in my place. Scrutinise everything that is said and report it back to me. Put forward on my behalf the arguments in favour of a moderate, respectful approach, but be sure never to sound less than positive about the idea of putting Mary back on the throne. Howard will be left in no doubt as to my faith in you."

"The respectful way to invade a country and depose its sovereign— you may have to remind me how that goes."

Castelnau smiles, but his heart is not in it. He looks so drawn that I fear he may have taken some serious sickness.

"You know what I mean, Bruno. Just do your best to curb my wife's zeal for disembowelling Protestants when the glorious day comes." Another sigh racks his chest. He presses his hands to his mouth as if in prayer and for a long while he stares straight ahead in silence, apparently focused on nothing. I am not sure whether I am dismissed or not, and am about to clear my throat when he suddenly says, "Do you think my wife is making a cuckold of me, Bruno?"

"Your wife?" I repeat, like a fool, while my mind scrambles to catch up with the question.

"Marie. She has a lover, I am certain of it."

"What makes you say that?" I ask, carefully. He is shrewd enough to try and catch me off guard, if it is me he suspects. As so often, I harden my face into an absence of expression.

"I have suspected since she returned from Paris. Her moods—she has often seemed flighty, easily distracted. Younger, I suppose." He scratches at his beard. "Marie has not come willingly to my bed since Catherine was born, and I am not the kind of husband to demand her submission. But she is young still. I forget this sometimes. It was inevitable, I suppose."

"But—you have some evidence of her infidelity?" I ask.

"The other night—it was foolish of me," he begins, not meeting my eye. "I had another wakeful night and I felt—not unreasonably, I think—that I was entitled to some comfort from my own wife." He says all this to the backs of his hands. Castelnau has a strong sense of personal dignity; it must be painful to him to share a story which ends with his own humiliation. For a moment I wonder why he is telling me all this, if not to accuse me. "I don't usually abase myself to her in that way, but—as you say, the pressure . . ." He trails off sadly, his head still bowed.

"And so . . ." I prompt, after another silence.

"I went to her chamber. I knocked, tentatively. I don't think I even entertained thoughts of lying with her then—I only wanted some gentleness, a woman's touch. A soft hand on my brow. Not too much to ask of one's wife, is it, Bruno?"

I remember vividly the touch of that hand on my own brow only hours earlier; my skin prickles with the memory of it. I shake my head.

"Not at all, my lord."

He pauses again and takes a breath, as if steeling himself for the next part.

"She was with someone?"

"No. Well, possibly. She was not there, was the point. Not in her own bed."

"So where was she?"

"I don't know, Bruno," he says, his voice edged with impatience. "I didn't comb the house to find out whose bed she was in. It was enough that she was not in her own. Who knows if she was even in the house at all?"

"Perhaps she got up in the night to tend to her daughter, then?" I offer.

Castelnau gives me a sceptical look.

"You don't know my wife very well, do you, Bruno?" he says. "She has never been that kind of mother. Catherine has a nurse who sleeps in her chamber. Perhaps I should employ one for Marie as well."

"Do you suspect anyone?" I ask, trying to keep my voice light.

He shakes his head.

"Anyone and everyone now, Bruno. You have seen my wife. She conducts herself as if to give every man some hope of success—I do not blame her for this, it is just her manner. She is an accomplished flirt—I cannot pretend this was not what drew me to her in the first place. Henry Howard pays her court, of course, but I had thought enough of his probity to believe that he wanted only to secure her support in religious matters. I don't know, Bruno. I suspect everyone from the kitchen boy to the Earl of Arundel to my own clerk." He gestures toward Dumas's empty chair, then rests his elbows on the desk and presses his forehead into his hands. "Watch her for me tonight, will you? If I am not present, she may behave with less restraint. You may glimpse to whom she shows improper affection."

With difficulty, I drag my thoughts back from Marie's sinuous body pressing against me, her hand on my chest. Poor Castelnau. Whatever the temptation or the consequences, I determine that I will not be the one to confirm his suspicions.

"My lord ambassador, I will do as you wish. But if I might advise—

there is no profit in allowing yourself to be tormented by phantoms. While you have no proof against Marie, confine your worries to real problems."

He smiles thinly.

"You counsel well, Bruno." He reaches unexpectedly across the desk and places one of his large, black-furred hands over mine. "I don't mind telling you this now, but I did not want you in my house at first, though you were under the patronage of my sovereign. Supporting a known heretic, under my roof! I thought you had played upon Henri's weak nature to win his affection. But I quickly conceded my error. You are a good man, Bruno, and I am gladder than ever that you were sent to my house. There is no one in England I would confide in so readily." He gives my hand a squeeze.

"Thank you. I am honoured." But I must look away first. I am not the good man he believes me to be, and his confidences, that I so readily pass on to Walsingham, may well be his downfall. But at least, I tell myself, I am not the one having his wife. "Where is Léon?" I ask casually, nodding toward the empty desk.

"Léon? Oh, I sent him out this morning to catch Throckmorton before he left for Sheffield. I have written a personal letter to Queen Mary, refuting Howard's accusations and assuring her of my personal loyalty. I do not want Mary to believe this embassy is not fit to handle her secret correspondence. And I do not want to be sidelined in this enterprise in favour of Mendoza. We must avoid that at all costs." He sets his jaw and glances again at Dumas's chair. "I had expected Léon back by dinnertime. I hope he has not taken advantage of an unscheduled outing to stop off in a tavern. I don't want him ending up in your state."

"I don't think that is Léon's way," I say, mildly, though I feel a distinct pricking of unease. Where is Dumas? Where might he have gone in his overwrought mood? I dig my nails into the palm of my hand; if only Marie had not interrupted his confession.

"No, you are right," Castelnau says, pushing his chair back and crossing to the door. "There are plenty of clerks who would, mind. I am fortunate in Léon—he is a diligent boy, if a little prone to nerves. Well, Bruno," he says, holding the door open for me, "thank you for listening to an old man's troubles."

"My lord ambassador," I murmur, inclining my head.

He smiles, his face seeming to collapse inward under the weight of tiredness.

"Tonight, Bruno, you will be *my* ambassador. Don't let me down."

As the door closes behind me, Courcelles appears out of the shadows in the corridor a little too quickly.

Chapter *14*

Arundel House, London.
2nd October, Year of Our Lord 1583

Wind gusts sideways across the river, scuffing the brown water into serried rows of white peaks, buffeting the ambassador's private wherry and making its lantern swing wide arcs of orange light as dusk and the swollen clouds seem to press a lid down over the city of London.

The Earl of Arundel's town residence is one of these grand red-brick houses bristling with tall chimneys whose abundant lawns stretch down to the river's edge, where a high wall keeps them from the sight, if not the smell, of the Thames and its motley traffic. Though only a short distance upriver from Salisbury Court, the journey provides ample time for Courcelles to make clear his feelings about my role this evening.

"It's preposterous," he blurts, half rising out of his seat so that the boat pitches alarmingly to one side while we scull past the gardens of the Inner Temple, a drift of leaves blowing down over the wall to rest on the water's surface as the wind curls along the river and shakes the branches of the overhanging trees. Marie, beside him, lays a restraining hand on his arm. I took the precaution of allowing him to step into the boat after her, knowing he would take the seat at her side; I will have enough to tax my concentration this evening without fending off Marie's sly touches, her feet searching for mine under the table. Tonight, I intend to stay as far away from her as possible.

Courcelles swats her hand away impatiently. "Well, it is! If my lord ambassador is taken ill, I should rightly attend in his place."

"You are attending," I say, casting my eyes across to the south bank. "What is the problem?"

"The *problem*, Bruno—" Courcelles is obliged to pause as the wind blows his fine hair into his mouth. When he has extricated it, he perches on the edge of his seat and jabs a finger at me. "The problem is that *I* am his personal secretary. I know his business better than anyone at the embassy. I should be the one to represent his views to the party this evening. What are you, exactly?"

I deduce from his palpable indignation that Castelnau has taken him aside before we left and made clear that he is sending me to this parley in his stead. No wonder Courcelles feels usurped. I raise an eyebrow.

"No doubt you are about to remind me."

"I will tell you," he continues, the pointing finger trembling with pent fury. "You are a fugitive, living at my lord ambassador's expense because our weak sovereign has some misplaced affection for you, based on your shared disregard for the Holy Church! Not even a Frenchman!" he adds, shaking his head as if this single offence were beyond contemplation.

"Enough, Claude," Marie says, in a bored voice.

"Why?" Courcelles is too riled to back down. "Is he going to write to King Henri and report my words?"

"Who knows who Bruno writes to, in his secret little room," she says, batting her lashes at me with an insouciant smile.

"My lord ambassador asked me to voice one or two things on his behalf, that is all," I say, turning back to the far shore as if I were unconcerned either way. "I'm sure he would not object, Courcelles, if you were to offer your opinions as well."

"What does it matter, Claude?" Marie pulls her velvet cloak tighter around her shoulders. "Everyone will have a chance to speak, I'm sure."

"It is a question of protocol," Courcelles exclaims, his voice rising to a squeak. "If the ambassador is indisposed, I am his next in command, and I should be officially despatched to represent the interests of France in my lord ambassador's place. Not this—*impostor*."

"It's a supper party, Claude," she says, as if to a sulking child. "Not a council of war."

"Isn't it?" He rounds on her; immediately she slaps his arm, nods to the boatman, makes a frantic silencing motion with her lips. The boatman appears not to have heard, but you can never be too careful, is what Marie's gesture implies. You never know who might be an informer. I focus on the water eddying under the oars. Castelnau may think I am there as his eyes and voice, but I have a bigger plan. In my mind, everything converges on Arundel House and the Howard family: the invasion plot, the murders of Cecily Ashe and Abigail Morley, Ned Kelley, Mary Stuart, and—here I hardly dare to hope—the lost book of Hermes Trismegistus, the book stolen with violence from John Dee fourteen years ago. This unexpected chance to penetrate the Howards' domain must not be wasted; I must contrive a means of uncovering the secrets I am now convinced lie hidden somewhere behind the wall of mellow brick that looms up on our right as the boatman steers us in toward a narrow landing stage with a set of steps leading up to an archway and an iron gate. I have a plan half formed at the back of my mind; to work smoothly, it will require a generous handful of good fortune, the candle and tinderbox concealed in my pocket, and some impeccable playacting on my part.

A servant in Arundel livery attends us at the top of the water stairs, his head bowed as he holds open the gate. I stand back, allowing Courcelles his moment of gallantry in handing Marie out of the boat. She climbs two steps, hitching her skirts up away from the slime that covers the stones at low tide where the river licks them, then turns to me as if she has remembered something.

"Your friend the clerk, Bruno—what was his name again?"

"Dumas," I say, though I am sure she knows this. "What of him?"

"It appears he has run away. My husband sent him on an errand this morning and he has not returned. I wondered if you knew where he might have absconded?"

"I have seen nothing of Dumas"—since this morning, I am about to add, but check myself in front of Courcelles, who regards me as always with his chin tilted slightly upward, as if he is trying to avoid a bad smell—"today," I finish.

It is true, and has been a source of growing concern; several times this afternoon I have been to Dumas's little room under the eaves, only to find it locked. I have found excuses to disturb Castelnau in his office at intervals too, to find Dumas's desk still empty, until I was afraid my intrusions would look suspicious. By late afternoon, even the ambassador had grown troubled by his clerk's absence and talked about sending servants out to look for him; he feared Dumas might have fallen victim to some antiforeign assault, as I am supposed to have done, but my anxiety is more particular. He had been in a state of great agitation this morning, consumed by guilt and fear over his part in stealing Mary Stuart's ring; this much I knew. But what exactly did he fear? He had taken the ring for money, he said, but Dumas had never struck me as an opportunistic thief, so had someone paid him to steal it? The same person who then gave it to Cecily as a lover's gift? Denied by Marie the chance to confess and ask my advice, as he had wanted, what might Dumas have done in his state of desperation? Had he confessed his guilty secret to someone else? Had he named the person and, more importantly, did that person know? I feared for his safety, as I feared equally that a piece of the puzzle has disappeared with him.

"Perhaps he has run away," Courcelles says smoothly. "What he knows from my lord ambassador's letters might be worth a great deal of money to some people, and servants are always desperate for coins. You can never trust that sort." There is a provocative note in his voice that makes me look twice at him; could he know something about Dumas, or is he merely trying to rattle me? But I am never sure of the degree of complicity between him and Marie. How much might she have overheard outside my door this morning?

"Dumas is an honest man," I snap back, stepping precariously out of the boat and almost losing my balance on the wet stairs. "More honest than many I know." Courcelles makes no move to assist me. Marie shivers.

"Oh, stop bickering," she says, impatient. "He is only a clerk. He'll either turn up or he won't. Let's get out of this wind."

⚱

WE ARE LED by a steward through the great hall of Arundel House, past the rich linenfold panelling and the ornamental armour, into a narrow passageway with walls painted green and gold. At the far end I can see a heavy oak door, left ajar just far enough to glimpse inside a stack of shelves lined with handsomely bound books.

"What is that room?" I call to the steward, gesturing to the end of the corridor. He pauses and half turns, not pleased to have been detained.

"That is my lord of Arundel's private library," he says, almost without moving his lips. "Please, let us not delay. The earl and my lord Howard are expecting you." I do not miss the emphasis on "private," but my heart is hammering in my throat as I glance back at the door. Before we reach the end of this passageway, the steward knocks for the sake of formality on a door set into the panelling and proceeds with a bow into a warmly lit room, not broad but with a high decorated ceiling and two tall windows, reaching almost from the floor to the top of the panelled walls. Here a long table is set with silverware and wrought branching candlesticks, all reflecting skittering beads of light from the flames. I note, with relief, that the stone floor is thickly scattered with scented rushes. This is exactly as I had hoped. We are late, it seems; the party is already gathered and, as we enter, the gentlemen rise to greet us. Philip Howard moves from his seat, his hand outstretched. Beside him, a shaggy white dog, a Talbot hound by its appearance, stands warily, its nose thrust forward quivering, almost the height of its master's hip.

"Madame de Castelnau, Seigneur de Courcelles, *bienvenus*," he says, with a graceful bow. "And Master Bruno. *Benvenuto*."

"Be sure to give Bruno his proper title, Philip," Henry Howard remarks, sitting down again, having barely risen in the first place. "He is a doctor of theology, and he is most offended when people forget. Dear God, Bruno—what has happened to your head? I had heard of your reputation as a brawler, but I thought you had left that behind in Italy along with your religious vows."

I touch my fingertips to the wound at my temple—much improved since the day before, but still a raised welt of dried blood that must have looked alarming.

"You should see the other fellow," I say.

Philip smiles uncertainly. I sense that he feels a familial obligation to treat me with disdain but does not quite share his uncle's conviction in the matter. I incline my head politely in return. I am not surprised to find that it is Henry Howard and not the young earl who takes the head of the table. Though the Duchy of Norfolk was forfeit when Henry's brother the duke was caught in his plot to marry Mary Stuart, and the Arundel title now comes through Philip's mother, it is quite clear to any onlooker that Henry Howard is de facto head of the Howard clan, and that his nephew defers to him in status and judgement. And also in deed, I wonder, looking at Philip as he now gestures around the table. My spirits sink at the sight of Don Bernardino de Mendoza seated at Henry Howard's right hand; the Spanish ambassador merely grunts a brief acknowledgement of our party's arrival, before ripping into a hunk of bread with his teeth. Archibald Douglas is here, and Fowler too, and at the foot of the table, opposite Henry Howard, a pale young woman in a blue dress, her fair hair bound under a plain hood. She seems to sense my enquiring gaze, meets my eye for the space of a blink, then looks quickly away.

"Now we are all present, I think," Philip says, casting around the room. "I was most sorry to learn of my lord ambassador's illness, madame. I trust he is comfortable and will soon find his health improved."

Marie's eyes narrow.

"I thank you. I had not realised he had informed you already."

"Oh, yes," Philip folds his hands together and glances at me. "His clerk came this morning with a message, sending your husband's apologies and explaining that he had asked Doctor Bruno to attend in his stead."

"Weak constitution," Mendoza observes through his half-chewed bread, to no one in particular.

I smile graciously at Philip. That was smart of Castelnau, I think, to make my presence official in advance. But by "his clerk," does the earl mean Dumas? Did the ambassador send him with a message here as well as the delivery to Throckmorton? And if so, who was the last to see Dumas before he failed to return?

Philip Howard points me to a chair on the far side of the table, tucked against the wall, adjacent to the pale young woman, who glances up at me shyly as I take my seat and this time risks the faintest of smiles. The dog pads over and rests its muzzle in her lap; she strokes its head absently.

"I don't believe you are acquainted with my wife, Anne, Doctor Bruno?" Philip says.

"*Piacere di conoscerla*," I say, bowing low so that they will not see my face. A wife! It takes me a moment to absorb this information. A wife throws my speculations about the Howards and the murders off course; I had all but convinced myself that the Earl of Arundel must be the handsome, impressive young courtier who had wooed Cecily Ashe, and that he had done so at his uncle's behest to further the assassination plot. But if Philip Howard is married already, this cannot be. I take my seat, frowning.

"You all right there, Bruno?" Douglas, seated opposite me, grins affably, reaching for his glass. "You had a face on you for a moment there like a man trying to shit a turnip."

"A little stomach trouble," I say, composing my expression into a smile. "Probably hunger." I must give nothing away. What I must do is model myself on the man opposite.

"Aye, we're all bloody hungry waiting for you," Douglas says, waving his glass in the air for a refill. Immediately, a servant peels away from the far end of the room, where bottles and dishes are laid out on a wooden buffet, and stands at his elbow with a bottle of wine. When he has poured for Douglas, I hold my glass aloft too, by its delicate stem, and drink off the contents almost in one. Douglas watches as if impressed, and grins wider.

Supper passes uncomfortably, as Mendoza bombards Marie and Courcelles with questions about the factions at the French court, interrogating them closely about the degree of support for the Duke of Guise among the French nobles and the waning of King Henri's favour among the people. Frequently he hints at King Philip of Spain's growing admiration for the young Duke of Guise, while Marie simpers and bats her eyelashes at him as if the success of the conspiracy depends upon the power of her attractions. Courcelles seems torn between his anxiety to please the Spanish ambassador and his instinctive possessiveness over Marie's attentions. The silences in their conversation are broken by one or another of us attempting stilted small talk about court gossip or variations on the same compliments about the food. These, at least, are sincere; the Earl of Arundel clearly keeps a talented chef.

"Italian," whispers Anne Howard, when I mention as much to her. The countess is softly spoken, eats little, and prefers to toy with her food, studying it as closely as if it were a memory test, rather than look directly at me, but by diligent attention and gentle questioning I learn from her that she is of a fragile disposition, often sickly, and rarely attends court. Though this, she confides, leaning into me, is less because of her health than because Her Majesty, now that she stands on the brink of her autumn years, is jealous over the attentions of her courtiers and forbids wives from attending all but the occasional celebration. The only women the queen tolerates, Anne explains, are her own maids of honour, chosen for their modesty and virtuous reputations. She tells me this without a trace of irony, so I refrain from comment. Asked, in a lighthearted tone, whether she fears sending her handsome young husband into this fray, she responds with a pretty laugh, and tells me that she has known the earl since childhood, that she was in fact his foster sister and they were contracted in marriage at fourteen. She explains this as if their shared history is a self-evident guarantee against her husband straying; I would regard it as the opposite, but naturally I do not say so.

Dishes are carried in, richly scented and steaming: capons stuffed with fruit; venison; coneys in fragrant sauces, piled with thyme and rosemary; calf's-foot jellies and pies of larks and blackbirds with delicate latticed pastry. Servants duck and weave past one another balancing their trays, while the young man with the bottle silently and discreetly circles the table, making sure that no one's glass remains empty for too long. Mendoza eats and drinks with the same voracious appetite he brings to all his dealings, talking constantly through bulging mouthfuls as remnants of his supper gather in his beard. I note that Henry Howard barely touches his wine; neither does the earl, or his wife. Douglas and I, on the other hand, appear to be keeping the serving boy permanently busy, one or the other of us constantly lifting our empty glass to him with a subtle nod. Fowler drinks modestly and says little, though now and again he catches my eye with a neutral acknowledgement from the other end of the table; I smile briefly and return my attention to Anne Howard.

Given the company, I had expected a more direct approach to the matter of the invasion, but as more bottles are opened, dishes are cleared, and new courses brought, it seems that, for the moment, this is no more than a supper party. I wonder if the determined silence is because of Anne's presence, or the servants', and at what point, if at all, the table will turn to a council of war. Some sort of almond custard is placed in front of me. The small talk begins to wear thin.

"They arrested one of those pamphleteers today, did you see?" Douglas says, after a remark of Fowler's about the weather having turned is left hanging in the empty air.

"Which pamphleteers?" Courcelles asks.

"You must have seen them, Claude," Fowler says, folding his hands together. "Shoved into your hand for a penny in any marketplace or tavern. With their apocalyptic prophecies, forecasting the end of Elizabeth's reign, even her death. Saying these murders at court are signs of devilry, or the apocalypse. Treason now to write or publish them." He sucks air through his teeth and shakes his head. "I wouldn't like to be in that fellow's shoes."

"I don't frequent marketplaces or taverns," Courcelles says, with a flick of his hair. "So the gossip of apprentices and serving girls tends to pass me by."

"The common people in this country are fascinated by predictions of their imminent doom," Mendoza pronounces. "I have never seen anything like it. Even the servants in my own embassy begin to have their heads turned by these prophecies, if they venture out to the English taverns. It is to do with insecurity, I think. But all to our advantage, if the people believe the apocalypse is upon them."

Howard flashes him a warning look, then glances briefly at Anne. She appears to be occupied with the dog.

"This lad they caught was only the printer," Douglas continues. "The word is they found an illegal printing press in a private house up Finsbury way. They'll prick the poor bastard for the names of the authors before they hang him. That could go badly for people we know."

Henry Howard holds up a hand in warning, making a sharp motion for Douglas to be silent; the Scotsman looks puzzled, until Anne Howard raises her head and says, in a small voice, "Murders?"

Philip Howard and his uncle exchange glances.

"You remember, my dear, I mentioned the sad death of one of the queen's maids?" Philip says, his voice soothing. "There was speculation at court—there always is—that it might have been murder. You know how rumours can spread."

Douglas splutters into his glass, spraying wine across the table; Anne looks from him to her husband, frightened. It strikes me that she cannot know the first thing about how rumours spread, if she is not even aware of the murders at court, one of them committed barely half a mile from her own house. Does her husband keep her locked away here, I wonder, like a damsel in a courtly romance? While the company regards her awkwardly, I take advantage of the distraction to slip my hand under the table and pour away my glass of wine onto the floor under my chair. The rushes soak it up silently, as they have the previous two I have quietly tipped out at opportune moments when the company's attention was engaged elsewhere. To my knowledge, no one has so far noticed this, though I am pleased to note Henry Howard's slight frown of disapproval every time Douglas and I beckon the boy with his bottle. It is essential that Howard thinks I am at least as drunk as Douglas—though when I glance at the Scotsman, aside from his high colour he shows no ill effects from the quantity of wine he has already put away. The man must have the constitution of an ox.

"My wife suffers badly with nervous illness and other complaints," Philip Howard explains to the company in general, as if he had heard my unvoiced question. "She doesn't want to be troubled by the petty goings-on and intrigues of the court."

Anne continues to stroke the dog's ears, glancing at her husband with a mild expression. Marie's face darkens; I can well imagine what she would say to such a husband. At least she knows enough of diplomacy to keep her mouth closed. I watch Anne as she passes a piece of beef to the dog under the table; her skin is so white that under the candles it seems to give off its own light, like a snowy dawn. Perhaps a sickly wife need not be an impediment to a dashing young courtier; Philip Howard could easily engage a young woman's affections with the promise that his wife was of a fragile constitution and he might soon be on the lookout for a new one. And what kind of man refers to the gruesome murders of two young women as "petty goings-on"? My suspicions of the Howards recover their earlier force. Mendoza says nothing, which surprises me; he has been the first to voice his opinions on every other topic this evening.

When the dishes have finally been cleared away, Anne Howard

excuses herself, claiming tiredness, though to my mind there is something rehearsed about her departure. I wonder if she has any inkling of why her husband and his uncle have gathered this unlikely group around their dinner table; perhaps she knows but prefers to muffle herself in ignorance, as with the news from court. The servants place a new jug of wine on the table, within reach of me and Douglas, and refresh the candles. Henry Howard rises from his seat and takes one of the servants aside at the door; in the expectant hush that follows, Howard's low murmuring is overlaid with another sound, a curious wet rasping. I realise everyone has turned to look at me. When I glance down, I see that the dog is between my feet, licking at the floor with evident relish. I watch him, half apprehensive, half curious. I do not want him to give away my trick; on the other hand, I have not seen a dog with a taste for Rhenish before. Philip cranes his neck to see what I am looking at.

"Oh, that dog. My wife is always throwing him scraps at table," he remarks, dismissively. "The creature thinks it is some sort of prince in this house. For want of a child, you see." The contempt in his voice makes clear whose fault the lack of a child must be.

Henry Howard returns to his place; the last of the servants closes the door. There is a shift in the quality of the silence; in an instant we are alert, straighter, leaning forward expectantly. I blink hard, and shake my head; though I have not drunk anything like the quantity of wine they think I have, still I have been obliged to drink more than usual, and my thoughts are more sluggish than I would wish them.

"The developments with Queen Mary since we last convened have been greatly encouraging," Howard begins, drawing out a folded sheet of paper from inside his doublet. Douglas leans across and pours me another glass of wine before filling his own; Howard looks up, peevish, at the sound, but as a good host he refrains from comment.

"According to our friend Don Bernardino," he continues, indicating the Spanish ambassador, "the Duke of Guise has successfully persuaded King Philip of Spain to lend money and troops to our enterprise." Here he unfolds his paper and waves it as proof. While all eyes are on him, I quietly pour three-quarters of my wine onto the rushes, where the dog leaps upon it.

"My sovereign is pleased to be part of this great Catholic collaboration to restore England for the glory of God," Mendoza says, laying his great hairy hands flat on the table and allowing himself a modest smile, though there is a triumphant glint in his black eyes that makes me think Castelnau was right; it is not God's glory that interests the Spanish ambassador or his sovereign.

"We are now preparing in earnest, my friends." Howard pauses, allowing his smile to encompass the whole table. "I have here a list of English Catholic nobles whose lands comprise safe harbours. Our tireless colleague Master Throckmorton, together with one of Mendoza's envoys, is even now riding across country to visit every one of them and sound out their support. We will need as many landing places as possible for the troops." He passes the paper across the table to Marie, who studies it with an appreciative nod.

"At the head of this list, naturally, is my nephew," Howard goes on, gesturing to Philip and beaming. "We have determined that five thousand Guise troops will land near Arundel on the Sussex coast and come ashore through the earl's lands. We have almost secured the backing of the Earl of Northumberland, who is friendly to our case and whose seat at Petworth would allow the French army to advance toward London over the South Downs. Meanwhile, we estimate twenty thousand Spanish troops will land on the Lancashire coast, and will be joined by an uprising of the Catholics there. This force will head inland to liberate Queen Mary from Sheffield Castle." He stops for breath, and takes a brief sip of wine. "They will be joined there by Scottish reinforcements moving south from the border, I believe?"

He looks expectantly at Fowler, who nods.

"The Marquess of Huntley supports us and has promised men. I await confirmation of the exact number, but I am hopeful that he will turn more of the Scottish lords to our cause once they are persuaded the invasion is in earnest."

Douglas snorts.

"And where do you have this intelligence, old son? When were you last in Scotland?"

Fowler blinks at him, unperturbed. "I am at least *allowed* into Scotland."

Douglas has no retort to this, except a black glare; again I find myself intrigued as to the source of the antagonism between the two Scots.

Mendoza interrupts.

"Have you settled on a date?"

Howard inclines his head. "Commit this to memory, gentlemen— and madame." He smiles at Marie. "This glorious mission is planned for the thirtieth day of November."

"The *thirtieth*?" I blurt, before I can stop myself. From the other end of the table, I just catch Fowler's warning glance. I swallow; all eyes are on me and the silence feels heavy, accusing. I glimpse in memory the fragment of paper hidden in Cecily Ashe's mirror; the Accession Day date, 17th November. Had the plans changed, or had I misunderstood?

"The thirtieth not convenient for you, Bruno?" Howard says, one eyebrow lifting with chilly sarcasm. "Do you have some appointment that day? I'm sure we can rearrange it to suit you if need be."

Amid the smattering of sycophantic laughter, I hold up a hand to placate him.

"It's only that it occurred to me," I say, deliberately slurring, "that an invasion might be most effective if it took place on, say, a public holiday, while the country is distracted by revels. I'd assumed it would be set for Accession Day."

"It *occurred* to you, did it?" Howard's voice is stretched tight; his knuckles are white where his hands grasp each other.

"And," I add, bolstering my pretence of drunkenness, "would the assassination not have the most profound impact if it took place on that anniversary? The country would be thrown into turmoil." I sit back, expectant. The silence is overwhelming. The faces around the table register a universal expression of shock. Fowler keeps his eyes fixed on the table and remains very still, both hands clasped steadily around the stem of his glass. I have the cold, dropping sensation that I have made a terrible mistake.

"Assassination?" says Philip Howard eventually, baffled.

"Who is being assassinated?" Mendoza asks, looking around the table with a thunderous brow, as if someone has wilfully tried to deceive him. "Elizabeth? I was not told—"

"This was not the agreement, Henry!" Marie cries, her colour rising; Howard gestures at her to keep her voice down. "The Duke of Guise has expressly said—"

"Don't say I haven't offered," Douglas chips in laconically, grinning as he picks his nails, so that I am not sure whether he is serious or playing on his own reputation. "It'd be nae bother."

Henry Howard rises to his feet, his eyes burning.

"Please! Let us keep our heads. There will be no assassination. I think our friend Bruno has drunk too much wine."

"Anyway, he is from Naples," Marie says, shooting me a look that could turn the wine sour. "Where they are notoriously hotheaded. What put this foolishness in your mind, Bruno?"

Howard resumes his seat and leans forward, fixing his dark eyes on mine.

"Yes, Bruno," he says, with icy precision. "Where did you get this fanciful idea? Do tell."

"Well, perhaps I have not properly understood," I falter, "but to put Mary Stuart on the throne of England, you must first remove her cousin, no? So I assumed that if—*when*—the invasion happened, she would be—" I break off with a shrug, looking around the table, hoping that my pretence of naïveté will convince. Fowler still does not look at me, I presume because he does not want to betray his anger.

Howard laughs indulgently; to my ear there is a measure of relief in it.

"I see—you thought that to crown a new sovereign we must first despatch the old one? No, no, Bruno—that may be how you conduct things in Naples, but we are not barbarians here."

I almost point out that he has just announced an invasion of twenty thousand and more troops to wage war on a peaceful nation, but I refrain.

"This coup, if you will," Howard says smoothly, "must be conducted according to the rule of law. What you have perhaps failed to understand as a foreigner, Bruno, is that Elizabeth Tudor is not the legitimate queen of England, and never has been. The simple people of our poor country have been deceived into believing that she had the right of succession. They need to have this view corrected. Murdering her in the name of the Catholic faith will only make her a martyr in their eyes—it would be impossible thereafter for any Catholic monarch to restore order or command the people's affection. No, we must be a little more civilised about it." He smiles, pressing the tips of his fingers together.

"Oh, a civilised coup?" I say. "I have not witnessed one of those— how does it work? Do the troops apologise as they march on a town?"

Despite herself, Marie stifles a giggle; Howard's smile is wearing thin.

"The point my uncle wishes to make, Doctor Bruno, if I may," Philip Howard cuts in, "is that to bring England back to the true church, we must guide the people gently. It cannot be done with swords and crossbows alone, but only by showing England her error. We are pursuing a holy war here, and I think we are all agreed that no more blood must be spilled than is necessary to do God's work." A quaver creeps into his voice as he lays a sincere hand on his heart.

"My nephew is the saint in the family," Henry Howard remarks, drily.

"But he is right," says Mendoza. "The pretender Elizabeth must be arrested and publicly tried by a papal court as a traitor and a heretic."

"It must be proved to the populace, by due process, that Mary Stuart is the only legitimate heir to the Tudor crown," Howard explains, with excessive patience. "This is essential if the people are to accept her and her heirs as their rightful monarchs."

Opposite me, Douglas snaps his head up at this and stares at Howard. Fowler has also raised his head from his private thoughts to do the same, an expression of curiosity creeping over his features. Marie turns and narrows her eyes at Howard. He returns their looks defiantly, but he cannot help a slight colour creeping up his cheeks; he knows he has also said too much.

"Last time I looked," Douglas says, drawing out the words and leaning back in his chair, "Mary had just the one heir, and that is King James of Scotland. To my knowledge there has never been any question over his legitimacy or his succession." He keeps his tone light, but I catch a steely note in it. "His father was a peacock and a drunk who couldn't keep it in his breeches, but there was no doubting the lineage."

"No, indeed," Howard says hurriedly. "I am only speculating, if you will. Queen Mary is young enough still that she may, once she is restored to her throne, wish to marry again. We cannot rule out the possibility." He brushes something invisible from his doublet in order not to have to look at Douglas. I am seized by an urge to laugh at his evident discomfort, but I hold my face firm.

Douglas regards him with a mixture of disgust and incredulity.

"Christ, man, she's forty-two and she's the size of a fucking shire horse—if any man was going to tup her he'd need a serious reward for it."

"Being king consort of England might be reward enough for some," Fowler observes; somehow, his low steady voice is the more startling for being heard so rarely this evening. I wonder if anyone else notices the fury that flashes across Howard's face for the briefest moment, before he composes his ingratiating smile once more. From the way Mendoza watches him, his lip curled almost into a smirk, it seems that Howard's error has not escaped the sharp black eyes of the Spaniard.

By now, Howard's paper has made its way around the table to me, via Douglas. It shows a rough sketch of the outline of England, with harbours marked around it at various intervals, together with the names of the Catholic lords whose lands border the coast. Most of the names mean nothing to me, but a copy of this would be all Walsingham needs to have Howard arrested and charged. The question is how to obtain one. In the meantime, I bend all my powers of concentration to committing it to memory.

"We were talking of what should be done with Elizabeth after the invasion," Howard says, clearly anxious to change the subject.

"Yes. The Duke of Guise is adamant that she must be tried for heresy by a papal court," says Marie. I glance up from the paper for a moment; her eyes are shining with the special fervour she reserves for religious fanaticism and seduction. "This way it will send a message to the other Protestant leaders of Europe. Submit to the authority of the Catholic church or this will be your fate." She smiles with the anticipation of triumph.

"The duke has the unwavering support of Spain in this course," Mendoza says, half bowing to Marie; she simpers in return. "It would be the single most eloquent act the united Catholic powers could perform, an act that would echo across Europe and beyond. Particularly in the Low Countries," he adds, with venom.

"And if the Inquisition find her guilty, as they will? You propose she should be executed as a heretic, with all that that entails?" Fowler asks her, his face earnest as ever.

Marie shrugs. "That is hardly for me to say. There is an established punishment for heresy. I do not see why she should be exempt just because she is a royal bastard who calls herself a queen."

"The people won't like that," Philip says, rubbing his lower lip.

"There are precedents," replies his uncle. "Besides, the people are primed for cataclysmic change. Think of these pamphlets Douglas mentioned. The Great Conjunction, prophecies of the end of the age. The people cling to this superstitious folly, so we turn it to our advantage. Persuade them that the end prophesied in the heavens is the end of the false Protestant religion, bringing a new era of peace in a united Catholic Europe. In their hearts it's what they all want, even if they don't know it." He makes a little flourish in the air with his hand, as if he has just signed off a contract whose business is now ended. It is this sense of entitlement, the way he directs other people's lives, that hardens my dislike of him. I am willing to bet he is already picturing himself enthroned beside Mary Stuart.

Marie sits forward again as if to speak, but at that moment the dog under the table produces an unmissable liquid belch and everyone turns to look at me.

"Doctor Bruno," Howard says, forcing his smile again. "The paper, if you please?" He stretches out his hand for the map I am still studying. Reluctantly, I pass it back along the table.

"We have not yet given you opportunity to fulfil your duty and share with us the ambassador's thoughts," Howard continues. "Please do so—if you feel able." His civility could wither the grapes on the vine as he makes a point of looking at my wineglass. My pulse quickens; my plan now rests on my performance in the next few minutes. I can feel the force of Mendoza's scorn as he glowers from the other end of the table.

So I stumble, glass in hand, through Castelnau's by now well-worn arguments against rushing the invasion plot—the Duke of Guise is acting without the authority or approval of King Henri, there is still the chance of a treaty between Elizabeth and Mary, the diplomatic processes have not been exhausted, too much power would be handed to Rome, et cetera—but I deliver them in such a slurring show of drunken rambling that Howard turns his face away from me in disgust. Courcelles, I note from the corner of my eye, appears delighted with my display; I picture him scampering gleefully back to Castelnau to report what happens when you trust your affairs to a renegade Italian instead of your own private secretary, as protocol demands. I would mind the affront to my own dignity, but there is too much at stake to worry about that; besides, I am unlikely to be invited back to Arundel House in the near future in any case. Fowler simply watches me with his steady, concerned expression, his fingers steepled together and pressed to his lips.

I end this virtuoso display with an expansive hand gesture that sends my wineglass crashing to the floor beside me, as I intended it should, to account for the quantity of wine spilled on the rushes. The dog whimpers and retreats into the corner of the room. It doesn't look well. Henry

Howard can barely contain his outrage; his moustache twitches unnervingly as he sucks in his cheeks.

"Don't worry, Doctor Bruno—the servants will see to that in the morning," Philip Howard says, with utmost courtesy, waving a hand.

"And thank you for conveying my lord Castelnau's views in your own unique way," Henry adds, as if he is holding his breath. Mendoza only laughs, and pushes his chair back.

I sense that my performance has ruptured the tension in the room; people are fidgeting, as if impatient to leave. The candles have burned almost to stumps; I cannot guess at the hour, but it grows late, and it is time for my finale. I clasp my face with my hand, then slump forward on the table over my crooked arm, allowing my mouth to hang open.

"Is he all right?" says Philip Howard, after a moment. A hand tentatively nudges me.

"Oh, for goodness' sake," Henry Howard explodes. "They have no self-control, you see. It's what I've always said. Indulging the pleasures of the flesh." He curls his mouth around these last words with evident revulsion.

I wonder who he means by "they." Dominicans? Heretics? Italians?

Then Marie's voice, sharp and impatient: "How are we supposed to get him back to Salisbury Court in this state?"

"Well, I'm not carrying him," Courcelles says quickly. "Besides, he'd likely vomit in the boat."

There is some conferring in low voices; I resist the temptation to open an eye. Finally, Philip says, "There is nothing else for it. He must stay here and sleep it off. We have room. He can walk back to the embassy tomorrow when he's in better shape."

Inwardly, I give a little cry of triumph.

"I could almost pity him, poor fool," Howard says. Though I cannot see the sneer on his face, I can hear it and picture it vividly. "He has disgraced himself and the ambassador. That will be the last time he is offered any kind of responsibility. The man thinks he's untouchable with King Henri's patronage."

"That will not benefit him much longer." Mendoza's voice is thick with scorn.

"Shh, Uncle—he might be able to hear you."

"Him? He's out cold. Get him upstairs, someone. Fowler—you at least seem sober. Would you mind?"

A scraping of chairs, followed by a crunching sound, as someone steps on the fragments of broken glass scattered around my chair. I feel a pair of strong arms grasp me around the torso.

"Come on, you can't stay here," Fowler says gently, hoisting me to my feet; there is a kind of tenderness in the way he lifts my limp arm and wraps it around his shoulder. Henry Howard, I note as I dare to open my eyes a bleary crack, stands with his arms folded, his lips pressed together, the model of disapproving piety. But Henry Howard has his own weaknesses, and tonight I intend to discover them and bring back evidence.

"Howard," Mendoza hisses, and through half-closed lids I see him gesture abruptly to the door.

By watching the progress of my feet and Fowler's through my eyelashes, I make a note, as I am bundled along a corridor and up a flight of stairs, of the way back to the corridor with the dining room. Philip Howard goes officiously before us with a candle to show the way, while I lean on Fowler's shoulders and allow myself to be half dragged, half carried to a room where I am dropped onto a bed.

"Will he be all right, do you think?" Philip asks nervously from the doorway.

"He'll be right enough after a sleep," says Fowler, sitting on the bed beside me and pulling off my boots one after the other. "A jug of good wine never killed anyone." He rolls me onto my side; I allow him to move me like a dead weight. "You might give him a piss pot in case he wakes in the night," he adds, matter-of-factly.

Some scuffling follows; I hear footsteps in the corridor, and eventually someone—presumably the earl himself, since the servants have all been dismissed—places a pot beside the bed. It is by now safe to assume that I will never receive a return invitation from the earl and countess.

"Don't worry—I'll make sure he is comfortable," Fowler says; the earl murmurs something and from the other side of the room I hear footsteps die away. I decide the best policy is to feign a state of unconsciousness. Fowler leans across the bed and lays a hand on my shoulder.

"Quite a performance, Bruno," he breathes, his mouth almost touching my ear. "And risky. What is it you want?"

I open my eyes to find his face barely inches from mine, looking for all the world as if he is about to kiss me.

"Whatever I can find," I whisper. He regards me for a moment and in the candlelight his face is full of doubt; I can see he thinks this an unnecessary danger. Resentment tightens in my chest; Fowler is a partner of sorts in this enterprise, but it is not for him to direct me or question my methods.

"That list of havens would be a prize indeed," he whispers back, eventually. "But Howard took it with him—you can be sure he will keep it somewhere secure. And you could mar everything if you are caught."

I am well aware of this, but having him point it out only makes me angry.

"I will not be caught," I whisper. "And if you delay too long here we will rouse their suspicions."

"Henry and Mendoza have retired together for a private conversation," he hisses. "I would give much to eavesdrop on that. But for God's sake be careful."

"Trust me."

He squeezes my shoulder.

"Good luck, then, Bruno. You are bolder than I, that is certain."

The candle is blown out, the door clicks shut, and I roll onto my back, grinning to myself in the dark, alert and waiting.

Chapter 15

After perhaps two hours have passed like an eternity, I sit upright and listen. The silence that has fallen over the house has an apprehensive quality, a muffled stillness that feels tense with expectation. Or perhaps this is just how it seems to me, after lying on my back in the dark for so many slowly turning minutes, ears straining for the slightest sound that would betray anyone awake or abroad in the household. But now there is nothing; only the intermittent yelping of seabirds over the river and the wail of an occasional fox. Cautiously, I swing my legs over the side of the bed and immediately kick the piss pot Philip Howard left for me; it rattles like a series of shots fired on the wooden boards as it settles and I freeze, heart pounding, but the house makes no response. I wonder how far I am from the private rooms of the family, or the servants' quarters, and who might be awake to hear me. It also occurs to me, as I rise and pad across to pull back one of the wooden shutters on the window, that they might leave the white dog to patrol the house during the night.

Although the dog is probably in worse shape than I at this moment, I reflect, rubbing my temple. I have a pounding headache, but I feel wide awake, my nerves primed.

The candle and tinderbox are still safe in the pocket of my breeches. Without my boots, my feet in my underhose make no sound, though the boards are uneven and complain at every step. I open the chamber door, first a crack and then enough to slip into the passageway outside. Nothing stirs; as I feel my way back toward the staircase, I imagine I can hear the collective rise and fall of breath as the household sleeps. If anyone crosses my path before I reach my destination, I can always pretend I am still half drunk and in search of a drink of water or the closestool.

The corridor that leads back past the dining room is deserted; though I keep my tread as light as possible, there is no one to hear. The door at the end of the corridor is closed and as I approach it the blood drums faster in my throat; if it should be locked, and I am unable to turn the lock with the blade of my knife—tucked, as always, into my waistband—then this whole performance will have been in vain.

But the door opens smoothly, so easily that I half expect to find someone inside the library waiting for me, having guessed at my intention. Instead I find myself alone in a rectangular room lined on all four sides with wooden stacks of books and manuscripts, except at either end where two arched windows face each other. Pale moonlight slants through one of these, tracing faint shapes on the floor. With trembling fingers, barely able to believe that my luck will hold, I close the door as silently as I can, take out the candle, and strike a flame, once, twice; on the third attempt it lights, and I move closer to the books, trying to deduce Philip Howard's method of classification. Or perhaps the library is really Henry Howard's; the young earl does not strike me as much of a scholar. Henry might have moved his collection of books to Arundel House when his family lost their own seat. Either way, it gives me a frisson of pleasure to be poking about in the Howards' library without permission, just as I believe Henry Howard to have done in Dee's house.

The circle of light quivers along the lines of books as I prowl the length of the shelves, knowing all the time that the book I hope to find will not be openly displayed, if it is here at all. But if Dee is right and it was Henry Howard who ordered the lost Hermes book to be stolen from him in Oxford all those years ago, then it is most likely to be hidden somewhere in his own library. My best hope is that I have enough time undisturbed to search for some sign of it.

Even a cursory glance at the stacks shows that most of the volumes collected here are uncontroversial; works of classical scholarship, theology, and poetry such as any gentleman might be expected to be acquainted with, chosen more for the finery of their bindings, it seems, than for their content. But the long wall facing the door intrigues me; it has no windows, yet from the layout as I came in, it seems to me that this room should mark the end of the east wing of the house. Why, then, does it have no windows to the outside to increase the light, when this would clearly be an advantage in a room intended for reading? I move carefully along the length of this wall, and as I reach the farthest of the stacks, the flame of my candle gutters violently and threatens to cough itself out altogether. I hold out my other hand to feel a sharp draught, which appears to be coming from behind the wooden bookcase. This is curious, since the stacks have the appearance of being built into the wall. Bending to the floor, I can see faint curving marks scratched in the boards at one side and my chest gives a wild lurch; trying to hold the candle steady, I grope with frantic fingers up the panel that joins the stack to the corner of the room. Built into the latticework carving on this panel are small indentations; about halfway up I insert my fingertips into one of these and find it is cut deeper than the others. Feeling blindly, I touch metal; there seems to be some kind of latch. I probe as best I can until I think I have released it; the wooden stack shifts almost imperceptibly and with my breath held fast, I begin to pull it toward me, away from the wall. It is heavy, but moves with surprising ease and I realise that it is built on a hinge, carefully weighted; it swings out just far enough for a person to slip into the gap behind, where a small door is built into the wall, invisible when the shelf stack is in place.

My palms are sweating as I squeeze myself into the gap and try the latch of this new door. This one is locked, and does not yield easily to the coaxings of my knife blade; setting the candle down, I breathe deeply, knowing that haste and clumsy fingers will not help this operation. After some delicate manoeuvring, I feel the tip of the blade engage with the lock mechanism and very slowly, I manage to turn the bolt back, though my hand slips at the last moment and the edge of the blade catches my finger, leaving a trickle of blood running down the side of my hand. Cursing under my breath, I ease the door open.

The candle flame leaps and flutters in the sudden draught as I nudge the door wider with my foot and step through into a narrow room. It is like stepping into a mausoleum. The dank breath of cold stone wraps around my face and there is an odour of decay, of dead matter. When I hold up the light, I almost gasp aloud, but the sound freezes in my throat.

No ornate plaster ceiling or linenfold panelling have been employed to make this room warmer or more inviting. There is only the naked brick of the walls, the exposed beams of the ceiling that slopes sharply down, stone flags on the floor. This room appears to be built into the very wall of the house, its two arched windows bricked up. It is as if this room does not exist.

Lifting the candle, I push the door shut and examine my surroundings. On the wall opposite, between the two blocked windows, hangs a vast painting of the heavens copied from one of the Arabic astrological charts, with concentric circles divided into the various houses of the zodiac and marked with the influence of the planets. Beneath this painting there is a cabinet of black wood, its double doors inlaid with a pattern of tiny mother-of-pearl lozenges and its top strewn with papers and discarded quills. To my left, at the far end of the room, stands a rectangular block draped in a dark purple cloth. It has the appearance of an altar, with a silver candlestick positioned at either side, but in the centre sits a polished crystal in a brass tripod, pale with a faint rosy tint under the light. It looks exactly like John Dee's showing stone. In Oxford I saw one such hidden chapel and I have heard that the Catholic nobles of England often have them built into their grand houses so that they may hear Mass in secret, but this looks like no place of Catholic worship. Glancing down, I see circles marked on the floor in chalk, divided into pentagrams, with astrological and occult symbols marked in each division. As I turn slowly to follow the line of the markings at my feet, a glint from the corner of the room catches my eye; I lift the candle and jump back at the sight of a human head, cast in brass and elevated on a narrow stone plinth. Its contours are eerily lifelike, though its cheeks are hollow and cadaverous, as if it has been cast from the head of a corpse. The eyes are blank and smooth, the mouth hollow, like that of the brazen head supposedly owned by the friar Roger Bacon some three hundred years ago, the head that, according to legend, would prophesy by the power of spirits. My skin prickles and the hairs on my arms rise in goose bumps; this head is the clearest sign yet that this room is a temple to Hermetic magic. The writings of Hermes Trismegistus treat of animating statues and such devices by the power of spirits to make them prophesy; Saint Augustine condemned this as demonic magic, but the true adepts knew better. Has Henry Howard tried to make the bronze head speak, I wonder?

Above the head a set of shelves is attached to the wall, with glass vials and flasks arranged in neat rows, together with a number of what look like surgical instruments. Some of these vials are filled with liquids, others contain more curious items—what appear to be splinters of bone or fragments of hair or skin, the kind of objects you might expect to find in any Catholic reliquary or alchemist's laboratory. Opposite the altar, against the wall, stands a speculum made of polished obsidian, the height of a man and perhaps four feet across. The outline of my own form wavers across its surface, the candle flame jumping wildly in reflection as I keep it close. The showing stone, the black mirror, the brazen head— these are the instruments of celestial magic, of those who seek illumination from the spiritual realm. So Howard, the great denouncer of prophecy, astrology, and every kind of divination, is himself attempting to contact the powers beyond the stars. Dee has already guessed as much; I can't help a smile of triumph.

The candle is burning low, and the persistent breath of cold air continually threatens it; I dare not lose it, so I cross the room quickly and light the two candles on the altar. The new arcs of light ripple up the brickwork, pushing back the shadows a little. With every nerve alert, barely daring to breathe, I return to the cabinet and begin to sift through the papers. I can find no semblance of order among them; some appear to be complex astrological calculations involving the positions of the planets in the Great Conjunction and their movements through the calendar; others depict a series of tables showing what look like codes and ciphers. There are dozens of these; seemingly endless variations on the same table, meticulously copied, lists of letters, numbers, and symbols in different configurations, multiplying over and over. Beneath these I find a rough draft of the map Henry Howard passed around the table at dinner, with the list of possible landing places and names of Catholic landowners. I lift up the sheet with the map and draw out another paper. With a jolt, I see immediately what it shows. I hastily lay it on top of the others and smooth it out to study, the flame trembling in my hand as I bend to read.

The paper shows the Tudor and Stuart family tree, from King Henry VII, Queen Elizabeth's grandfather, and his wife, Elizabeth of York. The true line of descent—as judged by the author of this page, at least—is inked in bold and clearly shows Henry's eldest daughter, Margaret Tudor, who married King James IV of Scotland, as the grandmother of Mary Stuart. The Tudor line of succession continues through King Henry VIII, which this genealogy shows as having married Catherine of Aragon and produced the queen Mary Tudor—Elizabeth's half sister, the one they call Bloody Mary—who died in 1558. Of Henry's subsequent marriages and offspring, there is no mention. Naturally, I think—this is the Catholic view of the English succession, which does not recognise Henry's divorce and therefore regards his first marriage as his only legitimate union and his daughter Mary Tudor as his only legitimate heir. This is why they take such pleasure in referring to Elizabeth as "bastard." There are other potential Tudor successors from the line of Henry VII's younger daughter, another Mary, but there can be no doubt as to what this version of history wishes to prove: that Mary Stuart is the eldest living legitimate heir to the crown of England.

To possess a copy of such a genealogy is treason under English law, punishable by death. But this is not even the best of it, for beside the name of Mary Stuart is written that of her deceased husband, Lord Darnley (himself also descended from Margaret Tudor), and beneath them a line showing the fruit of that union, the present King James VI of Scotland. Next to it, in the faintest ink but unmistakably in the same hand is a line conjoined to Mary that simply reads "H." From it leads a line of descent, as if to denote a prospective offspring, but the space where the name of the child should be remains blank. I run a tongue around my dry lips as I hold the paper closer to my eyes, as if doing so might confirm the audacity of what is written here. There is no doubt that this is the same hand as the writing on the list of safe havens passed around the supper table earlier, that I had studied so intently—the loops and crosses are distinctive—and must surely be Henry Howard's. So my suspicions were right from the beginning: his ultimate plan is to become Mary's husband, to sit beside her on the throne of England and—most daring of all—he dreams of putting a son of his own into the line of succession. I find I am shaking my head, partly in disbelief but partly in admiration at the reach of the man's ambition. Of course, he has kept this from his coconspirators. Marie and Courcelles are working for the Duke of Guise, who must intend a stake in the new Catholic kingdom for himself; perhaps, as Mary's cousin, he may feel he already has a family entitlement. Douglas I have always assumed to be an opportunist; does he guess he is working for the advancement of the Howard family, and would he care, as long as he came out of it well? I wonder if even Philip Howard, with his mealy-mouthed pleas for limited bloodshed, has guessed at his uncle's ultimate plan.

Hastily I fold the paper and tuck it inside the waistband of my breeches at my side, under my shirt. Whatever else I may uncover tonight, this alone was worth all the risk: it is pure gold. A genealogy in Henry Howard's own hand, denying Elizabeth's right to reign and clearly showing his intention to marry the Queen of Scots—this is proof of Howard's treason beyond anything Walsingham could have hoped for. With a bit of judicious questioning, Howard might be expected to give up further details of the invasion plan with plenty of time to prevent it.

My blood is racing with the thrill of this success, but I do not have time to lose; next I crouch to try the doors of the black cabinet, but here for the first time my luck fails. The doors are locked. I cannot see any other place in the room where books might be hidden—and if Henry Howard has forbidden occult books, as he must, where else would he hide them but in this secret chapel? I unsheathe my knife and attempt to insert its tip into the lock, but the keyhole is too small and the blade cannot penetrate far enough to make any purchase. Frustrated, and anxious too, as I note that all the candles are burning lower, I set it down and return to the shelves above the brazen head to see if there is some smaller implement among the paraphernalia there that might serve, and as my gaze ranges along the row of vials that look like reliquaries, one in particular catches my eye. An ornate glass bottle containing a single lock of bright gold hair.

I reach for it and take out the stopper. I have seen more saints' remains in Italy than I could number—enough fingers and blood and hair to people the world with blessed saints seven times over—but usually those who sell fake relics make some effort to give their wares the semblance of antiquity. This lock of hair has none of the brittle, dusty look of those old trinkets; it appears fresh and springy, coiled behind the glass. Cecily Ashe had blond hair, I remember, with a lurch of the stomach.

"I see you have found the hair of Saint Agnes."

Henry Howard's voice, behind me, is polite, amused, as if he were not in the least surprised to find me here, in his occult chapel, rooting through the ingredients of his arts. He has appeared so silently that for one awful moment it seems the brazen head has spoken; I leap and whip round so violently at the sound that I almost drop the bottle. All I can do is stare at him, slack-jawed and shaking. In one hand he holds a candle, in the other, an ornamental sword.

"They possess powers to protect chastity, the relics of Saint Agnes," he goes on, in the same breezy tone, "and also over the favourable cultivation of crops. But of course you know all this. I find it fascinating, don't you? That the same force should exercise its influence over both chastity and fertility, two opposites."

"Opposing forces share a powerful connection," I say, recovering my voice. "If one believes in such powers."

"You do not believe in the power of relics, I do not think. But as a good disciple of Hermes, you must believe that certain elements in the natural world may harness particular powers mirrored in the celestial realm?"

I only look at him and shrug, affecting a coolness I do not feel. I am aware that I am at his mercy here, and that the best course is probably to keep silent. My eye drifts to the sword, which he holds loosely at his side.

"It's a pity," he says, moving toward me and kicking the door shut with his foot. He wears a heavy crimson robe over his nightshirt. "It would have been interesting to discuss the Hermetic magic with you, in other circumstances. In private I am willing to concede that you have a considerable reputation in these matters, though you will not hear me praise you for it in company."

"I am flattered." I incline my head. He misses the sarcasm.

"You certainly have more audacity than I would have credited, Bruno." His tone is almost admiring. "Your performance was entirely convincing this evening. You outdrank Douglas—that should have roused my suspicions. If I had not been so willing to let you confirm my worst prejudices about you, I might have been more wary. And I see you are extremely canny. Even Her Majesty's pursuivants have never managed to find this room, not on all the occasions it has pleased them to search my nephew's house." He paces softly across the stone flags in his velvet slippers to cast a casual eye over the papers on top of the cabinet. His foot is only inches from the bone-handled knife I left lying on the floor after my attempt to pick the lock. My muscles tense; the document beneath my shirt pricks my skin. Will he notice its absence from one glance?

"My nephew had this built as a private chapel. The Jesuit Edmund Campion said a Mass here once, you know. But after Campion was executed and the Privy Council came down harder on the secret priests, Philip lost his nerve somewhat. Can't blame the boy—he was only young when he saw his father executed for treason and his title lost. He doesn't want this estate attainted as well. So there were no more Masses after that and I took possession of the chapel for my private work. We never speak of it." His eyes drift to the altar at the far end of the room, as if remembering its more orthodox use. "The day they hung and quartered Campion at Tyburn—that was the moment I realised England would never be restored by priests and prayers alone. Faith would have to show itself in stronger action." As he says this, the muscles in his jaw twitch and his knuckles whiten around the hilt of the sword. Perhaps, I think, watching him, behind his desire for revenge and advancement lies some genuine religious feeling; or perhaps they have become one and the same. He snaps his eyes back to me, the memories dismissed.

"You feign drunkenness very well, by the way," he remarks, as if we were casual acquaintances making small talk at some tavern. "Did you feed good Rhenish to my dog, is that what happened? Poor brute's been sick all over the back stairs."

I say nothing. For a moment we watch each other in the candlelight and I give a sudden involuntary shiver. The room seems very cold.

"Well, Bruno." He looks me up and down, his tone finally asserting his mastery of the situation. "I do not need to ask if you recognise what you find here." He waves a hand that takes in the circles on the floor, the altar, the brazen head.

"You pursue secret knowledge, even while you publicly decry it," I mutter. "Dee suspected as much."

"Of course he did." Howard's voice betrays a touch of impatience. "He always knew I was a natural adept. But he had the arrogance to presume that he held the key to my progress and could simply shut me out from the higher reaches of that knowledge. He is guided by fear, you see, Bruno," he says, suddenly brusque. "The last thing Dee wants is a rival for the queen's faith in such matters. Matters that lie on the other side of religion, in its shadows. He wishes to be recognised as her magus, and he will thwart anyone who tries to come up behind him. You will find this out for yourself eventually." He shakes his head and takes another step closer to me, the sword still held idly against his leg. With his face barely a foot from mine, he breaks into a grotesque smile. "But he lacks the one thing that would make him the preeminent magus of our age, and he cannot sleep for yearning for it. Neither can you."

"The lost book of Hermes." My voice is barely audible, but my breath rises in a plume between us in the cold air. "You stole it from him in Oxford, then."

It is not meant as a question. Howard merely curves his smile wider.

"It found its way into my hands. Oh yes, you may well hang your mouth open, Bruno. It is, I presume, what you have come here to find? You are resourceful, I'll give you that." He turns sharply and crosses the room to the small altar, then turns and fixes me with those black eyes.

"But a man in exile, Bruno, is always vulnerable. Am I not right? Little wonder he seeks powers beyond his own temporal means. You and I understand this," he adds, with feeling. "My brother Thomas lost us the greatest dukedom in England. My family name is now stained with treason. I have been threatened with prison and banishment, and I am forced to live as a lodger with my nephew and feign loyalty to the usurper Elizabeth." He curls his lip. "I am shut out of the heritage that is rightfully mine as surely as if I were banished from English soil. But I am only biding my time."

"And your solution is to finish what your brother started?" I say, raising my chin.

He frowns at me for a moment, as if calculating how much I might know.

"Why do you say that? Because of my comment at dinner about Mary's heirs?"

"If she was once willing to marry your brother, why not you?"

He lifts the sword and points it at me, and I feel my bowels contract; for a moment I think he might be about to run at me. But eventually he nods.

"Very astute of you, Bruno. The Howards are descended from Edward Plantagenet, the first English king of that name. Did you know that?" Without waiting for a reply, he continues. "We are of royal blood. There *should* be a Howard heir on the throne."

"You mean to take Mary to wife, once she is liberated and crowned by this invasion, and get an heir by her?"

He grimaces.

"It is my duty to my lineage. I would not expect a common-born man to understand such an ideal."

Instinctively my fists clench, as they always do when confronted with such claims of the nobility's inborn superiority. But I keep my voice calm. "Douglas is right, though. Mary Stuart already has an heir with an impeccable royal pedigree and he is king of Scotland."

"Young men are not immortal, Bruno," Howard says, with a low laugh. "And James has yet to breed."

I look at him, and realise I have not even begun to understand the scale of his hopes. Howard's plans reach far beyond this invasion, far beyond the restoration of the Roman faith that the others envision; his scheming stretches into a future in which he is king of a Catholic England, his own son the heir, and the young King James somehow the victim of an unfortunate accident, like his father. I understand now why Howard keeps Archibald Douglas so close; if Douglas could kill the father so efficiently, why not recruit him to kill the son? For the right price, I have no doubt that Douglas would oblige. But the real fear clawing at my insides comes because I realise the only reason Henry Howard would have confided such an incredible—some might say insane—plot to me is because he feels confident I will not have the chance to repeat it. My right hand itches instinctively to reach for my knife, though it is not there, and I force myself to keep still. If Howard thinks I am armed he may search me and then he would find the genealogy. I look down at the glass bottle I had almost forgotten I was holding. Saint Agnes, he says. This hair belonged to someone more recent. But I cannot begin to understand how the murders at court fit into Howard's elaborate long-term plan.

"But enough of that," he says, unexpectedly lighthearted. "I was going to show you something to make you tremble, was I not? Come closer, Bruno."

To my great relief, he lays the sword on the altar, though he keeps his hand within easy reach as he lifts the purple cloth that covers it. The stone beneath shows a carved bas-relief of figures, their faces so worn by time that only a blurred outline of their humanity remains. It appears centuries old.

"Comes from one of the Sussex abbeys torn down in the Dissolution," he remarks, as if he reads my thoughts. "My brother bought it secretly and kept it in his own chapel. We had it brought here after he died. You cannot imagine the work it takes to move a thing like that. Illegal to possess it, of course."

His voice grows muffled as he turns his back to me and crouches in front of the altar. Set into the stone near the base is a narrow recess; Howard reaches in and draws out a wooden casket, its lid inlaid with an intricate pattern stamped in gold. He takes a key from somewhere inside his robe and unlocks the box. I take a tentative step nearer, my palms prickling with sweat; I am anxious to stay out of the range of that sword. As I pass the black cabinet I gently kick my discarded knife out of sight, just underneath it, while his back is turned.

"You won't see properly from there," he says, standing and turning. "Come."

He holds it out to me, an object wrapped in a layer of protective linen. As I move closer, he unwraps the coverings to reveal a book bound in faded leather. I experience a sudden weakness in my limbs, as if my body had been flushed with cold water, as my heart gives an impossible lurch and I rush forward, almost forgetting the sword.

Could this really be the book I had chased from Venice to Paris to Oxford, the fifteenth book of the writings of the Egyptian sage Hermes Trismegistus, brought to Cosimo de' Medici out of the ruins of Byzantium, given to the great Neoplatonist Marsilio Ficino to translate, and hidden by him when he recognised the awful power of what it contained? The book that, according to an old Venetian I had known in Paris, Ficino gave into the safekeeping of the bookseller Vespasiano da Bisticci, whose apprentice mistakenly sold it on to an English collector; the book that had lain unrecognised in an Oxford college library until a wily librarian saved it from the Royal Commission's purges; the book that an unscrupulous dealer named Rowland Jenkes had sold to Dee for a fortune, and which Dee held in his hands for barely a day before it was stolen from him at Henry Howard's command? By all that was sacred—could it be that I was finally in the presence of the book that was believed to hold the secret of man's divine origin, of how to recover that divinity? I hardly dared breathe.

"Open it, if you want." Howard's smile grows wolfish. His eyes glitter; he looks like a child flaunting a marzipan figure, determined that you should fully appreciate the wonder of it, secure in the knowledge that you shall never take it from him. He nods, encouraging. I reach out, my hand visibly trembling, and lift the book from the casket. In the moment of opening the cover, it is as if the world ceases turning; I can hear my own heartbeat as if it came from somewhere outside. The bound manuscript pages are old and stiff, the Greek characters so faint in places as to be almost illegible, but as I begin to read, there is no doubt in my mind that this book is authentic.

Howard nods again as I turn the pages, my eyes hungrily scanning the lines, thinking what I would offer for the chance to spend a day with this book, to study it, copy it, drink it in. Eventually he grows impatient.

"Read on, Bruno. Skip the prologue and the early chapters. Turn to the middle section."

Surprised, I obey, and as the book falls open toward the middle, I understand his slightly hysterical look of triumph. I read the Greek lines, then read them again. As my frown deepens, Howard begins to laugh.

"You see, Bruno? You see?"

I experience a disorienting sense of falling, just as Howard himself must have done when he first opened the book. I look down at the page, then back to Howard, shaking my head in disbelief.

"Encoded."

"Exactly! The meat of the book, its most secret and sacred wisdom, is so inflammatory that the scribe didn't dare write it without a cipher. In the prologue Hermes mentions the Great Key, the *Clavis magna*. But this must exist separately, and I do not have it." His eyes burn with a frenzied energy. "Fourteen years! Fourteen years I have attempted to break the code. I have tried every system of cryptography I have ever read about, but I cannot. I cannot make it yield."

I watch him, the book limp in my hands, my mouth open. Fourteen years of trying to decipher the book you believe will yield the secret of immortality. I almost pity him; small wonder his plans seem touched by madness. It is a wonder he has held on to his mind at all.

"But Ficino must have had it," I wonder, aloud. "The Great Key. Ficino read the whole book, according to the story I heard, else how would he have been so afraid to translate it?"

"It exists somewhere, or it can be deduced," Howard says, and I hear the years of weariness in his voice. "But how to find it, Bruno? Where to begin?"

"Dee has a great many treatises on cryptography in his library," I reply, holding his gaze. "But then you know that."

He merely raises an eyebrow.

"Ask Dee for help? And confess that I have the book he was nearly killed for? Naturally, over the years I have made attempts to discover whether Dee holds anything among his papers that he may not know to be the key of which Hermes speaks. I have sent servants and associates to his house to pose as travelling scholars. And, yes, I have taken the opportunity to search there myself if I knew he was absent. In all this time I have barely touched the surface of Dee's library." His face hardens and he looks at me as if he has only just remembered who I am. "But Dee is close to being ruined. Elizabeth will no longer be able to turn a blind eye to his practices. And when he is—even if his life is spared, his goods will be forfeit. I will have his library somehow." The cold determination in his voice belies the wild light in his eyes; if his sanity is doubtful, it has not affected his ruthlessness. But his reference to Dee's impending ruin is almost a confession.

"Is Ned Kelley one of these associates you send out to do your work?"

He rubs his pointed beard as if trying to recall where he has heard the name.

"Kelley. A crook, of course, but with a remarkable imagination and a curious ability to win the affection of strangers, though I must say it has never worked on me."

"Nor me."

"The servant Johanna brought him to me—she found him at some fair, cheating at card tricks. She thought he might prove useful to me. But no one could have foreseen how Dee would take Kelley to his bosom, and how easily Kelley would work on him." He smirks. A sudden rage rises in my chest and I grip the book tighter.

"You paid Kelley to lure Dee into conjuring spirits so that he could be publicly disgraced and punished," I say, through my teeth. Howard permits himself an indulgent chuckle.

"I knew if Dee believed he could truly communicate with celestial beings he wouldn't be able to resist telling the queen. She is still drawn to the idea of knowledge beyond mortal means, but that would be a step too far for those advocates of reason in her council. Walsingham, Burghley. Myself, naturally." He smiles, patting his breast. "Dee will be cut down faster than a cankered apple tree, you shall see. And I no longer need live in fear of his exposing the secrets of my past." He folds his arms across his chest and tilts his head back to appraise me down the length of his nose. "Which brings me to you, Bruno."

"And the girls," I blurt, ignoring him, a flush of rage spreading across my face, "they died for this? To lend credibility to Kelley's violent prophecies? To implicate Dee in murder, just to make sure you finished his reputation for good?"

Howard is too much of a courtier to allow his polished mask to slip for long, but I had thought the accusation might prompt some admission of guilt in his expression, however fleeting. What I see instead is confusion, then outrage.

"Girls? Good God, Bruno—you don't think I had anything to do with that?" He looks genuinely stricken—but I must not forget that he is a politician and an expert dissembler. "That would be insanity—murders that draw attention to threats against the queen at the very time we are trying to organise an invasion which depends on surprise? Why on earth would I jeopardise the plans on which I have staked my whole future?"

"Ned Kelley's prophecy foretold the death of Abigail Morley in almost every particular," I say, lowering my voice. "How else could he have known?"

He shakes his head impatiently.

"Kelley was a fool—he allowed his imagination to be coloured too far by the lurid reports he read in pamphlets. So when the killer repeats himself, it looks as if Kelley foresaw the event. No—these murders could have been catastrophic for our invasion plans. Increased raids on Catholics, increased questioning, more guards around the court, and they'll be watching Mary more closely, just at a time when I have Throckmorton riding around the country trying to stir the Catholic nobles into a spirit of war—you think I would purposefully bring all this down upon our heads? By the cross—it would be madness!" His eyes flash. "No. If Dee is implicated in murder as a result, some good will have come of it, but I assure you, Bruno, I am furious about the timing of these murders.

Besides," he adds, with a little preening gesture, "I would never engage in such a vulgar display. Death is occasionally necessary, but it ought to be discreet. That sort of grotesque spectacle is the work of a man whose vanity outweighs his sense of purpose."

I look at him and the thrill of my earlier certainty shrivels to a point and disappears. Despite the self-satisfied twitch of his smile, I think he is speaking the truth. Wanting to persuade myself that he was behind the murders, I have tried to make the facts fit, but I have never found a plausible explanation for the way the murders so overtly tried to imply a Catholic threat. And now that I know the extent of Howard's regal and dynastic ambitions, I can see that the assassination of Elizabeth would clearly work against his interests, so the theory that he set up Cecily Ashe to poison the queen also crumbles. But if Howard is not the killer, then who?

"You had better return my book now, Bruno," he says, holding out a hand. "I wouldn't put it past you to crack the cipher while my back was turned."

Slowly, I step forward, my arm leaden as I reach out and let him take the book. The rough grain of the leather slides beneath my fingertips as he pulls it from my grasp; I watch him tuck it back into its casket with a sense of desolation, as if I had found a lover only to lose her again in the same moment. Except that I have pursued this book across a continent and a sea with greater devotion than I have shown to any woman; to have held it in my hands and have it snatched away is almost worse than to have gone on blindly seeking it, never knowing if it even existed. Nor can I escape the insistent voice of my own vanity: that, given time, Dee and I between us could surely break the cipher that has defeated Henry Howard for fourteen years. My eyes follow it longingly as Howard locks the casket and clasps it to his chest. My chances of ever touching that book again look remote.

The sword glitters on the altar under the candle flames. If I were to lunge for it now, while Howard busies himself with the casket, I might just be able to grab it before he has a chance to react, though he is nearer. As if he senses my eyes on it, without looking up he reaches out and lays a proprietorial hand on the hilt.

"You leave me with a dilemma, Bruno," he says, as he tucks the casket under his left arm. "All of this"—he gestures around the chapel, taking in the chart, the brazen head, the altar—"you should not have seen. My greatest secret. If it were made known, it would be the final nail in the coffin of my family's reputation, and would certainly see me in the Tower. You were never a man I wholly trusted, even before this night. So what am I to do with you, now that you have found me out?" His thumb lightly strokes the hilt of his sword, though he doesn't yet pick it up.

A coldness ripples along my spine and through my gut; my throat clenches. I had half expected this, but stubbornly I still hope I might reason with him.

"Dee has guessed at your secret, and not divulged it—why do you think I would not do the same?"

He must catch the fear in my voice, because he laughs, without humour.

"Dee has no proof of anything. And he has a healthy respect for the reach of my influence, whereas you, Bruno, appear to have no respect at all." He rests his left hand on his hip and shakes his head. "I don't think I have ever witnessed such a cocksure swagger in a man of low birth."

My eyes flick again to the sword.

"Oh, don't worry, Bruno, I'm not planning to run you through, unless you try anything stupid. That would take some explaining to the ambassador." He tilts his head to one side again and smiles dangerously. "Fortunately, your little charade this evening gives me the perfect opportunity. It's very common, apparently, for a man who overindulges in drink to choke to death on his own vomit in the night."

"Let me go back to the embassy," I plead, my voice emerging as a croak. "I will say nothing to anyone."

"Nothing?" His lips trace a faint smile, which vanishes as he picks up the sword decisively. "Even when you see Dee imprisoned for sorcery, you would still guard my secret? I suspect not." He points the tip at my chest; instinctively, I step back. "The maidservant will find you in the morning, stone-cold and covered with vomit. God knows that hound's produced enough to spare. It will be an embarrassment to the French embassy, of course, but between us Castelnau and I will do our best to cover up the scandal. And in the great tumult of what is about to happen in this country, no one will remember the little Italian monk who couldn't hold his Rhenish."

He ushers me with the point of the sword toward the far end of the room with the obsidian speculum. The casket with the Hermes book is tucked tightly under his arm.

"I'll have to leave you here while I rouse the earl's trusted servants. I don't intend to get my own hands messy. You can amuse yourself, I trust. I suppose it doesn't much matter now what you find here."

He backs toward the door, the sword still levelled at my chest. For a fleeting moment I consider the possibility of running at him, attempting to wrest it from his grasp, but he is a big man, considerably taller than I, and he would be upon me the moment I moved. The sword may be ornamental, but even in the dying light I can see its edge is vicious.

At the door he pauses, one hand on the latch.

"I read your book on memory, you know," he says thoughtfully. "I can confess this now—I considered it the work of an exceptional mind. I am almost sorry things have to end in this way, but a man must look to his own survival in these times. And my destiny is greater than yours. Goodbye, Giordano Bruno." He gives me a long look, then backs out of the door. I hear the sound of a key turning, and the unmistakable scrape of the bookcase sliding back into place. I push my hands through my hair, take a deep breath, and try to examine the room with a clear head, though my blood is racing and I feel faintly nauseous.

The candles have burned almost down to their holders, but still their flames dance and weave in currents of cold air. The atmosphere in the hidden chapel is chill enough that I can see my own breath cloud in front of me as I try to slow it down. By my reckoning, this chapel has been created by partitioning the room that is now the library, closing off the far-thest wall, meaning that we are at the very end of one wing. The bricked-up windows on the wall opposite the door bear this out. But this constant draught must mean that there is another opening somewhere, and the only possibility is behind the speculum. Snatching one of the candles from the altar, my theory is confirmed as I approach the edge of the speculum and its flame is almost snuffed out.

I have very little time. The thick sheet of polished obsidian is broad and taller than a man—a man from Naples, at any rate—and is set into a solid block of wood at the base to keep it upright and give it balance. I put my shoulder against it and push with all my weight. It shifts a fraction of an inch and there is no doubt that the cold air is coming through the gap between the speculum and the wall. I wedge my foot behind the wooden base and attempt to push it outward, leaning my back against the wall, keeping one eye constantly on the door that leads to the library, expect-ing at any moment to hear the sound of a key turning.

Straining every muscle, I push the base of the speculum with both legs until I have shunted it far enough away from the wall to reveal a fire-place, boarded up with wooden planks. My heart sinks, but when I hold the candle close, shielding its flame with my hand, I see that the nails are only loosely hammered in; it would be little work to prise them free, if only I had time. I scrabble for the knife that I kicked under the black cab-inet, easing it toward me with my fingertips. Setting the candle out of the direct draught, I force the blade behind the nail of the topmost board and it comes loose easily; I am able to work my fingers in behind and pull the whole board away from the fireplace. I repeat this with the second, my hands shaking with the need for haste and my fingertips bleeding from the splinters. In a few minutes, I have removed three of the boards, leav-ing a space big enough to fold myself into and climb through into the fireplace. I have no idea how wide the chimney breast will prove to be, or if it is even possible to climb it, but I have no other choice. I sheathe the knife and bend myself double to fit through the gap, reluctantly leaving the candle behind and thanking Fortune that I have the physique of a

Neapolitan; one of these tall, broad Englishmen like Howard or Sidney would not stand a chance.

Inside the chimney breast the darkness is complete and wraps around me heavy as broadcloth, the smell of soot and must thick in my nostrils. I feel the rising panic in my chest that always comes when I find myself in tight spaces, the furious quickening of my heart and breath, the slick of sweat on my palms, the blind terror of being enclosed. Willing myself to stay calm, I feel the brickwork above my head, patting method- ically all around until I encounter what I hoped to find—a metal bracket set into the inside of the chimney, to aid the children when they climb to sweep it clean. No one has been up this chimney for years, I think, as I brace myself with one foot against the back of the fireplace and grip the bracket to pull myself up into the narrow flue, groping blindly above my head for the next one. Cobwebs cling to my mouth and nose; I try to bend my mind to some memory exercises to distract me from the sensa- tion that the walls around me are growing narrower as I climb, feeling for footholds where I can as loose bricks crumble and scatter to the ground below. Soon I can feel the sides pressing against my shoulders; I take a mouthful of sooty air, and it tastes sharper, colder, with the crisp metallic edge of autumn. I can only pray that there is no ornate pot on the top of this chimney, closing me in. The climb has been shorter than I antici- pated; I can feel night air on the top of my head, which helps to damp down the fear that rises as my shoulders become wedged for a moment where the flue tapers. With some judicious wriggling, I manage to raise one arm above my head and feel for the top of the chimney; half squeez- ing, half dragging myself, I emerge through the opening, rubbing filth from my eyes as the wind off the river slaps against my face, its perfume of Thames mud and sewage never more welcome.

Clouds chivvy one another across the sky; a bright moon hides its face briefly before reappearing from their blue-grey shadows. There is enough light to see and be seen as I heave myself out of the chimney stack and onto the roof tiles. Here at the back of the house, the building is a jumble of extensions and rooms added onto the main structure. The room that contains the library and Howard's secret chapel appears to have been built onto the end of the wing as an adjunct; it is only one storey and its roof slopes sharply downward to the left of the chimney breast I have just climbed. Though the tiles are treacherous from the earlier drizzle, if I can ease myself down slowly it would be a simple matter to drop the distance to the ground from where the roof ends; it cannot be more than fifteen feet. Checking that I still have the papers and my knife secure in my waistband, I hold on to the edge of the chimney breast and begin the slide down the roof on my backside. I have no way of knowing whether Henry Howard has returned yet with his servants and found me gone, nor do I have much idea of which way to run once I reach the ground, but at this point I can only keep moving forward; hesitation serves no purpose now.

In the event, I have no choice; the roof is so slippery that I cannot control the speed of my descent and I first slither and then fall the distance to the ground, landing awkwardly on my left side as I try to soften the impact by rolling. I have barely picked myself up and checked that I can still move my arm when a volley of furious barks splits the night air only a stone's throw from where I stand. Panicked, I begin to run guided only by instinct away from the noise; from the vigour of the barking I guess this is not the dog I plied with wine earlier but some other hound kept in the grounds as a guard dog. I should have anticipated that, I think, as my legs carry me surprisingly fast across the open stretch of lawn that slopes down toward the river. Without turning, I feel the dog gaining on me, its ragged breath and the sound of its protest growing alarmingly near at my back. At the foot of the garden an ornate boathouse is built around an inlet from the river where the boats are moored; if I can only reach them and get myself out to open water, the journey back to Salisbury Court is a short one and I might stand a chance of making it before anyone could catch me.

But the door to the boathouse is locked, and I can see the dog now, a tall loping shadow with long legs, barking fit to wake the dead; my body seems to act of its own accord, darting instead across the grass to the iron gate set into the boundary wall where we had entered from the water stairs the previous evening—though it now feels like days ago. The gate is locked too, but fired by the blood pounding through my limbs, I scale it quicker than I have climbed anything, saving perhaps the boundary wall of San Domenico Maggiore, the night I fled from the Inquisition. Hooking my leg over the top of the brick archway, I half scramble, half drop to the top of the slimy steps on the other side, where I almost slip into the water. By now I can hear voices from the direction of the house, and a flickering point of light that can only be a torch appears out of the darkness. I glance behind me at the ink-black river; even in the fractured moonlight I can see how fast the tide is flowing. But I must not hesitate even for an instant; the torchlight is approaching as the dog hurls itself repeatedly against the bars of the gate, forcing its snout through, lips curled back, demented in its frustration at not reaching me. I look down; the water sounds unnaturally loud in the stillness of the night. From the steps it is only a short distance along the boundary wall to the river entrance where the boats are moored, but the current is strong—if I should miss it and be carried downriver . . .

Closing my eyes, I jump; the shock of the cold water knocks the breath out of my body and the black water closes over my head so fast that for what seems like an eternity I am submerged, fighting the burning in my lungs as I flail my way to the surface. As my head breaks through and I snatch a mouthful of air, I begin to struggle with all the strength left in my limbs against the force of the flow, which has already dragged me almost past the edge of the archway leading into the boathouse. As a boy I was a strong swimmer, though these past years in northern lands have muted my enthusiasm for the sport; now determination and fear combine to overcome the stiffness already setting into my limbs and I force my way through the current until I can grasp at the edge of the boundary wall and propel myself into the calmer waters of the boathouse channel. The men's voices carry through the windows and the light of their torch casts shadows on the arched ceiling of the boathouse, but it seems from the angry tone of their exchange and their violent rattling of the door handle that they do not have the key to the boathouse either. My hands are so frozen I can barely bend them to grip the sides of the nearest boat, but I will myself to heave my weight over the edge and sit for a moment, gathering my breath.

I am shaking so violently from the cold that the chattering of my teeth echoes around the walls; attempting to untie the rope that secures the wherry to an iron ring in the wall is almost beyond my numb fingers, but perhaps fortune is smiling on me, because I stumble back into the boat as it finally comes loose, and with shaking arms I shunt myself back along the wall with one of the oars until I emerge again into the choppy waters of the Thames. From the shadows behind me, a man's protests join with the relentless barking of the dog in a chorus of anger, which fades as I set my face into the wind and bend the last of my strength to holding this little craft steady along the north bank, hoping that I can see enough to recognise the landing place at Water Lane and the garden wall of Salisbury Court. As the prow of the wherry catches a large wave head-on, the spray drenching me again with icy water, and a sharp pain arrows through my left shoulder as I try to wrench myself back on course, the prospect of the embassy walls has never seemed more enticing.

Chapter 16

I set the boat adrift into the tide as I leap from it into the soft mud that silts the cobbles where Water Lane slopes down to the river. The moonlight and the pale edge of sky against the eastern horizon allowed me to see enough to recognise the Temple Gardens as I passed and to steer my way into the bank in time to disembark at home. Soaked, chilled, shivering uncontrollably and fighting a fierce headache behind my eyes, I drag myself the few yards up Water Lane to the garden gate of Salisbury Court and almost weep with relief when I find it unlocked. I do not expect to have the same luck with the house; I am wondering if any of the servants are awake yet and how much consternation or gossip my appearance will occasion, when I pass through the walled garden and notice a light burning in one of the ground-floor windows. Creeping closer, counting the windows, I realise that the glow comes from Castel-nau's study. Sleep still eludes the ambassador, it seems, poor man. How Courcelles must have relished giving him the account of why I had not returned with them last night! I owe him an explanation of that at least, and perhaps it is preferable to waking the servants. I set my jaw and, crouching low, tap gently against the windowpane.

There is a cry of alarm from inside, and the sound of something falling. Then a shadow appears at the window, holding up an oil lamp.

"My lord ambassador—it is I, Bruno." I can hardly force the words through my rattling teeth.

A pause, and the window opens a crack.

"Bruno? Dear God, man, what on earth has happened to you? What are you doing out there?"

"Can I come in first?" I indicate the window; he pushes it wider and I hoist myself onto the sill before tumbling through and landing with a dull thud like wet laundry on the floor. Castelnau holds up the lamp and stares at me in wordless disbelief as I pick myself up. In the still air of his study I am aware of the fierce reek of Thames mud coming off me. The ambassador takes a step back. Eventually he shakes his head.

"I knew philosophers in Paris. They were quiet men with dusty beards who confined themselves to their books. They did not fall through windows in the early hours covered in blood and shit. I feel there are whole realms of your life that I cannot begin to comprehend, Bruno. What is that all over your face? It looks like soot." He sounds not accusing but sorry. "I thought you stayed at Arundel House?"

"I fell in the river on the way back," I gasp, wrapping my arms around my chest through a series of violent convulsions. "I can explain—"

"You will die of cold first—here, take those clothes off and put this on." He shrugs off the heavy woollen robe he wears around his own shoulders. Underneath he still wears shirt and breeches; it appears he has not even made a pretence of going to bed. "Get yourself by the fire."

He holds out the robe, nodding to indicate I should hurry; with some embarrassment, I peel away my filthy wet clothes and drop them in a heap at my feet. My dagger clatters to the floor and I pick it up hastily and lay it on the edge of his desk. It is only as I lift my shirt over my head that I feel the sodden paper plastered against my skin. Castelnau watches with curiosity as I unstick it and hold it away from me, my heart dropping like a stone. The ink has smudged beyond recognition. I curse aloud in Italian and find myself fighting back tears of fury at my own failure; for the second time I have lost a piece of vital evidence that would have been beyond price to Walsingham.

"Something valuable, I take it?" Castelnau asks, as I flap the paper uselessly back and forth. When I do not reply, he ushers me gently toward the hearth, where the embers of a fire are quietly dying. He takes the paper from my hand and spreads it out over the flagstones in front of the fire, but I can already see that there is no chance of proving that it once showed an illegal genealogy in Henry Howard's hand. All I had to offer Walsingham was the report that such a document had once existed; I would need to get this information to Fowler as soon as possible. Perhaps he was already preparing to take his report of last night to Walsingham at first light, to inform him of the invasion plans, the list of Catholic lords and safe havens, and tell him that I had contrived to stay the night, whetting his appetite for whatever further evidence I might bring. Again, I would let them down.

In the silence, the first birds strike up their chorus outside the window. The ambassador wraps his beautiful robe around my muddy, soot-streaked body and crosses to his desk to pour me the last dregs of wine from a decanter. I guess that he must have drunk the rest himself in the long sleepless hours. I clasp the glass between my hands, trying not to spill it as I shiver, while Castelnau comes to stand beside me in front of the glowing ashes. He gives another of those great sighs that suggest he carries the weight of the world on his shoulders.

"There is bad news, Bruno." He speaks without looking at me, and before the words are out of his mouth, I know what he is about to tell me. "Léon is dead."

I bite my lip. Part of me has expected this since Dumas failed to return yesterday, but I have tried to persuade myself that there could be some other explanation. If only Marie had not interrupted, if only I had been more forthright in prising out his story about the ring, if I had paid more attention to his fears instead of dismissing his nervous disposition. I take a sip of wine, feeling sick to the depths of my stomach, but find myself unable to swallow; I cannot avoid the certainty that Léon Dumas, like Abigail Morley, died because of me, and that I should have prevented it.

"What happened?" I ask eventually, after we have stared together into the hearth for a few minutes.

"The aldermen came last night, after you had all left," he says, his voice flat. "Some boatmen found his body in the river down by Paul's Wharf and reported it."

"Paul's Wharf?" I glance at him. "By Throckmorton's house, then?"

"Nearby. They think he was strangled by some cutpurse. It's a dangerous part of town for that—all the foreign merchants coming off the boats. He had nothing on him but the clothes he was wearing when they pulled him out. He had been in the water some hours, they said."

"How did they know to come here?"

"They asked the dockhands and boatmen at the wharf. Someone recognised him, knew he was French. Said he was a familiar face down there."

So he would have been, from all the trips to Throckmorton, I think. So where was the young courier now? On his way to Mary Stuart in Sheffield? If Dumas was killed near Paul's Wharf, did his killer follow him there, or lie in wait, knowing that he was a regular visitor to Throckmorton's house? In fact, the one person who would have known to expect a visit from Dumas was Throckmorton himself. I glance across at the window and recall the day I found Throckmorton in this office unannounced, the way he could not keep his eyes off the ambassador's desk. Dumas was killed because of the ring. Everything centres around the ring. Dumas stole the ring from Mary's letter before it reached Howard, someone paid him for it, and the ring ended up with Cecily Ashe. I rub my eyes; my tired brain gropes for connections, but again I come back to Cecily's mystery lover, the man who gave her the ring as a pledge of their pact, the same man who gave her a vial of poison for Elizabeth Tudor. Dumas had to die because he knew this man's identity; it is the only explanation. But why now—unless this man had new reason to fear that Dumas was about to expose him? At this thought, my body convulses so violently that the wine in my glass lurches and spills a drop on the flagstones, and the word that springs instantly to my mind is on my lips before I can stop it.

"Marie."

"What was that?" Castelnau turns to look at me with red-rimmed eyes.

"I—nothing." I had not meant to speak her name aloud. "Marie—she came home safely last night?"

"Yes, of course. And Courcelles. He was full of stories of how you disgraced yourself and the embassy. Of course, I realised that you must have been putting on a show." He inclines his head with a meaningful expression.

"My lord?" It is fortunate that I am shaking so violently that any show of anxiety is lost.

"I did not say as much to Courcelles, but I guessed that you took to heart my fears that Henry Howard is shifting his loyalties toward the Spanish. I supposed you had decided to take the opportunity to find out what you could while you were under his roof, disarm them into revealing something by a show of drunkenness. Courcelles would not have the subtlety to understand such a strategy." He laughs weakly. "Besides, last night I had other matters on my mind. Come with me, Bruno. I want you to see him."

"They brought the body here?"

"He has family in France, poor boy. They'll want the body back to bury him there, but I don't know if that can be arranged in time." He passes a hand across his brow. "I must write to them. In the midst of all this." He waves a hand imprecisely, but I understand: he means the invasion.

"I would like to see him," I say. The ambassador nods as if his head is too heavy to hold up. I am seized by a sudden urge to confide in him, to tell him of the counterplots eddying around him, of Henry Howard's ambitions, of his wife's machinations, of Dumas and the ring. In my exhaustion, I almost believe for one absurd, fleeting moment, the instant it takes to draw breath, that I might be relieved of this burden if I share it with him, if I tell this upright, fatherly man caught between so many conflicting factions that I am not what he thinks, that I have been deceiving him all this while, but that, ultimately, we both desire the same outcome: to prevent a war. I cup my hand over my mouth and lower my eyes to the floor until this insanity has passed and floated away like smoke. I have chosen to live a double life, and I must remain faithful to that choice, even when the strain of it almost fells me.

"You realise how little you know a man, though you sit beside him for the best part of every day," Castelnau muses, subdued, as he leads me along the passageway toward the rear door by the kitchen. "I never asked him about himself, you know. All I did was bark instructions at him from dawn to dusk. I don't think he was happy in England, but he never complained."

He takes a key from a chain at his belt, unlocks the door, and leads me across the small courtyard to the collection of outbuildings and storerooms that surround it on two sides. My feet are bare and so cold that they hurt against the cobbles, but the ambassador seems not to have thought of this and with a great effort of will I force myself to ignore it. The sky is light enough now to do without candles, and when he pushes open the door to one outbuilding I see clearly the form of Léon Dumas laid out on a trestle, his head contorted to one side at an unnatural angle. Castelnau stands in the doorway as if keeping vigil, without looking at the corpse; I pull the robe tighter around myself and approach the table slowly.

Dumas's large startled eyes have been closed, but his face is not peaceful. It is bruised and swollen, the lips puffy and parted. Gently, with one forefinger, I pull back the neck of his shirt to see the mark of a ligature around his throat. I picture him walking those streets by the dock, preoccupied with the guilt he had tried unsuccessfully to unburden on me, ambushed by the killer stepping out of the shadows with a cord or a twist of cloth.

"He must have been set upon in broad daylight," I murmur. I reach out and lay my fingertips on his cold arm.

Castelnau shifts his weight from one foot to the other.

"You know what it's like down at the docks, Bruno, it's a bad part of town. The boatmen always brawling, half of them drunk in the day. Thieves on the lookout for any opportunity. People turn a blind eye."

"But Léon did not go about looking as if he would be worth robbing on the off chance," I say, glancing down at Dumas's worn breeches, now filthy with river silt.

"What are you saying?"

I hesitate; the ambassador has enough weighing on him at the present time, perhaps it would be kinder to let him persuade himself that Dumas was the victim of a random assault by an opportunistic robber.

"You are wondering, I think, if he was not attacked by a street thief but by someone who knew of his business," he says, when I do not reply.

He glances at the door as he says this, chewing on the knuckle of his thumb, and for an awful moment I wonder if he is hiding something. I stare at him across Dumas's corpse, until he meets my eye.

"What I do not know, Bruno, is whether he got his letter to Throckmorton before he was attacked. The aldermen said they found nothing on him, but that does not mean it couldn't have been taken. If he was known as a regular visitor, perhaps someone might have guessed . . ." His voice trails into anxious silence.

"That he was a courier to Mary?"

"They say Francis Walsingham has eyes everywhere," he says, pulling at his beard. I turn my own eyes studiously back to the body on the table. "Suppose Throckmorton has been indiscreet? We may presume they watch Mary's servants closely in Sheffield Castle—what if Throckmorton has been recognised up there as he comes and goes? I will confess, Bruno," he murmurs, lowering his voice, "I have been wondering about

Léon's loyalty since I learned of his death. He wrote out my private letters, as you know—he had access to the secret ciphers, all of it. I never
thought to doubt him until tonight, but now I can think of nothing else.
What do you make of it, Bruno? Might he have been so desperate for
English coins that he would have sold me and the embassy?"

His eyes grow wide and behind the tiredness I see that he is genuinely eaten up with fear; immediately I see what I must do, though his
words strike at my heart and my every instinct is to look away in shame.
Instead, I shake my head.

"You have begun to jump at shadows, my lord." I make my voice as
reassuring as I can manage, remembering the tone my father would use
when I was a boy and woke with night terrors. "The burden you must
carry would have broken a lesser man by now, and this terrible business
has shaken us all." I lay a hand gently on Dumas's frozen body. "But Léon
was true to you and to France, I am sure of it. Let us not allow fear to distract us from our purpose now. As you said yourself, Paul's Wharf is a
dangerous enough place for a foreigner."

He grimaces. "But I have been a fool. That letter I wrote to Mary
assuring her of my loyalty in the face of Howard's accusations—I wrote
it in haste, to catch Throckmorton before he left, so I did not bother to
use the cipher. It has the embassy seal—if it should have fallen into the
wrong hands—"

His eyes are fixed on me, asking for some reassurance. I would like to
tell him that I think whoever killed Dumas would not have the slightest
interest in his letter, but I can't be certain of anything anymore. My mind
is a cat's cradle of connections and theories, but this habit of chasing one
idea until I begin to believe it is truth has led me into trouble before and I
must not repeat the same mistake I made over Henry Howard. Even so, I
cannot help returning to my encounter that morning—Dumas's almost-
confession and Marie's abrupt appearance—like a tongue probing a sore
tooth. *Marie.* Her devotion to the Duke of Guise and his cause; her ruthlessness; her intimacy with Courcelles. If Marie had overheard Dumas in
my room before she knocked, if she feared what he might confide—what

could that mean? That *she* was behind the theft of the ring? Dumas had certainly looked stricken when she appeared, though I had assumed that was just the awkwardness of the situation. But Dumas, as I had learned last night, also paid a visit to Arundel House on the day he died, before his errand to Throckmorton; in his agitated state, what might he have said there, and to whom, that could have led someone to fear his loose tongue?

The thought of Arundel House recalls in an instant the events of the past night, momentarily forgotten in the shock of seeing Dumas dead. I pass my hand across my brow and my knees almost buckle under a sudden wash of exhaustion, so that I have to put out a hand to steady myself against the trestle.

"Are you all right, Bruno?" Castelnau takes a step forward, offers me his hand. "You should go inside. I'll have the kitchen servants heat you some water to bathe."

I rub at my face self-consciously as I begin to walk slowly around the trestle, peering at Dumas's corpse as if intense scrutiny might yield some clue, as if his poor dead limbs might speak to me of who did this. I pause for a moment by his head and lightly touch his hair, matted and darkened from the river; perhaps out of tiredness, frustration, sorrow, or guilt, my eyes are suddenly filled with tears and I have to turn aside to rub them brusquely away with the heel of my hand.

"He was fond of you," Castelnau says gently. "He was an odd one, Léon—kept to himself. But he spoke highly of you. I think you were the nearest he had to a friend in this country."

"I should have been a better friend," I say, and it comes out as a croak.

"We could all have served him better. The pity is that we never thought of it while he lived. So often the way. Come," Castelnau says, gesturing toward the door. I whisper a silent farewell and am about to step away when my eye is caught by a mark on the front of Dumas's shirt. On the left side, over his heart, a crimson stain blossoms, barely visible under the grime left by the water. Cautiously I peel back his shirt to see the skin beneath cut and matted with blood, just in that one spot, about the size of a gold angel. I spit on my hand and rub it on the dried blood, using the mud-stiffened linen of his shirt to scrape away the scab.

"What are you doing, Bruno?" Castelnau moves closer, peering now as if his curiosity has overcome his aversion. I find I cannot speak.

On Dumas's breast, cut with the point of a knife, is an astrological symbol. A circle with a cross beneath, a semicircle balanced on top, curving upward. For a moment I can't fathom it; this sign is out of keeping with the others, it has nothing to do with the apocalypse prophecies or the Great Conjunction. But as I stare at the mark deftly cut into my friend's flesh, I understand: this is the sign of Mercury, the messenger of the gods. Whoever killed Dumas left this as a signature, a deliberate nod to his connection with the other deaths and surely a mocking reference to his role as courier. I clench my teeth; anger boils up and sticks in my throat. This murderer treats death as a game, carving signs into skin as a private joke—but meant for whom? Unlike the marks of Jupiter and Saturn on the bodies of Cecily and Abigail, this one is discreet, almost an afterthought. Dumas's death was a matter of necessity, not intended as a public display, and yet this mark stands out as a taunt, a message from the killer to someone he—or she—knew would understand its meaning, just in case they should see it. Is that someone me, I wonder?

"What is that?" Castelnau points a finger at the raw-edged cut.

"A knife wound, I think." I lift the dead man's shirt back into place and press my palm for a moment over his still heart.

The ambassador gives me a long look. His eyes are tight and bloodshot, the skin beneath sagging, but he regards me as father might a wayward son.

"You should clean yourself up, Bruno. Later, I want you to tell me your version of what passed last night at Arundel House. But first, I recommend you sleep."

"And you, my lord?"

"Oh, sleep refuses to keep me company." He passes both hands over his face as if washing; it is a gesture of defeat. "I must go to see Mendoza this morning. The Spanish grow closer to Mary Stuart by the day and if we are not careful, they will squeeze out even the Duke of Guise once the invasion is under way. I will have Courcelles start the necessary arrangements for Léon's burial while I am out. The aldermen have the sheriffs making enquiries in the borough, but I do not hold out much hope that we will find the villains who did this."

"There must always be hope, my lord," I say, touching him lightly on the arm as he opens the door for me. But in this instance I am not sure I believe it any longer.

BATHED AND DRESSED in a fresh shirt and underhose, I lie on the bed of my attic room, staring at the ceiling, a whole choir of pains singing behind my eyes. I have slept fitfully past dinnertime, though when I woke a small jug of beer and some bread had been left outside my room, a thoughtful gesture I guessed came from Castelnau. Washing away the layers of soot and Thames mud in a tub of hot water provided by one of the kitchen servants has revealed a colourful array of cuts and bruises, but my exhausted body cannot drag my mind with it into dreams. The shock of seeing Dumas murdered has made me forget temporarily the seriousness of my own predicament: Henry Howard wants me silenced.

"Rumour travels with winged sandals, like Mercury," Howard had said to me at the Whitehall concert, on the night of Abigail's murder. Mercury, the messenger of the gods. Was that part of his cryptic warning, or merely coincidence? Now our own messenger, Dumas, lies dead with the mark of Mercury cut into his chest. My only protection lies in Howard's fear for his own reputation and public standing; now that I have deprived him of his chance to kill me in a perfect simulation of an accident, he will at least—I hope—be cautious about anything that would cause a scandal or link my death back to him. Inside Salisbury Court, I ought to be safe, but I have little doubt that as soon as I step into the streets of London it will only be a matter of time before I am the next to be dragged into a side street with a rope around my neck. I could tell

Castelnau about the threat from Howard, but what could he do? The ambassador is already too anxious about making an enemy of Howard and pushing him into the arms of Mendoza. I should get a message to Fowler about the genealogy and through him I could alert Walsingham to Howard's intentions, but here I am torn because I feel an instinctive desire to protect the secret of Howard's chapel. If Arundel House were to be searched, his experimentation with magic would surely come to light and the Hermes book would be seized by the authorities, who might in their ignorance see fit to destroy it. At least while it is in Henry Howard's hands I know it will remain protected, even if for the moment it is also out of my reach; though in his eyes we are mortal enemies, we are also curiously bound by this secret and our shared desire for it. I close my eyes and summon to mind the feel of its stiff pages and rough leather binding under my fingertips; the loss of it hits me again like a physical pang. Given time and opportunity, I have no doubt that Dee and I between us could break the Hermetic cipher. It is just a matter of retrieving the book somehow. But if Fowler has already reported the previous night's meeting to Walsingham, as he surely must, perhaps the principal secretary is already drawing up plans for an official search of Arundel House. I can only trust that Henry Howard, who has taken considerable risks for that book and guarded it for fourteen years, will have the wit to keep it safe from the pursuivants.

Eventually I feel I must get up and do something. I pull on clean breeches, shake my damp hair into some sort of shape, and take a look at my reflection in the glass by my bed. The wound on my temple is healing well, but my beard is unruly and to my bleary eyes the past few days seem to have aged me by years. There is still a stubborn rim of soot around my hairline. I pour some water from the pitcher I keep on a table by the window into a shallow bowl and rinse my teeth with salt and water. Well, I think, if Marie's interest in me is genuine, she will not be deterred by the lingering scent of Thames mud. Now is the time to put her to the test. She is not the only one who can try to use her body to tease out information.

The house is silent as I cross the first-floor gallery, my footsteps echoing around the dark wood as I step through angled shafts of light. At any moment I expect to see one of the servants, or Courcelles, with his gift of appearing wherever I happen to be, wearing his most contemptuous face. But there is no one, and I reach the rear corridor of the first floor, where Marie and her daughter have their rooms, unimpeded. From behind a closed door opposite the back staircase I hear the high-pitched chatter of a little girl interrupted by a woman's voice, more severe. It does not sound like Marie. The second door must be her chamber. If she is not there, so much the better; I can at least make a search of her room and if she should find me there, I have a ready excuse. With a deep breath, I knock softly at the door.

"*Entrez.*"

She is seated at a small writing desk by the window, a pen in her hand. She looks up and an expression of confusion flits briefly across her face when she sees me in the doorway, as if I am out of context, an actor who has wandered onto the stage in the wrong scene, but she composes herself quickly and motions to me to close the door.

"Bruno." She stands and smooths down her skirt; she wears a dress of pale gold silk, the bodice sewn with pearl buttons. Her hair is unbound and falls around her shoulders; the light catches the curve of her cheekbone as she moves toward me. I remind myself that I am doing this to catch a murderer, and that this woman may even be the architect of those murders.

"You have heard the terrible news about the clerk, I suppose?" She does not immediately approach me but stands a few feet away, her hands folded in front of her. She seems more than a little discomfited by my unexpected visit, which is probably to my advantage.

"Dumas. Yes. I—I can hardly believe it." I pinch the bridge of my nose between my forefinger and thumb and lower my eyes. Let her think I am overcome with emotion; women are always glad of an opportunity to comfort a man in distress, I have noticed.

"One can so easily forget what a dangerous city this is." She gives a little shudder of distaste. "Especially if you are a Catholic. Poor—Dumas, was it? And how are you today? You must have quite a headache." She laughs, nervously, and glances at the door.

"Yes. I wanted to apologise for my conduct last night—" I begin, touching my fingers to my temple.

"Oh, please, think nothing of it. It was amusing to see the Earl of Arundel so shocked. He really is the most unbearable prig." She pouts, and this time her laughter sounds more relaxed. "I did not take you for a drinker though, Bruno."

"No, I am not usually," I say, allowing my gaze to wander around the room in a way that I hope is not too obvious. Against the opposite wall stands a bed with white curtains drawn around and beside it a dresser with a looking glass propped against the wall, strewn with pots of cosmetics, brushes, and glass bottles. If someone wanted to fill a perfume bottle with poison, here would be an obvious place to find one. By the window is the small writing desk; several sheets of paper lie covered in neat script where she left off at my interruption. I turn my attention back to her face. "It was out of character. I have a lot on my mind. Forgive me."

Finally she seems to soften; she comes closer, lays a hand on my arm.

"Nothing to forgive. We are all carrying a great weight at the moment—there is so much at stake here. Not just our lives, if we should fail, but the future of Christendom. Let us not forget that this is what we fight for." She looks up at me, her eyes wide and full of meaning. "We must all try to stay strong. There are so few of us—we will not succeed divided."

I nod with feeling as I glance again at her dressing table, and then I see it. Amid the pots and cloths and trailing strings of glass beads, a small green velvet casket, of the size that might hold a signet ring. Mary Stuart's ring was sent in a green velvet casket, I recall. I cross to the dresser and make a pretence of studying myself in the mirror.

"I must apologise too for my appearance," I say, bending as if to examine my own dishevelled face.

"Your appearance is as charming as ever, Bruno," she says, still smiling, but there is uncertainty in her voice; she would like me to get to the point. I meet her eyes in the mirror as I pick up a necklace and allow its stones to trickle through my fingers.

"You have some beautiful jewellery here," I murmur, trying to sound as if I am a connoisseur. "And this is pretty too." I pick up the green casket and hold it up to the light, turning it around in my hands.

"Yes, my husband is very generous with his gifts."

"May I see?" I open the casket; it is empty. "Is this from Paris? I have seen some similar—"

"I do not recall where it is from," she says, and this time her impatience is unmistakable. "Bruno—was there anything? Only, I am just writing some correspondence while Catherine is with her governess, and soon they will be finished, so if . . ." She leaves the implication suspended.

I replace the box and turn to face her.

"I am sorry. I have been confused by my feelings for you, Marie. I have been trying to fight something that cannot be fought."

She seems taken aback by this; again I have the sense that I am reading the wrong lines. For a moment I fear she is going to tell me that it's not a convenient time, that I have missed my chance. But she regards me with a kind of curiosity, then moves again toward me with a last glance over her shoulder at the door before laying a hand on my chest. I must get her talking about Dumas again while I have her attention.

"I have been distressed by the death of my friend, too." I lower my head toward her. She cups a hand around the back of my neck and strokes my hair. A simple gesture of reassurance; I do not fool myself that she is sincere, and yet this touch reminds me how long it has been since I allowed anyone to show me affection.

"Poor Bruno," she murmurs. "But there was nothing you could have done."

"Yet he seemed so anxious yesterday morning," I persist, curling my neck back like a cat as she caresses me. "I should have paid more attention."

"You were not to know," she whispers, soothing. "Did he seem anxious about something in particular, then? Did he tell you what was troubling him?" Her fingers slide through my hair and down my nape inside my collar, but I am alert now; she wants information from me, just as I want it from her without yielding anything myself.

"He didn't get the chance."

She tilts her head back sharply with a questioning look.

"That poor man," she says lightly, resuming her stroking. "I barely paid him any heed, except to worry what he might say to my husband about my visiting your chamber. I suppose that is one less problem now." She smiles up as if expecting me to share the joke. By this time I should not be surprised at her callousness, but somehow it shocks afresh with each new display. But I smile in return. "Besides," she purrs, as she takes my arms, still hanging awkwardly at my sides, and places them purposefully around her small waist as she presses against me, "my husband is out at the Spanish embassy this afternoon. Perhaps it would do you good to forget your worries for a while, Bruno."

And then her mouth is on mine and I simply let her; my conscience and my will seem to recede to a pinpoint at the back of my skull so that I stand there, almost inert with tiredness and resignation, while my body responds predictably. Among the detached thoughts circling my brain as her fingers slide along my collarbone and begin to unlace my shirt is the memory of the look that passed between her and Dumas the previous morning in my chamber. He was afraid of her. This woman, the one whose tongue is flickering over my lips and who is even now lifting my shirt over my head as her nails scrape lightly up my spine, might be the very person who decided at that moment to have him silenced.

She drops my shirt to the floor and runs a hand down my chest, then takes both my hands and leads me to the bed, where she draws back the curtain and pushes against me until I am lying across the sheet. She eases herself down beside me—a complex manoeuvre, given the volume of her skirts—and I close my eyes as her hair brushes my skin and I feel her lips on my chest, moving lower, as her hand massages expertly along the inside of my thigh, my skin fully alive but my thoughts still remote until a woman's voice from somewhere beyond the room distinctly says, "Madame?"

Marie leaps up as if she has been stung, motioning for me to pull up my legs inside the bed.

"What is it, Bernadette?"

There is a timid tap at the door.

"May I speak to you, madame? About Catherine."

"Can't it wait?" she calls back, peevish.

"I fear not, madame. She complains of a fever and a pain in her stomach."

"Well, I am not a physician. Tell her you will fetch the barber surgeon—that will soon put an end to these games."

A pause from the other side of the door.

"Madame, I do not think she pretends. She feels very hot." The governess's voice is strained. "She is calling for her mother."

"Oh, very well. Give me a moment."

Marie rolls her eyes, stands, and brushes down her dress. "Stay there," she mouths, then draws the curtain around me. I lie motionless as I hear the door click shut, then with an almighty effort of will, I bring my thoughts back to the task in hand. Adjusting my breeches, I scuttle to the writing desk and scan the sheets of paper Marie has left there. "*Mon cher Henri,*" the letter begins. At first I assume she is writing to Howard, but as I scan through the papers, I am startled to find a reference to taking the Crown of England followed by the French throne. Is this King Henri of France, then? Convinced I must have misread it, I force myself to look again, more thoroughly, and I see that in the same paragraph she writes of "your Scottish cousin" being easy to move aside in due course, and "the reign of our weak king" facing its last days. I feel my face stretch in disbelief as I take it in. This is meant for Henri, Duke of Guise, and the letter is full of scattered intimacies; a mention of the pain of separation, the cruelty of distance, remembered embraces, a wish to be reunited as soon as God allows. At the end of the letter she has scribbled a postscript, in a hand that looks as if it was done in haste: "I do not know when you will receive this, as I cannot send by my usual means." Beside her signature she has drawn a picture of a rose.

I return the paper to the desk, slow and stupid with amazement. This invasion plan truly has become all things to all men; Marie may talk of unity but while Henry Howard contrives his own secret agenda, so too does she scheme to turn it to her own profit. So she is more intimate than I guessed with the Duke of Guise, who evidently regards the English throne as his rightful spoils once the small matter of replacing the monarch is dealt with. What is Marie's ultimate ambition, I wonder—is she hoping her husband will be a casualty of the "weak" French king's demise, so that she can take her place by Guise's side? I wander back to the dressing table and pick up the green velvet casket again, still shaking my head. Behind their talk of religious purity and their duty to Christendom and the eternal souls of the English people, each of them is scrambling for dynastic advantage. You can be certain that Mendoza and the Spanish king are not lending their resources out of piety either, I think, turning the box over and over between my hands; if this invasion should really happen, they would tear England apart between them like street dogs falling on a scrap of meat. Elizabeth Tudor will certainly be a casualty, but Mary Stuart could also find her jubilant restoration turns quickly to a worse fate if the wrong faction gains the upper hand, and those good, rational men of the Privy Council—Walsingham, Burghley, Leicester—would all be destroyed. This small island, with its strange ways and the few precious freedoms it offers to those who, like me, have made an enemy of Rome, will be thrown into a turmoil that will make all the end-of-days prophecies of the penny pamphlets look like children's stories, and who will be left to restore order except the powers of France or Spain, funded by the pope?

The green casket tells me nothing. I am no expert in jewellery, so I have no way of knowing whether this little box could be Mary Stuart's and have made its way to Marie via Dumas, or whether it is the commonest sort of container. But thinking of Dumas, I suddenly stop and remember in a new light Marie's hasty postscript. She could not send by her usual means—could she have meant Dumas? If Guise is her lover, she could not send letters to him through the embassy's diplomatic packet; she would have needed another messenger, a secret means of conveying letters to France. Guise has his own agents and envoys in England—he conducts himself as if he were an alternative king already—and Dumas, forever trotting back and forth to the city with letters for Throckmorton and the official embassy correspondence, could easily carry one more set of messages. As I knew only too well, he was more than willing to run additional errands if there was a chance to make money—a willingness that eventually cost him his life. Did Marie imagine that he had told me her secret? I recall the Duke of Guise from his appearances at the court of King Henri when I was living in Paris last year; a handsome man in his early thirties, with exuberantly curled hair and a sweeping air of entitlement. The French king always seemed cowed by him; it is easy to see how he might seem, by contrast, like the charismatic leader France lacks, especially to a woman like Marie. I regard my own naked torso in the glass and cannot avoid wondering whether she does to him what she had been about to do to me if the governess had not interrupted; I dislike myself for the pang of resentment this produces.

When the latch clicks I turn in anticipation, but instead of Marie, it is Courcelles who stands in the doorway with a piece of paper in his hand. He blinks rapidly, looks me up and down, glances to the bed, and makes several attempts to speak before any words emerge.

"What—? Where is she?"

"Her daughter was taken ill."

He glances at the door, then back to me as if struggling to accept the evidence of his eyes. Then he tucks the paper away by his side.

"And you—she—?" He waves a hand vaguely in the direction of the bed. I find myself battling an urge to laugh at his evident lack of composure; I wonder if Courcelles is also her lover, if she amuses herself with him while she writes her scheming billets-doux to Guise. Certainly his demeanour betrays a very personal sense of outrage. I merely shrug and raise an eyebrow; my state of undress and evident arousal make any justification redundant.

"I might ask what brings you to her private chamber," I say instead, trying to sound casual as I bend to retrieve my shirt.

"A messenger has just arrived for her from Lord Henry Howard." He brandishes his folded letter at me.

"Is that your job now? Should you not be making the burial arrangements for poor Dumas?"

This seems to galvanise him; he strides across to me and jabs a finger in my face.

"You think you can get away with anything, don't you? You just talk your way into everyone's confidence, you show no respect for birth or position, you think you can carve your own path with no consequences, all because you can make the king of France laugh."

"Oh, stop—you are making me blush."

"How do you think the ambassador will respond to *this*, Bruno?" he hisses, poking my bare chest and leaning down so that his face is almost as near to mine as Marie's was a moment ago. "After the faith he has placed in you. I should not be surprised if he decided to send you back to France. Let the king protect you from what's coming there, if he can."

"And what *is* coming there, Claude?" I say, determined to keep my voice light. "Something King Henri should know about? Or my lord ambassador? Some sort of coup, perhaps? As a loyal subject, I'm sure you would share whatever you knew to protect your sovereign. Or do your loyalties lie elsewhere now?" I pull my shirt over my head and stare him down; to my satisfaction, he looks away first. I glance over his shoulder and see Marie standing in the doorway, her arms folded across her chest and her lips pressed into a white line.

"If my husband hears a word about this, you will both be on the next boat to France with such a stain on your reputations that you will never find a position in the French court again," she says, pointing between us. "Understand?"

"Marie—*I* have done nothing! I came to bring you this and found him here." Courcelles flaps his letter at her, aggrieved. She gives him a long, reproving look.

"Don't be disingenuous, Claude. We must all keep one another's confidences in this house." She looks from him to me and I realise then that Courcelles is familiar with this room, this bed. I watch Marie with rising anger. She certainly knows how to keep herself busy. The worst of it is that I am most annoyed with myself for feeling even a passing stab of jealousy. Then I think of Castelnau keeping his lonely night vigil in his study and the anger is displaced by a wave of guilt.

"How is Catherine?" I ask.

"She'll be fine." Her tone is clipped now, businesslike, as she reaches for the letter and breaks the seal. It is clear that I am no longer required. "You had better go, Bruno. And lace your shirt. We don't want the servants to gossip."

Courcelles aims a look of pure hatred at me as I reach the door, but my attention is fixed on the letter in Marie's hand. What can Howard have to tell her since last night, unless it is something about me?

"Bruno," she says, holding out her hand, palm up. "The box?"

I realise I am still clutching the green velvet casket. I pass it over with a muttered apology; she narrows her eyes, then her face softens and she squeezes my hand briefly. "Perhaps we will pick up our discussion where we left off another time."

Lifting her hand, I press it to my lips in a grand gesture, just to irritate Courcelles, who appears ready to explode with an excess of choler. I may not have achieved everything I came here for, but I have discovered Marie's underlying motive. What part does Courcelles play, then, I wonder, considering him as I stand in the doorway and he watches me with the face of a man who would gladly commit murder at this moment? Does he know about the Duke of Guise, or does he believe that he, Claude de Courcelles, is destined to replace the ambassador at Marie's side when the glorious Catholic reconquest is complete? Either way, I sense that the two of them have closed ranks against me, standing shoulder to shoulder as they wait for me to leave so they can discuss this message from Howard, and again I am furious with myself for feeling that she has toyed with me; absurd, too, when it was I who went to her chamber with the intention of tricking her in the first place. I give them a last look, then leave them to their plotting. As I pass the door of the nursery, I catch the muffled sound of a child crying.

Chapter 17

Back in my own room, my shirt laced, I grow increasingly troubled by the thought of that letter from Henry Howard, which Courcelles and Marie are reading even now. He will not have told them anything like the truth, but if I were to second-guess him, I would expect him to have concocted some story about having discovered my betrayal of them all, some reason why they should keep me within their sight until he finds another chance to remove the threat that he fears I pose for him.

I would give almost anything at this moment for the chance to see Sidney, to have him make light of my predicament by punching me in my painful shoulder, then draw his sword in my defence. But Sidney is miles away in Barn Elms, and with Howard's men on the lookout for me, I would not wager much on my chances of reaching Walsingham's house in one piece. Wind buffets the window frames, making them rattle like teeth, and through the panes I can see only churning grey clouds. At this moment my heart feels constricted and I cannot escape the thought that

England has been a mistake. I thought it would bring me freedom from persecution, but since I landed on this friendless island it seems I have done nothing but put myself on the wrong side of Catholics who want to kill me. I could have stayed in Naples for that, I think, gloomily, though I know the fault is my own; no one forced me to accept Walsingham's offer of a place in his network of informers. I chose it because I found him to be a man I respected, and because, as I had told Fowler, I believed that the freedoms Queen Elizabeth had established here were worth defending against the tyranny of Rome. And—let me not fool myself—because I knew that to serve Elizabeth and her principal secretary in this way was likely to bring me reward and patronage of a kind no writer can advance without. Now, as I pace the confines of my room, I fear my life will be in danger if I leave the embassy or if I stay here.

But I am not altogether friendless in London; in the absence of Sidney, there is one person a little nearer with whom I can share a confidence. If I can get as far as St. Andrew's Hill and reach Fowler without being attacked, I could at least stick close to him; I would be less vulnerable in company. I picture again poor Dumas grabbed as he passes the mouth of an alleyway down at the wharf, the cord pulled tight around his throat before he can draw breath to scream, his frantic struggle for life unseen even as his limbs give their last few spasms and fall to stillness, before his body is dumped like a sack of refuse in the river. If I can avoid that fate for long enough to find Fowler, I can solicit his opinion on my unfinished theory, formed in my restless half sleep this morning: that Marie, prompted by the Duke of Guise, was behind the plot to poison Elizabeth on Accession Day. She paid Dumas to steal the ring, while Courcelles, with his winning face, was drafted in to seduce Cecily and provide her with the means to kill; for whatever reason, Cecily lost her nerve and had to be silenced. Perhaps the graphic display pointing to a Catholic threat was meant to turn the court's attention to the known English Catholic sympathisers in its ranks. Either way, the one element missing from this equation is who actually carried out the murders. I don't doubt that Marie could be ruthless enough to take a life, but she would lack the physical strength; besides, she would regard butchery as servants' work. Courcelles has always struck me as the sort of man who would pass out if he cut his finger on his dinner knife, but perhaps he is a better performer than I have given him credit for. Even if that were true, both Marie and Courcelles were standing beside me at the concert when Abigail Morley was murdered, so who was their accomplice, their third man?

I snatch up my doublet in a moment of decisiveness; I will not stay here pacing this room waiting for Howard's thugs to come and find me. I pull on a cloak over my doublet and then remember that I have left my leather riding boots at Arundel House; I will have to wear the shoes I keep for finer weather, though the recent rain will have left the streets in a mire. Before I leave, I prise up the loose floorboard beneath my bed where I keep the chest with the money I receive from Walsingham. It is not a fortune—not compared with the risks I run for him—but it does at least allow me a standard of living in London that King Henri's sporadic stipend would not provide. I will need to have new boots made—no one can survive a London winter without them, I have been told. Perhaps I can persuade Fowler to accompany me. In any case, I will retrieve my dagger from Castelnau's study on my way out and take my chances in the city streets; that at least is better than cowering in my room with endless theories multiplying in my head and no solid evidence to prove or disprove them.

Only the ambassador's butler sees me slip out through the front door, my cloak pulled up around my head. He can tell Marie and Courcelles that I have left if he pleases; I have decided that if I keep to the main thoroughfares and stay among crowds there is less chance of meeting the same end as Dumas. On the other hand, it is easier to stick a knife in a man's ribs and disappear in a crowd. I keep the bone-handled knife at my belt, one hand on its hilt, my eyes raking the street to either side.

At the Fleet Bridge, I hear footsteps at my back and whip around so fast that my pursuer will not have time either to hide or to pounce, but the only person I see is a skinny boy who freezes, gaping at me nervously.

His eyes flicker to the hand beneath my cloak, and I recognise him as the kitchen boy Jem from the Palace of Whitehall, the one who had brought the fateful message to Abigail Morley that lured her to her death. I let go of the dagger and step toward him, trying to make my expression less forbidding. He draws a paper out from his jerkin.

"Jem? How long have you been following me?"

"From Salisbury Court, please you, sir. She told me to wait outside and catch you whenever you came out. She said I was not to be seen."

"Who did?"

"I am to give you this, sir," he says, holding out the paper.

I glance at the seal, but it means nothing. Quickly I tear the paper open and find, to my surprise, a summons from Lady Seaton, the queen's lady of the bedchamber. She is visiting friends at Crosby Hall in Bishopsgate Street and has something to impart to me; I am to find her there by knocking at the trade entrance and asking for her manservant. In any other circumstances, the imperious tone of this note would tempt me to ball it in my fist and throw it aside, but I suspected when I spoke to Lady Seaton that night at Richmond Palace, after the murder of Cecily Ashe, that she knew more than she was willing to say. Why she has suddenly decided to speak to me now, I do not know; neither do I discount the possibility that it might be a trap. The boy hovers uncertainly, unsure as to whether his duty is despatched.

"Thank you, Jem. When were you sent with this?"

"Only this morning, sir. After breakfast."

"I wonder you have the stomach to carry any more messages."

He looks at me with a pained expression.

"I must eat, sir."

"Yes, of course."

I squint up at the sky; in this thin light it is impossible to guess at the position of the sun, but the hour must be already past three. She will be awaiting me now, if the note is really from her. I wonder briefly about giving the boy a shilling to accompany me through the city but decide against it; anyone who wants to attack me would not think twice about getting the boy out of the way, and I cannot risk any further violence to anyone on my account. I reach into the purse inside my doublet and find a groat; he pockets it gratefully and runs back westward along Fleet Street, slipping easily among the people and carts. I scan the street uneasily after he has disappeared, but the Londoners walking toward the Lud Gate press on, heads down, wrapped in cloaks against the wind, passing me by without remark. No one is watching, yet I feel the city's eyes on me, from doorways and side streets and blank windows, as exposed as surely as if I were walking through the streets naked.

With Lady Seaton's letter in my hand, I turn and continue toward the gatehouse ahead, its turrets jutting above the high city wall, but my nerves are wound as tight as Dumas's were on our last journey together; I start like a hare at the slightest movement at the edge of sight. I cast my mind back to the night of the concert at Whitehall, to the hushed conference in Burghley's room when the boy Jem told his story. He did not seem to me bright enough to be anything other than honest, but there is an outside chance that he knowingly delivered a false message to Abigail to trap her, and that he might now have been used by the same person to draw me. The man in the hat—who was he? Marie and Courcelles's unknown third man? But if Jem was lying, the man in the hat may not even exist; he might have been given his errand by someone he knew from the court and would not name.

My thoughts preoccupied in this way, I pass under the Lud Gate, squeezing my way through a flock of sorry-looking sheep and trying not to glance up at the rotten hunk of human meat spiked over the central arch, a reminder to the citizens of the price of treason. Instead of heading down to St. Andrew's Hill, I make my way along Cheapside, the wide stone-paved thoroughfare that bisects the City east to west. Here I grow certain that I am being followed, though each time I turn I fear I am just too slow to catch him, and I have seen nothing to give flesh to my fears, except glimpses of a cloak whisked into a doorway which might have been imagined. It is more that I sense him, his movements shadowing mine, his eyes on my back as I walk. Between the ornate fronts of the goldsmiths' workshops, their colourful signs creaking and swaying like banners overhead, the alleyways offer ample opportunity to hide, but if I keep to the centre of the road, avoiding those on horseback and the peddlers' carts, I hope to give myself time and space to react if anyone draws too close.

At the eastern end of Cheapside, where the Stocks Market and the Great Conduit stand, I turn north along Three Needle Street, past the grand façade of the Royal Exchange, the Flemish-designed building that looks as if it has been lifted straight from the Low Countries and dropped in the middle of London. Immediately you see that this is the part of the City where wealth gathers; merchants in expensive furs and feathered caps hurry up and down the steps of the Royal Exchange and the large houses set back from the road behind their walls are either newly built with lavish windows or converted from grand monastic buildings refurbished after the queen's father had them closed down. Even so, where money gathers so does desperation; beggars with only the merest covering of rags between them and the October damp hover near about the steps, plaintively calling for alms from well-fed, fur-swaddled traders. At least here, with more wealth visible, people also seem to be more vigilant; outside the exchange are liveried guards with pikestaffs, and some of the well-dressed citizens go about flanked by menservants. If whoever is pursuing me has come this far—and some instinct tells me he is near at hand—he will need to move cautiously.

I find Crosby Hall at the southern end of Bishopsgate Street, a fine new house with a gabled front of red brick and pale stone trim. A narrow alley runs alongside the garden wall and I guess that the trade entrance is to be found here; as I turn the corner, a wave of cold fear washes over me and I draw my dagger, expecting that if the assault is to come, it will be now, away from passersby. A door clicks; I brace myself ready to lunge, the knife held before me as a young woman with a covered basket emerges from a small gate in the wall and screams with as much vigour as if I had actually stabbed her.

"I'm so sorry," I say, sheathing the knife as I scramble to help her pick up her fallen laundry, but she backs up against the wall and continues shrieking as if all the legions of hell were at her heels. I conclude that my accent is not helping. A large balding man in a smeared kitchen apron sticks his head out of the gate, his fists clenched.

"What's all this?"

"Forgive me—misunderstanding—I am here to see Lady Seaton? My name is Giordano Bruno."

"I don't give two shits for your foreign name, ain't no Lady Seaton lives here. Now get away before I kick you out on your dirty Spanish arse."

"He's got a knife," the girl says, pointing, as she tucks herself behind his meaty shoulder.

I hold my hands up.

"Lady Seaton is a guest of your master today, I believe. I am told she has an urgent message for me. If you would be so kind as to enquire? I can wait here."

"You will wait here and all. You're not coming in with a knife. Get back in there, Meg, till we sort this one out." He holds the gate for the girl and she scuttles back inside. The man gives me a last glare.

"Say your name again. Slow, like."

"Bruno. Tell her, Bruno."

He nods, and the gate shuts behind him. The alley remains silent. I lean against the wall, swivelling my head from one side to the other, convinced now that I have been tricked, that I am standing in this mud-churned lane quite probably awaiting my execution. Well, I think—I have looked death in the face more than once and I have learned a bit about putting up a fight from my years as a fugitive in Italy. If I have been summoned here to die, I will not make it easy for them.

Time drips past, so that I have given up trying to count the minutes. A gust of wind drives flurries of dead leaves up the length of the alley; some cling to my legs before whirling onward. When the gate opens again I leap against the far wall, hand to my belt. A grey-haired man in a smart black doublet and starched ruff appears in the entrance and looks me up and down.

"You are Bruno? Lady Seaton's messenger?"

"Er—I am." I allow my breath to slide out slowly; he does not seem about to run me through. Was the letter genuine after all?

"Step inside. I am steward to Sir John Spencer." He ushers me through the gate into a small courtyard at the rear of the house. Several chickens scratch around the yard, perhaps looking for grain spilled from the sacks waiting to be loaded into storehouses. "Wait here. But I'm afraid I must ask you to hand over your weapon while you are inside our walls." He reaches out apologetically.

Still I hesitate, but as I glance over his shoulder I see, with a flood of relief so great that my legs almost buckle, the prim figure of Lady Seaton appearing around the corner of the house.

"Oh, there you are, Bruno—I need you to take a message to the palace for me urgently," she calls in that same peremptory tone as before. This is clearly some cover she has devised for having someone of low birth visit her at her friends'; her acting is deplorable, but it seems to have the desired effect. I produce a sweeping bow; the steward glances at me curiously, then does the same and retreats back into the house without demanding my knife. A servant pauses to stare in the course of hefting a wooden pallet across the yard, but returns to his work at one stony look from Lady Seaton.

She offers a vinegary little smile.

"They have still not caught the brute who killed my girls," she begins, with an air of accusation. "Sir Edward Bellamy was released without charge after Abigail Morley was found, though you may imagine the whispering at court when he showed his face again, poor man. The stink of accusation takes a long time to clear. People wanted it to be him, you know, so they could sleep easy in their beds. But the court must hold its breath in fear once more, and some of my girls are near hysterical. And the queen grows impatient."

"They are hopeful of finding him soon, I believe."

"Pah." Her mouth shows what she thinks of this claim. "They do not know what I know."

"What?"

She beckons me over to a corner in the shelter of a low brick storehouse.

"They released Cecily Ashe's body to her father for burial last week. The rest of her family came down from Nottinghamshire. There was a service in the Chapel Royal. I took the opportunity to speak to her younger sister."

I nod to her to continue, aware that I am holding my breath.

"Of course, the father won't allow that poor girl anywhere near the court after what happened to Cecily and you can't blame him, although I daresay it won't make much odds to her marriage chances—it was Cecily had all the looks in that family, more's the pity." She sniffs. "But you know how sisters are with confidences."

I did not, but I nod in any case, anxious not to interrupt.

"I got the girl away from her parents and pressed her on what Cecily had written of this beau of hers."

"The one you assured me did not exist?"

She purses her lips.

"Never mind that. Apparently Cecily had been writing to her sister every week—the maids' letters are supposed to go through me, of course, but they find ways and means to smuggle them out. She was not keen to tell me, but I can be extremely persuasive."

"I don't doubt it."

She nods, as if appeased.

"Well—this beau. Cecily had written to her sister that she was soon to become a countess."

"So he was an earl?" My blood quickens again; in my excitement I clutch at her sleeve.

"Unhand me, please, Bruno." She smooths the silk down, but when she deigns to glance at me I see her eyes are bright with the relish of her tale. "So he said. I had to prise it out of the girl with threats in the end. Told her if she didn't give me the name and any more girls died, I would tell the queen in person that she was responsible for hiding the murderer. That put the fear of God in her, I can tell you. They're stubborn creatures at fifteen."

"I can well imagine." I picture the terrified sister cowering before Lady Seaton's waspish tongue. "She gave you a name?"

"Not a name, but a title. She claims Cecily never told her his name. She confided only that he called himself the Earl of Ormond." She leaves a dramatic pause for me to digest this. I shrug to indicate my ignorance.

"So—do you know this man?"

She turns to look at me directly and her expression is gleeful.

"That is the whole point, Bruno—there is no one of that title at court!"

"But then—he could be anybody claiming a false title," I say. "How will it help us?"

"I didn't say it was a false title, just that to my knowledge there is no one *known* as the Earl of Ormond at court. And I know *everyone*," she adds, as if I had tried to suggest otherwise. "I thought it might be something you could look into. I daresay it might be some old family name that has become assimilated into another house or become defunct—the annals of the English nobility are full of half-forgotten subsidiary titles like that."

"So—he was English, then?"

She frowns, as if unsure of my point.

"Well, I assumed so. How else could he have persuaded Cecily that he held an earldom?"

I push my hair back from my face, impatiently revising my theory; Courcelles speaks good English, but his French accent is so pronounced as to make him sound comical to native speakers. Lady Seaton is right; he could never have convincingly posed as an English noble, and Cecily would surely have mentioned either to her sister or to Abigail if this impressive suitor had been a Frenchman. No; much as it frustrates me to have to let go of the idea, though Courcelles's face may fit, I don't believe he was posing as the Earl of Ormond.

"But how would I ever find out about such a title?"

She looks at me as if I am being wilfully stupid.

"The College of Arms hold all the records. At Derby Place, off St. Peter's Street. I am sure they would know something."

"Where *is* Ormond?"

"How should I know, Bruno? I am not a cartographer."

"Did you tell Lord Burghley about this?" I ask, curious.

She sucks in her cheeks again.

"There is no love lost between Lord Burghley and myself. I never had the sense from him that he cared very much about the maids. Their deaths are a political problem to him, and he will find a political solution, you may be sure. Meanwhile my girls are terrified, Bruno, that this killer has his eye on more of them. My queen is afraid too, though you would never hear her admit it. These murders were grotesque threats against her. And it is poisoning the atmosphere at court—we look at every man now wondering, Is it *him*? Is it that one? He must be found and put where he cannot harm any more of us." She wraps her shawl closer around her shoulders as another gust scuffs up the leaves in the yard. "I was not willing to be dismissed yet again as a foolish woman by Lord Burghley. But you had a look about you, with your sharp questions and your sharp eyes. When I saw you with the French ambassador at court I realised at once that you must be one of Francis Walsingham's recruits. You need not answer that. I am as discreet as the grave."

I neither acknowledge this nor deny it.

"I can assure you, my lady, I am doing everything I can to assist with catching this man, and I am grateful to you for your trouble. But I think you are wrong about my lord Burghley. He lost a daughter himself, of about the same age. I think he cares far more than you would credit."

She ponders this as I nod curtly and move toward the gate.

"Bruno?"

I turn back, expectant.

"Don't forget your manners. *My* title is quite real, I promise you." But there is a mischievous twitch at the corner of her mouth. I make a low bow, apologising, and when I look up, she is already on her way back into the house.

AT A RUN through Bucklersbury, where the density of apothecary shops fills the air with a curious mix of savoury herbs from their remedies, I don't stop now to glance over my shoulder; if my pursuer is still behind me, let him show himself, for I feel there must be something significant in this information of Lady Seaton's, I feel I have this elusive killer's identity almost within my reach. He seduced Cecily Ashe with a handsome face and a title he had borrowed, or invented, or perhaps it is his own genuine title though not one he uses, but if the earldom of Ormond exists, or has ever existed, I will find out who among the remaining suspects might have any connection with it. Already my mind is leaping ahead of the facts and settling on Throckmorton. Though I encountered him only twice at Salisbury Court, I recall him as a personable young man, no great beauty like Courcelles, but good-looking enough to deserve the description. He is English, of good family—might he not have persuaded Cecily that he had a title?

My thoughts are flying faster than my feet; along Great St. Thomas Apostle I then cut down Garlick Hill to Thames Street and due west to St. Peter's. I thank my good fortune as I run that I spent much of the summer wandering the streets of the city, exploring its neighbourhoods, the haunts of its guildsmen and merchants, its wealthiest quarters and its slums. I wanted to know its streets, to piece it together in my head; since I meant to make it my home, I felt I should take the trouble to get to know it. Now, though I will never know it as intimately as those born with the stench of the Thames in their nostrils, I have at least committed to memory a good many of the main thoroughfares, so that I do not always have to stop and ask strangers for directions. London is not a friendly city to foreigners; better never to admit that you are lost.

In St. Peter's Street I do stop a smartly dressed man to ask if he knows where the College of Arms is to be found; he points me down the road to a large three-storied house on the north side. On the west range of the building I find a gatehouse with its portcullis raised; inside the quadrangle a man in a tabard bearing the royal arms steps in front of the main door and asks me my business. I pause, bent over, and rest my hands on my thighs, trying to recover my breath; he watches me with some concern.

"I need to find some information on a particular title," I say, between gasps, when I am able to speak. His eyes narrow.

"For what purpose?"

"To see if it exists."

"On whose behalf?"

I hesitate. Whose authority would serve me best here? I cannot risk associating myself with Walsingham, and if I claim Burghley he will ask to see some letter or seal of proof—not unreasonably, since my appearance is less than professional.

"I am personal secretary to the ambassador of France, the Seigneur de Mauvissière," I say, drawing myself upright and pushing my hair out of my face. I lean in and drop my voice. "It is a delicate matter."

A flicker of mild interest passes over his face; he nods and opens the door for me. I find myself standing in a paved entrance hall hung with silk banners in sumptuous colours, a menagerie of lions, eagles, unicorns, gryphons, and cockatrices gently undulating in the draught from the open door.

"You will need to speak to one of the officers of arms," the doorman informs me. We both look around; the hall is empty. "Hold on." He crosses to a door at the far end, his heels clicking on the flagstones, puts his head around and calls to someone inside. A few minutes pass in silence. I smile awkwardly at my guide; he nods encouragingly toward the door. Eventually a stout man appears dressed in the same tabard, his chins bulging over his ruff. He also regards me with suspicion.

"This gentleman," says the doorman, and I do not miss the edge of sarcasm in the description, "needs to look up a title. Says he's from the French ambassador on a personal matter."

"Do you have a letter of authority?" says the man with the chins, who I presume to be the officer of arms.

"I'm afraid not." I pat my doublet, as if for proof.

He presses his lips together and folds his hands. For a moment I think he is going to refuse.

"I have money," I blurt.

The officer gives a wan smile.

"Oh, you won't get far without that. What is the nature of your enquiry?"

I glance between them.

"My lord ambassador's niece has received a proposal of marriage from an English gentleman who claims to be the heir to a particular earldom," I whisper, as if to draw them into the intrigue. "But my master does not know of this title and wants to verify the young man's credentials."

The two men exchange a knowing smile.

"That old trick," says the older, suggesting he deals with such matters on a daily basis. He holds out a plump hand. "The college must generate income to preserve our archive, you understand."

"Of course," I say, patting the breast of my doublet, where I wear my purse slung under my arm beneath my cloak. The money I had meant for my new boots would have to be sacrificed to a nobler cause. "What is the price?"

"Depends upon how long it takes me to find the record," he says, and by way of demonstration he pushes open the door from which he entered to reveal a high room lined floor to ceiling with wooden shelves, each one piled with bound manuscripts and rolls of paper. "Records of grants of arms and pedigrees going back a hundred years, since the college was incorporated by King Richard III," he says proudly, indicating the collection as if it is his own work. "Which is this spurious title, then?"

"The Earl of Ormond," I say. Already it has taken on a sinister sound in my mouth.

"Oh, then I cannot help you," he says, looking crestfallen. "You had better save your money."

"Why not? It is not a real title?"

"It is not an *English* title," he says, with careful emphasis. "I believe it is Scottish, and we do not keep the records for the Scottish nobility. For that you will need to travel to Edinburgh."

A dozen expressions must have chased one another across my face in an instant, because he seems to take pity on me.

"There is someone who might be able to help you, though. Wait here." And he strides importantly away through another door. His footsteps fade and I am suddenly so overcome by tiredness that I have to sit down on the foot of the marble staircase that leads up from the entrance hall.

"To be honest," says the doorman, who remains propped against the wall, apparently too interested in my quest to return to his post, "most times, the ones that claim to be earls probably aren't. I mean, your actual earls don't need to make a song and dance about it."

I raise my head from between my hands. "Thank you. I'll bear that in mind."

After an interval I hear the officer's footsteps returning; behind him shuffles a white-haired man dressed in the same livery, who carries himself with an upright, military bearing despite his slow progress.

"This is Walter, our longest-serving officer at arms," announces the man with the chins. "He has the best part of our records committed to memory, you know. If—God forbid—we should ever suffer the ravages of a fire, we should be turning to Walter to re-create our archive from here." He taps his temple. "But he is Scottish by birth and he knows a great deal of the Scots titles too."

"Well," says the old man, in a rich voice with those curling vowels I have come to recognise, "I regret to say age is stealing the names and dates from me piece by piece. But the earldom of Ormond I do still recall, if you are interested?"

I leap to my feet, nodding.

"Please—anything you know."

"Well." He clears his throat, as if to embark on a long history. Uncharitably, I find myself hoping this explanation will be brief. "The title derives from Ormond Castle in the Black Isle, you know, but the earldom was forfeit in 1455 after a rebellion against the Scots king."

"So the title is extinct?"

"It became a subsidiary title of the Dukes of Ross, but that title was also lost at the beginning of our own century. Now"—he pauses, swallows, and raises a shaky finger like a schoolmaster waiting for his pupils' full attention—"the Dukes of Ross were Stewarts, but the earls of Ormond were all of the house of Douglas."

I scarcely hear the officer at arms naming his price; my fingers reach for my purse and hand over coins almost of their own accord while I continue to stare at this old man without focusing. *Douglas.* The name repeats in my ears; why had I not seen it sooner? Douglas, the proven killer for hire, with that lawless charm he could turn on men and women alike, his rakish smiles and winks, his dirty jokes. Had he thrown in his lot with Marie and the Guise faction because he thought they had the best chance of rising to power after the invasion, or did they just offer him enough money to make the murders worth his while?

I thank the officers and blunder through the gatehouse of the College of Arms into the street. The light is fading now, a chill early dusk settling over the city as thin fog rises up and wraps the buildings, turning the streets unfamiliar. Already lamps are being lit in windows along the street. I pull my cloak up close around my face, my earlier bravado dissipating; here in the darkening streets I am alone and vulnerable, and this new knowledge makes me feel even more exposed. I recall the day Douglas had come upon me so suddenly in the street as if by chance; he must have been following me, even then. The fog will be no deterrent to him, nor will it to Henry Howard's men, if they have been tracking me, and the watch will not start making its patrols until the bells have rung for eight o'clock. It is a matter of a few hundred yards along St. Peter's Street to St. Andrew's Hill; if Fowler is at home, we can hire a boat to Walsingham tonight, or at least as far as Whitehall and Lord Burghley.

Feeling bolder, I set out along St. Peter's Street, keeping close to the shadow of the buildings. A few lone riders head west out of the city along the middle of the street, and the last street traders trudge past with baskets and panniers over their shoulders. The cries of the gulls over the river sound remote and melancholic in the half-light. I walk briskly, my hood up; the creeping fog seems to muffle the sounds of the city, or echo them from unlikely quarters. I have scarcely reached the corner with Addle Hill when an arm grabs me from behind, tightens around my neck, and I am dragged backward into a gap between two houses; I try to cry out but he is pressing the breath from my throat. My assailant is a tall man, and strong; he almost lifts me off the ground and though I try to kick my legs behind me I cannot reach him. With his free hand he pins my left arm behind my back, but in this manoeuvre I am just able to twist my body enough to draw the dagger at my belt with my right hand. I have one chance at this stroke and a bare fraction of a moment to think about it as he chokes his arm tighter around my neck; I arch my back, curve my right arm, and aim the knife behind me at his midriff. He seems to sense the movement just before it happens and tries to dodge it, but he is not fast enough; he lets out a howl of pain and his grip loosens sufficiently for me to pull in a ragged breath, bend my knees, and then stand suddenly, so that the top of my head cracks against his chin. When he lets go of my left arm, I am able to wheel around and face him, the knife held out before me; he is limping but undeterred, though I am lighter and quicker, and I move back in a series of feints, drawing him out into the empty street, away from the safety of the shadows. He swings his arm to throw a punch and I duck, at the same time making a lunge with the knife, which I stick in the soft flesh of his upper thigh. As he roars and flails his fist for me again, I kick upward and catch him in the groin so that he staggers backward. But he is strongly built and not inclined to give ground; he swings for another blow, I dart back and my foot twists against a rut in the road. I fall backward, landing hard on the ground with him towering above me; he reaches for his belt, I catch a flash of steel and try to scramble away on my hands and heels but he is almost upon me. Fear floods my body; I brace myself for impact and then, inexplicably, my attacker lurches, as if under the impact of a blow. His hand falls and his solid form appears to crumple; I roll out of the way as he slumps first to his knees and then onto his face, like a broken marionette, and I see that there is a crossbow bolt sticking out of his back. Shaken, I lie still, trying to make sense of this intervention when, almost before I have had a chance to register his presence, a cloaked figure darts from the shadows and runs away fleet-footed up Addle Hill, where he is swallowed by the fog.

A low moan bubbles up from the body beside me; he is not yet dead, but soon will be if no one helps him. A different fear sweeps through me; if I am found here it will be assumed I have killed him. I sheathe my knife, rise unsteadily to my feet, and take a last look at this stranger who would certainly have despatched me if my equally mysterious guardian angel had not been at hand. The air clings damply to my face. Who was the man who fired the crossbow, and how long has he been following me? I glance around, peering again into the fog up Addle Hill where the man disappeared; the street is silent. In the distance, I see a wavering pinprick of light from someone's lantern approaching from the east: I brush myself down and hasten away in the opposite direction before anyone finds me here.

Fowler pours a cup of hot wine and hands it to me, frowning with concern. I crouch on a low stool by the fire in his small, neat parlour, while he stands, leaning with one hand on the mantel above.

"But look—Henry Howard is an ally of the invasion conspiracy,

Bruno," he says, when I have finished recounting my ambush in the street. "If he is sending men to attack you, you must tell Castelnau."

"Castelnau has no influence over Howard. He is useful to the conspirators only for as long as the embassy provides a clearinghouse for their correspondence with Mary Stuart." I take a mouthful of wine and warm my hands around the cup. "There is no respect for Castelnau nor for the French king among any of them. Henry Howard has plainly decided I am a danger and must be silenced. I will only be safe when he is arrested."

Fowler clicks his tongue impatiently. It is the first time I have seen his placid demeanour ruffled.

"I know what you are going to say," I preempt, holding up a hand to silence his unvoiced criticism. "You warned me that my escapade at Arundel House might end badly, and you were right. I should have listened. But it so nearly paid off."

He sighs and runs a hand through his hair.

"That is the nature of our work. At least you were willing to take a risk." There is a note almost like regret in his tone. "But it is a great shame you lost that genealogy from Arundel House," he adds, inclining his head. "It would have sent Howard straight to the block in his brother's footsteps."

"I had no choice. If I had not swum to the boat I would have been killed on the spot. You have sent Walsingham word of last night's dinner, I suppose? The date and the list of safe harbours?"

"Of course," he murmurs. "I took word to Phelippes first thing this morning. But of course I had no written proof to offer. Good God, Bruno—Henry Howard." He shakes his head and gives a low whistle, half in admiration. "Imagine the reach of that man's ambition—I can scarcely credit it. You think he even had designs on King James of Scotland? Extraordinary."

"He is ruthless. I have all the proof I need of that." I rub my neck. "But I have not told you the half of it yet."

Fowler raises his eyebrow and pulls up a cushion, where he sits cross-legged, awaiting the rest of my account. It is true that I have not told him everything; in the account of my night at Arundel House I left out any mention of Henry Howard's occult pursuits. Nor did I tell him about the mysterious stranger who felled my attacker in St. Peter's Street just now. This is partly out of pride, but also because I have an instinctive sense of unease about what happened. I have suspected I was being followed long before Howard decided he wanted me dead; perhaps there is a chance that the person who saved me tonight did not do so out of gallantry but to prolong the game.

Taking another draught of wine, I tell him about Lady Seaton's summons and my trip to the College of Arms. When I reach the part about the old Scottish officer's information, he places a hand over his mouth and simply stares at me.

"Good God," he says eventually.

"I can't believe I didn't think of Douglas sooner. Perhaps because he was too obvious as a killer. But he always seemed so detached from the scheming of all the others."

Fowler shakes his head, his jaw set tight.

"He plays that part well, the laconic mercenary. But Douglas is shrewder than anyone when it comes to his own advancement. It's how he's survived so long."

"But did you ever suspect him?"

"No," he says flatly. "I suppose he crossed my mind because of his history, but I didn't consider him seriously because I couldn't see what motive he could have had. He must have been sizing up the different factions among the plotters all along, deciding which had the better chance of power after the invasion."

"Why do you and he hate each other so much?" I ask, when I have drained my glass.

Fowler's mild expression hardens.

"He is a man utterly without principle. He curries favour among the Scottish lords that surround the young King James and plays them off against one another. He thinks nothing of taking a life. But most especially"—here a shadow crosses his face and his voice drops to barely more than a whisper—"he took from me my closest friend."

"Douglas murdered him?"

He lowers his eyes.

"No. Though he may as well have done—he is dead to me now. Patrick, Master of Gray. We were friends from childhood, but Douglas has turned him away from me and drawn him into his own influence to further his cause with James."

There is such quiet bitterness in his tone, this young man who rarely betrays any emotion, that I find myself wondering at the nature of this friendship. Fowler seems to feel its loss deeply. Watching him, I am struck by an unexpected affection for this man who has become, by necessity, my confidant. How little we know of another's inner life; perhaps the self-effacing Fowler carries a hidden weight of pain beneath his outward composure.

"I must take all this to Walsingham without delay," I say. "Only he can protect me from Howard's thugs. But I fear tonight has shown beyond doubt that I cannot travel alone. Will you come with me upriver?"

He hesitates. I wonder if he is afraid; he does not look like much of a fighter.

"We should not be seen too often in each other's company—" Then he appears to relent, and stands to straighten his clothes. "But you are right, Bruno—who else would you take? Come—I will fetch us lanterns and cloaks. Do you have money for the boatman?"

I nod. He disappears, leaving me to try and soak up the last warmth from the fire before I am obliged to step out again into that seeping London fog that works its way inside your bone marrow and chills you from the inside out.

FOWLER HAS STRAPPED on a sword belt under his cloak, I notice. We walk in silence down the incline toward Puddle Wharf, holding our lanterns aloft, though they make little difference in the smoky air. The moonlight is almost obscured by clouds and the city feels muted and otherworldly, as if under a shroud.

"We have no evidence against Douglas except this scrap of gossip from Lady Seaton," I remark as we reach the empty landing stage. "He will argue that anyone could have picked a defunct title out of the lists."

Fowler leans out, scans the river, and calls, "Oars, ho!" He turns to me while we wait to see if this has any effect. "At this stage, I do not think we have any choice. Douglas is notorious for slipping through the net in Scotland, but Scottish justice can be bought and sold. He has never yet come up against the determination of Walsingham. If anyone can extract a confession, it is he."

I say nothing; we both know only too well some of the principal secretary's methods for extracting confessions. Walsingham always maintains that God allows him to keep a clear conscience in this matter; that he would rather put one innocent man to the rack than risk the lives of many more by allowing a potential plot to go unchecked. He knows I disagree with him here, and that I question the value of any information wrested from a man whose limbs are being pulled from their sockets; coming from a country ruled by the lash of the Holy Office, I know only too well how easily a man threatened with pain will say whatever he thinks will please the one who can command it to stop. But Walsingham has made the case to his own conscience and found it satisfactory.

Fowler calls again; after some moments, the soft plash of oars comes through the night, followed by the blurry light of a boatman's lantern. As the wherry nears us, Fowler turns suddenly and grips my arm.

"I have a better idea—what if we were to take Douglas himself straight to Whitehall? Only—I know him of old. He has a knack of scenting trouble on the wind and making himself scarce—by the time we reach Walsingham and he decides to send armed men to find him, Douglas will have disappeared into the cracks, I could almost guarantee it."

"How would we persuade him, though? It would be sure to make him suspicious."

Fowler considers for a moment.

"I will tell him Mendoza wants to speak with him—that ought to prick his curiosity. He knows Mendoza's influence over Mary is growing—unlike poor Castelnau's. And Mendoza is always around the court."

"I don't know." I am doubtful of this new plan; it strikes me that Fowler is oversensitive when it comes to Douglas, though he is right that the journey to Walsingham and back will take hours.

"Think how much better it would look for us if we were to deliver the man himself direct to Burghley," he hisses.

"Where to, gents? Here, take this." The boatman throws a rope out from the bow; it falls with a wet slap on the jetty, where I pick it up and haul it in tight.

"Across the river," Fowler says, before I have a chance to speak, as he climbs in and arranges his coat. "Drop us at St. Mary Overy's dock."

"Oh, aye? Trip to Southwark is it, gents?" The lamplight exaggerates his lascivious wink. I follow Fowler precariously into the boat. The cushions seem to have soaked up all the damp and cold in the air and transferred them to my breeches. "You'll come back a few shillings the poorer, I'll warrant! Make sure you don't get bitten by a Winchester goose, eh." He winks again and cackles as he pushes off with an oar.

"A goose?" I frown at Fowler, bemused. He breaks into a thin smile.

"It's an expression for catching the pox. A Winchester goose is a bawd—named because the ward is nominally under the jurisdiction of the Bishop of Winchester, who licences the whorehouses."

I squint across to where the south bank of the Thames is obscured by mist. Southwark, the borough outside the city walls and its laws, where a demimonde of brothels, gambling dens, and taverns offering illegal fights—animal and human—has spread like a fungus along the riverbank. Those who trade in contraband goods and illegal books off the boats do so in the inns of Southwark; pirates, brigands, whores, travelling players, and undercover priests rub shoulders with aldermen, lawyers, and courtiers disguised to taste the borough's forbidden fruit. Castelnau warned me to stay away from Southwark almost as soon as I arrived in

England; streets where they'd cut a foreigner's throat for entertainment, he said, especially a man who looked like me. I saw enough of streets like that when I was a fugitive in Italy, so I had largely heeded his advice. Little surprise that Fowler expects to find Douglas here. As the boatman turns the wherry and pulls on the oars to direct us back downstream, I experience a deep sense of foreboding. If I can be attacked in a main street in the city before darkness has even fallen, where there is still the chance of being discovered by the watch, surely it is outright folly to head for the most lawless part of the city under cover of night. I glance at Fowler's profile; he looks out over the water, determined and intense, his gaze concentrated on the far bank, one hand resting lightly on the hilt of his sword. At least I will have someone to watch my back this time, I think, and wonder again who might have fired the bolt that saved me earlier.

The landing stairs at St. Mary Overy's dock are slimy and narrow; I pay the boatman his shilling and follow Fowler upward as he negotiates with one hand against the dank wall of the quay, his lantern held out in the other. One misstep and we could be plunged into the black water lapping beneath. We emerge at the top onto a muddy, open area where two narrow streets branch away southward, each lined with two- and three-storey houses crowded together and canted forward so that their gables threaten to meet in the middle, like the foreheads of two people conversing. A number of these houses are distinctively whitewashed to mark them out as brothels. Fowler motions to the right; I follow him, keeping so close that I am in danger of tripping him in the fog. Despite the cold, plenty of people are abroad; rowdy groups of young men, arms slung around one another's necks and roaring sea chanteys or their own filthy versions of war ballads; women in garish colours, usually in pairs and pitifully underdressed against the cold, and more sinister figures, those who stand in doorways with their cloaks pulled up around their faces, watching and waiting. Where there are whores and gambling, there will always be great demand for meat and drink, and this street boasts an abundance of taverns, each spilling out its scent of roasting meat and warm beer every time its door is opened. If I did not feel in such immediate fear for my life, I would enjoy the atmosphere of Southwark, I think; there is a kind of frisson to the night, as if those of us who slink through the fog are tacit comrades in our pursuit of illicit pleasures.

Halfway along this street, Fowler ducks under an archway between two buildings and down a narrow alley that opens into a small courtyard with houses on three sides. By the entrance to the building on the left, a girl with her bodice half unlaced lolls against the doorframe, winding a strand of hair around one finger. She regards us with mild interest through eyes cloudy with drink as we pass, looking us both up and down, but Fowler ignores her and pushes open the door. It gives onto the taproom of a tavern with a low ceiling and blackened beams, ill-lit and thick with the smells of tobacco smoke and unwashed bodies.

"How do you know to find him here?" I whisper to Fowler as he presses between tables where men argue or slump over their beer.

"This is where the disaffected Scots drink," he hisses back. "It's how he stays abreast of what's going on back home."

I guess from his tone that it is not only Douglas who scavenges information in this filthy room. At the far end of the taproom Fowler lifts the latch of another door and holds it open for me to step through.

In the back room, Douglas sits at a small table opposite another man, intent on a card game. A pile of coins sits in the middle by the stack of discarded playing cards and a pitcher of beer. Beside it, an oil lamp flickers in the draught from the open window in the back wall. Douglas sucks on a long-stemmed clay pipe that coughs out sour smoke; but for the open window, the room would be as foggy as the night outside. Both men have a girl on their knee; plump, giggling, interchangeable creatures with thick face paint and bare shoulders. Douglas glances up at the interruption, briefly acknowledges me and Fowler, and nods to the table.

"With you in a moment, friends," he mutters, holding the cards in his hand up to confide in his young companion. She points at one; Douglas laughs.

"Lucky I'm playing this hand, then, and not you, love."

He peels away and lays down a jack of hearts; I watch his long, broad hands with a macabre fascination, the delicate way he holds the card between thumb and forefinger. Those hands that squeezed Cecily Ashe and Abigail Morley around their slender white necks until the life choked out of them. The same hands that cut signs into their breasts, and marked the sign of the messenger on Dumas for a joke. My mouth is suddenly washed with sour bile at the image; it is all I can do to hold myself back from lunging at him.

His opponent curses in a thick Scots accent, and Douglas scoops the pot of coins toward himself.

"Sorry, Monty," he says, laughing. "I'll give you another chance later. Piss off for the now, though—these gentlemen have private business to discuss, by the look of their faces."

The other man grumbles, but shunts the girl off his knee and pushes past us.

"You and all," says Douglas to the girl on his own lap, who pouts and fusses but eventually accepts a coin and a slap on her behind to make herself scarce. He taps his pipe on the side of the table, stuffs it with fresh tobacco, and spends a few moments trying to make it take light from his tinderbox. When he is finally puffing out gusts like a blocked chimney, he turns to me.

"Will you take a drink, gentlemen?" He gestures to the pitcher. "I'll send for another if we've run out."

I glance at Fowler and he nods encouragement; puzzled, I realise he means for me to put forward our ruse. His dislike of Douglas extends even to addressing him directly, it seems.

"We're not stopping," I begin. "We are on our way to Whitehall and have a boat waiting—we came to see if you would join us?"

"Whitehall, is it?" He puffs thoughtfully. "And what business have you at Whitehall that would draw me away from this august company?"

"Henry Howard is meeting Mendoza there and has asked us to be part of the company, to discuss what happens after the invasion," I say.

My voice sounds too loud for the room. Douglas regards me through narrowed eyes and breathes in smoke as if he finds it nourishing.

"Really? Mendoza? At Whitehall?" He sounds idly curious as he examines the bowl of his pipe. "That doesn't sound very likely to me, Bruno. Are you sure all these blows to your head haven't confused you?"

I lower my eyes for a moment, cursing myself for having listened to Fowler; I should have insisted that this approach would only serve to make Douglas more suspicious. I glance over my shoulder for support from Fowler, but his eyes are fixed on Douglas.

"This was the message I had," I say, trying not to falter.

"When did you get this message—while you were staying at Arundel House? Did you find anything interesting there, by the way?"

His voice is still cheery, but there is an edge to it.

"I'm sorry?"

"Well, it's just that I could tell you were giving all that wine to the dog. You think I can't tell a real drinker from a fraud? So I guessed you must have a good reason for wanting to get yourself in for the night. What were you looking for? Evidence of Howard's treason?"

"Why would I want that?"

"Same reason any of us want it. To see him in the Tower."

I look at him, unable to untangle the implication of his words. Is this a confession that he has shackled himself to the Guise cause? What reason could he have for wanting Henry Howard arrested for treason?

"I—" I begin, but cannot think of what to say next.

"Bruno has been to the College of Arms this afternoon," Fowler says softly, behind me. I whip around to him, confused. What game is he playing now?

"Oh, aye?" Douglas looks amused. "There's a fancy hobby for a man like you, Bruno, armorial history. Turn up anything of interest there, did you?"

I am tired of his tone and his sense that it is he who is toying with us.

"Yes, I did. I looked up the Earl of Ormond's line."

"Really? Why was that?"

I glance at Fowler; this is not what I had intended at all, to face Douglas down in a seedy tavern. There may be two of us, but there is no knowing how many of the men drinking on the other side of the door are his friends and cohorts. My shoulders tense; I feel now that we have turned badly off course.

"It's a family title of yours, is it not?"

The room falls very still.

"Mine?" Douglas still smiles, but this time through his teeth. He lays down his pipe. "Oh, very probably. There are as many branches of the Douglas family in Scotland as there are stars in the sky, Bruno—we've won and lost more titles than you've said Masses in your sorry life. Why does it interest you?"

"Because I believe the young maids at court were killed by a man claiming to be the Earl of Ormond," I say, drawing my dagger. Behind me, I hear the sleek rush of steel as Fowler pulls his sword from its scabbard.

Douglas throws his chair back abruptly and jumps up, his body poised to spring either way in an instant. From the speed of his reaction I see that, despite his apparent devotion to debauchery, he is strongly built and carries himself like a man in good physical condition. But after a moment, he bursts out laughing.

"Oh, and you've decided that's me, have you? Because of a title belonging to some ancient forebear, that anyone might have borrowed? You think that would stand up in a court of law?" His laughter sounds aggressively false in the small room.

I move cautiously around the table toward him, as he backs against the wall, his hands held up, palms upward.

"If you are innocent, there is nothing to fear," I say, and realise with a chill that this is Walsingham's argument when he questions Catholic suspects.

Douglas continues to smile uncertainly. Eventually he lowers his hands, but I can see his body is still tensed and alert.

"Put the knife down, Bruno, and stop being a fool."

"You're coming upriver with us, Douglas—you don't have a choice." I make my voice as commanding as I can, my knife still held out in front of me, pointed at him. Douglas turns to Fowler, a pleading expression on his face.

"Yes—put the knife down, Bruno."

Fowler's voice remains gentle and expressionless, even as I slowly turn, amazed, still unsure that I have heard correctly, to find his sword levelled at me from the other side of the table. Douglas relaxes his shoulders. A long silence unfolds as we continue to look at one another.

"Come on, Bruno—you think a pretty wee girl like that Cecily would take a ring off a grizzled old drunk with a face like this?" Douglas asks eventually, pointing at himself. "You're joking. No, I could never pass myself off as an earl, despite the family name." He grins and folds his arms, as if he is watching an interlude, but my eyes are fixed on Fowler. He continues to look at me with that level, unperturbed expression and I realise, as I have not before, that he might easily be described as handsome. His face is perfectly symmetrical, his features neat and regular, and his eyes are clear and earnest.

"You." There seems little else to say.

He inclines his head a fraction but doesn't move the sword.

"The Earl of Ormond, at your service," he says, in the impeccably clipped tones of the English aristocracy. "You put us in a difficult position, Bruno," he adds, in his own accent. "I was relying on you to find something that would incriminate Howard or the Earl of Arundel in time to get them arrested before this invasion plan gathered too much momentum abroad. But you started poking about in the wrong corners."

I grip my knife; Fowler still points his sword at me. He would run me through before I could reach Douglas, even with the table between us, I estimate, and relax my arm slightly. Douglas, apparently satisfied that I am not about to lunge, reaches for his pipe and sets about relighting it.

"I don't understand," I say eventually. "You want the other conspirators arrested? You meant for the invasion to fail?"

Fowler glances at Douglas, who shrugs as if he could not care either way.

"You might as well satisfy his curiosity," he says, sucking hard on the pipe stem, his breath emerging in short, urgent puffs as he tries to coax the leaf to take light. "It's not as if he can tell anyone now."

"The last thing we want is for Mary Stuart to be released from prison," Fowler says smoothly. "She must come nowhere near the English throne. She must be condemned for treason."

"So—courting Cecily Ashe, killing her—all this was to frame the conspirators and betray Mary?" I shake my head. "Then who *do* you want on the throne—Elizabeth? I thought you meant for her to be poisoned?"

Fowler looks at me pityingly.

"We want the true heir on the throne, Bruno. The king who will unite this divided realm, under the guidance of his trusted advisers. The one descendant of Henry Tudor whose legitimacy has never been in dispute."

It takes a moment for me to realise who he means.

"King James of Scotland?" I turn to Douglas. "You have done all this for him? What about his mother?"

"Old, ill, overweight, out of touch, a bag of resentments and revenge," Fowler says. "No one wants a woman like that at the helm of a nation already precariously divided."

"No one wants a woman at all," Douglas offers, with a chesty laugh.

"But the English Catholics have used Mary as a rallying cry for too long to suddenly change their minds," I protest. "There would be riots if Elizabeth died and she were not released."

"You insult us, Bruno." Fowler breaks into a hint of a smile, showing his even teeth. "We are canny enough to take that into account. That's why it was so important that this invasion plot go far enough that the main conspirators could be picked up by Elizabeth's authorities. That deals with Mary, the Howard family, and Castelnau and his wife—all tried for treason, all imprisoned or executed by Elizabeth. Before she is tragically struck down by a mysterious illness on her own Accession Day."

"Without the Howards, the English Catholics couldn't organise a game of cards," Douglas adds, gesturing to the pile on the table. "Elizabeth dies, no heir, the English are rudderless—then bring on the only person who can restore order and harmony to the country, together with the Scottish lords and advisers he most trusts." He smiles and indicates himself and Fowler.

"Or who can best manipulate him," I say. "But Elizabeth is past bearing an heir now, so King James will inherit the throne anyway. Why so much risk to hasten the day?"

"Elizabeth could easily live another thirty years," Fowler says. "Or some Catholic plot will unseat her in favour of Mary—if not this one, then another. The Spanish would move in—my lord the king could be shut out of the succession altogether. There was greater risk to his sovereignty in waiting. One must take charge of one's destiny, Bruno, instead of waiting for Providence to show its hand, do you not agree?"

I shake my head, incredulous.

"My God, this was an elaborate plan. But contingent on so many elements, it was bound to fail."

"It would have succeeded, if not for the girl." He clenches his teeth and the muscles in his jaw stand out.

"Cecily." I stare at him. "So you drew her into your plot by making her fall in love with you. But she changed her mind, is that it?"

"She seemed spirited enough. The queen had intervened to stop a budding romance some months previously because she didn't consider the young man in question a significant enough match. The girl was furious and itching for revenge—I nurtured that and offered her the opportunity. But she was hotheaded—she didn't have the patience to wait until the right moment." An expression of regret registers in his eyes for a moment, but I am not fooled; any sorrow he feels is only for the failure of his own plans.

"So you had to kill her. But the display—the astrological signs, the witch's doll—all that was to cast suspicion on the Catholics? Didn't you run the risk of tightening security around the queen or being discovered yourself?"

He makes a dismissive sound with his lips.

"Once Cecily Ashe changed her mind about helping me, she had to be silenced, that was beyond doubt. And you could hardly hope that the death of one of the queen's own maids would go without scrutiny, so we decided we may as well use it overtly to sow fear and confusion in the court and the city. A frightened populace will be all the more eager to embrace a strong leader."

"It worked," Douglas remarks, tapping his pipe on the side of the table. "The way people were talking in the taverns, you'd think they expected Beelzebub to rise up out of the Thames and burn the city to the ground. Shitting themselves, they were, especially after the second one."

"I hadn't intended to kill the second girl," Fowler says, sounding almost apologetic. "But when I saw her talking to you at the Holbein Gate, Bruno, I started to worry. Cecily never knew my real name, but I was afraid she might have told her friend enough detail to identify me, and I guessed Walsingham must have asked you to look into the death. So I had to make sure she didn't talk either. I thought if we copied the first murder, it would smack of astrology and conjuring—people would think it was the work of a deranged madman trying to fulfil the apocalyptic prophecies."

"Deranged wouldn't be so far wrong. So it was you following me, then, all that time. Then you were the man with the hat at the Whitehall concert?" I am struggling to piece this together.

Fowler shakes his head.

"That was Douglas. I was waiting on the river in a boat. Once the concert had started, I knew it would be quiet at the kitchen dock. The girl came down as the message instructed. After I had despatched her, I took off the old smock I had over my own clothes and rowed around to the Privy Bridge, where I was admitted to join the concert."

"And Ned Kelley? Where does he fit in, with his visions and his drawings of the murdered girls?"

Fowler frowns; he and Douglas exchange an uncomprehending look.

"Who is Ned Kelley?" Fowler asks. I stare from one to the other; both are skilful dissemblers, as I know only too well by now, but they appear convincingly at a loss. Perhaps Henry Howard was telling the truth about Kelley after all.

"Never mind. But there is one thing I don't understand," I say, as I struggle to take it all in. "Without Cecily, Elizabeth still lives. What happens to your plan now?"

"Accession Day is a while off," Fowler says, with a half smile. "Time enough to set other wheels turning."

"You have another assassin?"

"There's no shortage of hot-blooded young men in France ready to martyr themselves for the Catholic cause—especially among those exiled supporters of Mary in Paris, where our friend the Master of Gray has been living these past few years, making friends. Poison would have been more elegant, but one expendable youth with a pistol in the crowd, especially one with links to Mary . . ." He trails off as if the subject bores him.

"I hope that's cleared things up for you, Bruno," Douglas says brusquely, rising and brushing the drift of ash from his clothes. "But that's probably enough talking, eh."

"Wait—what about Dumas?" I ask, my voice rising with the need to keep them talking.

"Before you came along and hired him with Walsingham's money, I'd slipped him a few coins to give me an idea of the ambassador's correspondence. When he told me Mary Stuart was sending private packets to Henry Howard through Throckmorton, I gave him a considerable sum to look out for their contents—any gifts or jewellery, anything I could use to make it look as if the girl had ties to Mary," Fowler says. Douglas flashes him an impatient look but Fowler seems to feel he owes me this explanation, perhaps in recognition of the misguided trust I once placed in him. "But I could see he was unequal to the strain of so much secrecy. He sold his loyalties too widely and he didn't have the temperament for intrigue. I knew he'd crumble and tell you about the ring eventually. He swore he hadn't when he was begging for his life, but I didn't believe him."

"Was I next on your list of people to be silenced?" I ask, moving almost imperceptibly away from him toward the window. Keeping his eyes on mine, he matches my movement.

"I was relying on you to convey the necessary evidence of the invasion plot to Walsingham first," he says matter-of-factly. "I even thought you might find a way to blame Howard for the murders—you seemed determined to. But I knew you'd discover the truth about the ring eventually and then I would have to decide what to do with you."

"What did King James promise you both?" I ask, looking from one to the other. "How many lives would you have cut down, to secure his throne? He must have offered you the moon."

"James knows nothing of this yet," Fowler says, as if proud of the fact. "He is young and confused enough in his religion to fall easy victim to stirrings of conscience. We will present him with a throne when he has no choice but to take it, and thank us."

"Whereas you don't know what conscience means, do you? What *is* your religion—aside from power?"

Fowler laughs unexpectedly at this, a rich, open laugh, and he sounds for the briefest moment like the man I had believed him to be.

"There is no version of faith that cannot be interpreted to fit the desired political ends. I would have thought you'd learned that much on your travels, Bruno. Personally, I would advise young James to favour the Catholic church, but only because that is where the balance of power lies in Europe, although—"

"*Enough* now, William." Douglas brings his hand down flat on the table. "We need to finish this business."

"There's a bar full of people the other side of that door," I say, raising my voice; it wavers a little mid-sentence. Douglas tilts his head and grins.

"Do you not know where you are, Bruno? The Liberty of the Clink, this ward is called. Half a mile to the southwest, we'd be under the jurisdiction of the high sheriff of Surrey. Half a mile north, across the river, they abide by the laws of the City of London. But this little patch of ground is governed by the Bishop of Winchester, and he doesn't care. We're all outside the law here, son. We could leave your body in the street outside a bawdy house and people will just step over you as you rot."

Fowler adjusts his grip on the sword; I have barely the space of a heartbeat to make my decision. Before he can respond, I grab the oil lamp from the table and hurl it at him; he tries to jump back but the flame catches his sleeve and he lowers the sword as he bats at it with his free hand. Just as Douglas lunges at me from the other direction, I lift one end of the bench beside the table and push it at him; furious, he throws it aside but he is obstructed for the instant it takes me to pull myself to the windowsill and hurl myself out. I land with a clatter among milk churns in a muddy storage yard; on the far side a gate leads out to a side street. Douglas jumps from the window just as I slam the gate behind me and take off blindly through the misty streets with no notion of where I am heading.

All I can do is run now, into the opaque night. I hear him—or both of them—close behind; several times I think I hear their breathing, or perhaps it is only my own, disappearing into the white mist as my heart hammers in my ears. The streets are no more than lanes here, ungravelled, churned by hooves and cartwheels; as I run, the cold air makes my eyes stream, but from the sounds and the drift of the mist I think I am running toward the river. Around a corner I collide with two men who bellow their indignation but are too drunk to do anything more; I disentangle myself and pray that they trip up my pursuers. At the end of this narrow street the houses give way to open ground; the mist is thinner and I can make out the shape of trees to my left. But there are pounding footsteps from behind and I plunge on, away from the buildings; a few yards ahead the ground appears to give way and I almost fall into an inlet, one of the channels cut inland from the riverbank. A fierce stink of refuse and sewage comes off it; I skid to a halt and run along its bank instead, looking at the ground, until I find a narrow wooden bridge built across.

I keep on running, my chest aching fit to burst, determined not to glance behind me as a large building looms out of the mist on my right, like a high circular tower with walls of flint. A thick, sharp scent of animal excrement and blood rises from the ground, where straw is trodden into the mud underfoot. Of course; I must be at Paris Garden, the Southwark bear ring. This might afford me a place to hide. Keeping close to the wall, I scuttle around until I find a low double gate where the animals are brought in from their enclosures. This is easy enough to climb over, and I emerge into a broad ring, hung with skeins of mist. In its centre, a sturdy stake fixed into the ground, with chains wreathed limply over it, and in a circle all around, three tiers of wooden seating with a canopy overhead. Exhausted, I haul myself over the brick wall dividing the arena from the stalls and throw my aching body to the floor beneath the first row of benches. Facedown, I listen to my ribs heaving against the floor, my ears pricked for the slightest sound.

It seems only a moment before I hear the timbers creak somewhere on the opposite side of the ring. Then the low murmur of voices, seemingly from the entrance behind me, though the mist distorts my perception.

"That side." Douglas's voice, low and urgent. "I'll take the other." I hear footsteps on the wooden steps behind me; I decide that keeping still will help me more at this stage than trying to crawl away on my belly. The tap of steel on wood; the boards creak as he approaches, feeling with the point of his sword under the benches to either side. This must be Fowler, then. In a fair fight, man to man, I think I could overpower him, but he has a sword and I have only my short-handled dagger. Only the sons of gentlemen were taught to duel with swords where I grew up, nor was it part of my training as a Dominican novice; learning to fight with my fists and a knife became part of a necessary education when I lived as a fugitive in Italy, but it would be no match for a good swordsman with a sharp blade.

A bead of orange light bobs through the milky air; as the probing sword taps its way along the boards, I preempt my discovery by rolling out and kicking swiftly upward, aiming for the lantern. I catch his arm;

he curses, but keeps hold of it. I scramble to my feet and dart away over the wooden benches, climbing up to the next tier.

"Over here!" Fowler calls, and I see a second point of light pause in the stands opposite, then start a descent. But the scuffling I heard earlier came from above, on this side. There is no time to think about this now; Fowler moves nimbly over the benches and more than once I feel the whip of air as his sword shreds the mist only inches behind me. I climb downward again until I reach the wall, meaning to roll myself over it into the arena. I have trapped myself here, I realise, cursing my own stupidity; I will be forced to fight the two of them like the bears that usually take to the ring here, backed up against the stake with a mob of baying dogs snapping at them from either side. I place one foot up on the barrier to jump over, but a hand catches my cloak and yanks me back; I lose my footing and fall over the side into the arena, landing hard on my side. The ground is sand and though I am winded I roll over as he jumps the barrier and lands a mere two feet from my head; he raises the sword, I cross my arms in front of my face and, in that moment, as I wait for the blade to fall, I find my mind grown suddenly lucid; in that moment I know for certain that the myths of the priests and the preachers are so many stories for children; that death, when it strikes, will not come as judgement but as liberation; in this moment I see myself standing as if on a threshold between worlds, on the brink of the known universe, ready to ascend through the orbits of the planets in their spheres, out to the infinite universe beyond with its million suns, that Hermes Trismegistus called the Divine Mind. I see my life briefly illuminated, and my body relaxes to receive the blow, when this trancelike state is pierced by a sharp whistle, a motion so fast it blurs past my eyes, and a blood-curdling howl from Fowler, whose sword falls from his hand, grazing my leg as he topples sideways, clutching his arm.

My instinct returns; I throw myself on him and pin him down; a crossbow bolt protrudes from his shoulder. He bellows for Douglas but the only response is a frantic scrabbling of feet toward the entrance. The other lantern lies motionless on the ground where it was dropped.

Fowler struggles under me, moaning softly and clutching at his shoulder, but I draw my knife to his throat and he falls limp. There are footsteps in the seats overhead and then the thud of someone landing in the arena. I look up and flinch, as a tall young man in a leather jerkin crouches beside me and examines Fowler.

"I went for the lantern. I was afraid I might hit you, though, sir."

"Who are you?" I hardly dare breathe out, my knife still at Fowler's throat. The mist softens the stranger's features, making him look younger still; he is perhaps in his early twenties, with a broad jaw, his beard still sparse.

"Tanner, sir, Joseph Tanner. At your service." He sweeps off his cap and bunches it in his fist. "I was sent to look out for you, sir. They said folk were trying to kill you. They were right and all." He nods at Fowler, then picks up his sword from the sand and weighs it in his hand with the appraising glance of a connoisseur.

"You serve Walsingham, then?" Exhaustion floods me and I am suddenly freezing.

"I serve Sir Philip Sidney, sir," he says, still twisting his cap. Fowler produces a strangled howl of pain through his teeth; I dig my knee into his ribs.

"Sidney sent you? How long have you been following me?"

"Since the night you came to Barn Elms, sir, after you was attacked on the road. Sir Philip said I was to mark who tried to follow you and make sure you was never left unguarded. But only to act if I thought your life was in immediate danger."

"Why didn't you make yourself known to me?"

The young man looks awkward.

"Sir Philip said you mightn't like the idea, sir. He said you were proud."

"Did he." I smile; half of me does not like it all, the idea of Sidney deciding behind my back that I couldn't look after myself and required a bodyguard. The other half must concede that, without the intervention of young Tanner, I would now have Fowler's sword through me.

"He also said it's no more than he would do for you himself, sir, if he didn't have other duties. Watch your back, I mean, like a friend should."

"I will thank him for it." I glance down at Fowler, whose face, even in this meagre light, has turned very white. A dark stain spreads over the cloth of his doublet where the crossbow bolt has pierced his shoulder. "This man needs a physician, Joseph. We must take him to Whitehall."

Fowler struggles briefly, but I can feel he is growing weaker. He must not bleed to death here, or too many questions will be left unanswered—not least the matter of whether the Accession Day assassination plot is still active, and who might have been charged with carrying it out. Tanner nods.

"We'll have to get him to a boat, sir. We can carry him to Bank End Stairs between us, I reckon."

I admire his optimism; at this moment I do not feel capable of carrying my own cloak as far as the gate, but I struggle to my feet as Tanner drags Fowler upright, occasioning a further protest, but his cries are weaker too; his body seems limp in our arms, and all the heavier for it, as we must manoeuvre him over the gates where we entered. As I bend my back to take his weight while Tanner hoists him up from the inside, I find myself scanning the liquid shadows on both sides in case Douglas should be somewhere nearby, waiting for his chance.

"There was another one," Tanner says apologetically, as he hooks Fowler's undamaged arm around his neck and drags him toward the river. "I couldn't stop him, sir—he took off and I thought it was more important to make sure you were all right. This was the one had the sword."

The sword I am now carrying, its weight unfamiliar in my hand, but lending me a good deal more confidence than I had on my way here. Perhaps I could learn to use it, I think, feeling it slice through the air as I curve my arm gently downward. If I am to continue in Walsingham's service, it would seem a useful skill. As we arrive at the stairs and I descend to call "Oars, ho!," I can only marvel again at the unexpected turns my life has taken. I had thought my tools would be only pen and ink. By the time a boat draws up, I am fully convinced that Douglas has no intention of returning to help his coconspirator. The man who left only his shoes by the corpse of Lord Darnley has once again slipped away into the mist-draped streets, out of reach.

THREE ARMED GUARDS in palace livery patrol the landing stage at the Privy Bridge outside Whitehall; as our boat approaches, they level their pikestaffs at us and demand our business. Tanner declares himself Sir Philip Sidney's man and tells them we have urgent need of Lord Burghley. He is permitted to disembark and stands in close conference with one of the guards while the others regard us with suspicion, as I sit with the sword unsheathed in my lap, propping up Fowler, who still has the arrow protruding from his shoulder. We look like refugees from a small skirmish. I have pressed the hem of my cloak around Fowler's wound to staunch the blood; I am no physician, but I do not think the injury severe enough to threaten his life. On the jetty, I see the guard lift his lantern as Tanner pulls a medallion on a chain from around his neck; it must show some insignia because this seems to satisfy the guard, who confides something briefly to his fellows and motions for Tanner to follow him inside the gate.

We wait in silence. The boat rocks with each wave and bumps against the piles of the landing stage. The boatman looks questioningly at me and grumbles about time wasted; I hand over another penny to keep him quiet. The two remaining guards watch us, leaning against their pikestaffs. Fowler shifts his weight with a low moan.

"This will make for interesting diplomatic relations with King James when the queen knows of your plot," I whisper, to break the silence. "Did you think of that?"

"I don't know what you're talking about," he croaks. "Everything has been done in the name of Mary Stuart. She is behind this conspiracy. Let them prove otherwise. Where is their evidence?"

His face cracks into a smile, weak but replete with self-belief. He still thinks his plan is intact.

"You think Walsingham couldn't make you repeat what you told me an hour ago?"

"He can try. But I'll die with the name Mary on my lips. You can't stop the wheels turning now. And *you*, my friend"—he pauses, effortfully swallowing before running his tongue over his dry lips—"you'd better sleep with one eye open from now on. Archie Douglas doesn't like to leave loose ends." He coughs and a stream of white spittle trails from the corner of his mouth.

Footsteps rattle the landing stage as it bends under the weight of newcomers: Walsingham, with four more armed men, followed by Tanner. The principal secretary wears a fur-lined cloak which swishes and wraps around his legs as he halts abruptly by the boat and looks down, his face inscrutable. For a moment he does not speak, simply regards Fowler with that same, unchanging expression.

"William." In his voice, you hear everything his face will not show: regret, anger, disappointment, betrayal—and impatience with himself, for the failure of his own judgement.

"Sir Francis," Fowler replies, his voice so faint as to be barely audible, but the sneer in it is unmissable.

"He is wounded," I say; Walsingham gives a curt nod.

"Bring him ashore. And take care with his arm," he barks to the guards. One of them steps toward the boat, and in that instant Fowler sits upright, pushes me hard in the chest so that I tip back to the floor of the boat, and launches himself over the side, sending a wave of freezing water spilling back after him. The guards glance urgently at one another; in their armour they are helpless. One begins unbuckling his breastplate; I scan the black water as far as I can to either side but Fowler has disappeared.

"Hold up your light!" Walsingham shouts to the boatman, running to the end of the jetty. Almost quicker than thought I glance up at him, unpin my cloak, squeeze my eyes shut, and dive after Fowler.

Again, the shock of the cold strips me of breath and as I kick back to the surface, it takes a moment to regain my bearings.

"There!" calls the boatman, hanging precariously over the side with his lantern aloft and pointing; I turn, snatching shallow mouthfuls of air, to see through the white webs of mist a sleek black shape break the water's surface a little way downriver. I strike out after him; although the current is carrying him, he cannot make much progress with the arrow still in his shoulder, even if he had been exaggerating his weakness. In a few strokes I have almost caught him; he seems to flag and his head begins to sink below the surface. Filling my chest with air, I plunge after him; there, in the silent, swirling blackness, my hands grasp blindly and make contact with something solid. Fingers close over my arm; I battle for the surface, but he has a fistful of my sleeve and won't let go, and his weight is greater than mine. I fight to get one arm under his shoulder, kicking wildly to try and lift him up with me, but he claws at me with his other hand and I realise, too late, that he was not trying to escape but to avoid the punishment to which I'd delivered him, to protect his secrets from Walsingham's expert probing by taking them with him to the bottom of the river. Perhaps he even anticipated that I would throw myself impetuously after him. His hand gropes at my face; he does not mean either of us to reach the air again. I flail against him, and my hand collides with the wooden shaft of the crossbow bolt, still jutting from his shoulder; I wrench it hard to one side, his grip loosens, and I give an almighty kick with my legs, reaching the air just as my lungs begin to burn. Snatching breath, I gulp down a quantity of foul Thames water and choke violently; I fear I shall go under again, but something bumps against my shoulder and I clutch at it in desperation with my right hand, my left still clinging to a fragment of Fowler's garment as his weight drags him back under.

"Take hold!" cries a voice, and I blink the water away to see the boat, now with two of the guards at the helm; it is one of the oars that they have pushed out to me. My hand slips, but he manages to drag me close enough to the boat to grasp a handful of my doublet at the back;

between them, they haul me over the side like a landed fish, where I am doubled over, coughing up water.

"F-f—" I cannot make my voice obey me, my teeth are rattling too hard; instead I point frantically to the water, where one of the guards pokes impotently at the waves with his oar. I lurch forward; they must not give up now, Fowler must not be allowed to triumph by choosing his own way out. I have let too many vital pieces of evidence slip away from me in pursuit of him; he will not rob me of this final proof. Half crazed with anger, I am almost ready to throw myself over again in pursuit, but the guard who pulled me out takes a firm hold of my arm, just as his companion shouts out and the ripple of light spreads over a black shape, bobbed to the surface. Fowler, despite his best efforts, is more buoyant than he anticipated. The guards pull the boat nearer, and reach over to grab the sodden bundle, almost overturning the little craft in their efforts.

"Is he dead?" I manage.

"Don't know. Sit back," says one, who has evidently dealt with such matters before. He turns Fowler over and presses hard several times on his stomach. There is no response. The guard leans down harder, tries again, and lifts Fowler's torso upright as a feeble spluttering breaks from his lips, followed by a watery stream of vomit. By the time the other guard has pulled us back against the tide to the landing stage, I am satisfied that Fowler is still tethered to this world by a fragile thread.

The guards manhandle him onto the boards and lift him between them; Walsingham gives him a cursory glance as they pass.

"Does he live?"

"Aye, Your Honour."

He nods, then stretches out one leather-gloved hand to me. Shaking, I step onto the jetty and my legs buckle beneath me. Walsingham crouches beside me and lays a hand on my shoulder.

"If I didn't know better, Bruno, I'd swear you'd made a pact with the Devil himself. You're indestructible. But I don't think the Devil would have the nerve to take the bet. He'd be afraid you'd outwit him."

I try to reply but I am so cold I cannot stop the violent convulsions shaking my frame. Walsingham smiles, and gives my shoulder a fatherly squeeze.

"Oh, I know you don't believe in the Devil any more than you believe in God," he whispers. "You've done well, Bruno, once again. I will put you into the care of the Earl of Leicester, and when you are warm and rested, I'll hear this story."

He rises to his feet; I tug at his cloak and draw him back.

"I believe in evil," I manage, through my teeth, when his face is level with mine.

He nods once; stands, turns, and is gone. A guard with a torch holds out his hand to help me up, crooks my numb arm around his shoulders, and leads me into the palace.

Chapter *18*

In Mortlake, the trees and hedgerows stand silvered with frost along the riverbank, motionless as painted backgrounds from a playhouse under the hard blue sky. The path from the river stairs is brittle underfoot, where the night frost has turned the pitted mud track rigid as if all its markings were carved from sparkling granite. The sun hangs low but bright, brushing the landscape and the crooked roof of Dee's house with a sheen of pale gold. But my heart is heavy as I open the garden gate, and when Jane Dee opens the front door to me, I see she has been crying. She embraces me briefly, then gestures over her shoulder.

"You talk sense to him, Bruno, because I cannot." Her words come out clipped with pent emotion.

I hesitate, but decide it is probably better not to ask her any questions yet.

The laboratory looks denuded; today nothing breathes or bubbles or stinks or smokes, and a number of the stills have been emptied and dismantled. Dee stands by his workbench, haphazardly throwing books into an open trunk. I clear my throat and he looks up, then his face creases into a wide smile in the depths of his whiskers.

"Bruno!" He hops over a crate packed with glass bottles, which clinks alarmingly as he catches it with his foot, and enfolds me in a bear hug.

"You're in good spirits," I observe. I hope I don't sound too bitter.

"How could I not be, my friend?" He grips me by the shoulders and looks me in the face, his eyes gleaming. "Bohemia, Bruno. Can you picture it? Prague! Even you have not seen Prague in your travels. The court of a philosopher-emperor, himself a seeker of hidden truths, where those of us who pursue ancient knowledge not written in the books of the church fathers are not persecuted and condemned but revered and encouraged!" He gives my shoulders a little shake, as if this will clarify his vision. "The Emperor Rudolf is the most enlightened ruler in Europe. They say his court is filled with rare marvels. Wooden doves that really fly, and—"

"You don't have to go, you know," I break in. "Henry Howard is under house arrest and shortly to be removed to the Fleet Prison. Fowler is arrested on suspicion of the court murders. Your name is clear now."

"It is not so simple as that, as you must know." He looks down, regretful. "I had a visit yesterday from the Earl of Leicester's secretary."

"What did he want?"

"He brought me a gift from the queen. Forty gold angels, if you can believe it."

"Then you are still in her favour!" I say, brightening.

"Hers, yes." He pulls at his beard. "But not the Privy Council's. It was a going-away present, Bruno, and I would be a fool to regard it otherwise. A token of her esteem, yes, but also a way of thanking me for making her course simpler by leaving quietly. After this recent business at court, Burghley will draft yet more laws against astrologers and those who lay claim to prophecy and revelations—she could not continue to show me favour publicly. She has offered me a way out and I accept it with gratitude. I am fifty-six years old—is this not an extraordinary opportunity for me?" He forces the enthusiasm back into his voice.

"But what about—?" I wave a hand vaguely around the room. *What about me*, is what I really want to say, and chide myself for being so selfish. The prospect of London without Dee, now that Sidney has also become so distant, is a bleak one for a foreign heretic in exile. Seeing his laboratory stripped down like this, his books in the chest, I realise how much I will miss him. "All your books," I finish, unconvincingly.

"Jane's brother will live here and take care of the library," he says airily. "Of course, you must use it whenever you wish, Bruno, don't worry about that."

I am tempted to ask him whether Jane sees this as an extraordinary opportunity, the chance to uproot her family and travel halfway across Europe with two small children. From her face I know the answer—but I do not know what she expects me to say. Dee is right; the rumours that still persist about the murders at court, the unrest over the prophecies— all this must be quashed by the government if order is to be restored. What other choice has he? My friend would automatically find himself on the wrong side of the new laws; Elizabeth is subtly banishing him to save his life and his reputation. It is to his credit that he has determined to embrace this banishment as a new beginning. It is what I have tried to do for the past seven years, but it becomes harder with each year. Age and distance bring a yearning for home that all the freedom I enjoy in England—to read, to write, and to publish without fear of the Inquisition— cannot quite outweigh.

"Come," Dee says, beckoning me through to his private study, where I had once stood by and watched Ned Kelley invent the apocalyptic words of spirits. Here too, Dee's magical paraphernalia is in the course of being packed up and boxed for travel. The showing stone and wax seals lie in a decorated casket wrapped in the square of crimson silk; the notebooks and diaries are stacked beside it.

"Tell me, then," he says, patting the lid of one of the chests and motioning for me to sit down. "Have they charged Howard?"

"He is still being questioned. All they have against him is the map of safe harbours and the list of Catholic nobles they found on Throckmorton when he was intercepted on the road. They want to claim these are in Howard's hand, but he denies it, of course. And the queen is anxious to proceed carefully with him." Elizabeth's caution is a source of great anxiety to me, though I do not tell Dee this. Her refusal to allow what she pleases to call "hard questioning" of Howard has left him and the Privy Council at an impasse, and if he is not formally charged with offences of treason there is every chance she may choose to free him to appease her Catholic subjects. If that were to happen, I have no doubt that he would waste no time in looking for me.

"But they must have searched Arundel House?" Dee continues to potter about, lifting objects, replacing them, seemingly disconcerted among his half-packed belongings.

"Top to bottom, Walsingham told me." I hesitate. "They didn't find the book, John. He would have mentioned it if they had, I'm sure."

Dee shakes his head in sorrow.

"To think you held it in your hands. Listen, while I am in Bohemia, Bruno, I will seek out every treatise, every last manuscript and antiquarian tract on cryptography that I can find. I will consult the Emperor Rudolf's most celebrated scholars. And in the meantime you must get the book back." He points a finger at me.

"There was no evidence to incriminate Philip Howard when they searched Throckmorton's house," I say. "The earl and his wife have wisely retired from court until his uncle's fate is decided. I would wager any money Henry gave him the book for safekeeping before his arrest."

Dee tilts his head and considers this. "Well—there is a task for you while I am gone." He smiles sadly. "Throckmorton will hang, I suppose? And Fowler?"

"When they have finished with them in the Tower," I say, and we both fall silent. Fowler, true to his word, has confessed nothing; the Tower's most skilled interrogators could not persuade him to repeat the boast he made to me in the back room of that Southwark tavern. As a precaution, Walsingham is to undertake a diplomatic mission to Scotland after Accession Day, in the hope of prising the young King James away from the vying factions of advisers and persuading him that peaceful relations with Elizabeth will serve his kingdom best. For now, all the Privy Council's energies are bent on discovering whether anyone else might have taken up the supposed Accession Day assassination plot.

"This country," Dee begins, and then spreads his hands as if he cannot find the words. "When I was your age, Bruno, I believed that Elizabeth Tudor would make us truly free from the superstitions and the tyranny of Rome. But when I see what they are willing to do to preserve that freedom, I must question what we have gained. Walsingham would say you cannot defend the good of the many without spilling blood, but I don't know." He sighs. "I can only say I will not be sorry to leave this island behind me for a while. Except that I shall miss our conversations, Bruno."

"And I," I reply, with feeling. I want to say more, to let him know how he has become the nearest thing to a father in my exile, but at this moment I catch a movement behind me and see his gaze flicker over my shoulder to the doorway; he nods in recognition. I turn, and for a moment I doubt the evidence of my eyes, for there is Ned Kelley, a fraying red scarf tied around his neck and a crate of books in his arms.

"This one's ready to go," he says. "Oh, hello, Doctor Bruno. How's your head? I heard you took quite a blow." He breaks into a sly grin, showing his crooked teeth.

"You little shit." My anger boils over; I rush at him, grabbing him by the shirt front so that he drops his box and the books tumble to the floor. I swing my right arm back; Kelley bleats something, but it is Dee's hand that closes over my clenched fist before I can land it in the scryer's mocking face.

"Now, Bruno. I understand your feelings. But Ned and I have spent long hours dissecting everything that has passed between us, and he has repented."

"Repented?" I drop Kelley and turn to Dee, incredulous. "He sold you! He took money from Henry Howard to destroy you—and you still let him into your house? In God's name, John—have you lost your mind?"

"Bruno." His voice is sad and gentle as ever; he lays a hand on my arm. "Ned was too much under the influence of that woman. Now she is gone, he is returned to himself, and I have forgiven him, as I would a prodigal son. I think you can understand as well as anyone how a man might be diverted from his good conscience by the charms of a woman?"

"It was the charms of Henry Howard's purse and you know it." I shake his hand from my arm. So this is what Jane meant about talking sense. All the affection I felt for Dee a moment ago seems strangled by my fury at his obstinate faith in Kelley. "And he tried to kill me, while you were at the palace. He threw a rock at my head." I rub my temple, now healed but for a crooked red scar.

"That's slander, that is," Kelley says, stepping back out of my reach. "You've got no proof."

"Are you really so deluded?" I say, turning back to Dee. "He has no gift, John. He has no special language to speak to spirits. He is no more than a sideshow charlatan—I see it, your wife sees it, why cannot you?"

I had not meant to raise my voice to him; he looks hurt, and I am both remorseful and glad. I do not want to make this my farewell, but I cannot apologise for what I know to be true.

Kelley stoops to pick up his fallen books and dusts them off. "Are we taking all of these, sir?"

"I don't know." Dee passes the back of his hand across his forehead. His earlier cheer seems to have evaporated and he sounds weary and confused. "Put them on the desk, Ned, I will go through them in a moment. Perhaps you could leave us for now?"

Kelley bobs his head and scurries away with a last triumphant smile at me. I stare at Dee.

"You are not taking him with you?"

"I am. Oh, do not roll your eyes at me like that, Bruno. Ned has a volatile temperament—it goes with his gift. But he has confessed his deception and cut all ties with Howard and Johanna. Now he is determined to continue our previous work. He says he feels he is channelling a renewed energy from the spirits. They are eager to communicate."

"The only thing he is channelling is an eagerness to leave England before he is picked up by the constables for his debts," I say, with venom.

"Oh, my dear Bruno. I know we shall never agree on Ned, but let us not part like this," he says, and I see he will not be turned from his course. "I have a gift for you." He rummages on his desk among the papers and emerges with a volume beautifully bound in tawny calfskin, which he passes to me, almost bashfully. I open it to examine the flyleaf and discover that it is a copy of the *Commentaries* of Erasmus, the same book I was obliged to throw into the privy on the night I had to flee my monastery in Naples, seven years ago. Dee had always enjoyed that story and asked me to tell it repeatedly.

"I thought you should have your own edition," he says, not quite meeting my eye. "It is not forbidden here. Mind you don't drop it in the privy."

"It's beautiful." I stroke the cover and this time I have to look away, to hide the fact that I am blinking back tears. At the door I turn and watch him there, among the implements of his magic, his long beard illuminated in the sunlight streaming through the window, and I wish I had the gift of painting; I would capture him like this, as he stands now—stubborn, perplexed, a little sad, and wiser than most—just in case I do not see him again in this life.

In the hallway, Jane embraces me again. Little Arthur clings to her skirt.

"I must love him,' Bruno, or why would I put up with it?"

"Maybe Kelley will fall overboard on the journey," I say.

She laughs, and rubs away a tear with the back of her hand before it has a chance to spill.

"He might if I have anything to do with it." She pauses, twisting her apron in her hands. "Go with God, Bruno. You're a good man. Christ knows there are few enough of those."

"Look after the one in your care, then," I say, with a bow. "And raise up another." I ruffle Arthur's hair and he ducks behind his mother, gig-gling.

"And mind you keep yourself out of trouble."

"If only I knew how to do that. I do not seek danger, Jane—it follows me." As I say this, I recall Fowler's warning about Douglas, as I recall it every night when I lie down to sleep. The murders are solved and the invasion averted—for now, but the danger has not passed. I wonder if I will ever know what it is to live without fear of the knife at my throat—but I tell myself not even the Queen of England knows that peace. This is the nature of our age, and it needs no ancient prophecy nor conjunction of planets to explain it.

Epilogue

The royal standard is raised aloft; for a moment it ripples sharply in the breeze, crimson and gold against the watery blue of the sky, and the crowd audibly draws breath together. Time seems suspended, fates hang in the balance—until the standard falls and from either end of the tiltyard comes a crescendo of hooves and a blur of primary colours as the contestants gallop toward one another full pelt, the elaborate plumage on their helmets and harnesses coursing out behind them. I brace myself for the moment of impact; I have never learned to like this as a sport, though today of all days I am willing to be swept up in the collective celebration, the pageantry, the near-hysterical atmosphere of adulation for the woman who sits high above the skirmish in her gallery overlooking the tiltyard, her head dwarfed by an enormous stiff lace collar. From our seats in the stands, her every movement is a scattering of light as her jewels wink in the sun.

Beside me, Castelnau also tenses; the rider nearest us, his horse decked out in an azure-and-white-chequered costume, raises his shield expertly to deflect his opponent's lance; there is a sickening crack as the other is caught squarely in the shoulder; he tries, for agonising moments, to hold his seat but the momentum is too strong and he topples back, landing with a crunch of metal in the sand. A roar of applause breaks out; we the spectators rise to our feet, whooping and stamping, so that the wooden stands shake precariously beneath us. The victorious rider slows his horse and reins it around, trotting casually back up the field before removing his helmet and bowing deeply to the queen in his saddle. From somewhere farther east a peal of church bells joins the cacophony.

I glance up at the gallery window. We are too far away to see the royal party in any great detail, though as a foreign dignitary Castelnau has been given advantageous seats for the tournament. But I can make out Elizabeth in the centre, surrounded by her maids of honour, all dressed in white. I lower my head for a moment and close my eyes, not in prayer but in silent tribute to Cecily Ashe. If her conscience had not triumphed over her infatuation with the man she believed to be the Earl of Ormond, the Tudor line might have ended this very morning. And if she had never met Fowler, I think, if she had not harboured a girl's passing grudge against the queen, if he had been less persuasive or she more guarded, she might have been sitting at Elizabeth's side now in her white dress. Abigail Morley, too; if she had not been Cecily's confidante, if she had never met me or passed on the ring, she might be clapping her hands and shrieking with delight in the gallery with the rest of the girls. If, always if.

Glancing around the great crowd in the tiltyard, I wonder if anyone else has noticed the number of armed guards amid the heralds, the guildsmen in their liveries, the aldermen and lawyers in their gowns of office, the bishops and nobles arrayed behind the queen, wreathed in gold chains. In the past month, the searchers at every port along the south coast have been kept busy picking up young Englishmen and Scots coming out of France or the Low Countries; one who was caught trying to bring a loaded pistol through customs at Rye also carried Catholic relics concealed in his belongings, but Fowler's stubborn silence persists even in the Tower, so there is no way to be certain whether he was bluffing about finding a replacement assassin or whether, even now, some shadowy figure might be moving among the thousands of spectators or waiting patiently among the thousands more Londoners gathered behind the barriers that have been erected all along Whitehall and the Strand, where the queen will process after the jousts to hear a sermon at St. Paul's. She may carry herself as gracious and poised as ever, but for Walsingham, Burghley, and Leicester, until she is safely delivered to her chamber this evening, this day will be one of the most fraught they have known. Walsingham pleaded with her to abandon the public procession, but she insisted her people must see her, radiant, proud, and strong, undaunted by threats either from planets or Catholics.

We climb down from the stands, a laborious business among so many guests, all vying to take their places along the route by the Holbein Gate for a better view of the queen as she begins her procession.

"Marie would have enjoyed this," Castelnau remarks, as we shuffle forward in slow increments, pressed on all sides by eminent citizens in their furs.

"You must miss her," I say. We are so close in the crowd that I feel his torso rise and fall as he sighs.

"It was better for everyone that she return to Paris. When they arrested Throckmorton and Howard, I knew they would be knocking on our door next. I felt I had a better chance of keeping the embassy in the clear if Marie were not questioned. Besides"—he glances around and lowers his voice—"my wife has been absent to me for a long time, whether she is under the same roof or not. It was a mistake to bring her here. I do not doubt there are others at Salisbury Court who feel her absence more keenly than I do."

I look over my shoulder to where Courcelles trails behind, separated from us in the crush by a handful of people. He catches my eye and gives me the sulky, defiant look that has become his permanent expression since Marie left. I wonder if Castelnau guesses that he has sent his wife straight back into the arms of the Duke of Guise, whose ambitions, I feel sure, are only thwarted temporarily. I would wager Courcelles certainly knows it, and tortures himself with the thought daily.

"Still, we have been fortunate, Bruno," Castelnau says, as if to convince himself. "My interview with Francis Walsingham was the most uncomfortable moment of my career, I don't mind telling you. As I feared, it seems they had been watching Throckmorton's movements for some time, and we do not yet know how much of the correspondence he carried was intercepted. But so far I have not been directly accused of anything. I feel I have got off very lightly," he adds, and I hear the tremor in his voice.

More lightly than he knows, I think; when Throckmorton was arrested, as well as the map of safe havens and the list of names, he was also carrying Castelnau's last, rash letter to Mary, in which he assured her of his loyalty to her cause against Howard's accusations. It was only my arguments to Walsingham on his behalf, and the queen's reluctance to create a diplomatic storm with France, that have kept the ambassador from more severe repercussions.

"Mary was always shrewd enough never to make any outright acknowledgement in her own hand of the plot to free her," I reassure him. "Let them conclude the whole thing was a reckless fantasy cooked up by her supporters in Paris. If they had anything against you they would have used it by now."

He shakes his head, his lips pressed into a white line.

"They have barely started with poor Throckmorton. I dread to think what they are doing to him, and what more may come out. If King Henri should be brought into this, Bruno—can you imagine the consequences?"

I can well imagine the consequences of the French king discovering from the Queen of England that his ambassador has been involved in a Guise plot to topple her. But then King Henri will be fully occupied with the Duke of Guise's designs on his own throne, I reflect. I pat Castelnau's shoulder and murmur reassurance.

"All because I cannot say no to my wife," he says bitterly. I could tell him he is far from being alone in this failing, but I doubt it would be much comfort. "She thought it was you, you know," he adds, turning to me.

"Thought what was me?"

"The traitor in our midst—she and Courcelles were adamant you were the one who betrayed us. But you know what I pointed out to them?"

"What?" I aim to keep my face as neutral as possible.

"Where is Archibald Douglas? Eh?" He nudges me, pleased with his own powers of deduction. "No one has seen or heard from him since the arrests. There's your answer, right there. And he's just the sort whose loyalty could be bought for a shilling. Don't you think?"

"Absolutely."

"No, I never trusted him. Mind you, there is William Fowler arrested on suspicion of the murders of those girls at court, though I cannot imagine how they came to that conclusion. I always thought him such a mild man. And who knows what he might tell them on the rack." He sucks in his cheeks. "I shall not feel safe from accusation in England, Bruno, not for a long time. That, I suppose, is the price of a guilty conscience. But I tell you this—I shall never again involve myself or His Majesty's embassy in secret dealings of this nature, no matter who tries to persuade me." He sighs. "Sometimes I doubt whether it is ever possible to know the truth of another man's mind behind the face he shows."

I murmur in agreement, turning my own face aside so that I do not have to look him in the eye.

As we near the end of the tiltyard, there is a jostling among the crowd; people fuss and complain as someone attempts to shove his way through toward the gate. When he draws level with us, he turns and I realise it is Mendoza, the Spanish ambassador, with a face like granite behind his black beard. He jabs one hairy forefinger almost into Castelnau's face.

"My sovereign is furious," he spits, through his teeth.

Castelnau draws himself up with dignity.

"When is he not?"

"I am summoned"—Mendoza lowers his voice further, the effort of suppressing his fury turning his face puce—"I, Don Bernardino de Mendoza, am summoned to stand before a committee of Privy Councillors to account for myself like a schoolboy! Are you?"

"Not yet," Castelnau says evenly, as we funnel through the gate and into the street, where official stewards and more armed guards usher us into orderly lines to pass under the Holbein Gate to a place behind the barriers.

"The queen accuses King Philip of conspiring against her," Mendoza continues. "You realise I could be expelled over this?"

"As could I."

"But I do not see you being questioned. And yet it was someone at Salisbury Court who betrayed our plans to Walsingham."

"Walsingham arrested Throckmorton. They searched his house. As I understand it, he was carrying as many letters between you and Mary as he was from me. Perhaps your letters were less cautious." Castelnau remains admirably calm. Mendoza bristles and turns his glare on me.

"I am not the one who keeps a known enemy of the Catholic church under my roof. I have said this before, Michel—you are being played for a fool. If I am banished from England, my sovereign will make sure you and your king pay a high price for it."

I am about to defend myself, when I glance across the street to the crowd on the other side and my heart misses a beat; among the massed faces, I am certain that I saw him: the briefest instant, a flash of recognition, that mocking grin under the peak of an old cap, the laconic wink, and then he is gone, slipped away in the tide of people. I blink, try to find him again, but there is no sign, so that I wonder if I conjured his face out of my night terrors. But I cannot take the risk; I duck behind Castelnau, pushing my way through irritated spectators to the fringe of the human stream, until I can grab at the sleeve of the nearest guard.

"Find Walsingham," I gasp, shaking him.

"Eh? Who are you? Get your hands off me." He moves to lower his pikestaff; I hold my hands up.

"Please—you must get to Sir Francis Walsingham. Tell him Douglas is here. Tell him the queen must not pass through the streets—you must find him urgently. Her life is in danger. Tell him the Italian says so."

He looks at me in confusion for a long moment as he weighs up how seriously to take this; I nod frantically, urging him to act. Eventually, he raises his pike and calls out, "Make way, there! Make way, quickly now!"

By the time I am assured he means to convey my message, I have lost Castelnau and Mendoza in the crowds. I slip into the press of people unnoticed, my eyes darting from face to face, my hand, as ever, resting on the handle of my knife under my cloak.

LATER, IN THE great court at the Palace of Whitehall, I stand in the shadows with my neck craned back, breathing frosty air as fireworks scatter orange-and-gold sparks against the ink-blue curtain of the sky, plumes of coloured fire that flare briefly and dissolve into smoke as the guests coo and squeal like children. This display is almost the finale of the day's celebrations; once it is over, we will retire to the great hall to watch a series of pageants, variations on the theme of Elizabeth's greatness and likeness to various mythical heroines. I wanted to go home, but Castelnau would not hear of it; what is required, I am told, is a show of faultless devotion to the queen for as long as the ambassador is obliged to try and win back a place in her favour. But Elizabeth is still alive, and that is worth celebrating; her procession, though delayed through my intervention, went ahead at her insistence, but passed without incident, and from the sounds of riotous street parties from beyond the walls and the incessant clamour of church bells across the city, her subjects are united in noisy celebration of their devotion. Perhaps Douglas was never there today; perhaps this is how I will live now, imagining his face in every crowd, skittish as poor Léon Dumas, and look how much good that did him.

I raise my eyes beyond the glitter of the fireworks to the infinite sky beyond. The night is clear and the stars so bright they seem to pulse. What would I need to calculate their distance, I wonder?

"How many new worlds have you discovered, Bruno?"

I start from my reverie and wheel around to see Sidney leaning against a wall, a glass of wine in his hand. Guiltily, I glance about me to see if Castelnau is nearby, but there is no sign of him.

"Infinite numbers," I say, feeling my shoulders relax.

"Where is God to be found, then, if there is no sphere of fixed stars?" He speaks in a whisper. "Beyond where the universe ends?"

"An infinite universe by definition does not end, you dullard," I point out with a grin.

"Then where? Beyond the stars?"

"Or in them, perhaps. In the stars and the planets and the rain and these stones under our feet, and in us. Or perhaps nowhere."

"Well, you had better keep ideas like that out of your book," he says, "because Her Majesty is anxious to read it."

"What?"

He laughs. "That is your reward, my friend. Walsingham told her you were writing a book about the heavens. She asks that you have a copy bound and present it to her in person at court when it is finished." He slaps me on the shoulder and offers me his glass. "Her Majesty is a woman of prodigious intellect, it is well known, but I wish her luck trying to grapple with your theories." He looks up again to the tracery of milky vapour overhead. "If I try for one minute to imagine a universe that never ends, I fear that my brain will overheat and explode."

"Then don't risk it." I take a drink and hand the glass back to him. "Please pass on my thanks. I am honoured."

"You should be. A royal endorsement will make this book the talk of every academy. Just try not to write anything too inflammatory."

"You know me, Philip."

"Yes, I do. Hence the warning. She won't give her patronage to any writer who implies there is no God, no matter how many times you save her life."

I acknowledge this with a nod, and for a long while we stand there, looking up at the vast unknown reaches above us.

"I was sorry to hear of Dee's departure," he remarks, eventually. "I didn't have a chance to say goodbye. I shall miss the old conjuror."

"And I," I say, with feeling. "It seems hard, since he had done nothing wrong except be taken for a fool. The scryer Kelley had no connection with the murders, in the end. I read into that what I wanted to be true. Some things are just coincidence, though."

"But people gripped by fears of planets and prophecies will not believe that. Dee was too inflammatory a figure to be tolerated at court, even before this dreadful business." Sidney sighs and pushes a hand through his hair. "His hunger for hidden matters will be his undoing, I fear. As it will yours, *amico mio*."

He turns to me and squeezes my shoulder briefly. For a moment we regard the sky again in silence.

"Wouldn't you give anything to rise up through the spheres, Philip, to travel beyond the reaches of the heavens and understand what is out there?"

"Anything except my soul," he says emphatically. "You have not given up, then. You still believe this book of Howard's will teach you the means to do that?"

"Howard believes it will make him immortal."

"It may be too late for him to test that, if he's charged with treason. Where is the book now?"

"I don't know. Only Howard can tell us that. Or perhaps his nephew."

He turns to look at me. The fireworks are almost ended now, and only the torches in brackets around the courtyard give any light. His face is patched with shifting shadows.

"You already have it in your head to search for it, don't you?" When I do not reply, he claps a hand to his forehead and steps back. "Christ's blood, Bruno—let it go, will you? You have the queen and her senior ministers in your debt, you have an income and the leisure to write a book that will send waves through Europe, like Copernicus before you. This is everything you wanted, isn't it?"

I acknowledge the truth of it with a dip of my head.

"Well, then! Don't throw it away chasing will-o'-the-wisps. Howard's already tried to kill you and Dee for that book, and I can't keep watch over you all the time."

"You're right, I know."

"Promise me you will let the Hermes book go? Henry Howard cannot touch it where he is, and the Earl of Arundel is too pious and cowardly to look into it himself, if he has it. It is out of harm's way. So leave it alone."

I hesitate. Sidney points a finger in my face, assuming the expression of a schoolmaster.

"Very well then."

"Good man. Now I suppose I had better find my wife. Still no sign of an heir, you know," he adds, as if he can't understand why someone doesn't sort this out. "Not for want of trying, neither. Here, you finish this, I've had enough."

"I'm sorry to hear that," I say, as he hands me the glass. "Still, you've only been married two months."

"Huh. That ought to be plenty of time for the Sidney seed to do its work."

I grimace, and he laughs, clapping me soundly on the arm again, then walks backward a few steps. "Don't forget what I told you," he calls. "I have your solemn oath."

In the emptying courtyard I stand very still and look up again, my head as far back as I can stretch so that I am almost bent backward, and I imagine the whole of the heavens spinning around as if on a wheel with me as the fulcrum. I have promised nothing, and as I watch a shooting star fire its trail across a constellation and wink into blackness, I recall the sensation of that leather binding, the stiff ancient pages, the coded truths in a hidden book that might one day show me what lies beyond the visible world, out there, among the mysteries of infinity. As I stare upward, a final burst of fireworks pierces the dark with crimson light, scattering sparks like a shower of bright rain so that, for an instant, the sky is illuminated, stained the colour of blood.